A STEEL TOWN

A GATEWAY TO LOVE NOVEL

CHLOE T. BARLOW

A STEEL TOWN - A GATEWAY TO LOVE NOVEL

http://chloetbarlow.com/

ISBN-13: 978-1518808463 (Traditional Paperback)
ISBN-10: 1518808468 (Traditional Paperback)

First Edition Published January 2016

Cover art by Complete Pixels and Eisley Jacobs. Cover models: Nick and Cassandra Martinez

Editing by Marilyn Medina of Eagle Eye Reads Editing Service
Proofreading by Kara Hildebrand

DEDICATION

To my wonderful husband,

for giving me the courage to try to fly, while never failing to catch me every time I fall. I love you more with each minute of every day.

To my dear friend Micaiah,

and others living with diabetes, as well as those who love them, for the quiet strength and fortitude, which you bring to all you do.

And to my mother,

for constantly inspiring me, and for always being eager to help light my way on the many paths I have taken in life.

PROLOGUE

"A.J., get over here and sit on my lap," Trey urged, turning from his computer so he could reach a hand out to his girlfriend.

"There you go, ordering me around again," she teased from her spot on the lone twin bed in his dorm room.

He'd spent one sleepless night during his freshman year infiltrating *Stanford's* housing protocols to get himself assigned to a single room for his sophomore year. That effort was really paying off, because privacy was turning out to be vital.

"That's right," he answered. "And I'll be even more demanding if you don't get that cute ass of yours over here…now."

"Oh yeah? Well, maybe I want to keep saying 'no,' then I'll see how far I can push you before you break…"

"You've already broken me, so now I just want you near me. Come here. Look at what we were able to get."

She unfolded her long legs, and quickly made her way across the room to stand next to him.

"Holy hell, Trey, it worked! Look at all this data."

"It's not just information. Our plan to get control over the whole university mainframe and its servers worked, too — all that power is right here at our fingertips. And there's no tracing it to us because we've perfectly mimicked the system."

"Wow! All this with just our little program?"

"Little? I think it's pretty big," Trey corrected.

"Not as big as I'd hoped, but I guess you're right."

"That's because I reined it in some."

Frustration streaked across her face, hardening her voice when she blurted out, "What the hell, Trey? I thought we were doing this together?"

"We are. I'm sorry I didn't tell you I made this change. But this is just for fun, right? To see if we can do it?"

"You're right, I'm sorry. I just…I want it to be amazing, like what you told me you'd done when you were in high school."

"What I did was *too* amazing. The hardest thing with a virus like this is containing it. We don't want it to get away from us. It's how shit gets out of hand."

"I know…" Her voice was distant, fading off as her eyes began darting quickly around the room and back to the glowing screen in front of Trey. He could almost feel the nervous energy emanating from her.

"A.J., calm down." He grabbed her wrist and dragged her on top of him, letting his hand slide up her arm, then down her shapely torso, settling finally at her waist. She giggled in response, relaxing against him.

"Sorry. It's hard not to be excited. I've never done anything like this before. I spent all my days before I met you doing the right thing. It never even occurred to me to try something like this. If I hadn't been partnered with you for this project, I would've kept on living my boring life, doing the actual assignment, creating antivirus software. But making a super virus? This is so much more fun!"

"I definitely enjoyed corrupting you, A.J. — both your brain and your body."

A.J. met his eyes, then pulled Trey's arms around her waist and said, "I enjoyed it, too. You were very good at bringing me to the dark side." She kissed him quickly, smiling against his mouth, before turning back to the screen. "What else should we do with it?"

"What do you mean?"

"It seems like such a waste to use it as just a little school prank. Why can't we do more?"

"Like what?" he queried slowly, concern spreading through him.

"Whatever we want. If we're always scared of what bad thing might happen down the road, we'll never find out what we can really do," she persuaded.

"We have to be careful, A.J.," he warned. "If *Stanford* gets wind of what we did with our 'little' sophomore year project..."

"We'll get expelled?"

"No. We won't just get kicked out of school. We'll go to jail. Trust me, I know how much you want to take the credit...how you want to prove yourself...but I also know what it's like to get picked up by the cops."

"You were only fourteen."

"Exactly, and they'll be much less forgiving this time."

"But your dad owns most of Silicon Valley. There maybe wouldn't even *be* a Silicon Valley as we know it without him. He can get you out of anything."

"I'm not asking that of him again. I gave him my 'word,' as he called it — swore I wouldn't let shit get away from me like I did before."

Trey made sure to keep his voice gentle, because disappointing her actually physically hurt him. Her sexy mouth twisted into a pout and his stomach immediately tightened in response. He'd never loved anyone before, but he was pretty sure what he felt for A.J. had to be it.

Yet, losing control of one of his little games almost broke whatever was left of his family once before. With the genius of the Adler line, came its own particular strain of madness — an almost pathological need to create and rule over your own reality, one separate from everyone else's, and completely subject to your control.

This urge thrived inside of them, whether it was in relation to the collection of mortal beings in their lives, or over a pattern of ones and zeroes, such as those his father developed. One of them had even become the most important operating system of its time, revolutionizing the world in the 1980s.

This Adler "gift" was great for building an alternate world, but it was also perfect for devastating relationships in a real one. Trey was intent on controlling this side of himself so he wouldn't lose A.J., but he had to balance this desire against the promise he'd made to his father.

"Fine. But I can't help but want to shove it in that asshat, Professor Cooper's, face. I'd love to show him a girl actually *can* be a hacker."

A.J.'s face turned into a mask of angry resolve.

"You're still pissed about that?"

"Hell yes, I am. He spends every day of class acting like everyone who ever did anything with a computer had a penis. Especially stuff like this." She waved her hand toward the screen, a vibrant symbol of just what this sexy, and voluptuous, girl could accomplish. "I mean, the school could be taken down with one keystroke...*we* did that. And you need to calm down, because we aren't going to get caught."

"You won't rest until you prove the whole world wrong, will you?"

"Damn straight, I won't. I showed *you* what I can do, which was hard enough. Taking on the rest of the world seems like a good next step."

Trey smiled and stroked slowly over the length of her long, blonde ponytail, taking a moment to bury his nose into her neck.

"All I want is to feel you close to me, A.J. World domination is not really my thing," Trey whispered against her skin.

"Oh, really? You seem pretty comfortable telling *me* what to do. Maybe simply lording over me is what you're into."

"I like the sound of that. But, even if I may need to dominate some things, the rest of the world can wait."

A.J. giggled again. "Hey, remember when you told me every good virus needs a cool name?"

"I do. What should we call ours?"

"Hmm..." A.J. intoned. She crinkled her nose and squinted her pretty, light blue eyes, a sure sign she was deep in thought. "I was thinking we could call it 'Starling.'"

"Like the bird?"

"Exactly! They are gifted mimics, and will actually take over another bird's nest and control it."

"They're also beautiful, just like you," Trey whispered against the soft skin of her cheek.

"You're gonna turn me into goo, Trey. Before I rip your clothes off, we need to record this moment of triumph, *partner*," A.J. said gleefully, grabbing Trey's digital camera from beside his keyboard. She quickly turned it around and snuggled up to him before snapping several shots.

Flipping through the pictures, Trey's heart squeezed at the sight of them together — smiling, laughing, and sticking their tongues out. It was the most normal he'd ever felt, and it was amazing.

Her face turned serious when she looked over to him, wrapping her arms around his neck, the camera still dangling from her hand.

He pulled her flush against his chest and said, "I'd love to be able to give you whatever you want, A.J."

"You make me so happy, Trey. That's enough, I swear," she whispered in his ear.

Five Weeks Later

"Trey…*Trey*. Wake up. *Please*."

A distant, pleading voice was breaking through Trey's sleepy brain as hands shook him vigorously. He slowly opened his eyes to see A.J.'s face. Even in the darkness, he could see her eyes were wide and frenzied.

"A.J.?"

"I packed you a bag. We have to get out of here, *fast*."

"Are you messing with me? Come back to bed." He reached for her, but she shook him off quickly. The movement jarred him fully awake. He sat up, running a hand through his hair, trying to will his brain to process how crazy A.J. was acting.

"What's wrong, A.J.? You're shaking."

As his eyes adjusted to the lack of light, he saw her bite her quivering bottom lip and look away from him. She was breathing rapidly and spun her head back to the door, but she let him hold her briefly.

A feeling Trey assumed was fear, accentuated by a hint of panic, started to pour through his veins like liquid mercury — slippery and toxic.

A.J. had become increasingly erratic over the last few weeks. The logical part of Trey's brain sensed she was hiding something from him. Every aspect of her had been changing more by the day, and she would disappear for hours on end. Trey's practical instinct told him to demand A.J. tell him the truth. He'd even considered spying on her and reading her emails.

Yet, he'd repeatedly let the stupid lovesick part of himself win out — choosing to trust her and their feelings for each other. He deliberately ignored whatever signs were warning him something terrible was coming to destroy what they had. Fury with his own stupidity started to boil that mercury coursing through his body — making him embrace his own form of insanity.

He gritted his teeth, desperate to take control of the situation. Maybe if he'd been more tough with her before, rather than let her have her way all the time, they wouldn't be in this situation — whatever it was.

With firm hands, he grabbed A.J.'s upper arms and twisted her body to him. Her silence enraged him, and he could feel his self-control slipping away.

He sensed the code of his Adler-family DNA taking over his body after so many weeks of suppressing it. Leaping to his feet, he stood her up roughly, shaking her body and shouting at her brusquely, "Goddamn it, A.J. — I'm not going anywhere until you tell me what the fuck is going on. *Now!*"

Her mouth dropped open, clearly shocked at how he'd changed with her.

"We don't have much time. Can't I tell you on the way?"

He just growled in response, squeezing her arms harder.

"Trey, you're hurting my arms."

"You're hurting *me.* Tell me…please," he said, his voice somber and pleading.

"I-I started playing with the Starling virus. I wanted to see what it could do…"

"What?"

Trey's hands fell, and the fury in his veins turned to chilling terror in an instant.

"I wasn't trying to hurt anyone. It was just to see if I could do it. I thought if I made it bigger and controlled it…you'd be so impressed."

"Why would you want to do that? You already know I think you're amazing."

"But we created the virus together. When you scaled it back without telling me, I thought you were just trying to protect me. I wanted you to see I could handle all this on my own — to make you really believe in me."

"I told you — you can't push it. Did the school find out? What happened?"

He rushed to his computer and started damage control — deleting every file and all the information they'd received, desperately trying to turn back time.

Her voice came through the room, thick as cotton candy, "Then I saw how much money we could make. I thought we could be set for life…"

Trey's fingers stopped and he turned to her. It was suddenly far too clear to him.

"No, A.J. Please tell me you didn't. Who?"

"Trey…"

"Who did you try to sell it to?" he roared.

"I don't know their names, but they're from Russia."

"Holy shit. Russians?"

Trey felt like someone had kicked him in the gut. He bent at the waist, running his hands through his hair so hard it hurt his scalp. The world he'd been trying to build with A.J. was shattering right before his eyes, as though a catastrophic earthquake had split the ground beneath them — wreaking havoc on everything in their vicinity — and all he could do was helplessly watch.

Trey swallowed roughly around the strangling sensation from the destruction of his own stupid reality, and choked out, "Are you nuts, A.J.? You're going to get us killed."

"I swear, I had it all set up. I was using dummy accounts, fake identities, and everything. But I never got the payment yesterday. I was going through all the information today and they accessed it from just a few miles away. They're here, Trey. I mean it…we have to leave."

"Yes. We have to get fucking gone," he answered stonily. Trey felt his head nod involuntarily along with his words. He moved quickly through the dorm, grabbing his computer and other necessities, as A.J. collected the bag she'd packed for him. Her mouth was moving, but all he heard was static and noise, like he'd been punched in the head and his ears were still ringing.

He took her hand and led her out the door. He felt his feet break into a run, bringing A.J. along with him. None of his motions felt real, he'd switched over to running a program — his own internal survival software was clicking through his muscles and joints, setting the pace of their quick steps.

Whatever force controlled his movements, also shot them out of the building to the deserted parking lot. Their feet slapped over and over on the wet pavement, but he felt them being directed to his parked car. It waited to transport them to the safety of a different world.

Trey released her hand so he could unlock his car with his key fob, the accompanying blinking light reflected off the wet droplets covering its dark blue paint, creating a halo of safety. He could feel his chest relax slightly as he reached back for A.J.'s hand to help her get in the car. All he found when he grasped for her was empty air, and the terrifying sound of her scream.

As Trey turned, he saw the forms of two men; one was holding A.J. around the waist and she was sobbing uncontrollably. He lunged for them, but the other man grabbed him from behind.

"Say good-bye to your girlfriend," he ordered, his accent thick and unmistakable.

"Help me, Trey, please," she whimpered.

"I promise, I will. I promise!" Trey shouted. He tried to lunge for her again, but a fierce blow to his lower back doubled him over in pain. An elbow came down on him from above, hitting at the base of his neck. He fell to the ground, the wet pavement jarring his knees and seeping through his jeans. The cold didn't even register in his brain, because his body had already turned to ice.

"Sorry, but you asked for that. It's not nice to lie to a woman, Mr. Adler," the man holding A.J. said, taunting him. "You will be fine, the ransom we can get for you is too high to pass up. Now this one here, though? We aren't sure what she'd be worth. Probably too much trouble, right, Ivan?"

"Your choice, Vlad."

The one called Vlad chuckled, "I like that. Choices are good."

A.J. turned her head to find Trey's eyes. Her face became fierce with power and strength. He tried to shake his head at her, tell her not to do anything stupid, but he couldn't tell if any part of him had moved — the glacial chill of doom had already frozen his whole body.

She slammed her heel down hard on the top of Vlad's foot, and then elbowed him in the stomach. He growled furiously, grabbing her hair in his hand, making her cry out in response. He yanked her body around by the hair repeatedly.

"A.J.!" Trey shouted after them, finally finding his voice. He heard a gunshot and saw the bright flash of the bullet's report. A.J. made the oddest sound — a combination of shock and pain, then her body crumpled to the ground.

Before he could see her face one more time, Trey felt a brutal impact against the back of his own head.

Blackness invaded the edges of his eyes, and with his last conscious thought the crushing reality hit him: this was what it really meant to be an "Adler" — he was not a creator of worlds, but a destroyer of them.

CHAPTER ONE

Approximately Ten Years Later

Claudia McCoy slammed the driver's side door of her car shut behind her so hard it sent reverberations through the metal handle, rattling her hand and jarring the length of her arm in response. For good measure, just in case the offending automobile wasn't perfectly aware of how supremely pissed off she was, she delivered a firm kick to her front left tire. The rounded tip of her leather boot connected perfectly, bringing a grim smile to her tense face.

The satisfaction faded quickly, leaving her with jangled nerves. She cringed at her lost temper, taking a moment to peer at the door and make sure it was okay. It wasn't *really* her car, after all. It was the safe and reliable ride her brother, Wyatt, had bought for her as a college graduation present — another gift she'd never asked for, but could certainly not decline.

On a good day, Claudia treated such things with much more care.

But this was in no way a good day.

In fact, it was a terrible day and she was tempted to scream so loudly she broke every one of her dependable *Volvo's* tempered glass windows.

Instead, she turned and leaned back against its front fender, forcing her emotions into check until she'd calmed down. Claudia pushed her purse strap back onto her shoulder and made her way to the apartment building in front of her.

Claudia had been thrilled when her brother's girlfriend, Dr. Jenna Sutherland, had invited her to her old apartment for a girl's night in, complete with Jenna's two best friends.

Jenna was a beautiful orthopedic surgeon from Georgia, who also happened to be the only person in the world Wyatt ever seemed to listen to about anything. This fact alone was proof Claudia needed to get to know her better.

Maybe Pittsburgh wasn't Claudia's first choice of places to start her FBI career, but she'd been really trying to make a go of it, and new friends seemed like just the boost she needed. Which meant, she should probably stop acting like an angry eight-year-old in the parking lot and start socializing.

She entered the code Jenna had given her to the building, a free-flowing sense of excitement filling her body as she made her way up the steps.

Claudia pressed the doorbell of the apartment, now inhabited solely by Jenna's best friend, Aubrey.

The door opened and Claudia fought to soften her features so she didn't scare off the grinning cool-looking woman in front of her.

"Hi. I'm Claudia. You must be Aubrey. We haven't actually met, but..."

The tall beauty grabbed her and pulled her into a hug, which planted Claudia's face into her small bosom, knocking the wind out of her.

"Of course I know who you are! You're practically family, girl. Get on in here," Aubrey said cheerfully, pulling away enough to give Claudia some air before dragging her through the door. "Jenna's not here, yet. She called to say she's running late with one of her patients. Girl's night has already commenced, even if we're still short one girl."

"As long as it's no trouble, that would be great."

"Of course not. If I always waited for that workaholic to drag herself from the office, I'd never get a drink in me, and wouldn't that just be a shame? Our friend, Tea, is already here, too."

Aubrey's words came at Claudia like rapid-fire shotgun pellets of happiness, punctuating just how lonely and desperate she'd been for friendship over these last few frustrating weeks.

Claudia responded with a smile twitching at her lips, "Thank you. I really appreciate you guys including me."

"Don't be silly. We just feel bad it took three weeks to get us all together. Whenever your brother has an away game, Tea and I finally get to spend some time with Jenna. Don't worry. Tea can be a really bad influence, just like me — when she wants to be. Follow me," Aubrey ordered, walking with grace and ease toward the counter lining the open kitchen, where the woman they called 'Tea' was fussing with strawberries, mixers, rum, and a blender. She was stunning in her own way, shorter and more curvaceous than Aubrey, with full lips and big hazel eyes.

"Tea, we've got company, and she looks thirsty. Claude, would you like a daiquiri? Jenna bought a new blender for her and Wyatt's place, so I got to keep this one. We're celebrating with sugary 1980s girly drinks, so it was this or mudslides. You want one?"

Claudia hesitated, concerned at the prospect of what so much sugar and alcohol could do to her blood sugar.

"It's okay if you want something else," Tea said quickly. "I'm sure we can dig up some ingredients for a cocktail people actually drink in *this* decade."

Irritation welled inside her. Jenna claimed to understand when Claudia told her she didn't like people to know she was an insulin-dependent diabetic. *Jenna wouldn't really have told these girls without permission, would she?* Claudia worried.

"No. It's not a problem," Claudia insisted. "I'll have whatever you're drinking. I just need to use your bathroom first?"

"Of course, right through there," Aubrey answered and pointed down the hall. Claudia's feet moved her forward, while her brain quickly worked its way through the familiar insulin game so many type 1 diabetics knew how to play. Surviving college with a moderately normal existence required she maneuver a world full of junk food and alcohol — a minefield where the only armor was a well-trained eye for sugars and a good insulin pump. As far as she was concerned, this night was no different.

With the door shut behind her, Claudia reached to her waistband to reset her insulin pump. She wasn't sure how many carbs were in the sweet drink awaiting her, but it was probably a lot. Confident she'd upped the insulin amount enough, she made her way back to the kitchen to see the icy treat awaiting her.

Their smiling faces, which greeted Claudia, assured her she'd made the right choice. Ever since she'd graduated college, Claudia had missed being in the same town as her friends.

That sense of loss had been tempered by her fierce excitement at the prospect she could get assigned to the cybercrime division of the FBI's Washington, D.C. headquarters. She was eager to be a part of the action, taking on the toughest cases and worst bad guys in the country. Even though she'd learned years before her juvenile diabetes would prevent her from serving the military in combat, she was convinced this was the way she would achieve the next best thing.

Yet, one unfortunate day during training at Quantico had derailed all of those hopes. Claudia had passed all her medical and physical tests with flying colors, and even though her insulin dependency had given some pause, her internship with the Bureau had seemed to dispel all that — at least until her blood sugar dropped dramatically during a raid simulation exercise. As the room filled with the loud alarm of her glucose monitor, she'd clumsily tried to manage the situation on her own, but they wouldn't let her.

The medical staff simply fed into the hysteria, and before she knew it, a challenging D.C. assignment was off the table. They'd at least been kind enough to let her choose between several other locations. Though it risked putting her smack dab under her brother's watchful gaze, Claudia knew Pittsburgh was the most suitable compromise. It was close enough to D.C. to not completely eliminate the possibility of a real future, and it had a very respected cybercrime unit, with more than enough action to keep her busy. If only they'd let her actually do anything.

Instead it felt like everything she'd fought for over the last several years, and dreamed of throughout her life, had all been ripped from her. Now, she was in a strange city, acting as a glorified desk clerk, with no friends to keep her company, unless one counted the presence of her own steadily growing need to prove to the world she could really be a successful field agent.

"Here you go, Claude," Tea said, waving her hand at it, before taking a seat at the counter with them. "Jenna said you work at the FBI. How cool. What do you do there?"

Claudia took a long sip before speaking, "Not much it seems."

"What do you mean?" Aubrey asked.

"Sorry, I swore to myself I wouldn't bitch about work tonight."

"That's one of our main pastimes here, come on, bring it," Tea commanded.

Claudia chuckled, explaining, "Well, Pittsburgh wasn't my first choice assignment, but I've been trying to make the most of it."

"Good for you," Tea said encouragingly, toasting her glass to Claudia's.

"A lot of good it's done me. They keep sticking me on these bullshit low-level investigations, and today, one of my friends, Drew, said the word around the office is no one wants to see Pittsburgh's star quarterback's little sister get hurt."

"Is that true? Can they do that?" Aubrey asked incredulously.

"I'd like to believe they couldn't. But Drew's been in the office five years now and knows pretty much everybody, so if there's a rumor, he's heard it. Even if it's not true, anyone even thinking *it* is so humiliating. And Wyatt didn't help, sending everybody signed jerseys and footballs, coming by and taking pictures. I told him to stay away… I explained no one would take me seriously, but he just blew it off."

"Did you tell him what Drew said?"

"Yeah. He claimed not to have any kind of influence over the FBI," Claudia dropped her voice to impersonate her brother, *"'But if my swinging by makes people second guess getting you killed, then that's great.'"*

"Aw, I bet you wanted to punch him in the face!" Tea said loudly, slurring slightly. "Sorry. I actually had two cocktails while I made these. Aubrey, help me out with the advice here."

"No, I agree. I was going to propose punching him somewhere else. Wyatt is definitely a leopard who won't change his stripes…or spots, which one is it Tea?"

Claudia laughed, a heady and giggly feeling filling her body.

"Focus Brey. Damn Claude, you must be so frustrated."

"I am! I just want to do my best — really kick ass. If they'd only let me try, they'd see I know what I'm doing! Um, by the way, could I have some water?" she asked, her mouth incredibly dry from thirst. Aubrey quickly fetched Claudia a glass of ice water, which she slurped gratefully, before continuing with her story.

"It's probably even more aggravating because you're in a new city, living a life you may not have planned or chosen for yourself," Tea stated carefully.

"You're exactly right. How'd you know?" Claudia asked, honestly surprised at how insightful this woman's words were.

"My husband, Jack, died almost seven years ago, during my last year of law school. He mysteriously drowned late one night. I was a little older than you, and in an instant, I'd lost everything. I was alone in Jack's hometown, with nothing to call my own. Then I found out I was pregnant without any warning. Aubrey and Jenna moved here to help me after Johnny was born, but..."

"Wow, that was so great of them to do," Claudia enthused.

"Yeah, we're really amazing. You'll see," Aubrey added slyly, Tea just rolled her eyes before continuing.

"They helped me so much. We were like our own little family, but it took me years to really find my way and not feel like I was missing something."

"That and meeting Griffen Tate," Aubrey added.

Tea laughed, "Yeah, Griffen was a big part of it."

"He's your fiancé right?" Claudia clarified.

"Mmm hmm. I had no idea when I'd met him last year, but he'd actually been Jack's best friend when they were growing up here in Pittsburgh. He's the one who helped me find my heart again, even though I fought like hell to hold on to my grief. And he did everything in his power to figure out how Jack really died — that he'd been murdered by his boss and mentor, David Murphy," Tea explained, as she shivered slightly.

"That son of a bitch, David, even had the nerve to hang around and moon over Tea for years. He helped her with little Johnny, and everything..." Aubrey growled.

"When all the while, he was hiding the fact he took money from some unknown bad guys to steal information from the *CMU* robotics department where they worked. Jack was just caught in the proverbial crossfire, I guess," Tea mumbled, sadly.

Claudia remained silent. She was very familiar with the continuing efforts to learn which "bad guys" actually paid Professor David Murphy to betray his employer and kill his protégé. In fact, it was an obsession of hers to get to help on the case.

"It wasn't easy for Griffen to break through and convince me I was able to have a life of my own, believe me," Tea continued, a little emotion still coming through her voice.

"But Griffen got the girl *and* busted David, because he's a bulldozing investigative journalist who refuses to quit when it comes to what he wants to know, or whom he wants to get," Aubrey interjected, smirking at Tea.

"The point is, you never know where this life will lead you," Tea interjected. "Jack's death was the most horrific tragedy, but it was also like a stone falling in a pond. Each ripple from that one act has touched so many people, many of them here in this city now with me. So you may find your own little derailment in life could lead you to something really great...something you never even knew you wanted."

"She writes fortune cookies in her spare time if you're interested. Good thing Jenna's not here to listen to you get all *'one-to-grow-on,'* Tea. She'd be making so much fun of you right now," Aubrey teased.

"I know. Well, guilty as charged. I'm the big softy in this group. Sorry, Claude," Tea responded, taking a healthy slurp of her daiquiri.

"Oh no, I think it's great advice! It's what I keep trying to tell myself. In fact, I found the perfect opportunity, too. There's this case I want to work on…"

Claudia paused, watching her words carefully. She didn't want to compromise any sensitive information by sharing details about active cases, especially as it was an investigation into the very acts, which had stolen Tea's first chance at happiness so many years before. The case may be the biggest thing happening at the Pittsburgh office, but she needed to be sensitive to the human tragedy behind it, especially after Tea had been so open with her.

"Did you ask to get on the case?" Aubrey inquired, disturbing Claudia from her fuzzy thoughts.

"I did! I may be new, but it's the biggest cybercrime case going right now. Other junior agents have been allowed to help, even though they're in other departments. After I scared up some of the non-confidential files, I came up with ideas about what might help the investigation. I swear, if I had a chance to show them what I'm capable of, I might finally get back all that progress I made when I was in D.C. I'm worried if I don't make it happen now, I never will."

"You don't take no for an answer do you?" Tea asked.

"No. It's kind of not in my vocabulary. Today, after Drew told me what people were saying about me, I got an anonymous email with a tip. I figured that had to change my boss' mind. But when I went to him about it, he said no way. That it's too dangerous for me and someone else should do it."

"Well that just sucks," Aubrey stated definitively. "There's got to be some way you can make them come around."

"I agree," Tea added, "you must've worked really hard to make it this far. If they can't see what you have to offer, then you have to make them."

Claudia nodded and smiled.

"Thank you," she answered, but she was suddenly having trouble forcing the words out of her mouth. Her eyes felt so heavy as they tried to focus on her newly-filled drink. She couldn't process how much of this sugar bomb she'd put in her body. Claudia wondered if she'd misjudged the amount of carbs when setting her insulin, but it was too hard to figure it out as her eyes started to close independent of her own will.

"Are you okay, sweetie?" she heard Tea ask in the distance.

"Damn it, you're so tiny, maybe you have a really low tolerance? Come on, you can lie down in Jenna's old room."

"That sounds nice," Claudia muttered slowly, feeling two arms lifting her off her stool.

"Jenna's room is still set up? Wow, Aubrey, are you in denial much?" Tea asked, helping Claudia from her seat.

"Shut up, Tea. Focus on Claudia."

"I'm fine," Claudia forced through her lips.

"Poor thing. Aubrey, I think I should text Jenna. She'll want to know Claude's not feeling well."

Claudia's eyes closed as they laid her body down on a soft mattress that felt as dense as the syrupy blood running through her veins. Once they left, she reached to her pump, quickly upping the insulin amount, before closing her eyes and waiting for it to take effect and battle the powerful sugar clogging her bloodstream.

It seemed to Claudia like only a moment had passed when cool hands began touching her hip.

"What's going on? What are you doing?" Claudia mumbled, her lips stumbling over each sound.

"I'm giving you insulin."

"Jenna?"

"Yes, it's me. Hold still while I give you a shot."

"But my pump…"

"Is almost empty. And you're pretty hyperglycemic. Jesus, Claudia. You have to know drinks like those daiquiris you had are so bad for you."

Claudia felt the needle enter her body, releasing the insulin she hated and loved simultaneously, into her body. What a fool she'd been — trying to live a regular life. That realization didn't change the furious sense of impotent anger coursing through her body, just as powerfully as the injection Jenna was giving her.

"I am *not* a child," Claudia huffed out to her.

"I know that, but..." Jenna trailed off, clearly searching for the right words to say.

"I thought I had everything under control…"

"You probably would've been okay, but why even risk it?" Jenna muttered. "Wyatt's already so worried about you."

"This isn't about Wyatt. It's none of his business," Claudia insisted.

"That's your decision to make. I understand wanting to keep issues with your health to yourself, believe me… Besides, I have ethical obligations to protect your privacy. Still, I'm sure he'd want to know."

Claudia's mouth felt hot and cloudy as she worked it around her words.

"I'm sorry, Jenna."

As the insulin started to take effect, Claudia already felt more like herself — enough to sense Jenna sigh and lie down next to her.

Jenna stroked Claudia's hair gently, making her feel safe enough to let her eyes flutter back closed.

"Don't be sorry, Claudia. You've had a rough few weeks, these things happen. Nobody's perfect, and I'm not asking you to be. You'll feel better soon. You can stay here tonight. Just rest. I took care of you. No matter what happens, I am always going to look out for you."

Trey thanked the barista for the two drinks she handed him, adding a quick smile and wink, which made her red lips curl upward into a grin. The soft light in the small, hipster coffeehouse Jenna had invited him to glinted off the woman's lip ring, while her smooth cheeks quickly blushed.

She was hot, and the hungry look her black-rimmed eyes were giving his whole body promised an afternoon full of distracting trouble. The busy street outside hummed with a frenzied activity akin to complex circuitry. This untapped energy of the accompanying world around him seemed to be transmitting directly into his body.

That same nervous tingling continued through his limbs, bringing with it a familiar sense of wanting to command something — anything, anyone — for a brief moment. That urge was in his blood, and no matter what he did, it never seemed to go away. The only cure was to keep his "relationships" short and meaningless, to ensure he didn't give a shit what happened to the woman — or women — beneath him on any specific night.

If Trey had more time, he would take this barista up on her flirtatious look — see if he could make other parts of her skin blush. Yet, the powerful impulse to get back to Jenna was far more important than his unquenchable frustration. Jenna needed him. That was clear in her voice when she'd asked to meet him.

He'd settled into a cozy, albeit temporary, way of life in Pittsburgh, with friends, including Jenna, who mattered to him. This meant playtime with a dirty little coffee-slinging minx was going to have to wait for another day.

Trey made his way back to the table where Jenna waited for him. Her face was schooled into its most serious expression, which was saying a lot since she'd already cornered the market on intensity.

"Damn, woman, you look all worked up. I hope this helps." He placed her mug in front of her before sitting down. "It better be how you like it, because if you need more of that pumpkin spice shit in your drink, we've got problems."

Trey gestured with his head to the line that had grown since they'd arrived. The place was pretty packed, but it was close to where Jenna had her *UPMC* sports medicine practice, and her schedule was too tight for much more than coffee.

"The world calls them 'lattes,' Trey. And most of America has been drinking them for ages now," she teased with a slight smile, but she wouldn't meet his eyes.

"I know. I'm still protesting the entire concept, no matter how long they've been around. I fought them growing up in San Francisco and I'll keep doing it here."

"You're such a baby," she teased.

"I'm not a baby, I'm a *man*...so it's *coffee.* I drink coffee." Trey made a tough guy face, hoping it would loosen her up a little.

Jenna rolled her eyes dramatically and released a burst of laughter from her mouth, but quickly let worry streak her face again.

Trey touched her chin for a second, forcing her to look at him before leaning back in his seat.

"All right, Jenna, if it isn't your *latte* that's bugging you, why'd you have to see me so urgently?"

Her sharp light-blue eyes darted between his and her frothy drink, while her long fingers twisted the cup in little half-circles — back and forth so many times he worried she might saw through the wooden table beneath it.

"I know you helped Tea's fiancé, Griffen, with investigating Jack Taylor's…you know…murder… And you told me you've been working with the FBI on it since then. Are you still doing that?"

"Yep."

Trey had agreed to work on that case, and possibly any others the FBI needed help with. In return, they'd overlook how he'd played a bit fast and loose with the precise letter of the law, when helping his good friend uncover the facts behind Jack Taylor's mysterious end — which turned out to be a tragic murder at the hands of David Murphy.

When Griffen and Trey handed them Murphy on a silver platter over a year ago, the FBI hadn't been able to make any immediate headway in determining which nefarious folks had bribed Murphy to help them steal the sensitive, and valuable, robotics work, occurring at *Carnegie Mellon University* on behalf of both governmental and private groups.

The list of who would want such information, including both foreign states and shadowy crime syndicates, was long, but evidence was scarce. That's when they'd come up with Trey's "deal."

Normally Trey would've told the feds to kiss his ass, and deal with whatever repercussions came. It wasn't the first time he'd bent some laws, and it wouldn't be the last. Yet, they'd dangled the promise of keeping Griffen completely free of any consequences related to their actions if Trey sat at a desk in the

Pittsburgh FBI field office and helped them figure out their asses, versus their elbows, in the Taylor case.

Trey couldn't bring himself to refuse. Fact was, even though Trey had nothing left in life to lose, he knew Griffen had a brand new future nestled precariously in his grasp. He was about to be a stepfather and a husband. People needed him, and as much as Trey wanted to avoid complications, he'd figured doing Griffen this additional favor wasn't too big a hardship.

Yet, weeks of helping the FBI had turned into months, and Trey had been hitting roadblocks of his own since he'd joined the investigation.

"So, does that mean you're still spending a lot of time consulting at the Pittsburgh FBI office?" Jenna inquired.

"Yes. I was there today, actually. It's how I made it here so fast," Trey answered slowly.

"Oh, good. I didn't know since you left town recently, for God knows where."

"I had a little side issue to look into, but I'm back now, at least until I can finish helping them sort out the Jack Taylor case."

Trey looked into the dark liquid in his cup, letting the import of his recent trip to Shanghai enter and leave his mind. When he'd accepted the FBI's offer, Trey had promised Griffen he'd use the arrangement to guarantee *all* those who'd lead to Jack Taylor's murder would be found and punished. Trey never broke a promise to a friend. Well, not anymore.

Yet, a different vendetta had taken him to Shanghai — an unresolved debt still lingering after the loss of A.J. His buddy, Stephen, the leader of a CIA task force, had brought Trey to the glamorous Chinese city to follow up on a lead. It turned out to be good enough to drag him away from the Taylor case — if only for a few days.

Trey had wanted to keep the trip to himself. Even though his Pittsburgh friends didn't know where he'd gone, the fact they knew he'd left at all was still more information than he was accustomed to sharing about himself with others. It seemed like every day he spent in Pittsburgh he was becoming more wrapped up in other people's lives, which never turned out well.

His heart clenched whenever he thought about the last time he'd made that mistake. His mind would follow on its own dark path, tormented by memories of A.J.'s desperate screams, followed by the vision of awakening in a dark cell, waiting for his own solo rescue, which did not extend to the life of his helpless first love. His father had paid Trey's ransom and managed to make yet another hacking crime disappear. After he'd pulled every string — and lined many pockets — at *Stanford* to keep them from pressing charges related to the Starling Virus, it was as though nothing had ever happened.

The school may have cooperated with protecting Trey's freedom, but they didn't want him back. The feeling was mutual, because when no amount of effort or money had managed to recover whatever was left of A.J., Trey couldn't bring himself to step foot anywhere near that campus. He certainly didn't want to see the building housing the "Adler School of Computer Science," erected a year after a bullet ripped into A.J.'s beautiful body a mere one hundred yards from where they broke ground.

Despite knowing what a waste it was to let himself care for people, he wasn't quite ready to go back to his closed off existence. Another month or two of pretending to be an ordinary person who had a beer with his friends on the weekends, and listened to their problems, was just too tempting.

After taking a deep breath, Jenna met his eyes, breaking him from his own maudlin reverie. "I was hoping to talk to you about someone."

"Who?"

"Claudia McCoy, Wyatt's sister."

"What about her? Not sure what she has to do with me."

"She's in Pittsburgh…assigned to the FBI office here…"

"I heard that," Trey said slowly, regaining his cool as he took time with his words.

"Can you look out for her, Trey?" Jenna blurted.

Trey almost choked on his coffee at the sheer mention of that family in relation to him.

"It's not crazy for me to ask. You helped Wyatt before."

"No. I did that for you. I helped him try to fix things for you after his stupid ass broke your heart and almost ruined your career."

"And I'm still so grateful. For all you've done since we became friends this past year, but I think you're being a little dramatic, Trey."

"*Right.* Well, it seemed pretty fucking dramatic at the time when everyone in the world was saying he seduced you as the consultant on his shoulder to save his starting quarterback spot. And even though I worked with him to protect you from all the crap he put into motion, it doesn't change how I still think he has the capacity to be a piece of shit. I don't know if I'll ever think he's good enough for you or that he's made up for the harm he caused."

"He's not like that. If you two would just give each other a chance and not fight every time you're in the same room, then you'd see that. I don't get why you're so hostile still about him."

"I get it. You're happy now, and living together, and all that shit. I'm glad you're crazy about each other and everything, but I don't have to like him, and I sure as hell don't have to do anything for his fucking family. Some people only know how to hurt the ones they love," Trey added, disgusted to hear how much his words about Wyatt sound like the ones, which had rattled in his own head over the years about *himself.*

"You're such a poet, Trey. He doesn't hurt me, though. We love each other, and I want to look out for him and his family as much as I can. You know I wouldn't come to you about anything involving Wyatt unless I were really concerned."

"I feel like I should've made a New Year's resolution or something to keep me from the McCoy family and all their bullshit — but it's fall now, so I guess I'm screwed. Either way, I'm pretty fucking done after what happened with you and Wyatt."

"I know that. I hate even asking you for this, Trey..." Jenna twisted her cup between her hands again, this time with a precision consistent with her occupation as a surgeon.

"Thanks. Then you should also know I'm pretty sure I've already had more than enough of Wyatt McCoy — a feeling which extends to his relatives — so I'm not sure why you'd want me to do anything for his sister."

"Then do it for *me*," she pleaded, placing her hands together as she begged.

"That's not fair," Trey said with a laugh. "Fine. What's wrong with her — other than being a McCoy."

"I'm going to ignore that last part. There's nothing *wrong* with her. She's awesome, actually, but she can be hardheaded and Wyatt will have an aneurysm if anything happens to her."

"Like what?"

"She's very young and is going through a tough transition with moving here and starting at the FBI. I want to make sure she's...taking care of herself. I can't say any more, but I wouldn't come to you if I didn't trust you. You know that."

"Why don't you ask her boss at the Bureau — *Assistant Director in Charge Jacobs*?" Trey's voice dripped with snide disdain at the title. Jacobs was a pompous ass, who wasn't qualified to look after a lemonade stand, but he *was* Agent McCoy's direct supervisor.

"I don't know him. I know *you.* I don't want to humiliate her, or mess up her career. I just want to get her through this rough patch. She's stubborn…"

"And you know *all* about stubborn McCoys."

"Exactly. Look. You have relationships in her office. You're there all the time, but you aren't in the FBI."

"So, you want me to babysit Wyatt's spoiled little sister? Even if I were willing, I'm not sure your boyfriend would appreciate my oversight — seeing as he and I have such a kick-ass relationship, and by that I mean, we want to kick each other's asses."

"He doesn't have to know. Actually, it's better if he doesn't." Trey arched a brow at her, but she dismissed his facial expression with a shake of her head. "Please, Trey…"

He could hear the desperation in her words — her feeling of helplessness, even if he didn't know what was causing it.

"Fine, I'll do it…like you said, for you, not for him."

"I'll take it. And Trey…"

"Yes?"

"Don't sleep with her."

"With Claudia McCoy? Don't worry. Seriously, Jenna, who do you think I am?"

"I know exactly who you are, which is why I'm telling you not to sleep with her."

"I didn't sleep with *you.*"

"Wow, you amaze me with your self-restraint. And you know the decision was mutual."

"True, neither of us wanted to screw the other. That definitely helps with abstaining. But I'm trying to turn over a new leaf in general. I'm practically a model citizen these days."

Jenna let loose a rough laugh, before adding skeptically, "That would take a lot of leaves, Trey."

"A whole tree's worth, huh? But seriously, I'm almost a brand-new person nowadays — you should be more encouraging."

"I'm really proud of you, Trey," Jenna teased.

"I'll take that as a thank-you for the huge favor I'm about to do for you. You're welcome. I better get going if I want to get this errand over with."

Trey stood to leave, but Jenna grabbed his sleeve to stop him.

"Thank you so much for your help with this. You're the best," Jenna said quickly, standing to give him a hug.

He squeezed her back, and laughed. "You're right. I *am* pretty damn awesome. You're lucky I like you, blondie, because you are seriously a lot of trouble."

CHAPTER TWO

Claudia's boots made a cringe-inducing crunching sound as she treaded over a smattering of dried leaves and gravel. The sound was almost thunderous against the silent backdrop of the abandoned steel mill site to which her very first tip had led her, forcing her to pause for a moment as the echoing noise dissipated. The delay was also helpful in allowing her racing heart to slow, if only a small amount.

Insidious shadows overtook the many nooks and crevices of the metallic wasteland surrounding her. Ribbons of violet, yellow, and dusky orange, which had been streaking flamboyantly above the length of the Ohio River, were rapidly surrendering to the much more inky, and menacing, dark shades of impending twilight.

With a shaky breath, she took out her phone to look at the satellite map images she'd collected before leaving her duplex. Claudia relied on the glow from her phone and made a quick left turn between two small buildings.

They appeared to have once been designated for storage during a now bygone era, the idea of which felt almost wistful on that desolate night. Yet, in the brutal present, after years of neglect, the decrepit metal structures had become merely broken-down artifacts of a way of life long-since departed from the former "steel town" she was now calling home. It was hard not to be depressed by the rejected and disgusting relic of a world no one seemed to want any longer.

It had been decades since generations of dutiful workers reported to this place every day to craft some of the metal, which formed the backbone of Pittsburgh's development. Now, its only visitors were graffiti artists, and perhaps the occasional drunk hoping to find a peaceful spot for their escape…and at that moment — apparently — her.

The entire scene was lonesome and anachronistic in a way, which made her uncomfortable with the task she'd put upon herself. It also seemed like a damn fine place to get tetanus, so Claudia was treading carefully.

She put her phone away and zipped up her light leather jacket, her fingers quivering with a treacherous, uncontrollable energy. The evening autumn air was crisp, and had been seeping through her jacket and thin tee shirt, chilling her blood. It seemed to be so much colder down by the river, the rusted-out hulls of dozens of aluminum buildings creating a whistling wind tunnel, which buffeted her small body with merciless, cutting gusts.

This collapsing, metal ghost town seemed a universe away from the sparkling high-rises of downtown Pittsburgh, and the tree-lined brick streets of its historic neighborhoods. Her nerves started to get the better of her, causing her heart to race and breath to quicken.

Calm down, she chastised herself, before panic could set into her blood. *I'm the one who wanted to be tough — a real field agent. That means I need to suck it up, find the box the tipster told me about, and then I can get the hell out of here.*

This private pep talk seemed to work, steeling her nerves enough to keep walking with more confidence in each step. With another sure-footed step, she turned sharply to maneuver between two more buildings.

Her feet, and her pulse, stopped short when a shadow flashed across the corner of her vision. At first, she could almost convince herself it was just her imagination, but she whipped her head around and caught sight of a form ducking behind a corner. She caught enough of a view to see it was a man — tall and broad-shouldered beneath his hooded sweatshirt.

Claudia made sure her *Glock* was quickly accessible, but she wanted to do all she could to avoid using it. This interloper could either be dangerous, or the person behind her tip — or both. Seeing as she wasn't even supposed to be there, discharging her FBI-issued weapon was not a good idea. She took advantage of her own petite frame and maneuvered forward delicately, venturing toward a more open area of the mill site.

When the light was bright enough, she caught his shadow move more closely behind her.

Perfect.

With one quick motion, Claudia spun around with a roundhouse kick to his stomach. The muscles of his abs were firm beneath her blow, but she'd thrown him off-balance, and the force elicited quite a few expletives from under his breath. Taking advantage of his distraction, Claudia moved herself closer to the ground, to increase her body's leverage for a more effective attack. Supporting herself with her hands, she spun around with a low kick, taking him off his feet and landing him on his ass.

Worried he'd get back up, Claudia pinned his arms to the ground, as she stretched her body out on top of his. He didn't fight her at all. Perhaps he was still winded from her stomach kick. Securing both his hands with one of her forearms, Claudia used her free hand to pull his hood back from his face, and her breath skipped in her throat. The shadowy figure she'd just taken down was freaking gorgeous.

Dark hair framed his tanned skin. His face was so close to hers, she could feel his hot breath just barely brush against her skin. He looked vaguely familiar, but she couldn't quite place him. Especially when she was distracted by the way his twisted curve of a half-smile, and sparkling gray eyes, made it clear he was laughing at her. Still not uttering a word, he grinned fully at her and began to move his large torso to sit up and face her.

Oh, hell no, she thought. Moving her hands to his chest, she pushed him hard to the ground.

"Hey, easy, little tiger," he grunted out. "I let you have your fun, but this ground is starting to get uncomfortable. Even for a tough guy like me."

The smoothness of his voice, even through his clear annoyance, was almost hypnotic. His face held a few piercings and she could spy some tattoos peeking out from underneath his hoodie, but he didn't look hard or scary — just intensely sexy.

Finding a man so attractive was new to Claudia. It was really pissing her off how her own eyes were more interested in his strong jaw and chiseled cheekbones, rather than with trying to determine if he was aggressive.

She couldn't help herself, though. His face had a couple days of stubble, and she wondered what it felt like. Would it be prickly, or smooth?

"Are you done?"

"Excuse me? Done doing what?"

"Staring at me?" he teased with a smile, which revealed a row of perfect, straight teeth resting behind his distracting lips.

"I-I'm not staring at you. I need to ascertain what kind of a threat you are."

"Fine. Play it that way. You don't need to worry about me. I'm on your side."

"What? *My* side? Did Agent Jacobs figure out I was still going to follow up on this tip? Did he send you?" Claudia asked rapidly, worry overpowering all other thought.

"Jacobs? Hell no. Your dumb-ass assistant director wouldn't recognize a tip in a urinal."

"You're disgusting," Claudia snipped out, but his crass joke made a smile twitch at her lips.

"Besides, I'm not a Fed. Well, not really."

"Then who are you? Tell me who you are right now, or so help me…"

"So help you, what? You'll swat at me with those little mitts of yours again?"

Claudia lifted a tiny fist and went at him hard. She wanted nothing more than to show him how this tiny paw of hers could do some serious damage, but he grabbed it in one of his large hands before she connected. She shook her hand out of his, fury pumping through her.

"You son of a bitch! Tell me who you are."

"Calm down. I'm Trey," he answered, awkwardly moving his other hand from his supine position to shake hers. "Nice to meet you, Agent McCoy, I guess… I'm one of Jenna's friends."

Claudia leaned back, sitting fully on his midsection as she processed this information.

"Wait. Trey? Trey *Adler*? Are you the one that's in love with my brother's *girlfriend,* Jenna?"

"The Adler part is right. But I'm not in love with Jenna. What gave you that idea?"

"That's what Wyatt says."

"What your brother is wrong about is a lot."

"That may be true, but you still haven't told me what you're doing here."

"Um, first, do you mind moving? I know you're just a little thing…"

"I'm not little!"

"If you'd let me finish, I was going to say, no, you aren't that small. But if you don't climb off me we're going to have a situation on our hands. Or in my lap, to put it more accurately."

"You're a pig."

"You're the one who won't climb off of me."

Claudia huffed at him as she stood, pushing off his chest hard enough to hear him release a satisfying *oof* sound. Trey lifted a hand to her, his crooked grin never still in place.

She stared at him for a minute, finally grabbing his hand with hers and helping him up from the ground. His hand fully enveloped her much smaller one. It was rough and cool to her touch. As soon as he was standing, Claudia dropped it like she'd been bitten. Now that he was standing fully in front of her, she had to crane her head back fully to meet his eyes.

"Impressive," he said softly. "You really are a little one. It was quite a pleasure letting you take me down."

"*Letting* me? Screw you." He just laughed gently in return. Claudia tried to bring reason back to her mind. "Why did Jenna ask you to follow me? What did she tell you?" Claudia demanded.

Shame coated Claudia's throat at the memory of letting herself get even remotely sick in front of her brother's girlfriend. A stunning and confident physician, she knew a diabetic who may not be able to handle her shit when she saw one.

Trey looked down at her, his eyes turning warm and reassuring. Claudia decided she preferred his teasing manner to this unnerving, caring demeanor.

"Jenna didn't tell me anything. She didn't have to. She just asked and I said yes. I'm around the Pittsburgh FBI office a lot. I'm helping with the ongoing investigation into Jack Taylor's murder, so she figured I could keep an eye on you."

"I know that case. I've been trying to get in on it. But they keep sticking me on the FBI equivalent of cat-stuck-up-in-a-tree types of cases. That's what..."

"This supposed lead is about? I know. I also know you were instructed not to follow up on it."

"Yeah. I get told 'no' quite a bit."

"I'm not a fan of being told what to do either, Claudia." It was the first time he'd said her name, and it was like he'd poured warm honey down her body. "But that doesn't mean you shouldn't be careful. You were planning to follow up on a shady tip like this all alone?"

"I was doing some digging of my own when it came through directly to me. It didn't seem completely suspect, plus I tried to get support, but they said it was too dangerous for me to pursue."

"So instead you decided to come out here by yourself — a place that looks like Murder City, population of you? Forget the danger factor for a second, do you know how much trouble you'll get into with your boss?"

"So? Look who's talking? From what I hear about you, all you do is get in trouble."

He stepped so closely to her he towered completely over her. The heat of his body came over her in waves, almost overwhelming her. Trey stared down at her until she met his eyes completely.

"*You* aren't me," he whispered.

"Thank goodness for that," she huffed out, turning to walk away briskly. Claudia raised her chin, desperately trying to remember her original path before this tattooed pain-in-the-ass interfered with her evening, but it seemed like her brain just wouldn't work. A sudden tug at her right arm spun her around, forcing her to look up again, straight onto his chiseled features.

"All right, that's it. This whole feisty thing is cute, and all. But I promised Jenna I'd keep you alive, so I'll tell you right now — this shit's going to get old really quick."

"I'm so sorry to inconvenience you. Here's a solution. How about you leave me alone then? It's a win-win, for both of us."

"Oh no you don't, little one. Trust me, being Wyatt's little sister's designated hand-holder is not appealing to me in the slightest..."

"I don't need you holding my hand — or anything else for that matter," Claudia interrupted gruffly.

"Are you sure about that?" he taunted. "Regardless, Jenna is a good friend and I can't say no to her."

"That does a lot for your whole 'I'm not in love with Jenna' game."

Trey pressed a hand at the small of her back, stilling her.

"Are you scared that I'm in love with Jenna, or that I'm not, and I'm available?"

"Oh, please. I know your game, and your type. You just want to torment me. Thing is, if I don't get going, it will get too dark to find anything, and this whole night will have been a waste."

"Not a *total* waste," he answered with a smile, "you got to meet me."

"Ugh, no wonder my brother hates you."

"Trust me, my feelings toward your brother are mutual. It doesn't change why I'm here, or what I promised to do. If you won't give up, then I guess you're going to have to get used to me going everywhere you do... Face it kid, I'm your new — much taller — shadow."

Claudia turned away from him and her stomach turned when she noticed night had almost completely fallen. The mill yard had seemed manageable before, but now, all she saw was a vast archipelago of hidden alleys and easy hiding places. She'd come too far to turn back now, but doubt had crept into her bones, as insidiously as rust had slowly overtaken the building in front of her. "What do they say in the movies?" Claudia muttered to herself. "Oh, right. I've got a bad feeling about this."

"Me too. Do you want to leave now?"

"I'm not giving up. I never give up."

"Me neither, little one," he answered.

"Stop calling me —"

A loud bang in the distance made her jump. She swallowed hard before choking out, "Fine. If you really want to come, I guess I can't stop you."

"How kind of you, because unfortunately for both of us, you're stuck with me. And I'm not going to let anything happen to you, little one."

Trey watched as Claudia's shiny, dark ponytail bounced behind her. She was blowing out little indignant breaths in time to each of her steps from just a short pace in front of him. Wyatt McCoy's little sister was already proving to be the pain in the ass Trey had anticipated she'd be, but the image of her tight little body and pretty face had a potent way of taking the sting out of his own practiced annoyance.

Although he'd looked up a picture of her before tracking her down to this deserted steel mill, it definitely hadn't done her justice. Her frame was tiny, but shapely enough to make him wonder how she hid such strength under all her tempting curves

— much less, how the hell she'd managed to knock him right off his feet. She was practically *Smurf*-sized. She may have planted him on his ass, but all he wanted to do was bite hers. Yeah, that would definitely be an awkward conversation to have with Jenna.

"You'd be proud of me, Jenna. I didn't sleep with Claudia...I just bit her butt."

Another bratty and adorable sigh emanated from the sashaying form in front of him, bringing his wandering brain slightly back to reality.

Her delicate, yet sensuous features and body were completely inconsistent with their surroundings, which at best could be said to resemble a George Orwell fever dream. Yet, somehow her obvious drive and fierce resolve made her seem right at home in the perilous world in which she'd insisted on thrusting herself.

The whole package left Trey feeling a little unbalanced — a sensation he hadn't experienced in almost a decade.

Sure, he knew she was the daughter of a model, but nothing could've prepared him for the effect of feeling her pinning him down on the ground and finally seeing her perfect face, free of even a hint of makeup.

Trey's heart still raced at the thought of Claudia's wide, dark eyes peering down at him, their disturbing beauty matched only by the shape of her full mouth, which was at once innocent and indecent. It felt like he'd been sucked into a parallel universe, one full of endless hope and goodness — a place where he could never live, but dammit, he'd love to be able to visit.

Trey mentally shook some sense into himself. He needed to keep those kinds of thoughts in check. Nothing good would ever come of indulging the dirty thoughts still rattling around in his brain ever since she'd sat astride him. Any other woman would've been on her back beneath him in a second, but he'd let her have her victory and suppressed his urge to take control of the moment.

Noticing her head whipping back and forth, he looked over her shoulder to a map she'd apparently prepped for the trip.

He tapped her shoulder, and she jumped, quickly setting her face in a frustrated scowl.

"Looks like we go this way," he said, pointing to the left, down a dark path along the river. It would keep the steel mill to their left, and preserve their ability to escape, if necessary.

"Right…um, yeah, you're right," she mumbled, her voice sounding different from the last time she'd spoken to him — almost confused, though he couldn't imagine her ever showing that kind of weakness to him. Her face then twisted back to irritation, and she clomped quickly to her left.

Trey grimaced at the echoing sound her march was creating through the emptiness. Leaning down to her ear, he whispered, "You might want to keep the petulant stomping to a minimum. It really fucks with whatever element of surprise you may be going for."

She inhaled deeply and spun her face and shoulders away from him, gifting him with a distracting swipe of her fragrant, soft hair against his face. Trey's mouth quickly went dry from the contact.

"I don't get why Jenna is even friends with you," Claudia stated roughly, looking straight ahead again.

"I'm a great friend. It's all the other stuff I'm shitty at."

"I guess I can believe that. I'm not too good at those other things either."

"We have something in common? Shocking," Trey teased, and she rolled her eyes, releasing an odd giggle that seemed almost surreal coming from her mouth.

She was clearly impulsive, coming out to this place by herself, but her ambition was a pleasant surprise. Claudia may have the smoking hot body of *Catwoman*, but underneath that she was all *Tasmanian Devil.* Maybe on paper she seemed like an indulged young woman, whose brother coddled her as if she were a child, but at least the impressive real-life version of her appeared to want some form of autonomy, in whatever brazen way she could find it.

"What I'm worried about is that we also have insanity in common."

"What do you mean?" she asked, bringing her hand to her mouth to put something in it.

"The reason you're here. A lead shows up in your email on a case you aren't even handling... Doesn't that seem suspicious?"

"Of course it does. I'm not an idiot."

"Are you sure about that? You seem pretty stubborn," Trey grumbled through clenched teeth, which were suddenly gritting with worry. He could feel his hands curling with the urge to grab her and shake some sense into her.

"I won't deny the latter. But those are two very different things."

She stumbled slightly and her voice slurred somewhat over the last word. Though she quickly looked away from him, he caught her sneaking one of her small hands into her jacket pocket. Her hand shot back out, and she stuffed something in her mouth again.

"Are you okay?"

"I'm fine," she retorted sharply, but her steps were slowing down and her hand was trembling when she tried to look at the map on her cell phone. Her breaths were coming out in rapid, almost-panicked bursts, and her eyes appeared as if swimming around, not focusing on anything.

"You don't *look* fine. How about we get out of here?"

"I already told you, I'm not doing that…"

"Yes, you did, but I don't have to listen to you." Worry was starting to fill Trey's brain — a sensation that was quickly turning into an insistent need to take over this whole ridiculous situation, as well as this obstinate woman.

She ignored him, and took a small, unsteady step, before turning her head back and forth.

"What was I going to say? Oh, right, even if the email is fishy, that's all the more reason to figure out why I got it and if it could mean something. I've looked into it and this Taylor case has been going nowhere new — fast — for months."

"And you think *you* could make all the difference?"

"What good detective w-wouldn't, um, think that?"

Her words were suddenly coming out somewhat garbled. After stuffing another handful into her mouth, she averted her eyes from him and chewed whatever it was with an almost desperate determination.

Claudia took several steps forward, but stumbled slightly. After reaching her arms out for stability, she managed to regain her balance; yet, the sight brought him no comfort. The itty-bitty thing didn't have far to go before making it to the ground, and he had no desire to see if that cute ass of hers would eventually smack hard on the gritty gravel beneath her. As she took another wobbly step, Trey lunged to her, grabbing her waist.

"All right. That's it," he declared angrily, under his breath. With quick movements, Trey put her arms around his neck, and pulled her hard against her body.

"What the hell are you doing?" she demanded, but he ignored her protests. With one hand under her ass and the other around her back, he lifted her into his arms and began heading briskly back to where he'd seen Claudia park her car. "Talk to me, little one," he ordered to her. "Can you hear me?"

"Yes, of course I hear you," she grumbled with irritation, but he felt her head move to rest lightly on his chest, and she didn't fight his grip. "I'm okay, just put me down."

"Not a chance," Trey grunted out, as if the words were fighting to get through his clenched teeth. Fear was squeezing at his chest in a viselike grip. Though she was very light in his arms, it felt like he couldn't get her to safety fast enough.

Finally, her *Volvo* came into view. He pressed her fully against his chest and reached for the car remote and keys sticking out of the pocket of her jacket. The automatic door responded to his hand and he eased her into the passenger seat. He rushed around the front of the car, quickly sliding into the driver's seat and moving it back to accommodate his much longer legs.

"You almost passed out back there. I'm taking you to the hospital, Claudia," Trey stated brusquely, using his finger to engage the car's push-to-start ignition. The force with which his body and mind demanded he rule the situation with an iron fist shocked him. Trey took a deep breath and relaxed his grip on the steering wheel before turning to her and softly adding, "Okay?"

"No..."

Trey slammed his right hand against the steering wheel and let his frustration take over again. "I don't have time for your shit. I'm taking you, whether you fucking like it or not."

"I'll be okay," she muttered, as she twisted her body, reaching a shaky arm toward the back of the car. Trey stilled her, easing her back on her seat.

"What do you need?"

Claudia turned her face to look at him. Her cheeks were flushed and breaths rapid, but she was clearly fighting to maintain some kind of composure.

"In the backseat… Go in my purse. My candy wasn't enough. Can you grab my glucose pills? Please."

She closed her eyes for a moment, and Trey quickly twisted around to grab her bag. Diving into the tote and pushing aside her wallet, he saw a vial of insulin and other medical supplies. A plastic cylinder with cartoon-looking grapes on it, boasting *Fast-Acting Glucose* came into view, and his twitchy worry subsided a little. He quickly grabbed it and opened it for her, shaking out some of the quarter-sized discs into her awaiting palm.

"Four," she stated weakly, taking one after another into her mouth, until she'd eaten all four. Trey watched her intently, his hands itching to get her somewhere safe. But after a matter of minutes, she was already looking more like herself. The dramatic change seemed almost magical.

Shakily, Claudia sat up in her seat. "Thank you, it must have been all the activity. I'm better now. Come on, let's get back out there."

Trey snorted, and reached over to buckle her seat belt. Claudia turned her head a touch, brushing her soft cheek against his rough one. Trey's heart froze, his chest feeling uncomfortably full with pain. She turned more, sliding her nose against his cheek. Her dark lashes fluttered as her wide, chocolate-brown eyes met his, and she whispered, "I'm fine, Trey. Trust me, I know my body. We've got to go back and figure out what's going on. I don't want to lose this chance."

She tried to unbuckle her seat belt and quickly became woozy again. Trey grabbed her arm, and pressed her back down.

"Hey! Didn't you hear me?" she protested.

"You're not going anywhere. I don't completely understand what's going on with you, but I know you're not leaving this car except to enter your home, or a hospital. This is not negotiable."

She opened her mouth to speak — or more likely yell — when a booming crash resounded from the distance.

"We have to figure out what that explosion was! I must really be on to something."

"Only thing you're onto is a healthy death wish. I know that crazy single-minded look in a woman's eye when I see it. As long as I'm here, there's no fucking way you're going back out there. Do you understand me?" Trey stated crisply. He eased his face away from hers, immediately noticing the absence of her warm skin against his. With a hard swallow, Trey looked straight ahead and peeled out of the rocky drive where Claudia had hidden her car.

"What about *your* car?" she asked, her voice quieting down noticeably. He sensed her breath was quickening from their moment of closeness.

He turned to see her staring out her window. Deep worry was etched across her delicate features. Trey turned away as fast as he could, eager to push down whatever feelings were swirling inside him.

"Forget about it, I can get it later."

"But what if it gets stolen?"

"I'll have *Uber* pick me up after I drop you off. My car is replaceable. *You're* not."

He glanced sideways to see Claudia blush faintly and nibble at the corner of her slightly upturned lips. Her face was twisted into the most adorable image of shyness. For the first time, he noticed that underneath all her cocky bluster was a confused, yet powerfully sexy woman. Trey squeezed the leather of the steering wheel, as he reminded himself he couldn't let her get to him.

"I can't fail Jenna right out of the gate, can I?" he attested, with a coolness he didn't feel.

"Right. For Jenna. I'd hate for you to let her down on my account," she gritted out, irritation quickly returning to her voice. "I don't have to go to the hospital. You can just take me home."

"Are you sure?"

"I'm sure. Might as well end this week on a complete losing streak," Claudia muttered to herself. "Maybe everyone's right about me…it looks like I can't handle the tough stuff, after all," she added, her tone heavy with defeat and shame.

Trey glanced over to see her studying her folded hands, with a lost look in her eyes.

All her fierce strength had given way to an almost visibly crushing self-doubt and it shocked him how much he wanted to make it go away. She was ambitious, and impulsive, but she was also clearly feeling thwarted, and there was no telling what kind of risk she'd take next in her mission to prove herself to the world.

Claudia needed a chance, and Trey suddenly felt the strongest desire to make sure she got it.

CHAPTER THREE

Knock, knock, knock…ring. Knock, knock, knock…ring.

Claudia sighed, willfully continuing to ignore the thirty seconds of commotion emanating from her front door. Instead, she focused on reading her blood sugar monitor, relieved to see it was still registering as 'normal.' The night before, she'd used all her energy to eat a good meal, test her blood sugar levels, and then crash.

After almost two months without either a hyper or hypoglycemic diabetic episode, she'd now had one of each almost back-to-back. Her life had evolved quite a bit from when she was diagnosed at seven years old, but what never changed was how these diabetic glucose roller coaster rides were never any fun.

The brutal, almost hungover sensations, which came with the hypoglycemic and hyperglycemic swings she'd suffered through over the past few days were still swirling through her body. Yet, that struggle had nothing on the lingering embarrassment and disappointment she had in herself.

She'd tried to blame her latest failure on her boss shoving her aside, as well as her brother's — and now Trey's — intrusiveness, but she knew it was a lost cause.

Managing diabetes is tough for anybody, and the transition to her new career was making it all the more challenging. Yet, she couldn't deny if she'd been stricter on herself, she would've turned down those pure-sugar cocktails her new friends had offered her. She also would've had enough confidence to scarf down her whole damn bag of *Skittles*, just as she would've done if she'd been alone. Instead she'd given into the prideful desire to hide her need for a quick sugar rush from Trey's prying eyes.

Ever since she was a little girl, lying in a hospital bed as doctors and nurses desperately tried to get her juvenile diabetes under control Claudia had known her life would be different from everyone else's.

This fact didn't stop her from wanting a real life of her own. Rather, it only made her more insistent on fighting for one — resulting in a series of battles since she was a kid, which she'd lost more times than she'd won.

But she wasn't a child anymore.

How will anyone treat me like an adult, if I'm too damn stubborn and foolish to show them I can actually take care of myself?

When she couldn't tune-out the sounds blasting from her front door anymore, Claudia stood from her bed and tied a bathrobe around her body, covering the tiny tank top and panties she'd managed to strip down to the night before. She grabbed her insulin pump before it could clank against the floor, looping it around the side of her short robe and tucking it tightly into the sash.

After clomping down the stairs of her small townhouse, Claudia gazed through the small window in her front door to see who had the nerve to invade the sanctity of her personal pity party. She groaned and leaned heavily against the wall next to the door when she saw Trey's handsome face on the other side. With a deep breath, she stood again, undid the dead bolt and turned off the security alarm her brother had installed before she'd moved in, and opened the door to her fate.

Trey's strong, tattooed hand held a cardboard tray supporting two paper cups. He proceeded to look her up and down, settling on her bare left leg in a way, which caused her throat to tighten. She frantically slapped her hand against her leg, attempting to hide the bare flesh from his intent, gray eyes.

"Morning, little one. Looks like I woke you up, or caught you coming out of the shower..."

"What makes you think it's okay to just show up here like this?" she stammered, yanking her pump out of her robe sash, allowing the fabric to flutter down and cover her more fully. She chose to hold the pump in her hand instead of letting his stare potentially burn a hole into her exposed skin.

"I brought you a Cuban coffee from that coffee shop you like in Oakland."

"How the hell do you know that about me!" Claudia exclaimed.

"You're kidding, right? I've used my skills to learn enough about you to know you'll use yours to find out everything you can about me."

"Fine. Yes, I may have planned to spend half of today trying to figure out who you really are."

"Don't hold your breath on that being successful. My life is best served by trying to manage information, including what's out there about me."

"Ooh, you're *sooo* mysterious."

"That's what they tell me. I thought you women liked that in a guy."

"Not *this* woman, but that's just one reason why I want you to leave. Look, I've had a couple of seriously humiliating days. I don't need you here making me feel worse about myself."

Trey ignored her, pushing past her into her home. Her mind filled with fast and hot indignation, but her stupid body tingled at the sensation of the quick brush of his forearm against her shoulder. The crisp morning air was still leaving cool remnants on the leather of his jacket, making her skin feel like it was sizzling in response.

"What the hell do you think you're doing, Adler?"

"Making myself at home, or at least finding a place for the coffee I brought you."

Claudia's mouth watered at the thought of the much-needed caffeine, but she tried to fight through it so she could get back to being pissed at him.

"Are you going to keep following me around like a creep? If you leave now I promise to help you out and leave one blind half open so you can watch my refrigerator with a pair of binoculars."

"Nope. Stalking you only managed to get me knocked on my ass. I've decided this approach works better."

"Oh...*you've* decided? Well, I've got news for you — no, it doesn't, because I need to get to the office. Which means, you're slowing me down."

"No, you don't."

"Don't what?"

"Have to go to work."

"What would you know about my job requirements?"

Trey looked past her into the main area of her first floor. He'd dressed nicely that morning, with gray slacks and his black leather jacket layered over a blue button-down shirt. It was open just enough to reveal a distracting amount of his neck and the very top of his muscular chest, which featured the hint of more ink. She stared at the spot where his skin met the cotton, and it was like water stroking the sand on a secluded shore.

Claudia squeezed at the pump in her hand and sucked lightly on the middle of her lower lip. She couldn't help but wonder what he would look like shirtless on a beach — the sun finding the few strands of lighter brown hair amongst his otherwise dark waves.

"You're staring at me again, little one."

"What? At you? No, I'm not. Shut up," she blurted out, prattling on defensively.

Truth was, she *had* been ogling him. How could she not? It felt as though her eyes were connected to his body by a string, which she couldn't cut. For some reason, every time she was close to him, some part of her brain turned into a horny puddle of goo — a feeling she had absolutely no experience with before she met him.

"I talked to Assistant Director Jacobs."

"Huh?"

"I told him you weren't feeling well and wouldn't be coming in to the office today."

"Wait…you did *what*? Christ, do you have any idea how bad this is for me? I can't have Jacobs thinking there is something wrong with me!" She yanked herself back from the brink of momentarily basking in her dirty thoughts to process his ridiculous words.

An all too familiar surge of irritation and helpless fury began tingling in her fingertips and moving up her arms. Without even realizing it, her right hand curled into a fist, poised to fight back in any way she could. Trey looked down at her and curved his mouth into his signature sly grin, which creased his cheeks in a completely frustrating way.

"Breathe through it, little one. It's for your own good. You look like shit..."

"That's it!" she screamed, pointing a finger toward the door. "Get out of my house!"

"Whoa, easy there. Hot coffee here, you maniac," he chastised. After pausing to look around her foyer, he stated, "This is a nice place. Not too far from mine, actually. I guess your brother didn't do his homework when he picked it for you."

"Please cut the crap about my brother for at least one morning. I chose this place myself and I pay the rent. I do have an actual job, you know — even if you're trying to mess with it."

"You're doing fine trying to fuck it up all on your own, little one."

"Fine, so you think I'm a rotten little brat. I get it. But you're wrong."

"I don't think that about you. Stop rolling your eyes. I mean it. Calm down."

"I was perfectly calm before you showed up in my life."

Trey snorted at her derisively, "I find that hard to believe. Look, on top of needing to rest, if you go in and face Jacobs and his team today, they'll want to know where you ran off to yesterday. Do you really want to answer that question right now? I've covered up for you, but I need it to sink in with him for a day or two. Do you want a future with the FBI or not? Well?"

"I do," she muttered, trying to unclench her teeth.

"Good. Now calm down and show me where your kitchen is."

Claudia sighed, pointing toward the kitchen area. She turned and helplessly shuffled behind him. After he placed the cardboard tray on the counter, Trey turned around and crossed his arms, presenting such an air of authority Claudia suddenly felt like a guest in her own home.

"What was your excuse?" she asked.

"With Jacobs? I lied and told him I caught wind of a lead and didn't want to risk being seen, so I used you. He believes I sent you an email as a test to see how you'd handle it, because you look innocent, and you weren't officially on the case as of yesterday. It was better than telling him you decided to go rogue and conduct your own investigation and then follow up on a lead with no backup or clearance, and it works perfectly for the plan I have for you."

"A plan for *me*? What does that even mean?"

"It *means* I got you on the Taylor case. Letting Jacobs keep you off it clearly only makes it harder to keep you safe, and now I can make sure I have an eye on you. I looked at what you accomplished as an intern at D.C. headquarters. You've got a real gift for cybercrime investigations. Jacobs is wasting your talents. So I talked to him and he agreed — you're now on my team."

"*Your* team? What the hell are you doing for the FBI? *Really*?"

"Let's just say I'm kind of an indentured servant to the federal government. They need what I can do to crack the Taylor case, and I would rather not go to jail for what I've done already. Plus, I have enough friends where it matters that I'm given the leeway to at least make my servitude effective." Trey paused, looking into her eyes intently enough to make her heart race a little. "Which means, when I see something I need, I get to have it. And like you said, this investigation has hit a dead end, and it's driving me crazy. So maybe right now what I need…is you."

"Oh." Claudia breathed out softly. Turning toward the kitchen table, she fought to gain some balance within herself. "So, you do care about solving the case? Not just because of your deal?"

She turned back in time to see his face turn to stone and his jaw twitch with frustration, "I may not be working on this case on my own terms. I may not have known Jack Taylor. But the people who mattered to him matter to me, which means, I can't let his death go unpunished… This isn't a game for me, Claudia."

Claudia crossed her arms and again found that vein full of fierce energy, which Trey's presence had temporarily blocked since he'd barreled into her home.

"I'm glad to hear it, *boss*," she said tersely, "because I don't play *games*."

"Good. So, you'll do whatever I tell you?"

"That's not really what I had in mind," Claudia responded, her arms falling to her sides and nervousness tickling at her throat.

"Listen to me, *Special Agent* McCoy. You're going to have to accept sooner or later that the world's not going to do everything the way you want it to. So you might as well get over that idea right now. It's this way…*my* way…or nothing."

"With you babysitting me, and all?"

"Until Jenna takes me off my assignment of keeping you safe, you are going to have to take things on my terms. Unless you want to chase after strung-out Russian credit card thieves all day…"

"You know I don't."

"Good to know you have at least one reasonable bone in your miniature body, because I have another condition for you."

Claudia couldn't hold back an exasperated sigh, but she did manage to ask, "What?"

"You need to take care of yourself. I do think Jenna was right to be concerned about you, and now I am, too."

"I don't understand."

"I think you do…" Trey touched her elbow lightly, shooting electric shocks throughout her body. "How are you feeling today?"

Claudia wasn't sure if she could form words, with how frazzled each of the neurons in her brain had become.

"I feel fine. Thank you for bringing me home."

"You scared the shit out of me. I didn't like it. You hear me? Plus, I'm fucking exhausted after staying up all night figuring out what happened to you. I'm not a fan of that feeling, you understand?"

"I do," she whispered, almost choking on her tongue when he leaned down, bringing his face closer to hers.

"Then you agree with my conditions?" he asked quietly, his breath just barely touching the skin of her forehead.

The warm scent coming off of his skin was at once soothing and unsettling. Claudia closed her eyes for a second, searching inside herself for the ability to understand why this man made every muscle in her body tighten and her breath stall in her throat. It didn't work, because when she opened her eyes again, all those feelings had simply amplified in power.

"Why do I feel like I'm making a deal with the devil?" she asked quietly, conceding enough to allow her eyes to lock with his.

"It seems your instincts really *are* good. But it doesn't change how few options you have."

"Okay. I'll do what you tell me."

"Good. That's what I like to hear. Now grab your laptop and have some coffee. It's time for me to…debrief you."

Trey moved the bag of food he was holding to his left hand and rang the doorbell to Claudia's home. It had been a week since she'd started working with him on the Taylor case, and he worried she was spending every waking minute on it, potentially putting her health second to her career — again.

He also was getting used to seeing her at the office several times every day, and was surprised to discover he had no interest in breaking that streak. Seeing as it was a Saturday evening, this meant he found himself appearing at her front door uninvited for a second time.

With each new day, Claudia was opening up to him more and more, revealing she had a wickedly-sharp mind to go along with the bluster and sass, which had greeted him when he'd first met her.

Trey only knew a few other people who could work the kind of magic with a computer that Claudia did with such ease — himself, his father, and the other…well, she was gone. It seemed like Claudia just needed someone to believe in her. Then, before he knew it, the floodgates opened, and her abilities quickly poured out of her. Trey felt simultaneously excited and terrified to be a part of her progression.

Being around her beautiful face and tight body was also making it very difficult to remember why he'd promised Jenna he wouldn't sleep with Claudia McCoy. Though, he could probably keep that precise commitment, since he'd been fantasizing about her constantly over the last few days — and sleeping was not involved in any of those flights of his imagination.

"Hi, Trey," she greeted cheerily, as she opened the door in a pair of pajama bottoms and a tightly-fitting matching tank top, which showed just enough of the tops of her breasts to make it hard for him to recall the reason he had for showing up there in the first place. "Are you working over the weekend, too. Can't get enough of me, can you?" she teased.

Even though her words were light, he caught her eyeing him up and down — in the end, resting her gaze on his mouth in a doe-eyed stare. Every time she looked at him that way, it sent a powerful shot of desire through his body, straight to his bones. Trey's awareness of her desire for him only managed to drive him more nuts.

And unfortunately, his craving was getting stronger with each of her innocent glances, as well as the way she'd unknowingly lick and gently suck on her plump lower lip whenever their eyes met.

"I guess not," he answered eventually, having to clear his throat a bit to force the words out of his mouth. "Can I come in?"

"Oh, of course. Jeez, I'm sorry. I probably shouldn't leave you at my front porch all night, huh?" she said quickly, the words stumbling over each other, as she stepped aside to let him enter.

"Thanks, little one," he answered, and winked. "Aren't you cold in that?" he asked, nodding at her chest and raising an eyebrow. He tried his damnedest not to look at her hard nipples poking into the thin fabric, and begging him to give them a proper hello.

Perhaps she sensed his own interest in them, because she immediately crossed her arms over her chest, which made the agonizing view of her cleavage just another reason he regretted not wearing looser jeans before heading over to her place.

"I'm okay. I can get a sweater if it will make you more comfortable," she teased.

"Don't cover up on my account. Just looking out for you is all."

"Thank you," she said slowly, letting her disobedient eyes wander all over him again. If their seemingly endless path made their way to his crotch, he might be the one needing to cover up, in case those quick glances of hers turned less sweet. He almost exhaled in relief when they landed on the bag still dangling from his left hand like a white flag of surrender to his own resistance of actually liking the sexy package in front of him.

"Trey?"

"What?"

"Did you hear me? I asked you what's in the bag," she clarified over a sweet, yet nervous, laugh that matched those big eyes of hers, too well.

Trey felt like a horny kid with a crush all of a sudden. Desperate to shake off the sensation, he barreled into her kitchen and placed the bag on the small part of her table left unoccupied by papers, scribbled notes, and her laptop.

He turned to look at her, comforted by the effect his stern look had on her.

"Why do you look mad?"

"I'm not," he said, and the little smile she gave him almost pushed him right back into eager puppy category. Standing straight, he crossed his arms to ward off the temptation to pick up her supple body, push her back up against her kitchen wall and lick every inch of tantalizing skin he could get to — immediately.

"I brought you dinner," he said, adjusting his stance to give his dick some room in his suffocating pants.

"Oh, thanks. What is it?"

"Grilled salmon and asparagus, with steamed herbed brown rice pilaf," he responded.

"Wow, I didn't know you were a chef for the *American Diabetes Association.* I think that's on the cover of one of their cookbooks," she joked.

"It is," he answered seriously, glancing around the kitchen to see empty coffee mugs on the counter and one dirty bowl in the sink. "That's how I found it. I gave the recipes to the chef at *Viola.* He's now got a list of meals from me he'll make for you whenever I have a request," he said, letting his mouth curl up in a cocky smirk.

"*Viola*, why does that sound so familiar? Is it..."

"Jack Taylor's family's restaurant? Yes. They feed me regularly. It's a benefit of the case, trust me. Now I'm making sure they feed you, too."

"Wow, what a nice gesture. You didn't have to do that for me, though. I *have* food."

"Having food doesn't matter if don't pause long enough to eat it. I need to be sure you use this kitchen table for more than just nonstop work. And besides, you promised to follow my rules," he said, clenching his teeth slightly.

Her forehead crinkled. "Are you okay, Trey?"

"I'm fine," he grunted, throwing his jacket over a chair.

"You sound like me," she teased, revealing hints of her softer side, which had been coming through more and more throughout the week. "I'm always 'fine,'" she said with a grumble, intended to copy his, "even when I'm not."

"You won't be fine if you don't make sure to eat and take care of yourself."

Claudia let out a sigh. "I get it, okay? You've already won. I've been eating and looking after myself, I swear. But enough of that, I really want to show you what I've started today. Have you gotten any results from the remnants you collected from the steel mill blast? I'd like to include them with my analysis."

"Not yet."

"It feels like it's taking forever," she lamented, almost petulant in her impatience.

"I know. Being patient is a bitch," Trey mumbled.

"Have we at least been able to confirm whether it was a sophisticated incendiary device?"

"All evidence is pointing to that. I've been more concerned about making sure my story about why you went to the steel mill sticks."

"Oh yeah, thanks," she murmured.

"Luckily it was small enough and in a sufficiently remote location not to spark too much interest in the noise."

"Was someone trying to kill me? Another fed?"

"I can't be sure. It seemed to be deliberately contained, at least from the blast pattern."

"So it was either meant to harm or send a message — but what?"

"Hopefully the tests help us there, too."

"So, back to being patient, damn," she grumbled. "Oh well, I still have plenty to keep me busy. Come on."

She confidently walked to her chair and turned the screen of her laptop toward him. Her quick fingers moved feverishly, and she only paused to take a sip of water and look up at him, as he towered over her.

"I used a virus to manipulate the email I received leading me to the steel mill. I call it the 'Tongue Louse.' It's one of the first tools I made back when I was thirteen."

"And you called it 'Tongue Louse'?"

"Yes. I named it after a parasite who eats the tongue of the host and remains there, so it can hijack all the food the host eats."

"Pretty gross, Claudia."

She laughed, snorting a little. "Yeah, I know. I was kind of weird… Every good hack should have a cool name though, right? Even if it's being done for enforcing the law instead of breaking it… This virus does the same thing. Once I determined the email's source server, I implanted the virus. Right now, it's absorbing all the information going into it, as though it were the server itself."

Each of her passionate words were sending chills along Trey's flesh. His fingers twitched from the urge to protect

Claudia from the dangerous thrill of this chase. The twinkle in her eye was only intensifying the power of his tormented memories. She continued speaking, rapidly turning back and forth from the computer to him with each motivated sentence.

"We've been thinking too small, Trey... Everyone so far has assumed the group who paid Taylor's former boss, for the *CMU* robotics secrets had to have been Chinese military or someone in the government, but that's gotten us nowhere." Her brows furrowed as she blew a few stray hairs away from her face. "I think it's because that's not the answer," she continued. "There are numerous new companies in China — Shanghai, especially — making billions of dollars using the kind of technology and data David was paid to get. David still claims to have no clue who was behind it. Maybe that's because he actually doesn't know. There are also underground groups for hire who could easily have the firepower and wherewithal to be the go-between on a theft of this magnitude. If we could figure out which one was used, and work backward, then infiltrate it..."

The determined look in her eyes filled his brain with uneasiness. Just her complying with his terms wouldn't be enough. He knew she had a point, but he needed more control — to pull her back from the ledge he saw her teetering on right before his eyes. Knowing firsthand how quickly a small scheme like this could go terribly wrong, he knew he had to put a stop to her inquisitiveness. Letting her fall was not an option.

"That could work, but you're not doing it," he stated firmly.

She gaped at him for a second, before jumping out of her seat and throwing her arms up in frustration.

"You've *got* to be kidding me, Trey! I thought we were past this stuff."

"We'll never be past it, so just deal with it."

Her face turned a deep shade of angry red, "You're invested

in this case, and damn it, so am I. This is my best shot at proving everyone wrong about me. Why can't you understand that?"

Her words cut into his chest like a hot dagger. Before he knew what he was doing, Trey grabbed her shoulders and blurted out, "You'll never be satisfied if all you care about is making the world take you seriously."

As soon as his fingers touched her bare flesh, she lowered her voice and allowed her breaths to become more measured. Fire entered her eyes, but from a very different source — molten lava bubbling up from the same fault line fueling Trey's intense response to her.

"That's easy for you to say," she whispered. "You break every rule there is, and *you're* still alive and kicking."

"So you *were* able to figure out something about me?" Trey unpeeled his hands from her shoulders, and Claudia heaved out a deep, disappointed sigh in response. "You promised to follow *my* rules, and that means you help me keep you safe."

Her tank top strap had slid down her shoulder, leaving Trey transfixed with the soft curve of that small piece of completely exposed skin.

"But I *am* being good. I'm complying with your requests. I've connected my glucose monitor. It hurts like hell, but I use it anyway. Plus, I keep the alarms turned on these days, because it's the best way to keep a close watch on my glucose levels. Look!" she exclaimed. Trey's eyes jerked back to her face. Claudia lifted up her tank top, revealing her taut abs, her insulin pump tucked into the waistband of her pajama bottoms, a plastic knob secured into her flesh, and a thin cord completing the complicated circuitry of her life.

Trey couldn't look away from the juxtaposition of her young, athletic form next to so much machinery working to keep her alive.

Unsure how all this equipment even connected to her lithe body, Trey found himself touching the area gently with his fingertips before he could stop himself. Her sharp intake of air and stuttering breaths shocked him, causing him to jerk back his fingers quickly, but Claudia didn't pull down her top.

Staring at him again, her chest rose and fell with each deep breath she took. Trey tentatively touched the cotton of her shirt, smoothing it back into place lightly, all the while hating to cover that smooth, olive skin and mechanized evidence of how many challenges she faced just existing day-to-day, let alone trying to make something great of her life.

Trey couldn't take her silence any longer. With a sure hand, he grabbed her chin and asked, "Cat got your tongue?"

She shook her head, allowing her soft, pink tongue to peek out and lick her lips.

"I thought you said you were being good?" he asked her, squeezing her chin slightly. Trey slid his thumb across her swollen, bare lower lip. On a shaky breath, she let her mouth fall slightly open.

"What am I doing that's bad?" she finally responded, her eyes large and filled with confusion.

"You are being *you.* And that's making *me* want to be bad…and to do bad things."

Trey slowly moved his hand from her chin, and gripped the back of her slim neck. Claudia perched on the balls of her feet, head thrown back, her face trained on his. Trey kept her eyes locked to his, leaning down to allow their breaths to mingle with each other's, becoming one warm burst of arousal between them.

His lips were tingling with the urge to touch her full mouth. His tongue was eager to stroke hers. But, more than that, he needed to taste some part of her perfect skin.

He bit her chin — a little harder than he'd intended. Then

licked across the brief red mark it left from his teeth and the pressure of his lip ring, and ran his tongue along her jawline, causing her to release a shocked exclamation, and then a distressed moan.

Trey released her neck, slid the errant strap of her tank top back onto her shoulder, and backed away from her. After a deep breath of his own, Trey said, "That's better. Now sit down with me and eat."

Claudia's eyes were swimming with lust and confusion, but she grabbed the bag with a shaky hand and nodded.

With that gentle motion of her head, Trey finally felt the fist of worry, which had been squeezing around his throat start to loosen.

CHAPTER FOUR

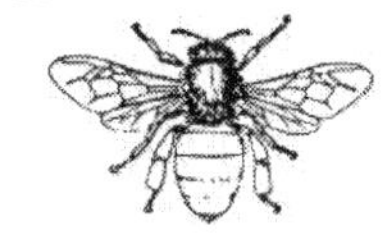

An imposing twenty-foot-high wrought iron gate had been flung open at an entry way nestled along an especially fancy portion of Pittsburgh's lovely Shady Avenue. Its powerful gray rods loomed against the dusky sky, competing for dominance with the elegant trees just beyond them.

Once Claudia coasted her car through the opening, the residential urban pageantry continued into a broad Governor's driveway, already dotted with numerous cars. Behind them stood Tea and Griffen's new home together — a three-story red brick Victorian palace — and the site of their housewarming party.

It was nestled in the east end of Pittsburgh, a part of the city still so visually heavy with the weight of its own past, Claudia wouldn't have been surprised if she looked in her side-view mirror to spy a turn-of-the-century steel magnate pulling up in a chauffeured *Model T.* Maybe he'd be sipping grumpily from a monogrammed flask, while his valet apprised him on the latest mill production numbers, or warned him of rumblings of an uprising from his hundreds of oppressed workers.

Claudia actually had to give her head a physical shake to rid it of the effects of her overactive imagination. The ghost world she'd temporarily conjured disappeared from her mind, revealing the clear image of present day, and her eager anticipation for an impending confrontation with Trey.

For days, she'd been planning precisely what she'd say to him, when she finally got to corner him outside of the FBI offices. It had been a week since Trey Adler, of the *We-Invented-The-World-of-Computers-That-Claudia-McCoy-Loves-So-Much* Adlers, had bitten her — yes, he had taken *an actual nibble* of her.

Trey clearly had tried to keep the fascinating identity of his father a secret. Despite those efforts, she'd figured it out pretty easily. Claudia had a personal understanding for anyone's yearning to distance their life from their father's. Yet, she was curious to a fault, which made Trey that much more dangerous. No one had ever sparked her desperate urge for discovery as much as he. After only one day of working with him, she'd found herself sitting in front of her laptop all night, determined to figure out who in the hell Trey really was.

His whole life, especially the period after he dropped out of *Stanford* his sophomore year, was a total mystery. Somehow, the more she learned about Trey, the more she found herself longing for him to bite her again.

What Claudia wanted didn't matter to Trey, though — which was a far too familiar feeling for her.

Her mind went to its dark place, the one it visited every time she felt different…broken. Because no matter how hard she took risks to make the most of her life, rejection never sat well with her. It hurt her deep inside to think Trey would just be one more link in a long chain of things she wanted, but would always stay just out of her grasp.

Trey had been all business since their passionate moment in

her kitchen. In fact, he'd barely spoken to her since, and the resulting sense of brutal disappointment it instilled in her came with an almost acidic aftertaste, as though she'd thrown up and brushing her teeth had only made it worse.

His recent ice-cold behavior had left her deeply confused, because Claudia truly believed Trey wanted *her*, just as much as she did him.

She knew he'd probably *already* been with tons of women. A jolt of jealousy shot through her blood at the idea of how many women Trey had touched, or bitten, or licked before her. Hell, as far as Claudia was concerned, anyone who didn't want to have sex with Trey had likely just not met him yet.

None of that mattered now, because Claudia wasn't going to put up with his crap anymore. He could treat her like a professional, or he could touch her like — well, she didn't really know…but she was going to *make* him choose one of those two options.

What did she have to lose? Claudia had been going into the office every day — reviewing old files and searches, running through Jack Taylor's flash drive repeatedly. But Trey was practically avoiding her, and he was still refusing to let her use her hacking skills for the investigation. He'd suddenly decided to be a complete angel with her, but she found herself missing the devilish side of him.

They'd spoken in crisply efficient bursts, but the only real conversation they'd had — about her interviewing David Murphy — had been…unproductive. In fact, Trey had almost lost his shit when she'd proposed the idea of meeting with the man.

Everything about Pittsburgh and the FBI was feeling like the most oppressive waste of time. Claudia knew she could always join a security company. The demand for her cybersecurity skills in the private sector was high, and the pay was certainly better.

But it was never about the money for her. It was about using her brain to help the world — showing the other lonely, scared young diabetics in the world they could accomplish anything they set their mind to do.

She'd already found out the sheer force of her desire couldn't overcome everything, though. If it could, she'd be in the Marine Corps instead of being rejected when she'd insisted on serving in combat. Besides, leaving the FBI was also the surest sign of defeat, and Claudia was no quitter.

"Stop whining, you big baby," Claudia quietly growled out loud to herself.

Claudia only knew of one strategy to employ in life — advance until you can't move forward anymore. It was time to take Trey on and make him deal with her, regardless of the outcome. If she had to knock him on his ass again to whack some sense into him, so be it. Claudia was always more comfortable with blunt force, instead of words, anyway.

Pushing through the slightly ajar front door, Claudia was immediately greeted by Tea's sweet, but somehow always sultry sounding, voice.

"Claude! You made it!" Tea exclaimed, running to her and giving her a quick one-armed hug, leaving her other hand free to hold a glass of wine.

"Hi, Tea. Thank you for inviting me."

"Of course! Come on in. Did you end up feeling okay after the last time we saw you?" Tea added quietly, so only Claudia could hear her.

"Um, oh, great, thanks. About me having to lie down…"

"No need to explain. We've all been there. Jenna said you had a little bug that night. I wish I'd known, or I wouldn't have forced my crazy fruit concoction down your throat. I'm not really the best bartender. Sorry."

"You're awesome, don't be silly. Yeah, a bug… I guess you could call it that. But tell me about this house? It's so beautiful!" Claudia paused to take in the whole effect of the expansive foyer — and to peer around surreptitiously in the hopes of spotting Trey.

"Thanks! I couldn't be happier with the renovations. I imagine Jenna told you what a mess it was when we got it. It had been completely neglected for decades, but we could tell it just needed a second chance — like it was waiting for us to come and make it whole again."

Tea's eyes scanned the room, falling on her handsome fiancé. He turned and smiled at her, his deep-set dimples creasing his cheeks. Claudia could almost feel Tea's heart respond to him. Their obvious connection was touching, though it ran a shot of envy through Claudia, as well.

"Tea, are you being all dramatic again?" Jenna asked, appearing from behind Tea to give Claudia a kiss.

"What would I do without Jenna here to keep me from getting all mushy?"

"It's a gift," Jenna answered. "The place really does look awesome, Tea. Please tell me you weren't in charge of any remodeling. I know how obsessed you get with doing things yourself, no matter how disastrous it can be. Do I need to be scared of turning on any lights?"

"Don't worry. Griffen had to hold me back from doing anything to it, so I didn't hurt myself — or damage the house. He knows I'm a certified spaz."

"Is that a technical term?" Claudia teased.

"It should be when it's the level of clumsiness Tea has. Hey, girl!" Aubrey grabbed Claudia from behind in a bear hug, which almost knocked her over. Jenna stepped to her other side, giving her arm a quick squeeze. "How does he keep you from trying to become a handy man, Tea? Do tell," Aubrey continued.

"Lucky for me, he has several surefire ways of distracting me. And each of them are far more satisfying than any of my DIY urges."

"I knew it," Aubrey exclaimed. "Good thing you have all these rooms now — more private places for you two to break in. Considering how you used to do it in every random place you found while you were keeping the two of you a secret."

"This is much better, and more convenient."

"Come on, you two. Don't terrorize Claudia too much. Look at her, she's blushing," Jenna chided, pursing her pink lips and narrowing her cornflower blue eyes. Her long, blonde hair was done in lovely waves, accenting her simple formfitting dress, which did wonders for showcasing her *Playboy* centerfold bosom. As always, she managed to make everything she did look effortless.

"Oh, no, you guys are great. I love the bad impression you've given me. Please don't change," Claudia responded quickly, an easy smile stretching over her face for the first time in days. Large crowds always had a way of making Claudia feel uneasy and awkward, but these women took the edge off a little.

"Good, then we will continue to be on our usual worst behavior. It's such a shame Tea's mom, Vivian, couldn't be here. She's a blast, and talk about someone who can make you blush!" Aubrey exclaimed.

"No kidding," Tea added. "She's giving a talk in Singapore tomorrow, but Griffen's mom, Valerie, is going to videotape anything memorable for her," she explained, with a twinkle of anticipation in her eye.

"Can you tell Tea is excited, Claude?" Aubrey interjected.

"And why shouldn't she be, right? What do you think? Isn't this place stunning?" Jenna asked.

"It's incredible. I may never leave," Claudia enthused.

"We have to thank all those dead-steel magnates, for building so many beautiful homes in the 20s. I'm going to pour out a tumbler of scotch on the yard for Andrew Carnegie later," Aubrey enthused.

"She means it," Jenna added calmly. "Brey's taken so many pictures of this house, it's like she's casing the joint."

"Who said I'm not? Griffen's loaded, I could rob worse…if I were so inclined."

"Well, it's my house, too, and I would rather you not," Tea declared with a sassy chuckle, but it turned into a delighted squeal when Griffen hugged her from behind. He kissed her neck and whispered something to her, which made her face turn scarlet red. She turned to kiss him so deeply Claudia had to look away.

Still holding Tea around the waist with one arm, he reached his other hand toward Claudia, "You must be Claudia, I'm so glad you could make it. Trey told me he's been working with you while he's consulting for the FBI. He's really impressed, and that's saying a lot. Almost nothing impresses Trey."

The compliment made warmth crawl from Claudia's back, all the way up to her neck and cheeks.

"Wait, you've been spending time with our sexy international man of mystery? You have to tell us everything you learn," Aubrey instructed her.

"I'm sure I don't really know anything about him," she mumbled out, suddenly aware of Jenna's appraising gaze sear the side of her face. "Is Trey here, yet?" she asked Griffen, trying desperately to keep her tone steady, even as she felt Jenna's intent gaze practically burning a hole in the side of her head.

"Yeah, but he's playing with Johnny in the backyard right now. He should be in any second though, because we have an announcement to make, right, gorgeous?"

Tea smiled, kissing Griffen on the cheek and nuzzling her nose into one of his dimples. His deep blue eyes sparkled like sun glinting on an ocean.

"Why yes, we do. And I can't wait anymore."

"Thank you all for joining us in our new home," Griffen announced to the crowd of guests now gathered in the main room, eager to hear Griffen and Tea's big news. He held Tea's hand, drawing her flush against his side. "We're so excited to share our house with you. You all might know this woman by her nickname, *Tea*, but to me she will always be Althea — the woman I met my first night back here after so many years away, who quickly turned out to be the best thing that will ever happen to me. Lucky for me, she's taken a chance on this Pittsburgh boy…a chance on us."

Griffen paused briefly to lean down and kiss the top of Tea's head, smiling when his lips grazed her lush hair.

"I'd traveled the world, written books and articles, but I didn't know anything truly important until I met Althea, because she taught me falling in love is the most important thing we do in life. Finding that person, creating a life with them…a family…nothing else will ever measure up."

The room filled with a combination of gentle "ahhhs" while a couple guys let out some happy hollers. Griffen and Tea laughed, each wrapping their arms around the other's waist, eyes locking and smiles matching in a way, which was almost embarrassingly intimate to watch.

Claudia scanned the room full of numerous unfamiliar faces. Her own nervousness began to take root again, until her glance fell on Trey. He was at the far end of the room and hadn't spotted her yet, as his eyes were intently focused on his friend. Yet, seeing him made her forget any of the shyness, which usually plagued her when she felt out of place. Instead, all she could think about was the strong lines of his handsome face.

Griffen's voice broke through her thoughts, as he continued his speech.

"To the Pittsburghers who know me from back in the day, you'll be happy to hear my mom made lots of great food, but sorry, no chipped chopped ham or pierogies, this time. And listen up, if any of yinz get too drunk n'at, there's a Pittsburgh potty dahn in the basement for ya' jags to get sick in. Now, for all you non-Pittsburgh natives, such as my beautiful fiancée here, I'll be happy to translate that part of the speech for yinz later."

Tea elbowed him, but she was still beaming with pleasure. She turned to the guests and added, "Now that Griffen is done teaching me some more 'Pittsburghese,' we can get on with the big news of the night. What really makes us so happy tonight is knowing you all are the first to hear we have set a date for our wedding!" Tea blurted out rapidly before Griffen twisted her into his arms affectionately. Everyone in the room cheered, raising their glasses with excitement.

"When is it?" one partygoer asked loudly.

"August twenty-third. The anniversary of when we first met a little over a year ago. It will be at the Outer Banks, in my home state of North Carolina. So y'all had better bring your bathing suits," Tea yelled back, a southern drawl invading her husky voice.

"That's right, because we've decided everyone here is invited!" Griffen boomed as he wrapped Tea in his arms more closely before dipping her slightly. He kissed her passionately, even as some of her long hair got caught in her mouth, muffling her girlish laughter.

Griffen hugged her once more before placing her back on her feet. Tea laughed, leaning against him before saying, "It's kind of a *chicken and the egg* thing, Griffen. They were invited here tonight *because* we wanted them at the wedding."

"Shhh, you cute nerd. Let me act like it's a crazy, spontaneous thing we're doing, gorgeous."

"I guess you don't have any crazy things in your life anymore, Griffen," Tea responded, crinkling her nose.

"Oh, I do. You're nuts in all the right ways, lady."

Tea giggled uncontrollably until a slow and deliberate clap broke through the din, silencing her. Tea peered toward the front door. Her face suddenly turning a weird shade of pale and her smile twisted into a distressed frown.

"Althea, what's wrong?" Griffen inquired, before following her gaze. His face turned red with fury, but the clapping continued, growing louder as its source moved through the crowd toward them.

A man Claudia didn't recognize was making his way toward the happy couple from the front door, staggering with each step. He appeared to be about Claudia's age, and even though he had the expression of someone about to be completely awful, there was no denying the young blonde guy was equal parts disruptive and distractingly handsome. When he made it to Griffen and Tea, he brought his face closer to theirs than was appropriate.

Several in the crowd gasped and began whispering to each other. Trey's face turned a hot red before he left Claudia's line of sight, quickly replaced by various people trying to move closer so as to better eavesdrop on the drama unfolding before them.

"Don't stop all the fun on my account," the intruder slurred at Griffen and Tea, his voice much louder than necessary. "What a *pretty* goddamn picture you two make...Jack's wife and Griffen Tate. I wouldn't have missed this for the world."

"Baxter, cut the shit, right now..." Griffen growled in warning, but the interloper simply laughed and started clapping again, a bitter smile contorting his face. "Bax. You're loaded," Griffen continued, his face mere inches now from Bax's, "I was patient with you at Carol's Christmas party out of respect for you and what you've been through."

"I don't need your pity, *Griffen*."

"No, you don't, because you're acting like a spoiled child and I'm thinking I need to shut you up the hard way," Griffen threatened. Trey suddenly appeared alongside Griffen, his hands curling into fists. Wyatt made his way through the crowd, pulling Griffen and Trey back. Claudia breathed out in relief. She didn't know who this Bax guy was, but she was sure Trey didn'y need any more run-ins with the law.

"Aw, hell no. I can't believe he pulled this shit again," Aubrey muttered.

"Who is that guy?" Claudia whispered to Jenna. "And why is he being such an ass?"

"He's Jack's surviving brother. Griffen's mother just made a run for it...hopefully to go grab Baxter's mom, Carol, from the kitchen. Hopefully Carol will come through for a change."

"Aubrey, be nice," Jenna chastised.

"Why start now?" Aubrey inquired.

"Oh my god, he's Baxter *Taylor*," Claudia thought out loud, amidst the madness. She'd come across the transcript of his FBI interview in one of the Jack Taylor files, but the old student ID hadn't captured his handsomeness.

"The one and only," Aubrey grumbled. "Wouldn't you know it — just in time for Halloween, Baxter shows up and proceeds to haunt the whole party like some kind of douche bag ghost. I don't even understand why he came."

"He's gorgeous," Claudia blurted. Trey's fire-breathing fury next to Griffen was keeping Claudia pretty distracted, but she wasn't completely blind to anyone else.

"Hell yeah, he's hot as hell. The Taylor gene pool has always been made up of ridiculously sexy males. Too bad Jack was the only Taylor brother to have any class. Jack would be furious if he could see Bax now."

"Well, Griffen seems angry enough for the both of them. Why is Baxter being like this?" Jenna fumed.

"I guess he thinks because Jack and Griffen were best friends growing up, Tea being with Griffen now is the ultimate betrayal. Who knows, though? It's hard to understand the mind of an ass." Aubrey interjected.

"We should get Tea out of here. Come on, Aubrey," Jenna whispered. Cautiously, they made their way over to Tea, with Claudia following at their heels, unsure what else to do.

"Tea, sweetie, come on," Aubrey whispered to Tea, with a sweetness Claudia had not previously seen from the brash brunette.

"No. I need to handle this," Tea answered, her hand shaking slightly as she smoothed a lock of hair off her face. Tea breathed slowly, calming herself, before turning to her guests and stating, "We're sorry for all of this ruckus. Griffen's mom, Valerie over by the door will show y'all to the living room so you can start eating dinner. In addition to Valerie's delicious treats, Carol's restaurant, *Viola*, has catered tonight's dinner. Please get started, and we will all meet you in there shortly."

Valerie began shepherding the guests out of the room. Once they were gone, Tea stilled Griffen with her hand and focused her gaze on Baxter, silencing his obnoxiousness for a moment. Griffen looked like he would explode with all his pent-up fury, but he let Tea have her chance to deal with the situation.

Baxter opened his mouth, most likely to release another

snide comment, but Tea put her finger in his face and burst out with, "No! It's my turn to talk, Bax. One night! One night! All I asked for was *one goddamn* night where Griffen and I could celebrate our life together and our future with the people we love. I was hoping you could be grown-up enough by now to be one of those people."

"Tea, you're always going to be my brother's wife. No matter what you run off and do with Nicky *Griffen* Tate."

"Shut up!" she shouted, and it seemed so unlike her that Jenna and Aubrey audibly gasped. "I wasted away for almost *six* years, alone and heartbroken after you brother died, Baxter. I refuse..." Her voice cracked, and Jenna put a hand on her shoulder to calm her for a moment. The touch apparently gave her enough strength to go on, and she finally added, "I refuse to allow you to come into *my* house and act like I am doing something wrong. Tell me, Baxter, when would the length of my pain have been enough for you? Ten years? Twenty? Did I need to die alone to prove my loyalty to your brother? Because I never saw you sacrifice anything — not one freaking thing — you wanted in his memory. No. I guess you think that's only *my* job for eternity."

A lone tear slid down Tea's cheek and Griffen turned so red Claudia worried he might actually kill Baxter.

"That's it! You made my fiancée cry, Bax. Now I'm going to make you cry. I don't care if you're like a brother to me. Sometimes you need to kick your brother's ass. And if Jack were here, I feel pretty sure he'd help me."

"Sounds like a great idea," Trey added, pushing his sleeves up to reveal his dark and menacing tattoos. He was also clearly ready to do serious damage. "Jack may not be here, but I can sure as hell help teach this kid a lesson for you, Griff."

"Bring it, Griffen. I've been looking forward to this for a

while," Baxter responded, his voice still slurring.

Wyatt stepped between them, pressing one hand on Baxter and the other hand against Trey's chest. The force of it elicited an exclamation from Jenna, "Careful with your shoulder, Wyatt! You don't need to keep grabbing everybody."

"It's okay, Doc," he answered, smirking slightly at Jenna. "Just trying to do my part here."

Trey threw Wyatt a mean look, and knocked his hand away, "Back off, McCoy. I fully intend on helping my boy here."

Panic set into Claudia's bones, and she grabbed Trey's other arm, stopping him in his tracks, "You can help Griffen by *not* getting arrested," Claudia murmured. Trey met her eyes and she could feel his arm relax under her palm. He must have seen the worry on her face because his eyes softened and he stepped back slightly from the fray, careful not to break her hold on him. Time slowed down around them — the battle raging only inches away, faded to a speck, leaving only the sensation of Trey's gentle gaze on her face.

"That's it! Cut it out, the lot of you." An older blonde woman ran up, silencing the bunch of angry men immediately. Claudia released Trey, the madness of the moment crashing back down around her, as the woman continued. "Baxter, you may look like a grown man but I am still your mother, and I demand you stop this nonsense immediately. I have let you get away with this long enough."

"Mom!"

"No. I am telling you right now — you are going to apologize to Griffen and your sister-in-law, then you're going to behave yourself. You do that or you leave. There is no third option," Carol threatened softly.

"I can't believe you're just accepting all of this."

"We are all trying to move on. I don't understand why you

have to be this way."

"*Move on*? It's like you're killing my brother all over again."

"Enough. He may have been your brother, but he was *my* son, and you don't get to tell me, or anyone else, how to grieve his loss. Come outside with me so you can cool off." Carol grabbed Baxter's shirt, leading him out of the room.

Claudia was still transfixed by the sight of Trey. He was still close enough to touch. His gaze found hers again, a flash of hot desire crossed his face — a sight she'd so desperately wanted to see from him again. She couldn't hear any of the clamoring discussion around her over the beating of her heart. Its pace became more frantic when the smallest smile creased Trey's handsome face.

"Come on, let's get in the kitchen, ladies. Give Tea a chance to collect herself," Jenna interrupted, grabbing Claudia's arm and giving Trey the oddest look, almost like a warning.

"What the fuck is he even doing here?" Aubrey demanded. Everyone was still serving themselves and eating in a separate room, giving the women some privacy.

"Carol invited him," Tea answered, taking a seat at her kitchen table.

"She did *what*?" Jenna shouted.

"Shh," Tea responded. "Carol was so upset and embarrassed about Baxter's behavior at her Christmas party, you know that. She felt bad for not telling Baxter about us. She's been trying to get him to come around ever since."

"Classic Carol. Even when she helps, it still causes stress."

"You saw her dealing with him. She's trying."

"Well, maybe if she'd tried before, instead of indulging him with all his tantrums, then we wouldn't be in this mess," Aubrey responded, irritation dripping from her words.

The kitchen door swung open, as Griffen's mom, Valerie

made her way in, quickly giving Tea a warm hug.

"Oh, Tea, honey. I'm so sorry you had to deal with that."

"It's okay. And thanks for being so great. Are the guests okay?"

"They're fine, maybe a little worried about you and Griffen, but the good food is a distraction. I'm still concerned about you, though."

"I'm okay, just a little jittery, I guess. I've never really yelled at anyone like that before."

"I couldn't hear what you said, but I know it was certainly warranted."

"It was, Val," Jenna assured her as she handed Tea something brown and stiff to drink. "Damn, Tea, that was some serious Southern girl attitude you brought there. I'm so proud of you," she continued.

"Baxter may want to mess with our night, but I refuse to give him the satisfaction of succeeding."

"Why would he do something like that?" Claudia asked, honestly confused by such a selfish display.

"He's always been such a moody thing," Aubrey answered. "Losing his brother made it so much worse."

"Well, he won't be able to get away with it anymore, I hope," Jenna added. "Baxter broke Griffen's number one rule — don't ever make Tea cry."

Tea chuckled lightly, before standing up and attempting to open a series of champagne bottles, but she was clearly still distraught and had little success.

"Hey, is it okay if I open the champagne bottles? I need something to keep me occupied," Claudia said, eager to help in some way.

"Yes, Claude. That would be awesome," Tea answered, easing back from the bottles. "You guys don't need to worry about me."

"But it's what we do," Aubrey responded, hip-checking Tea in the arm.

"I know, and thank you a million times over for it. But, I'm so happy tonight. I'm not letting Bax bring me down. It's just... He looks so much like Jack. When he comes here pissed like that, it sucks. Carol said he's been unhappy, trying to take over decision-making for *Viola*, but she's not ready to let go of her family's empire."

"He doesn't seem mature enough," Valerie interjected.

"No, and he's only just started business school... That doesn't excuse anything though."

"It doesn't. Forget about him. I'll make sure Bax is occupied," Jenna assured her.

"No, I can do it," Aubrey offered.

"Are you sure? When you saw him last year at Carol's Christmas party you almost punched him."

"*Almost*, being the key word there. I didn't *actually* kick his ass. I can handle this. You and Tea both have your guys, I should probably help you actually get to spend time with them."

Claudia saw what seemed like the slightest hint of sadness streak across Aubrey's face, but it was gone so quickly, she couldn't be sure if it was all in her imagination.

"Thanks, Brey," Tea answered.

"No problem," she said with an abundance of cheer, before rushing out of the kitchen.

"At least no one can claim our parties are boring," Tea stated. "Thank you for taking care of the champagne, Claude. By the way, how is work going? Does it still bite?"

Claudia's hand slipped when pulling out a cork in response to Tea's choice of words, which had evoked the memory of Trey nipping at her chin a week before. Before she could collect herself, a torrent of bubbly liquid spilled over her hands.

Jenna grabbed a dishtowel and started to clean it up. "If we wanted a spaz to spill it everywhere, we would've let Tea keep opening the bottles," she joked.

"Sorry, I think I got a little distracted," Claudia muttered.

"I can help you, Claude," Jenna offered.

"Don't worry about it. This will give me a chance to get settled. I always feel kind of awkward when I meet so many new people at once."

"If you're sure… When you're done with that, can you find Wyatt and me? Hopefully you don't feel too overwhelmed already, because we have even more people for you to meet, sorry," Jenna told her quickly, before heading out with Tea.

Claudia simply nodded, licking some of the champagne off her hand. Jenna and Wyatt may have another sea of faces to thrust at her, but all Claudia really wanted was to find Trey and pick up where their last enticing look had left off.

CHAPTER FIVE

"Hey, Wy. Jenna said you guys wanted me to see me..." Claudia explained to her brother with a smile. Her feelings may have been mixed about him and all his protective hovering, but she did love him.

"There you are. We sure did. Come over here," Wyatt responded, beaming with a joy, which immediately put Claudia on alert. Even so, she allowed herself to be dragged away, all the while scanning the room for Trey, yet to no avail.

Wyatt pulled her over to a group of people, including his agent, Gabe, Jenna, and a very good-looking blonde guy.

"Come here. You remember Gabe..."

Claudia nodded shyly, feeling her usual discomfort becoming amplified by her brother's boisterousness.

"Claude, hi again," Jenna greeted her cheerfully. "This is Jason, we were friends in high school when he played on my dad's team."

"Wow, what a coincidence," Claudia responded, skepticism dripping into each word, yet Jenna barreled on shamelessly.

"You may have met Jason before when he played with Wyatt at *Texas*."

"Oh! I remember you now," she answered, recognition coming in a flash and overriding her prior skittishness. "Go *Longhorns*!"

"Hell yeah. I gotta say, you're amazing. That was ten years ago, you must have been barely a teenager back then," Jason responded, an adorable grin spreading across his handsome face.

"Yes, pretty much, but I still could tell a great wide receiver when I saw one. Do you play football now?" Jason, and his connection to her beloved home state, managed to immediately put Claudia at ease, in spite of herself.

"Jason plays in the *Canadian Football League* for the *Toronto Red Wings*. He came all the way down here to come to this party. Gabe's his new agent, so hopefully we can get him on a team here in the States, soon," Wyatt said, inserting himself back into the conversation quickly. "Jason is *also* single."

"Wow, great segue, Wy," Claudia mused sarcastically.

"All right, Wyatt, let's try not to be so obvious, you've made them both feel embarrassed," Jenna stated, catching the completely mortified expression on Claudia's face. "But he *is* cute, right," Jenna whispered, pinching Claudia's upper arm.

"Jenna!" Claudia sputtered out, her cheeks flushing bright red.

"Don't worry. You can tell her I'm ugly, I won't mind," Jason declared to Jenna, and Claudia almost spit from laughing.

"How diplomatic of you. It's very nice to see you again, Jason, sorry if I seem unwelcoming," Claudia said.

"No problem at all. Wyatt was never the most subtle person."

"You can say that again," Jenna agreed.

"Jenna, you're no better," Claudia retorted.

"She's got you there, J," Jason answered laughing.

"Oh, screw the both of you. I have other friends... Look, there's, Laney. Get over here, girl."

"Hi, Jenna."

"Laney. I'm so glad you made it. I want you to meet some people. I was going to introduce you to Brey, too, but I can't find her anywhere. You'll see her later, I guess. You know Wyatt...this is Jason...and I don't believe you've met Wyatt's agent Gabe." Jenna stated.

Claudia felt almost claustrophobic with all the new names swimming around her head. She may have wanted to make new friends, but this was starting to feel ridiculous.

"No, she hasn't," Gabe interjected. "But she's your doctor, right? Wyatt says he owes her the world."

"All I did was give Jenna a routine exam," Laney corrected. Claudia's throat constricted realizing this must be the physician who discovered the lumps in Jenna's breast a year ago, saving her life. "Jenna's the brave one here," Laney continued. "But, so you know, Wyatt, I do accept gifts. The more lavish, the better."

"You got it," Wyatt declared, reaching for Jenna's hand, with a determined look in his eyes.

"Oh no you don't. I need you to go back to being frugal for a while, Wyatt. Gabe, please make sure he doesn't *actually* give Laney the world. We're looking to buy a house closer to Tea and Griffen and I'm all about saving money right now."

"I'll try, but I couldn't even get him to accept doing that *ESPN* special. I don't know how much pull I have with the guy."

"What special?" Jenna asked, dumbfounded.

"The one they asked him to do about his career turnaround," Gabe explained.

Jenna pivoted to Wyatt quickly, a stern look quickly overtaking her pretty features. "Wyatt, why am I just learning about this now?"

"Because it wasn't a big deal. Don't worry about it," he answered, throwing an arm around her shoulders and kissing her cheek.

"It sounds like a seriously big deal."

"Doc, please, calm down. I knew you'd want me to do it, and we've finally gotten a chance to relax together, so I went ahead and said no."

"Um, Laney, how about we head over there and get a drink?" Gabe asked Laney, clearly recognizing the strain of the moment. Jason tried to catch Claudia's eye, too but Claudia wasn't ready to go anywhere. The familiar feeling of irritation with her brother was more powerful than any discomfort she may be feeling.

"Wy, this is just like you to think you know how to run everybody's lives," Claudia fumed, bursting into the conversation. Wyatt glared at Claudia, but she simply met his eyes, digging in even further. "You always do this — make decisions for everyone else, thinking it's for our own good. It's infuriating!" Claudia added.

"This is none of your business," Wyatt responded harshly, before turning back to Jenna.

Jenna quickly took over the conversation. Her tone was even and firm. It still amazed Claudia how only Jenna seemed able to shut Wyatt up.

"Wyatt, maybe I would've realized that, too, but you didn't even give me the chance. This is exactly what you promised you wouldn't do anymore," Jenna added with a whisper.

"I'll never apologize for protecting you," he grunted, staring in the distance.

Jenna wrapped her arms around his waist. "Look at me," she whispered.

His eyes met hers, jaw tight, "They wanted to focus on you and what happened last year. I'm not going to put you out there like that…again…no matter what."

"You should've told me and let me be a part of this decision," Jenna responded roughly. "At the very least, talked to me about it. That's the whole point. We're in this together."

Wyatt's deeply worried face sent a shot of guilt through Claudia. Of course he was zealous about keeping his girlfriend from the world. Wyatt had always been an overprotective caretaker of the people he loved, which led him to take some serious chances with Jenna's trust.

When his secret relationship with Jenna became the stuff of headlines, he'd almost lost her forever. Those few months had been painful for Claudia, too — the speculation about their family, especially what role, or lack thereof, their long-absent *NFL* quarterback father had really played in their lives.

With that mess finally behind them, Wyatt was probably obsessed with keeping Jenna away from all the pitfalls of a public life with him. Claudia started to apologize for butting in, when Wyatt moved a hand to Jenna's neck, running his fingers upward into her hair, forcing her face closer to his. "Mi belleza, listen to me. I do this because I love you."

Jenna sighed softly, "No fair, Wyatt. I get that, but we *will* be talking about this later," Jenna said thickly.

"Claudia, I am also going to go grab a drink at the bar, want to join me?" Jason whispered in her ear, providing her an out, which she was now very ready to take.

"Good idea," Claudia breathed out in relief. "It's probably better if we let them work this out in whatever way it is they do," Claudia joked.

"I imagine a bedroom is part of that resolution."

"Eww, that's my brother," she chastised, slapping him in the arm as they walked away. She was touched that Jason had shown the class to wait for her while she had it out with her brother, even though it couldn't have been a comfortable situation to endure.

As they made their way across the room, and put some space between themselves and the latest round of drama pinballing around the evening, Claudia lamented, "It looks like my brother hasn't really changed a bit. He still displays type A obsessive behavior when it comes to looking after the people he cares about."

"My understanding is he's type *triple* A when it comes to looking after Jenna," Jason added.

Claudia burst out laughing, relieved to finally talk to someone who understood her brother and all the craziness that came with him, including his huge heart.

Jason handed her the drink she'd ordered from the bartender and continued speaking, "I can't blame Wyatt for wanting to protect Jenna from the dangers and pain, which can come with how overexposed the world of pro football can get. It doesn't mean I would use his same methods, but his heart's in the right place."

"I guess so…"

"And he's smart to keep her close. Jenna's great. If you're lucky enough to find someone special like that, it's your job to do all you can to keep them safe, no matter what it takes."

Claudia turned to Jason and said, "Sounds like you and my brother have at least one thing in common besides football."

"We've been friends for a long time, and know each other very well — the good and bad of it."

"It's hard to imagine you doing anything bad, Jason," Claudia teased, waving her free hand to refer generally to his overall aura of respectability.

"I wouldn't bet on that if I were you, Claudia. Though your brother does have a *pretty* positive view of me. I'm sure it's why he wanted us meeting like this."

"About that…I'm so sorry for what Wyatt and Jenna did just now — trying to fix us up, I mean. You must have been so uncomfortable. My brother has always been in my business, but now Jenna is in on the act, too. I am starting to feel pretty outnumbered."

"Don't be too mad at them… In fact, I should probably confess something."

"What?"

"I saw your picture when I came down a few months ago for Jenna and Wyatt's housewarming party. You were in Quantico in training at the time. Wait, am I not supposed to know that?"

"It's okay," Claudia responded with a chuckle. "I'm not *that* kind of federal agent. You're allowed to know I'm in the FBI. I have a badge and everything," she teased.

"Good to know. Well, thing is, I've been pushing for a chance to meet you ever since."

Claudia almost dropped both her jaw and the low carb vodka martini she'd been holding. Her pump was full of insulin, but the spike of olives jostled in the clear liquid for a different reason — quivering right along with her own shocked nerves.

"Wow, Jason, how…flattering," she stammered out.

"It's just the truth. What man would be stupid enough to see someone as beautiful as you, who also happens to be a kick-ass FBI agent, and not move heaven and earth to get a chance to talk to you?"

Claudia glanced across the room and caught sight of Trey talking to Jenna. Despite their previous heated glance, now she could barely catch his eye when she looked his way.

Apparently Jenna had decided to take a break from her dust-up with Wyatt, because Trey and Jenna were chatting comfortably. It was as though he was a totally different person from the intensely confusing man who'd invaded her life. The ease of his relationship with Jenna drove the knife of his recent indifference toward her even more deeply into Claudia's heart. As far as Claudia could tell, nothing ever seemed to be easy between her and Trey.

In defeat, she looked back to Jason and sighed. "I can think of a few guys who are immune to it."

Jason leaned toward her, whispering so his warm breath washed over her ear, "Whoever they are, they're idiots."

She turned her head back to look into Jason's remarkably light blue eyes, giving up on catching Trey's eye. Jason was tall, blonde, sexy, and clearly very interested in her.

Claudia couldn't help but wonder what it would be like to stop fighting a never-ending series of fruitless and exhausting battles for all the things she would probably never get to have in life, and instead enjoy what was actually right in front of her.

"Trey? Did you hear me?" Jenna demanded, and he wracked his brain to figure out what she'd been saying to him.

"Yes, I know. It's bullshit. You did the right thing," he blathered out, fixated on the sight of the big, blonde all-American asshole leaning over Claudia like he had something worthwhile to say.

"Thanks for the support, Trey," Jenna retorted with a cranky bite to her tone. She grabbed his shoulder and twisted him to look at her. Before he could look back to check up on Claudia, Jenna added, "I asked if you'd been to Tea and Griffen's new house before tonight."

"You did? I mean, of course you did... That's what I said, um..."

"Save it, Trey. I know you weren't paying attention," Jenna responded with a stiff laugh.

Trey used all his strength to pretend to focus on Jenna's angry face, but he could feel his own eyes straying away again.

"Man, you're in a shitty mood all of a sudden, Jenna."

"I have some stuff on my mind, but you're changing the subject," she answered. Trey glanced quickly over to Claudia, concerned he couldn't see her face anymore behind the guy she'd been glued to for longer than what seemed appropriate. "Cut it out, Trey. Could you stop pretending not to stare at Claudia for a second and talk to me?"

"What? Who is that guy with her anyway? She keeps leaning over, is she choking?"

"She's laughing and enjoying herself. Jason is very funny. I think they look great together, don't you?"

"Yeah, fucking wonderful," Trey grumbled. They *did* look like they were made for each other — both clean-cut and gorgeous. Jason seemed to be just the kind of guy Wyatt and Jenna *would* choose for her. He likely had no tattoos or piercings, and probably possessed an innate ability to follow the rules, without any history of destroying sweet, innocent young women.

Jason also was clearly capable of talking to Claudia without losing his mind — another stark and irritating contrast to Trey. For the last week, Trey had been trying his damnedest to do the right thing with Claudia. He couldn't believe he let himself touch her — taste her — even if only for a moment.

He'd told himself it would help him manage her willfulness, but all it had done was make him all the more out of control himself. She possessed his brain on the inside, while each day he'd been working hard to be professional on the outside. All his good behavior only seemed to upset her though. Leaving her to someone else — an apparent choirboy like this Jason guy, was probably just what she needed and deserved — and the last thing in the world Trey wanted for her to have.

The battle with Baxter had gotten his blood pumping, throwing off his restraint. As soon as he saw Claudia again, looking so stunning and concerned for him, it took all his strength not to grab her right in front of everyone.

"Trey? Are you still with me?"

"Yeah. I'm right here." Trey turned back to Jenna. He knew he should change the subject, but he couldn't. "His name's Jason, huh? Glad to hear he's funny. How do you know that?"

"Wyatt and I are trying to fix Claudia up with him. He plays for the *Canadian Football League* and is really awesome. He'd be good for her. Why are you all worked up?"

"I just need to make sure Claudia's okay… Like you asked."

"I call bullshit, Trey. I thought you were dreading doing me this favor. Is something going on with you two? I saw her mooning over you like a girl with her first crush. Are you already sleeping with her? Christ, Trey. You promised me."

"Easy. I haven't slept with her, Jenna. I've been keeping my distance."

"The way you two keep looking at each other all night doesn't look very distant. Jesus, you two are practically eye-fucking each other."

"Shit. Nice language lady. Claudia is part of my team on the Taylor case now. I need to keep an eye on her."

"*Humph.* Then why are you glaring at poor Jason like he just cooked a puppy in Tea's newly renovated kitchen?"

"Poor Jason? You're kidding, right? What do we even know about this guy?"

"I went to high school with him and my dad coached him, so I know a fair amount."

"You could say the exact same thing about Chase, and you had no idea just how bad *he* was. No offense, but from what little you've told me, you don't really have the best judgment with men all the time."

"Hell, Trey. *Yes*, offense. Offense definitely taken."

Trey regretted the words as soon as they left his mouth. Chase was a bastard who had tormented Jenna since high school. That bully was gratefully out of the picture now, but the wound was probably still raw.

"Shit, I'm sorry, Jenna. I shouldn't have said that. I don't know what's wrong with me tonight." Though he did know what was wrong, or more accurately, *who.*

"It's okay. I know you didn't mean it. If you really aren't involved with her, then what's the problem if Jason talks to Claudia? Wyatt is trying to loosen up on her and I think him agreeing to set them up is a good sign."

It didn't sound good to Trey at all. In fact, it made him feel like punching in the pretty dude's teeth.

"He looks awfully shady to me, and all that *Canadian Football League* crap sounds pretty fucked up. Let me see if it's a cover."

"What the hell is going on with you, Trey? I trusted you to look after Claude because you don't give a damn about anything, but now you're here acting like a total lunatic. Oh hell, Wyatt is going to lose his shit. Look, maybe I should call all this off. She already looks better..."

"Because of what? Christ, Jenna, don't you get it? Claudia is better because *I* am taking care of her. And who the hell do you think *you* are telling me what to do? You don't fucking know everything about me."

"Jeez, Trey, calm down."

"No. I won't. I'm tired of being told what to do...by you...all of you. Everything is on your terms and I'm pretty fucking sick of all of it."

"Trey, you're being an ass right now."

"Am I? Well, then it's probably good I go home. I'd hate to mess up your and Wyatt's plans, or fail to comply with all your orders. I made my appearance. I smiled at Griffen's speech about getting his fucking dream life. I didn't interfere with Claudia's cute little fix-up... I guess I should go before I say or do something to upset *your* perfect evening."

Trey turned quickly, making it out of the beautiful home, its surreal, flawless life pressing down on his shoulders like a collapsing ceiling. His shoulder knocked into one happy, normal partygoer after another on his way out.

"Trey, wait..." Jenna pleaded quietly from behind him, always so afraid of making a scene. She didn't really know him, no one did — and because of that, they couldn't truly care for him.

Trey caught Griffen eyeing him with worry, but he quickened his pace before Griffen could leave his nice, jovial, bullshit conversation to follow him.

He knew his friend would try to convince him to stay and celebrate the happy bubble he'd created. Yet, Trey didn't want to be around when all this magic disappeared, because that's how happiness works — it is always doomed to be tragically inconstant.

Griffen had unexpectedly gotten everything one could want in life — a girl who loved him, a family. The poor bastard wasn't prepared for any of this to end — but it always did, because nothing good ever lasts. Griffen was likely due for the rug to be pulled out from under him soon enough. Trey may not be able to stop it for his friend, but he could try to avoid his own fall, before it was too late.

He was almost at his car when a hand grabbed his jacket sleeve.

"Back off, Griffen, I've had a seriously fucked-up night," he growled, turning to make sure Griffen saw the face to go with his angry words, but all his fury fizzled when he looked down instead to see Claudia's huge, confused brown eyes staring up at him.

"Trey, what happened? Are you okay?" Claudia asked sweetly.

Trey couldn't speak. That same suffocating force was still bearing down on his shoulders — crushing his muscles, bones, and will in the same prolonged press. He tried to force his face into a stern expression, like he'd done so many times with Claudia, but he was too happy to see her in front of him. The jarring jolt of pleasure at the sight of her face made him even more irritated — but this time it was with himself.

"I just needed a break."

"I know, all those gorgeous, happy people being so nice was starting to wear me out a little, too," she teased. "Seriously, did they all have to be so friendly?" she asked, with the most deliciously sarcastic look on her face.

Trey rubbed his thumb in the space between his eyebrows, as his mouth worked over the loop in his lip.

"Yeah. Jason seemed really nice. You two would make a great couple — like a commercial for *Sandals Resorts*, or something. Just...fucking perfect."

"He *is* very sweet. But maybe I don't want sweet or perfect. Maybe I want you…"

"What? You can't know what you're saying. You don't want me," he stammered, though the words filled his stupid heart with something like joy.

"I sure do. I *want you* to stop jerking me around…"

"I'm not jerking you around," he countered, feeling a touch of defensiveness prickling along his spine.

"Trey, you know that's a lie. I don't know which way is up or down with you. Right when I thought we were making some progress, you cut me off again. And now you're leaving without even saying hello or goodbye to me?"

"Would you believe me if I told you it's for your own good?"

"I have faith you're telling yourself that. But I refuse to believe you ignoring me, or treating me, at best, like some coworker you barely know, could ever be good for me."

Trey tried to swallow, but something was clogging his throat. He wanted so much to hold her, he had to clench his hands in fists at his sides to stop himself.

"I've had a lifetime's worth of people telling me what's for my own good. I'd like to have a chance to do something, which may be stupid, or great, but it'll at least be *my* choice. No matter what you think is right for me, you *will* deal with me…*right* now. Otherwise, I'll just stop even trying to make sense of you and hang out with Jason all night…"

"You know I don't fucking want you talking to him…day or night. Stop being like that," he ordered.

"You're giving me credit for psychic powers I don't have, because I never know what the hell you're thinking."

"Trust me, I don't like seeing you with that fucking guy."

"Then stop this hot and cold crap. I may be young and I figure I'm not the most experienced person in the world… Hell,

I'm not even the most experienced person in this driveway, but I know I don't like how you've been ignoring me lately. I thought you were becoming my friend, or at the very least — we're a team."

"I could never ignore you, Claudia, and whether or not I'm your friend, has nothing to do with why being around you is making me act this way."

"Then why?"

"I like you, a lot…more than is safe for me. It messes with my head… I thought if I was all business with you it would fix things…"

"But it hasn't?" she pleaded.

"No. I guess I'm fucked," he stated with a chuckle, then adding, "but I promise I'll try to be different with you."

His hands were itching again with the urge to touch her, and he didn't try to stop them this time. They were on her cool cheeks before he could control them. The way her pretty, red lips parted in response made his chest hurt.

He'd spent the last week keeping his hands off her, but it was too much to deny now — if he was going to spend his life crushed under the pressure of a world he couldn't control, why couldn't he have a few moments of pure bliss? Trey had done the purely sex thing already and it hadn't worked. Perhaps enjoying the sheer *rightness* of this lovely, guileless young, woman could bring him some peace.

"Trey?"

Her sweet breath flickered across his lips and he realized how close her mouth was to his.

"Yes?" he whispered.

"If you don't kiss me, I may have to kick your ass."

"That's scary, because I know you can do it," he answered, letting his thumbs run gentle circles on her smooth cheeks, before sliding his fingers into her thick, soft hair.

"Trey? Are you out here?"

"Fuck, that's Griffen," Trey grunted.

"Ignore him," Claudia answered, gripping the fabric at his waist, with the same sexy stubbornness, which had been keeping him up at night. Her small hands then reached up and slid into his hair, until he felt like there was no one in the world but the two of them. He leaned down, her nose brushing against his like warm, soft velvet. He shouldn't do it. He should let her go, but she was so close — almost his.

Trey was close to experiencing the beautiful mouth he'd denied from himself for what seemed like an eternity when a cacophony of additional voices broke in.

"Wyatt, get in here. Leave her be. Claudia probably just went home."

"Busted…that's Jenna," Claudia whispered, a giggle breaking into her voice.

"I'm not a crazy person, Doc. I just want to make sure she's okay. Her car is still here."

"And *that* would be your brother. Mood killer, for sure," Trey whispered back, his hands leaving the thick length of her hair.

"Maybe Trey took her home. Both their cars are here, though. It doesn't look good. Dammit."

"That's Griffen again. He sounds worried," Claudia whispered.

"Yes. That ass. I guess we should get back."

"It sucks when people love you," Claudia grumbled.

"No shit."

"We better get moving. It only gets worse if you ignore them."

Trey nodded, even though he knew she couldn't see it.

He allowed his traitorous hand to rest at her tiny waist for a moment before they moved toward the glimmering light awaiting them. After managing to sneak her back into the home without anyone becoming suspicious of he and Claudia's almost tryst, Trey's mind began to wander.

Maybe he felt lost, but so did she, and that made him somehow eager to see if they could get found — together.

CHAPTER SIX

Claudia pushed her front door closed behind her with one foot. She almost lost her balance in the process, as she struggled to carry the stack of new files Trey had dumped unceremoniously onto her desk that morning.

After mere moments of pleasantries about their lives, he'd brusquely instructed her to review all the materials, and then quickly left the FBI offices for the rest of the day.

She still had yet to get the kiss she'd demanded from Trey the night before at Tea's party, but from her review of the documents he'd given her, it was clear he'd finally started to entertain her theory that industrial espionage and greed could be the real motives they should be exploring in their investigation.

This also meant she was now buried under piles of research on every Chinese company, which might have been behind the plan to steal robotics technology from *Carnegie Mellon University*, by way of the egomaniacal, yet witless David Murphy.

After placing the stack carefully on the bench by her front door, she moved toward her alarm keypad, rubbing her sore eyes along the way. All tiredness left her body when she registered it had already been disarmed. A sound from the kitchen put Claudia on even higher alert. Reaching for her pistol, she eased her body along the wall, until she could peek quietly through the kitchen doorway.

Claudia froze at the sight of Trey's long legs on her kitchen floor, his body lying supine with his head and chest hidden underneath her sink. Her blood was flush with a combination of relief it wasn't an intruder, and the usual all-encompassing thrill, which always managed to knock her silly whenever she was in Trey's general vicinity. If a person truly could be a force of nature, then this guy was the whole San Andreas Fault.

Even though his head was tucked away under her sink, his white tee shirt had ridden far up his torso, revealing much of his flesh. She would recognize his ripped stomach, with its intricate tattoos, anywhere. Despite never seeing it fully, occasionally he would lean over to grab something, pulling his shirt up just enough to turn Claudia's brain into mush, while simultaneously adding to the image of his body, which she'd been burning into her memory.

She indulged herself for a moment, gazing at his bare stomach and jean-clad legs for longer than was probably okay. His feet were bare and even they were making her body feel uncomfortably warm, as her mind filled with thoughts of other possible ways he might someday be in her house with no need for shoes.

Claudia began to worry she might be frozen in place. Finally, she managed to squeeze out a few words.

"Glad to see you made yourself at home."

She heard a loud "bonk," as he hit his head on the underside of her kitchen sink. His hand slipped, pouring a burst of water over his torso. A few colorful expletives followed. Shaken from her surprise at his obvious breaking and entering, and her own lascivious staring, Claudia managed to gather her wits enough to throw the nearest towel directly on his crotch. The gray cotton rag gave her a helpful distraction from her obsession with his southern hemisphere.

"Ouch. That sounded like it hurt. Are you all right? Do you have a concussion?" she asked quickly, crouching down to check on him.

Trey eased out from under the sink, revealing the rest of his muscular, tattooed chest at a slow and unnerving pace. His shirt was soaked, rendering it almost transparent as it clung to his body with as much steadfast commitment as her fixated gaze.

He moved one hand to rub his head, gifting her with a broad smile, which made her worry she might be the one who'd just had her bell rung.

"Why does it seem like so many of my interactions with you, risk me ending up on my back, close to being injured?"

The thought of him on the ground underneath her again sent a slew of confusing sensations through her brain at a frenzied speed.

Forcing down her wayward thoughts, she answered, "Maybe because you're always doing things that make you deserve a whack on the head? What are you up to under there anyway? I thought you just fix computers."

As he bent his knees to hoist himself to his feet, Trey stated, "I fix a lot of things… I break a lot of things, too." Before Claudia could process his statement, he continued, "You mentioned this morning your kitchen sink was messed up, so I decided to swing by and take care of it."

"I appreciate you coming by to fix it. You know, if it were by invitation, I might not have been so surprised when I found you. How'd you get in here? What about my security system?"

"That was nothing for me to get past. It barely slowed me down."

"Imagine that..."

"Improving your souped-up alarm clock is next on my to-do list in here."

"Um, thanks, I think. But you didn't answer my question. *How* did you get in here?"

"Why ask me a question, when you may not like my answer to it?"

"Humph," she grunted. After a beat, she allowed the mischievous fun of the moment to override her common sense. Claudia added with a smirk, "So, you felt pretty confident I wanted you here invading my pipes?"

"Another question you don't want to hear my answer to," he quipped, before peeling off his wet tee shirt so he could use the kitchen towel to dry off his chest.

Claudia released an awkward laugh, hoping it would mask the sound of her nearly swallowing her own tongue at the sight of his half-nakedness. She leaned back against her kitchen table, crossing her arms over her chest to hide the nervousness tingling through her arms, "Fine. Be that way. So, did you learn how to be a plumber at *Stanford*?" she teased.

"What?" he grumbled, his muscles visibly tensing. His brows furrowed and all the joy left his face.

"Oh, I'm sorry. I was just joking. I may have snooped into you a little. I'm sorry. I'm sure you don't like that. I was just being..."

"Curious. I get it. I figured you would try to learn about me. I have *met* you, after all. I just don't like to talk about *Stanford*."

"You don't seem to like to talk about yourself, period."

"No. And I know you like to figure things out. I did say I'd be different with you. So, how about you get to ask me *one* question. I promise I'll answer it."

Thousands of questions had been swirling through her brain since she'd met him. Yet, her mouth didn't seem to work. All she could do was stare at his naked chest, transfixed by so much artwork and his pierced nipples — the way his skin was still shiny with the remnants of his unintentional shower.

After her silence continued for an almost interminable amount of time, he looked down and smirked at her. The twist of his lips yanked her back into reality.

"Did it hurt?" she finally asked, tilting her head up to meet his eyes.

"When I fell from heaven?"

"*No.* All this stuff on your chest," she said, waving her hand back and forth in the direction of his chest. "Did it hurt?"

"Yes, but it was worth the pain. Come here," he purred, before taking her hand and placing it gently against one of his pecs. His skin was damp and warm against her palm, and the cool pressure of his metal piercing caused something deep inside her stomach to clench and relax repeatedly. "Does it feel like it hurts now?"

"It feels…" Her mouth was dry and her throat spasmed in a way she couldn't control. She peered down at her olive-toned hand as it rested against the tanned skin covering his heart. She could feel its beat beneath her quivering hand. Though his face was still, she sensed the pace of his pulse quicken the longer she touched him, and the knowledge made her hand quiver in response.

Then something struck her, and she couldn't hold the thought inside. Looking up into his sharp gray eyes, Claudia licked her lips and asked, "Why don't you have a tattoo here,

Trey? You have them all over your chest, but not here where your heart beats."

Trey's face twisted slightly and he backed away from her. The sudden removal of his warm skin from her touch filled her with a chilling sense of loss.

"I told you — just one question," he stated so sternly it felt like she was being chastised for something.

Trey turned away from her and reached for his shirt off her kitchen counter. Yet, her frustration with his repeated bullshit and her own abysmal inability to manage any moment she shared with him was impossible to deny. Before she knew it, Claudia grabbed him by the waistband of his jeans and spun him back around to face her.

"I never agreed to you being an ass afterward."

Claudia didn't know who she was more aggravated with — Trey for being so stubborn, or herself for always having such a knack at killing a mood. Other girls seemed to know how to get a guy's attention, and hold it without saying something stupid, but Claudia just couldn't help herself. Her mind always had to get in the way, and in this instance, her body was getting the losing end of the stick.

"More conditions, little one?"

"Yes. You're not the only one who gets to lay down ground rules. You always want to boss me around…"

"Oh, so it's your turn now?"

"Maybe it is."

"I happen to like bossing you around. Why do you think I should share all the fun?" he asked, a smirk playing on his face, making him completely unreadable to her. Claudia crossed her arms over her chest and huffed out a hard breath.

"You'd better think about it, because you're pissing me off. I don't know what else to do to reason with you, or make you talk to me, unless you want me to go back to potentially wounding you."

"I don't think that's why you're upset."

"Oh, you don't? Because you know everything there is to know about the world?"

"I didn't say that. And that was *another* question. You're going to owe me a lot if you keep trying to change all the rules."

"You're in *my* house, you son of a bitch…"

"Shh… I'm sorry. How about this…" Trey eased toward her, a sly grin creeping across his face.

Before she could collect herself, Trey grabbed her by the waist and hoisted her onto her kitchen table, so her knees just barely grazed the sides of his denim-covered thighs.

"Fine. I'll answer your question about the bare spot over my heart, but you have to answer one for me. It's been bothering me ever since I met you."

"Okay, shoot."

"Are you sure? You won't like it, but you'll still have to tell me the truth."

Trey's fingers were slipping back and forth against her thighs, caressing her lightly.

"What?" she sputtered out. "Of co-ourse. It's a waste of time for me not to tell the truth. I suck at lying."

"Being bad at lying and being honest are two very different things."

"Fine. I promise to be *honest*," she answered, her throat drying with each persistent press of his hands, punctuated by the gentle circular motion of his thumbs against her inner thighs.

"Good. Then this will be an easy way for you to get what you want."

"Um, okay. What do you want to know?"

"Are you a virgin?"

"*That's* your question?"

"Yes," he answered, letting his hands squeeze the sides of her legs, hard, sending a new set of shocks and tingles along her nerve endings. "Last night you ordered me to *deal with you.* Well, then I deserve to know what I am dealing with."

She swallowed roughly, trying to use her prior irritation to pull herself back to reason.

"It's a ludicrous thing to ask. Plus, it's such a dumb male thing to care about or think you have the right to know."

"Uh-uh, little one. You're not answering my question. If you want to start making rules, then you have to be able to play by them, too."

"What do you *think* is the answer? I'm twenty-three…" she said, her breaths coming out in short puffs of air. Claudia pressed her palms on the table, trying to get up. Trey slammed his hands over hers and met her eyes with a blazing fury that made his gray irises look like swirling, melted steel.

"You're doing it again, Claudia. I've got all the time in the world, nowhere to be…and no desire to answer *your* question. If you want to back out so I don't have to tell the truth, then so be it."

She moved her face to avoid his eyes, "You're ridiculous."

Trey leaned in closer to her, using his nose against her cheek to force her face back toward his. He slid it across the length of her face, pausing to briefly brush his lips over her skin and suck on her earlobe, making her gasp out loud. When his teeth bit down on the flesh gently, Claudia couldn't help but release an embarrassing moan.

His warm breath tingled against her moistened skin, when he asked again, this time with a whisper, "Are…you…a…virgin?"

"No," she breathed out roughly.

Trey moved so he was facing her, staring squarely in the eyes as he challenged her, "No — you've had mind-blowing sex that turned off that crazy, intense mind of yours and made you stop trying to control everything? Or you've had a dick in you?"

"You-you dirty piece of —"

"Eh, eh, eh. Answer the question."

"Fine. I had sex when I was twenty." Trey's hands clenched a bit over hers, but his stare didn't waver from hers. When he stayed silent, she added, "He was my best friend. His name is Trevor. I felt it was important to get it out of the way and he was comfortable with my viewpoint, I guess. Are you happy now?" Claudia barely moved an inch, but Trey made it clear she wasn't going anywhere until he let her.

"Yup, just like I thought. For all intents and purposes, you're a virgin, little one. And since we're being honest with each other, I would like nothing more than to be your *real* first… It could be the only way I ever get you to listen to me." Claudia swallowed a gasp until the air turned into an awkward bubble in her throat. The thrill in her chest dissipated quickly as Trey's face fell, and he added, "The thing is, your answer confirms you're a nice girl. The problem is — I'm *not* a nice boy. And that's something we *both* have to deal with."

His words simultaneously frustrated and saddened her. She took a deep breath and muttered, "Your turn."

Trey leaned away from her, and rubbed the left side of his chest a bit, looking away from her.

He turned his eyes back to hers. There was no wicked gleam in his eyes, or smirk to lighten the mood. All that remained was dejection, and something even darker — almost ominous, though she couldn't quite place it.

"I don't have any tattoos there because I felt it was important to leave the area around my heart bare. It doesn't deserve anything…it's my weakest organ." He moved away from her, but she didn't stop him this time. With his back to her, he grabbed his damp shirt and pulled it on before declaring, "Get your laptop. I arranged for you to question David Murphy tomorrow."

Claudia opened her mouth to speak, eager to express just how excited the prospect of her first real suspect interview was, but Trey cleared his throat and cut her off before she could make a sound.

"We've got a lot to do. I need to make sure you're ready to meet with him…and that kitchen sink of yours is still fucked up."

CHAPTER SEVEN

"You ready to do this?" Trey asked Claudia, as he turned off the rumbling engine of his black 1967 *Ford Mustang Fastback*. His hands were sore from reflexively gripping the steering wheel during the entire drive to the federal courthouse downtown where the FBI was detaining David Murphy in advance of his trial.

"I can't wait… You know I was born ready. The real question is whether *you're* ready for me to go in there, Mr. White-Knuckler," she responded lightly, though her rapidly drumming fingers belied her nerves.

"Always such a smart-ass," Trey grumbled out. The soft weight of her hand alighting onto his bicep made the muscle twitch, but it also calmed him slightly.

"Seriously, Trey…are you okay? You seem kind of, um, tense."

He took a sharp intake of breath before turning to meet her intent and worried gaze. It touched him how even with her visible eagerness to take on this new challenge, she still stopped to express concern for him.

"I'm cool. I just need you to appreciate how dangerous this guy is. I've interviewed him countless times and it's never gotten anywhere."

"I've read the transcripts and it's clear he likes to toy with you, but he does know something more than he's letting on. I'd bet my *MacBook* on it. He's smart, but he wasn't smart enough not to be a patsy for the bastards behind all this."

"And you can't wait to go in there and meet this *patsy*?"

"Yes, absolutely. But I won't leave this car until I know you're not going to have a heart attack over all of this."

Trey let out a rough chuckle, pausing to enjoy her soft features and serious expression. The parking garage provided them an odd degree of privacy. In spite of all his continuing efforts to keep some semblance of distance from her, Trey yet again found he had to touch her...to connect with her.

He slid his right hand around her neck, letting his fingers graze over the strands of her hair, stretched taut on the path up to the tight twist of her bun, while his thumb rubbed back and forth along the curve of her jaw.

"I trust you, Claudia...and your instincts. I just need you to be careful. Got it?"

She licked her lips and nodded gently. He wanted so much to kiss her, and throw away his own self-imposed discipline. Yet, he had to be strong, because if he took that step, there would be no turning back, not with her.

Trey reluctantly removed his hand from her face and reached across her body to open her door. She threw him a quick, relieved smile before bounding out of the car, barely grabbing her bag on the way. He moved much more slowly, locking the car and following her to the elevators.

"Are you nervous?" he asked.

"No," she stated, entering the elevator with her head held high.

"You were right, you *are* a terrible liar," Trey muttered, pressing the button for the floor that would lead them to David Murphy's containment area.

"I'm not lying!" she answered, but her words sounded hollow, punctuated with an anxious laugh. "All right," she added, turning her body to his, "the truth is I'm kind of worried, but I'm also super excited. I can't describe what it feels like to finally have a chance like this…"

"That's better. You can always be honest with me, little one. Besides, I'm never going to fall for it anyway if you try to bullshit me."

She gave him a sheepish half smile, resting her hand lightly on the side of his stomach. He looked down at her, and could feel his face easing into a small grin.

"Mmm," she hummed. "You know, you should smile more often. It suits you," Claudia added with a teasing tone.

Trey beamed at her before briefly, before he squared his shoulders and schooled his face into a serious expression again. "If David tries to pull any legal shit about being in here too long, ignore it. He's waived all his speedy trial rights so his lawyers can file motions on his behalf. And he's a posturing ass, so he doesn't actually know what he's talking about most of the time."

"Got it," she responded, nodding quickly. The two fell into a pensive silence as they made it through processing and finally were escorted into a room with murder defendant and ex-professor, David Murphy.

He sat at a long, nondescript table, his hands resting on it in a thoughtful, clasped position, almost concealing the shackles at his wrists. Even in a prison jumpsuit, he still looked like a pompous ass. His hair was perfectly combed and his face free of worry. The guy didn't have a single wrinkle, even though he was forty-five years old.

"Well, if it isn't Mr. Adler, my favorite college dropout. You're back to chat again, I see."

"It's not my interview to take this time, David. Though ours have never been productive. I'm being assisted today by FBI Special Agent McCoy here."

"Well, well, what a pleasant surprise. I would stand and shake your hand, Agent McCoy. But, you understand..." he cooed at her smoothly, spreading his hands to showcase the metal containing him.

"That's perfectly fine, Professor Murphy," Claudia responded and her respectful demeanor irritated Trey to no end. David loved it — beaming in response to her deliberate effort to show him deference. "Are you sure you don't want your lawyer to be present?" Claudia continued calmly.

David smirked at Trey, before responding, "Oh, it appears Agent McCoy is both beautiful *and* conscientious? You should try to be more like her, Mr. Adler. She's *quite* impressive."

Trey laughed mirthlessly, keeping his eyes glued to David's obnoxious face. Without flinching, he said, "I know what you're trying to do. Just answer the questions she asks you, David."

"My pleasure. Though I have a few of my own, first. Specifically, how is Tea? I've written letters to her, but I'm not sure the mail system here is particularly accommodating to a gentleman in my position, no matter how pure the intentions," he stated, his eyes never wavering from Claudia's impassive face.

Trey pulled out a metal chair for Claudia, and one for himself.

"Can't you give this shit a rest for one hour?"

"What do you mean?" David asked with a simpering look, which showed he was ready to play.

"You're fucking kidding, right?" Trey could already feel the familiar aggravation brewing inside him at the mention of his best friend's fiancée.

"Of course I'm not kidding. How are Tea and Johnny? Do they talk about me at all?"

"They're fine," Claudia said quickly. Trey shot her an exasperated look, before turning back to David.

"David, you know the rules, talking about them is off-limits when I'm here," Trey stated.

"Oh, what a silly rule," he countered, and turned to Claudia. "You must understand, Agent McCoy, I never wanted to hurt Tea. She and Johnny were my family after Jack passed away."

"After you killed him," Trey grunted.

"Eh, eh, I'm still not confessing anything to you, Mr. Adler." And a lascivious grin ran across his lips as he took another quick glance at Claudia. "You understand the closeness of family, don't you, Agent McCoy," he cooed.

"Of course."

Trey threw her a stern look, before growling at David.

"Cut the bullshit, David, everyone knows you killed Jack and tried to kill Griffen. You confessed it to Tea," he stated roughly, furious he'd already lost his cool again with the son of a bitch. "Let's get to work. Agent McCoy is new to my team. She's a gifted computer scientist and white-hat hacker. You know the drill, if you cooperate with us, you may be able to make a fresh start with the U.S. Attorney."

"New to *your* team? Well, isn't that something. You really do fascinate me Mr. Adler." David's voice turned acidic when he added, "Because you aren't really a team kind of guy, are you? You seem like more of a bomb thrower to me."

The boiling red blood coursing through Trey's blood made him so hot, he thought he might explode.

"David, you better..."

"I'm just saying, seeing as you behave as though you enjoy working alone, this is quite interesting. I think I'm going to need to learn more about this person who is important enough to make you change so dramatically. Tell me, Special Agent McCoy, where are you from, because your exotic beauty is quite a non sequitur for your pedestrian name."

"I'm Mexican and Irish."

"Oh my, certainly a fiery background. I imagine you are quite passionate, in addition to being as brilliant as Mr. Adler claims. Tell me of your other accomplishments."

"Well, that's part of why I'm here. This is my first big assignment."

"Come closer. I can't quite hear you."

"David, let's take it down a notch."

"Does this bother you? Me talking to your new special friend? I mean special *agent* friend."

"I'm not going to let you bait me this time."

"Oh, really? Not even if I move my hands just a little bit closer to this stunning teammate of yours."

"Damn it, David, I know what you're trying to do..."

Claudia threw Trey a look of warning, and intoned, "Mr. Adler, can I go over something with you outside for a moment? Professor Murphy, please excuse us."

"By all means, take your time. I'm not going anywhere," David answered, spreading his hands in a show of supplication.

Claudia walked briskly out of the room and Trey followed behind her with slow, measured steps. As soon as the door closed, she spun on him, her eyes wide with confusion.

"Trey, what the hell was all that? You know he's just trying to get a rise out of you, and you're *letting* him. I sensed it was happening when I read the interview transcripts, but this is much worse."

"Sorry, I'll try to behave myself. So far, he's refused to talk to anyone but me. Our conversations are usually just that pointless. Each time I go in there, he says he'll only talk if I bring Tea and Johnny here to see him... But, this was different. I don't know why, but he got me even more pissed than usual."

"Maybe it would be better if you leave me alone with Professor Murphy for fifteen minutes."

"No way. And don't call him *Professor* Murphy. He's not a person to be respected and you shouldn't treat him like one. You need to refer to him as 'piece-of-shit-David,'" Trey said quickly, leaning away from her to press his back against the wall, bringing his arms calmly in front of his chest.

"Fine. I'll put that on his name tag," Claudia grunted out.

He could see her teeth were clenched with barely leashed rage, but he didn't give a shit. She might be ready to pounce, but he was too worried to care.

"You said you trust me, right, Trey?"

"I do."

"Then give me a chance with him. You see there's a guard right out here with you, and you can watch it all on the monitor right there," she added, pointing to the live feed into the examination room.

Trey's jaw was twitching, and his arms had clenched even more tightly across his chest.

"Claudia, that *professor* in there is a very *evil* man. You have no idea what evil people are truly capable of...and what they are more than happy to do to someone like you. I do know — too fucking well. And I'm here to keep that from happening to you."

She rolled her eyes, and retorted, "You need to make up your mind."

"About what?" he inquired, honestly confused.

"You're giving me these great opportunities, and I really appreciate it. But it's bull shit the way you give me an inch, and then yank me back a mile when the time actually comes. This place is monitored better than a new *iPhone* reveal. I have complete faith I'll be safe in there with him. What I can't trust is he'll talk while you're in there. Trey...please?"

"Fine," he growled. Claudia smiled, but Trey held up a finger and instructed, "But I'll be watching the whole time and I will absolutely stop it if I need to."

"I know," she whispered, her eyes softening. "Thank you."

Claudia disappeared back into the interview room and the seconds ticked by at such a torturously slow speed that Trey wondered if the passing of time had ceased altogether.

He wanted to pace up and down the hallway, but didn't risk peeling his eyes from the monitor above him. David appeared to be responding well to her, but Trey couldn't see her face. All he could do was hope she was okay.

Suddenly the image of Claudia's small black and white figure stood, and in a flash she was out of the frame. He couldn't tell if she'd fallen, or just walked to a corner of the room. Fear grasped at his heart.

Several terrifying scenarios played out in his mind each painful moment she was out of his line of vision.

What if she was having a hypoglycemic episode in there and couldn't get to the door?

What if David threatened her and she needs to get away from him? She could be grasping at the door handle now — desperate for my help!

"Kevin, can we get audio?" he asked the guard.

"Yes, but we'll have to go to the AV center down the hall. This feed is just for visual security purposes. Sorry."

"Right. I understand…"

Trey tried to take a calming breath, but he choked on it once he caught sight of David laughing, his eyes crazy and hands slapping the table, as though he were keeping a drumbeat.

"Man, that dude just gets more messed up every day," Kevin muttered.

"No shit. Can you let me back in there?" Trey asked, forcing his voice to sound normal, as his throat tightened and his heart raced.

"Want me to come in with you?"

"No, I don't want to end the interview. I'd like to give Claudia a chance to question him some more. I just need to get in there and make sure everything is okay."

"If you say so."

When the door finally opened, Trey quickly looked around the room.

"Oh, what a shame. Claudia, it appears your babysitter has returned. I suppose he's not comfortable letting you out of his sight for a minute? Mr. Adler, this is quite disappointing, seeing as Agent McCoy and I were really starting to get somewhere. I suppose you aren't happy unless you have her squarely under your thumb."

"Shut up, David. Are you okay, Claudia?" he whispered to her. "You went out of frame. I couldn't see you."

"I'm all right," she answered, but he could tell she was a little shaken.

"What did he do to you? What did you say to her, you son of a bitch?"

"It's okay. He was answering my questions. He just said something that made me uncomfortable, so I walked away."

"And I couldn't see you." Trey tempered his tone. Claudia's wide eyes said enough about how nuts he must seem.

"Relax. As you can readily discern, she's perfectly fine, Mr. Adler. Honestly, you are exhausting me today. Why don't you take another break and give us some more alone time. I think it would be delightful to continue to learn about this remarkable mujer encantadora."

Trey battled his intense desire to strangle the arrogant ass seated at the metal table in front of him.

"What does that mean? Are you talking in code, David?"

"Yes," Claudia retorted quietly. "It's the code of my Spanish ancestors. Christ, chill *out*, Trey," Claudia whispered.

"Fine, where'd you leave off?" Trey growled, his shoulders tight with irritation. "How about some more questions?"

"I've decided I only like talking to Agent McCoy. Run along, Mr. Adler."

"Professor Murphy, I thank you for your faith in me, but I can't exclude Mr. Adler. It's his case too."

"Those are my conditions. I like being alone with you. I don't have much in my life to enjoy."

"Then we're leaving," Trey commanded.

"Trey…" Claudia murmured.

"He answered some of your questions. Let's go."

"So pushy. Well, hasta luego, Agente Especial McCoy," David said smoothly.

"Sí, adios, Profesor Murphy," Claudia answered, having already recovered her usual bravado.

"I *will* see you again, my dear, I promise you," David added.

"What the hell does that mean? You're fucking full-on bat-shit now? Is that it? All this fucking time with nothing but your own messed up brain to keep you company finally getting to you?"

"Trey, that's enough," Claudia stated with an impressive amount of authority, but they both ignored her.

"Tea has moved on. Maybe I should, too. I would love to meet with Agent McCoy more. Even in here, I can learn things about people. For example, I can see your lovely Agent McCoy here is committed to solving this case…figuring out who paid me so much money to ruin my life, and I must say, she has a real knack for loosening my lips."

"You talk about her like that again, I'll fucking destroy you. You hear me? I will end you."

David laughed, and the brittle sound only served to make Trey angrier.

"I'm just being honest. It *is* why you keep bothering me, isn't it, Mr. Adler? So I'll prattle on one truth after another?"

"About your murderous tendencies, nothing else."

"See, and this is why I feel so much more chatty with the charming Agent McCoy over here. Though I am very angry with you for distressing her so much. I hope you treat her better when you are out of my presence."

"Shut up, David…" Trey growled out, but David was clearly on a roll.

"Everyone has a weakness. Your beautiful, young compatriot here? She's desperate to prove she has what it takes to solve this case. Desperation is the most toxic and dangerous emotion in life, even more than love. I should know… And you? I think your weakness is *her*. It's nice you indulged her and let her see me alone. I know you regret it now. It's really quite fascinating to watch. I can't blame you for enjoying her company. I know I do. If it means I have to keep opening up to see her again, then so be it."

"That's it! We're done here. I warned you, David."

"What are you going to do, Mr. Adler? Kill me? Please, because if you let me live I'll do all I can to manipulate these weaknesses, until I make your little conniption fit in here look like a hiccup… I do have to keep myself entertained *somehow*," he added with a feverish chuckle.

Trey knocked the metal table to the side. Claudia pulled at him from behind, but he shook her off quickly. He grabbed David by the front of his jumpsuit and yanked him as far off his chair as his shackled ankles would permit.

He could feel Claudia trying again to yank him back, as the guard rushed into the room, but all his senses could focus on was the smirk on David's face. He might've seemed like a weakling before, but his simmering menace was fully present now.

"What's going on in here?" Kevin demanded.

"Trey! Let him go, *now*!" Claudia commanded again, and this time he listened.

"It's okay, Kevin. We were just talking," Trey stated.

"I don't know, Mr. Adler. On the video it looked like you attacked the inmate." Kevin's hand was resting at his holster, ready to immobilize one of them, and it was unclear to Trey if he was the more probable target at that moment.

"Oh no, nothing like that. I had something on my jumpsuit collar," David said to the guard, never removing his taunting eyes from Trey's face.

"Yeah, everything is great, Kevin. No worries at all," Trey answered, removing his hands from David and stepping back so quickly he almost fell against the metal table, which was still askew. "It's nothing. Agent McCoy and I were just leaving," he added before calmly turning and leading Claudia out with a gentle hand on her elbow, and a pounding heartbeat in his chest.

CHAPTER EIGHT

"Trey, what in the *hell* was all that crap you just pulled?" Claudia demanded, before flinging her purse on the bench by her front door as she stormed into her townhome. A slight Texas drawl had invaded her voice, eagerly accompanying the heavy dose of anger in her tone.

"Oh, so you're speaking to me again?" Trey asked, before clomping behind her with the type of useless rage usually reserved for a twelve-year-old boy whose bike just got stolen. "I thought you'd lost your voice on our drive here, what with all your silent stewing," he countered, releasing his own personal batch of indignation to match hers.

She spun on him, eyes blazing, "I wasn't *stewing*, you big jerk! I was trying to collect myself…you know, so I wouldn't *accidentally* strangle you while you were bringing me home. Do you have *any* idea how unprofessional you were back there?"

"Seeing as I'm not a *professional*, or a fed…no, I don't know, and I don't really care. I couldn't see you on the video. I had no way of knowing if you were okay," he added with a shrug, which felt practiced, even to him.

"So, it's my fault?"

"Of course it is," he retorted.

"You can't be serious!"

"I'm completely fucking serious. You should know better! You promised me you'd stay in my line of sight."

"*You* also promised *me* I'd be able to go in there and do my goddamn job. When are you going to realize I can't be right where you want me every second, and I can't possibly follow your every random command?"

"They aren't random and they aren't commands, they are just what's right. Christ, look at what happened today. I got in there and he says all that shit. He's not allowed to talk about you that way."

"But you get to act like an idiot and break every protocol I've sworn to follow? This is the life I've *chosen*, Trey. Don't you care about me and what I want at *all*?" she pleaded, and the hurt in her voice tore him apart.

"I do care about you, Claudia," he whispered, moving closer to her. "You know I do. That's why I can't play by these stupid FBI rules you're talking about. It won't make you any safer. We're going to do this my way…all the way."

"There you go again…"

"Exactly. I'll keep doing what I can to help you with this job and life you want, but I know how risky it is, in a way you don't. You think you understand, but you're wrong."

"We were just talking. And it was going somewhere. I had it under control."

"Then why did you stand and walk away from him?" He bit his tongue at scolding her again for leaving the camera's range.

Her face softened. "I decided to tell him Tea was doing well, but she would rather not see him. I think it helped him to open up. But he started asking some really personal questions about me. I was…uncomfortable. I moved away from him to try and get the power back."

"What did he say to you?" Trey growled.

Claudia took a slow breath. "It doesn't matter. He's arrogant and delusional, but he does regret taking the bribes, and more so, what happened to Jack Taylor. I think underneath everything he's scared."

"I don't doubt he regrets getting busted, but I'm more concerned about the delusional part. He was totally fixated on Tea, and now he's trying to make me think he's transferred his unhealthy obsession over to you."

"If it helps to solve the case, who cares?"

"I care!"

"I'm a special agent, right? I can do this."

"I know you can. I brought you there because I believe in you. But leaving you in a room alone with him was stupid. I shouldn't have done it."

"I'm glad to see you realize you acted stupidly today, we will just disagree on which specific part," she teased with a surprising amount of ease before walking into the kitchen.

He followed her, noticing her sneak a peek at her continuous glucose monitor, before opening the refrigerator to grab a bottle of orange juice and what looked like a premade sandwich. He was glad to see she was taking care of herself, but he was still filled with an oppressive sense of dread, which wouldn't subside.

Trey immediately started to pace around her kitchen. Claudia poured herself a cup of orange juice and watched him cautiously. Unable to leave her, but incapable of knowing how to behave if he stayed, he ran a hand through his hair, glancing from one appliance to the other because he couldn't figure out where to rest his eyes. He decided to commit to the window, eying the gray, moody weather outside, which mirrored his own internal unrest.

Every time he thought he'd figured out how to handle Claudia, something else twisted him up all over again. Maybe the person he couldn't manage was himself — which was the most terrifying part of it all.

She leaned back against her kitchen counter and stared at him, her face becoming more still as she sipped her orange juice, then placing the half-empty cup on the counter. Claudia finally broke the painful silence.

"I won't lie, I'm glad I got to talk to David alone, but I'm sorry I upset you. I was so focused on the fact he was opening up to me, I lost track of everything else. When he started to get too intense, I got flustered and a little scared. I tried to distance myself from him, but I also forgot how worried you'd be. Thing is, I had no idea you'd overreact like that. I guess I should know better by now," she added with a rueful smile.

"I know I'm not the only person who has ever tried to protect you," he answered, moving so close to her he could've dipped a finger into her drink.

She met his gaze and whispered, "Maybe not, but you are the first one who I actually wanted to."

"I must confuse the hell out of you, little one," he responded, allowing himself to laugh a little.

"You won't get all worked up again if I agree with you, will you?"

"No promises," he answered, running his gaze over her upturned face, and resting on those big, brown eyes of hers.

"What did he say to you?"

"David?" she asked. Trey simply nodded. "About the case?" she added.

"No. What did he say to you in Spanish? When we left."

"Oh, that. The *code* you were so worried about?" She laughed a bit and answered in the most beautifully perfect Spanish, "He said 'mujer encantadora.'"

"Yes. When he said it, you blushed."

"It was only because it was such a silly thing to say about me. It means a girl whom everybody loves. All people are enchanted with her. So you see, not me at all. He probably said it to throw me off."

Trey moved a hand to her face, running his thumb slowly back and forth across her pronounced cheekbone.

"David is supposed to be a genius. I mostly think he's crazy and full of shit, but he's absolutely right when he calls you that."

"You're being crazy again," Claudia said with a forced chuckle, looking away, but he moved her face back to his.

"Maybe I am. Even so, I wish I could speak Spanish, because it would've given me words for the spell you have over me…how you make me feel. You have enchanted me, Claudia, and I don't know what the hell to do about it."

"Just do *something*, Trey. Because you have me completely turned inside out. I don't know what I'm supposed to do next. I'm putting all my faith in you, so how about you have a little in me? What if we just let go? If we screw each other up, so be it."

"It's very tempting."

"Is it?" Claudia swallowed, sucking on her upper lip for a moment. The sight transfixed him. She continued with a tremor in her voice, "Don't you want to hear what else he told me?"

Trey didn't answer her. His eyes searched her face to see if she understood just how scared she'd made him.

"Not yet," he whispered.

"Why not?"

Trey grasped her upper arms. "Because I'm still freaked out. You have to be more careful. Do you have any idea how hard it was for me to leave you in there with him?"

Claudia licked her lips and it made him feel completely exposed.

"But you have to trust me, Trey. I know it scares you to let things go, but I'm not crazy. Well, not *totally* crazy."

"This isn't about me somehow not trusting you, or not believing in what you can do — because you already know that's not possible. It's not even about you figuring out I really am a controlling ass. The fact is, I have no trouble letting *things* go. Hell, I've spent most of my life losing *things*, and I've tried hard to be really fucking okay with it each and every time… But you…"

Trey took a deep breath, loosening his grip before bruising her. Backing away from her, he continued, "Claudia, *you* are a very different story. David was also right about something else — I do refuse to allow you out of my sight for too long. Maybe I don't have a clue how not to mess all of this up with you, but I know this — no matter what happens with us, this case, you name it…the one thing I can promise you is I won't be able to breathe if I don't know you're safe."

"Trey…" Claudia answered before pausing briefly, her lips parting before she started to continue her rejoinder.

"Shhh," he countered, silencing her. Once more, Trey moved his hands to her face, holding her in place. He watched her lips part and heard her breath quicken. He had no idea what he was doing and he knew it wouldn't end well. But it was too late to stop now. His fingers twisted into her hair and his lips were on hers in an instant. He wasn't slow or gentle. He was too desperate. Just when he thought she might back away, her arms were around his neck.

Their kiss wasn't sweet and romantic like he knew she deserved. Instead they had both become nothing but eager lips, teeth, and tongues. He knocked his hip against the kitchen table on his way to pushing her against the wall — moving her upward slightly and pressing his own body against hers. She slid her arms down to clutch his face in return, pausing to suck on his lip, licking the metal loop with her quick tongue. Trey groaned into her mouth, slipping his hands under her top.

The thrill of her hot flesh under his fingertips quickly morphed to concern when his hand caught in the cord of her insulin pump. The rapid reminder of her delicacy — how perfect and fragile she was — rocked him back to reality. He eased away from her, breaking their connection.

Her eyes were burning with a potent combination of passion, confusion, hurt, and fury. The emotions were swirling within the velvety brown irises, singeing him like acid. Claudia clutched at the front of his shirt, forcing him to face her.

"No! Don't you dare stop. Not because of that. *Never* because of that," her voice dropping from an angry demand to a devastated plea.

"I don't want to hurt you…"

Tears threatened to choke her words to death before they escaped her mouth, and the knowledge of how much this show of emotion must have hurt her cut into Trey. She bit her lip and met his eyes with a steady gaze.

"Don't you get it? If you ever let that be the reason you stay away from me, then you *will* hurt me…more than I could ever say. Touch me, Trey… Please…"

His hands clenched and then relaxed at his side, drawn to the intoxicating peace, which only came from the sensation of his skin on hers. Before he could figure out what was the right thing to do, her fingers were in his hair and she was pulling his mouth back down to hers.

Trey gave in to her, but this time he controlled himself a bit more. His arms held her close to his chest, and his kisses were gentler as he savored the soft fullness of her lips. Running a hand over her back, he twisted the ends of her hair into his fingers. She might have been petite, but he could feel her lithe muscles under her shirt. With each turn of his head, he would leave her mouth for a moment before immediately tasting her again.

He moved his left hand slowly down her neck, then over the curve of her shoulder, finally allowing himself to stroke the edge of her breast. She gasped immediately with surprise and lust. The sound broke through the haze in his brain.

It took all his resolve not to take it any further. Her inexperience was apparent to him, but it was also heady and arousing. Just when he thought he couldn't hold back anymore, her fingers made their way to the button of his slacks. Reluctantly, Trey moved his hands to hers and stilled them.

"What are you doing?" Claudia looked up at him, her eyes swimming with lust and her lips were impossibly plump and red.

Trey pushed down the image of other parts of her body becoming red from desire and attention.

"We should slow down."

"I told you..." she began, her voice sharp with that temper of hers.

"This isn't because of your pump."

"Then what *is* it about? I figure you've been with a lot of women, you probably know what you're doing."

"No argument. I've been with more women than I probably should have."

"I can follow your lead..."

A chuckle escaped his mouth, which only made her look more irritated.

"Always so practical."

"I'm not a little girl. Seriously, I can't believe this is how my sexual life begins. You're being such an asshole."

"I know it seems like that. And maybe I *am* an asshole. But if we're really going to do this, then you need to listen to me, because I also know a lot of this is new to you. No matter how much you think you have this figured out, I don't want you waking up tomorrow and worrying about how fast we moved tonight. I want you to enjoy everything I do to you. And trust me, I would like to do so many things to you, Claudia."

"Oh," she breathed out, a desperate look of desire washing over her features again, and hints of red streaking her smooth cheeks.

"But I don't want to fuck this up with you — whatever it is. It's almost guaranteed I will somehow. I'm not good for anyone, little one. But I can't stay away from you. And if I'm going to be weak, I want to at least give myself a fighting chance to get something right. Which means, I need you to let me be a domineering jerk, okay?"

"Okay, as long as you promise to kiss me again," she answered.

"I guarantee it, Claudia," Trey promised. He took her face in his hands and brushed his lips against hers, as he let the fog descend over his mind once again.

CHAPTER NINE

Claudia pressed her right index finger firmly against Trey's doorbell, and couldn't help but think about how odd it seemed for him to have one at all. A front door with a little round button to alert him to company seemed far too pedestrian for someone as remarkable as him.

When she thought of Trey at home — other than picturing him in bed — she generally imagined him in some kind of swanky penthouse from a James Bond movie. In the feverish recesses of her brain, the mysterious Mr. Adler was suited more to a lair than a house.

Guys like Trey weren't supposed to have a zip code and junk mail in the box next to their carved wood and stained glass entryway. Yet, he did have mail, and her nervous, grabby hands snatched it up while she waited for him to open the door.

The late October breeze ruffled lightly against her skin, but her cheeks were burning red, thinking of being inside his home for the first time. Before she knew it, the door was open and Trey was standing in front of her. He was dressed comfortably in a fitted tee shirt and jeans. He looked sexy as hell, as always, but she was fixated on what was beneath his clothes.

Now that she'd touched his chest — if only through the cotton of his shirt — her palms seemed magnetically drawn to stroke it again. Right when she built up the nerve to throw herself at him, he stepped backward to let her inside.

"Come on in. Is that my mail?"

"Uh, yeah, *Pottery Barn* is having a sale on their *Harvest Collection.* You should get right on that." Claudia thrust Trey's rubber banded mail against his stomach so hard he huffed out a breath of air in response. After taking the bundle from her hand, he tossed it on the built-in bench just inside his door.

He'd rented an old row house from the 1920s and every inch of it was lovely — the kind of home she'd like to share with someone…with him.

"I've been thinking this place lacked a certain element of farm-related charm. Did you find it okay?"

She could barely hear him over the pounding in her ears. Her brain was still flush with the memories of him finally kissing her the evening before. The sensation of loss, which came from him stopping was just as fresh, and had left her desperately wanting more of him. Ever since he'd walked away from her, it seemed all she wanted to do was kiss him until her lips were raw.

The firm outline of his pecs and the impression of his nipple rings were pushing provocatively against the thin material of his shirt with each of his breaths, and suddenly Claudia wanted to kiss more than his lips.

"Claudia?"

"What? Oh, getting here? Right. Yes, I found it, no problem. It was easy."

Faking nonchalance, she strutted through his front door. When he leaned down and kissed her cheek, the pressure was light though when he pulled back, his eyes were smoky and intense. A jolt of desire passed through her and she leaned her face eagerly toward his mouth, like a tiny flower tucked away alone in a kitchen window, yet still seeking the sun.

He pulled away from her and her own body lurched forward just enough to be awkward. Feeling downright silly, Claudia desperately attempted to fill the void between them with words.

"I actually remember finding this address for my brother when he needed help with Jenna," she added.

"So *that's* how he tracked down where I lived. Well, it explains a lot. I knew he couldn't have done it on his own."

"Trey…" she warned. Even though he supercharged her libido enough to turn her into a complete idiot, she was still a McCoy, and no one talked crap on her family when she was around.

"Right, only you can bitch about your brother. I remember the rules," he answered, a playful half smile gracing his face.

"It's nice to see you lighten up a little for a change."

"You think I need to lighten up?"

"Well, duh…"

"Did you just say *duh* to me?"

"I sure did."

"You truly are a poet."

"You better believe it. And I'm right, you're way too wound up."

"I gotta say, no one has had to tell me that for a really long time."

"Come *on*…"

"It's true. Whether either of us likes it or not, I can't help it, I'm only this way with you."

"Does that mean you can give me a taste of the more easygoing Trey?"

"I'm happy to give you plenty more tastes of me, Claudia."

"Um," she muttered dumbly, leaning toward him again. He rested his fingertips on her waist gently, though the pressure still seared her skin, even through her jacket. She licked her lips and he groaned slightly, bending forward to press his mouth on hers. Her arms wrapped around his body eagerly, but he eased away from her before she could trap him in her clutches.

With his face still close to hers, he whispered, "The rest of the world gets a very different man. Everything *that* man does is light. But I can't pretend to be him with you, Claudia. You're far too special to me. So you're just going to have to accept the heavy." Stepping away from her, he softened the blow of disappointment, which always came when he wasn't plastered against her by taking her hand in his. "Come on, we've got a lot to do. I was up all night updating my work with your research. I really like the database you built on newly minted Chinese billionaires who might want to pay top dollar for the robotics information David was trying to steal."

"Thank you. But why do you need it here?"

"This is where I do all my analyses."

"Why not at the Bureau? I mean, you have an office and everything."

"I do. It's nice. I sit in there and read sometimes, I even use the computer, but not for anything sensitive. I've never felt comfortable sharing my work with the government."

"What about me?"

"You're different. Which is why I want you to be just as careful as I am. Trusting the wrong people can get you seriously hurt, and I won't let that happen."

"Don't you think you're being a little paranoid?"

"It's not paranoid if you're right. Come on. I want to show you something."

Her mouth was working its way around a sensible rejoinder, but when he opened the door to his study, any intelligent thoughts left her brain. What little she'd seen of his place was beautiful and chic — clearly expensive, but it all paled in comparison to this one room.

It was spacious and he'd tricked it out like some kind of outlaw version of *NORAD*. Multiple monitors and processors curved into a horseshoe around two chairs. Much of the technology was military grade, and not all American. Part of her wanted to scold him for clearly having contraband equipment in his home, but the rest of her was itching to touch it.

"You like it?" he asked, rubbing the back of his neck and avoiding her eyes. He seemed oddly eager for her approval all of a sudden, and it made her descend even more into a pit of madness over him.

"Like it? Hell, I love it, Trey. Seriously, this setup is incredible."

"Good. Then have a seat." He smiled with pride and the innocent cuteness of it all made her heart feel like it might burst.

She stumbled into the chair he rolled behind her and gaped some more at the electronic possibilities laid before her. She eventually stated inelegantly, "Thanks. This must be how normal girls feel when they walk into *Tiffany's*."

He chuckled, answering, "I've met more than my share of normal girls. Trust me, I find you much more interesting."

Claudia had to stifle a silly giggle, but she couldn't hide the blush rushing up from her neck to her cheeks at his sweet sentiment. Luckily he hadn't looked away from his screens as he continued to speak.

"This is nothing," he boasted as he entered passwords into the various units in front of him. "You should see my war room in New York. I have two of them. One I share with people like

Griffen, while the other is behind several levels of security systems."

Claudia realized she'd been so caught up in her own career struggles, she'd completely forgotten Trey was displaced, too.

"You just left it all there?"

"Nothing sensitive. All that is here with me. The equipment is a lot more secure than it would be in your house, or even in the Bureau, I'll tell you that."

"I'd love to see it."

"Maybe I'll take you there someday. I'll make you get all dressed up and we'll go to the *21 Club*. I'll show you off. You can be my own miniature Latina Grace Kelly."

"Don't tease. Now all I can think about is acting out *Rear Window* with you."

"I'm not teasing, just motivating. How do you know *Rear Window*?"

"I love old movies! I had to spend a lot of time recovering in bed when I was little, and they kept me occupied. That and commercials of *Wilford Brimley* talking about 'Di-a-bee-tus.'"

"So, you and the *Quaker Oats* guy have something in common. I bet *that* made you feel good," Trey added with a laugh.

"Like a princess," she said slowly, throwing Trey a roll of her eyes before turning back to the computer screens.

"I can make you *really* feel like one, and I'll keep you company better than an old movie. Let's wrap up this Taylor case and then we'll see. Want to be a New York tourist while we're there, too? Have you ever been?"

"A few times when Wyatt played in New York… I didn't really get to experience it. I saw enough to know I can picture you there."

Trey laughed. "Why's that?"

"Because it's larger than life…like you."

"I love how you're still too young to know you shouldn't think so highly of me."

"Hey! You only think I'm young because you're so ancient." She laughed and punched his arm, probably harder than necessary, but it was fun to see him jostle back and forth in response.

"Right, because thirty-years-old is ancient," he groused.

"Okay, enough about your old age… Do you miss it?"

"What?"

"New York?" she clarified.

He shrugged, focusing instead on the screens in front of him, "I guess."

"Isn't it your home?" she asked.

"Home?"

He stared intently at one monitor, but she could see his jaw twitch repeatedly, even though his cool gray eyes never wavered.

"You know what I mean."

"New York is where I live most of the time. I've been there for a while now. I suppose it's as good a place as any." He turned to her for a moment, and his silver gaze was such a combination of warning and internal hurt, it was almost painful to behold. "I haven't had a real home for a long time. It doesn't help to love a place. Everything changes. And the things, which stay the same, are never as good as you remember. It's a waste of time to worry about shit like that. I've done better to just *be*."

"Well, now you're being silly. Home doesn't have to be a certain place. It's just what you can always go back to when you don't have anything else in the world," Claudia responded, her back stiff with determination.

"Little one, I hope you never see how fucked up the world can get when you believe you have a home to go to, only to realize there's nothing really there."

She leaned over and hugged him awkwardly, their seated positions impeding their connection.

Claudia moved away from him quickly, but she spied a small half smile creasing his face.

"You'll work here…at least for the time being. It's the only place you can make real headway," he instructed, clearly eager to talk about something less emotional.

"What about the Bureau? Won't Assistant Director Jacobs be wondering why I'm not showing up every day?"

"Don't worry about it. I told him you have field investigations and other offsite work to do for me, so he won't be looking for you. We can swing by every once in a while if it makes you feel better."

Trey fell silent, pulling up various folders on Jack Taylor and potential criminal hacker groups. Some names she recognized, others were completely new to her.

One grabbed her eye because it was the only one on the desktop of the far left monitor, yet he didn't open it. The title was simply — "Operation Lexis."

"What's that one?" she asked, pointing to the screen, while trying to keep her voice even.

"Nothing. Just one of my side projects…something else I need to wrap up before I can deliver on all your Manhattan fantasies."

"Maybe I can help. Let me see."

"No," he answered gruffly.

"What's the big deal?"

"I…said…*no.*"

"Don't you trust me?"

"It's not about that."

"Then what is it about? Because it *feels* like you don't trust me."

"This isn't about feelings. It's something else I'm messing around with, which is none of your business."

"Fine, but you're being such a butthead."

"Right, and that's why *I'm* ancient and *you're* a kid."

"Move over, Grandpa, and let me get to work on the case I'm *allowed* to know about. I'm sure my young eyes will catch something you missed, you know, in case you forgot your bifocals."

Despite her lighthearted teasing, suspicion was gnawing at the edges of her brain like a bored dog with nothing but an old rawhide to keep it company. She ran her tongue across the backs of her teeth as they clenched in her mouth. She'd felt a lot of emotions since she met Trey, but this one was the most upsetting — disappointment.

"Do you hate me now?" Trey probed roughly.

"Of course not. You have boundaries, and I crossed one of them."

"The Taylor case is plenty to keep you occupied. Operation Lexis is just…my own personal battle. I wouldn't wish that case on my own worst enemy. So please forget about it, okay?"

"Forgotten."

"Still a shitty liar, but I'll take it. I'm not picky… Tell me what happened with David. What did he say when you were in there?"

"You're ready to talk about it? You aren't going to get all worked up again, are you?"

"I thought you liked me when I got worked up?"

"True," she laughed lightly, already feeling the hurt his stern denial had caused begin to disintegrate.

"David still swears he never got any names associated with the group who hired him, but I did get him to admit it seemed to be a solo operating faction, not a governmental unit. All phone communications he had were from locations he couldn't determine, but his contacts were all speaking in American English. They used voice distortion technology, but he did feel it was a woman on some calls, and she was pulling the strings."

"Why?"

"He said it was just a feeling at first, but in one call, the contact referred to a 'she.' Said 'she was getting impatient,' that 'she was happy to eliminate any dead weight, and he was getting pretty heavy.' This was right before Jack revealed to David his suspicion the robotics department had been compromised, and..."

"Then he killed Jack."

"He still didn't go so far as to admit to murder, but it sure felt like he was getting close."

"It's still a hell of a lot more than I ever pulled out of David. Good work."

"Why thanks, *boss*," she joked. "What really had me interested was when I asked him why he thinks they contacted him instead of going for the big guns. I mean *CMU* actually has a whole division, which works specifically for the Department of Defense. He assumed it was because the robotics department was a softer target, but he agreed it didn't explain why they specifically reached out to him. It was apparently very calculated."

"He had a painkiller addiction after his car accident. He was desperate."

"But he insisted he'd kept it secret, and all our records support that. It had to take some serious legwork and psychological focus to uncover so much about him — not the kind of thing you see from your run-of-the-mill 'smash, grab, and sell' we see committed by hackers operating out of a dirty Moscow basement. This group is sophisticated, and ruthless. That's the thread I want to pull. We figure out how they found their mark, then maybe we can finally get somewhere."

"That's my girl. I have a lot of data for you to sort through, including internal discussions from the *CMU* IT department. I may hate the government, but there's something to be said for a search warrant broad enough to really let me loose. I've managed to get a lot of data beyond the warrant recently, too"

"How?"

"I used your Tongue Louse virus. It's honestly pretty cool, especially how you came up with it when you were so young. It just lies there and absorbs everything, without the messy warning signals of a more aggressive worm. Pretty badass ninja shit."

"Holy hell, Trey, that's the most romantic thing anyone has ever said to me."

"Your standards are either very low, or pretty odd."

"Maybe they're both. I don't care. You believed in me, Trey, which is all I ever want from people — to understand I can actually do something."

"Of course I do. Are you ready to get cracking?"

"But I've never worked with any gear like this before... It's not exactly FBI issue."

"You'll get used to it. If I'm really going to take you deep into this investigation, you're going to need more than the crap the FBI provides you."

Trey stood and moved behind Claudia's chair, deftly rolling it and repositioning her directly in the middle of the monitors. She felt like a queen at her throne, ruling over an electronic kingdom full of endless possibilities.

"I built this one directly in front of you by myself. Reverse engineered the software from something I…borrowed… from the CIA."

"Is this one of those things you tell people they don't want to know?"

"You and I are way past that. Which means you're going to have to let your white hacker hat get a lot more fucking gray."

"I'm not afraid to get my hands a bit dirty," she answered, not hiding the strident confidence from her tone as she reached for the keyboard directly in front of her. Trey stopped her, placing his hands on her shoulders before sliding them inward to her bare neck. His fingers rested against the top of her chest, as he stroked his thumbs slowly over the sides of her throat.

She could practically feel the little baby hairs at the base of her ponytail standing on end in response to his strong fingers. Claudia never knew when he would touch her or how long it would last, but it drove her freaking crazy every time. Her breath stalled and she froze in her seat, willing him not to stop — not this time.

He bent over her, kissing her neck, before nibbling at the flesh gently. It elicited a deep groan from the deepest recesses of her core, which echoed against the plaster walls around her.

"I need you to understand... You spend this much time with me, little one, it'll be more than your hands that will get dirty…and it won't be just a bit."

"All right. I'm back. That means it's time to take a break," Trey bellowed, barreling into his own study, which Claudia had been occupying almost exclusively since he'd shown it to her.

"Just fifteen more minutes," she muttered, squinting intently at the phone records of calls to David during the period when he was attempting to sell information.

"You pulled the same line before I left two hours ago. I'll bet good money you haven't moved since." Trey began to rub her shoulders, and she purred in response, bending her head forward.

"No fair," she muttered, allowing her head to flop forward, giving his fingers access to her long, slender neck.

"Who ever said I play fair?" Trey removed his hands and stepped away from her, before his self-control got away from him. "Come to the kitchen. You need to be fed and watered. I have your blood sugar testing materials in there, too."

"Wow. You can't be serious? I'll take your silence to mean you are. Trey, you've got problems."

"Not denying that."

"I have my glucose monitor on, it's really not necessary."

"Humor me?" he asked, meeting her gaze and throwing her his most effective smile.

"Fine. Must say, you really know how to pamper a girl...glucose test *and* dinner. All this luxury could go to my head."

"Stop being such a smart-ass," he answered, though his voice was light. "Look, I know what it's like to get sucked into something, and there's no way I'm letting the work I give you translate into hypoglycemia on my watch. Plus, I have some new information for you."

"What? That's great. Tell me!" she exclaimed, jumping out of her seat with a spry jubilance, which always made him smile.

"I knew that would get your attention. Get moving. I'm not giving up the goods unless you get out of here."

"Okay. I guess this will be here when I get back."

"There you go," he said.

She moved toward him, sneaking a glance backward toward her work longingly and sucking on the plump curve of her lower lip in thought.

It still struck him how she always happened somehow to look so naturally beautiful. She didn't bother herself with flash or high-maintenance crap. Even today, her loveliness was packaged simply, with no makeup slowing down her eager need to get back to her mission.

No matter how effortless her appearance may be, it was still devastating to him, which was why he'd indulged in frequent bouts of brief, yet ardent, kissing since she'd begun spending the bulk of her time in his inner world. He longed to taste more of her — a yearning, which only increased in intensity by the day.

That afternoon, her diminutive, but curvaceous body was showcased in tight jeans and a cocoa-colored sweater, which accented her large, dark eyes. It was fitted enough to show off her pert breasts, though he sensed the looseness at the waist was part of her insistence on hiding her pump from anyone's view.

Regardless of her intent, the entire effect was a welcome departure from the nondescript pantsuits she wore when working at the Bureau. Her unknowingly sexy displays of her perfect body were reason enough to keep her all to himself at his place, even without all of the progress she was making when allowed to work outside the restrictive bubble of official FBI procedure.

Trey couldn't help but wonder of what she'd be capable if she freed her abilities from the chains of rules — of right and wrong — and unleashed all her penned-in brainpower.

Yet, he had to fight any such nefarious urge. The last thing he needed was to bring her down in such a way. There was no way he could do such a thing again.

Claudia managed to pull herself away from her work, and he followed her to the kitchen. He patiently watched as she sat down, pricked her finger, and began her blood sugar test with the militaristic efficiency, which only came from performing a task so many times it became muscle memory.

After a minute, she showed him the digital reader with a smile, "Boom. Perfect. Now spill."

Her bright glow was too much to resist, especially since the silence of the moment and her delicate scent had driven him kind of insane.

Trey bent toward her, sliding both his hands roughly into her hair, securing her face in front of his. Her mouth opened slightly and he could hear her short little bursts of breath puff in and out at a quickening pace. The way Claudia would still in response to every one of his touches was almost as maddening as when she'd tried to climb him like a tree in her kitchen a few days before. It told him she was his when he chose to take her, and *damn* was he ready.

Yet, he'd made a promise to himself he'd do things the right way with her, and he'd already broken enough vows to the people who mattered to him. If she truly could be the second chance Trey had given up on ever getting, he'd rather die than let anything fuck it up — especially if that *thing* happened to be him.

Even so, taking it slow didn't mean he couldn't enjoy the deliciousness of her at a reasonable pace.

Her eyes sparkled with desire as Trey closed the small distance between them, until he inhaled one of her little, hopeful breaths as his own. Sealing his lips over hers, peace seeped into his veins, even as the passion of the moment pumped powerfully through his heart and into his arteries.

Claudia tickled his lips with the tip of her tongue, flicking her way inside his mouth. Trey had to grasp her head more tightly, holding her in place and bringing his tongue to meet hers boldly. She was sweet and hot and he wanted to taste every other inch of her. Settling for that scrape of her teeth against his bottom lip, Trey pulled away from her. The answering disappointed sigh emanating from her throat made his cock harden in response.

She leaned in, returning close to his mouth and cooed, "With positive reinforcement like this, I'll test my blood sugar ten times a day," Claudia murmured against his lips, and Trey had to laugh out loud.

"I might take you up on that," he responded roughly, struggling to pull himself together. Moving a kitchen chair in front of her, Trey leaned his arms on his knees and said, "I finally got back the analysis of the incendiary device components we recovered from the mill site."

"Awesome! What did Eddie Lockley say?"

"I didn't send it to Eddie. That's why it took so long."

"But he's great! I worked with him when I was interning at D.C. headquarters."

"I sent it to someone I trust."

"What do you mean?"

"It went to someone who won't have any obligation — or interest — in asking why we have remnants of a low-to-midgrade intensity bomb from a mission you decided on your own to pursue."

"Oh."

"*Oh*, is right. Part of me taking care of you is protecting your chance to have a career after all this is over. If this is the one you still want, it's what you'll have to do."

"My family did always say I don't think things through…"

"I'm okay with you being impulsive. If you waited for the FBI you'd never be satisfied, and we wouldn't have made any of this great progress. It's okay to be impatient with life — to want everything all at once — but living that way can have…unforeseen consequences."

"If I promise to be less eager, will you tell me what your secret, trusted friend found?"

"Absolutely. It was an amalgam of Chinese, Russian, and American components, each of which was a little outdated. I think it confirms your theory about mercenaries for hire, whether they were working for a government or private company."

"So if it is a team for hire, they could've worked for these governments before and kept their supplies?"

"Could be, but more likely they stole it. Or found vulnerabilities through hacking and stole the technology, or reverse engineered it."

"Including *human* vulnerabilities? Like David?"

"Yes."

"Is that what you'd have done to hack in? What these criminals did?"

"Yes. I would always find access somehow and take over from within."

Claudia's eyes darkened, and she backed slightly away from him. It was so subtle, Trey was sure she didn't even know she'd done it. The way he felt her prior admiration of him become slightly tainted was unpleasant, but he couldn't let it slow them down.

"What's keeping you chained to your chair in there? Anything good?" he asked.

"Maybe. I was sorting through the data the Tongue Louse virus brought in, and I came across something suspicious from about seven years ago in the *CMU* English Department. Someone had tried to remove it, but I could tell it was still there. It was hard to find, but I could see the remaining imprint of its code. The whole thing was pretty simplistic, but effective — it appeared to have been operating as a carbon copy of the main

CMU server — a shadow, really. I'm convinced it was a virus. I feel it in my bones, as they say."

"And how do you see it relating to the Robotics Department's infiltration?"

"I couldn't find any obvious link...at least nothing Jacobs would care about."

"Then it's a good thing Jacobs isn't here. I'm getting the feeling you're onto something."

"I was thinking hacking into a liberal arts department would be a great way to get back-door entry into the other more lucrative departments, such as robotics, but I don't know where to go with the idea," she sighed, leaning back in her seat.

"What's the problem?"

"It's just...I'm so damned frustrated. There are all these pieces…I keep finding more, but I can't seem to get any of them to fit with each other."

Trey could sense how truly thwarted she felt. Claudia needed a release, and he so desperately wanted to give it to her. It didn't help that Trey's mouth was still watering from his last taste of her. He needed more, and maybe he could have it, without breaking any promises. There was one thing he knew could help turn off that big brain of hers.

"Maybe you need to focus more clearly. I can help."

"Like with meditation or something?"

"Or something," he retorted, feeling his mouth tilt into a half smile as he stood and looked down at her confused gaze. "Tell me, have you ever come before?"

"Come?" she queried, then immediately blushed. "Oh, um, I think so."

"Then, no," he answered with a smirk. "Stand up."

She searched his face for a clue, but finally did as he said.

"Take off your jeans and panties."

Her mouth curved into a tiny "O," but she remained silent, slowly unbuttoning her pants and sliding her jeans down the length of her smooth, olive-toned legs. The light blue cotton of her panties was next to go, revealing a small, well-trimmed triangular thatch of dark hair at the juncture point between her legs.

After she straightened up, Claudia crossed her arms over her stomach and reached for the bottom of her sweater.

"No. Stop. That's all I need."

Trey kneeled in front of her.

"What are you doing?"

"Helping you."

The smell of her was destroying his ability to see clearly. He adjusted himself in his jeans, trying to ease the pressure of his own desire. If he was going to take things this far, it had to be about her, not him.

Separating the lips of her perfect pussy, Trey reached his tongue out and slid slowly up the seam of her delicate folds. Whatever he'd tasted of her with their kisses had nothing on this intoxicating experience. He had to break away to keep his sanity, and to continue with his crazy idea.

"Do you like what I'm doing?"

"Very much. I didn't know anything could feel like that," she whispered.

"Were you feeling worried about your work?"

"No," she answered with a soft laugh.

"Good. Now relax, spread your legs a little more, and tell me about what's rattling around in your head."

Trey sealed his mouth over her again, licking harder at her clit, until she slammed one hand on the table next to her and the other on his left shoulder.

"I, ah…oh."

He pulled back.

"No! Don't stop."

"Focus. Talk through it, or I will stop all over again."

"How can I? It feels too good."

"Breathe, use this feeling to help you see more clearly," he whispered, pulling away from her and using the first two fingers of his right hand to pleasure her. "Look at me. I'm here for you."

Her eyes were hazy, but her teeth gritted in determination. The way she rubbed herself against his hand made Trey's heart rate race with want.

"Let the pleasure bring you focus. Why is the shadow of this virus nagging at you so much?"

He removed his slick fingers and began licking her more briskly, moving down to thrust his tongue inside her. She moaned and squeezed his shoulder hard, but he could sense she was trying to follow his instructions.

"Something about it is so familiar."

Trey eased up with his tongue, allowing her to feel the rush, without it totally blinding her. Removing his mouth from her, he eased a finger back inside her.

"How so?"

"I don't *know*! It's why I'm so discouraged!"

Slipping a second finger inside her, Trey flicked his tongue against her clit for a moment.

"You can do better than that. You know it. What stood out to you about it?"

"It seemed so simple, ah, ah, al-almost juvenile, but it managed to be a perfect mimic of the system...."

Trey curled his fingers deep inside her and flicked his tongue roughly across her clit, making her scream in response, and pull at his hair.

"Oh, God, that feels so... I don't..."

Trey sucked against the hardened nub of her clit, and she gasped audibly in response. Pulling away for a second, he commanded, "Concentrate, Claudia. You're almost there."

"I am. Oh God. I've seen something like it before."

"Good, there you go," he muttered against her mound, stroking her gently, but slowing the pace to let her ride out whatever was happening in her mind.

"When I was in D.C.—" And she swallowed hard before continuing. She jerked slightly, apparently overcome by a growing revelation. Trey slowed his motions in response, letting her explore the inspiration. "For some reason I keep thinking about this virus my mentor had me examine. Someone had used it on a company in Sydney years ago. That's it! It was a perfect mimic, too…as though it *was a part of it.* An American Senior VP for the company, and his wife, were killed almost a year later, but no one could link them."

Trey backed away from her so quickly he almost knocked over a chair. Claudia was so thrilled with her discovery she didn't notice Trey was almost numb with shock. Instead, she kept talking.

"The murder was made to look like an average breaking and entering. They took some jewelry, but every hard drive was copied or destroyed. Why do that if you're just some garden-variety burglar? Wait, why did you stop? Are you okay? Did I do something wrong?"

"No. I mean...you're perfect. But I have to make a call."

He knew all too well what the crime scene had looked like. In fact, he still had a set of the photos in his hard copy Operation Lexis file.

After so many years of Trey chasing after a team of monsters, Claudia may have found a lead to them in a matter of weeks — thrusting her onto a path more treacherous than she could ever imagine.

"Damn it, Trey. How can you tease me like this? Are you kidding me?"

The desperate look in her eyes broke through his blind panic.

"You want me to make it better?" he asked, breathing slowly to regain control.

"Anything. Just don't leave me like this. It hurts."

Trey grabbed the back of her head so hard he worried he might hurt her, but he didn't stop. With his hands gripped tightly in her hair, he pulled her mouth to his, letting her taste her own essence on his lips. He kissed her hard, pushing two of his fingers back inside her, rubbing the soft front wall of her entry until she gasped into his mouth. He bit her bottom lip, causing her to scream out in response as he massaged deeply inside her.

His cock was hard, as eager as his own mind was frenzied. His emotions were a swirl of desire and desperate fear, but he worked hard not to let either be revealed to Claudia. The worst thing he could do was show weakness to her, because she had to trust him completely in order for any of this to work.

She gasped and clung to him.

"I guess I was wrong."

"About what?"

"I *definitely* have never come before."

Trey chuckled, and almost forgot how much he needed to do.

Claudia was still panting, holding him tightly to her.

"Sorry if I almost strangled you," she muttered, releasing him.

Trey grabbed her hands from his shoulders and kept them in his grip.

"Don't be sorry. I never want you to apologize for holding onto me like that."

He eased back to help Claudia put on her panties and jeans.

With a voice more steady than he felt, he asked, "Have you told anyone else about any of this?"

"All these scraps?" Claudia wondered, smoothing her shirt down over her waistband. "There wasn't anything really to tell before. Drew called my cell earlier because I haven't been in the office. He wanted to know what I'm working on."

"Drew Jaworski? That junior agent tool who sits near you?"

"Yeah, but he's not a tool to me. He's my friend. I can always count on him to be eager to help me."

"I'll bet," Trey growled. He was sure any twenty-something guy would be more than happy to be Claudia's "helpful friend."

"I asked him about the Australian Secret Intelligence Service, and if he knew anyone there. I didn't say why."

"Don't talk to him or anyone else about…anything…anymore. You should only speak to me."

"Why? What aren't you telling me?"

"Nothing. I just don't know anything about this Drew guy. Did he know you followed up on the lead, which sent you to the steel mill?"

Trey could barely get his thoughts straight. So much would have to be done now, but it took just as much strength not to let Claudia know how worried he was.

"Sure. He's my best friend there. He knew I wanted to be on the Taylor case, so when the tip came in and Jacobs shut me down, I went to Drew for advice. He knew I planned to check it out, but I didn't tell him what happened when I went there. Do you suspect he's dirty or something?"

"I don't know what to think about anything."

"I'm starting to sense you don't like much of anyone."

"You're one of the only feds I've ever liked, that's for sure. I have a friend of my own I want to visit. If anyone can help us with what might have happened in Sydney, it's him."

"Great!"

"You know, I think he's, um, in D.C. right now. We'll need to leave soon. Probably tomorrow night."

"But we have so much to do here still. I can..."

"No. Just keep working on what we've already found until we leave. Let me follow up on this lead. And it's important you only discuss this case and what you're finding with me. I can't risk anyone thinking you're a target for any reason… For now, until we sort this out, I'm your only friend…I'm your world"

"But…" she pleaded, before silencing herself. He could tell she was confused and overwhelmed by the influx of experiences barreling down on her. Perhaps she was even a little scared of him, but he had no other choice.

"Trust me, little one. It will all be okay," he whispered, holding her chin with his left hand, before planting a soft kiss on her lips.

Now, if only he could trust himself that his words would turn out to be true.

CHAPTER TEN

"Jenna, don't worry, I promise I'll be there. I've already got my costume on and everything. I can't wait to see you guys again," Claudia said into her cellphone, using her free hand to adjust the poncho she'd found online to complete her Halloween costume.

"Good, because Wyatt has really missed getting to spend real time with you."

"He's putting together the best season of his professional career. I can forgive him for being a little busy right now," Claudia joked.

Jenna chuckled lightly in response. "Right. Luckily it's a bye week, so Wyatt can relax a little."

"As much as he ever can," Claudia teased, before continuing, "You girls are doing a good job of making me be social, and not chained to a computer all the time. I really appreciate how welcoming you've been."

"Of course..." Jenna paused, her tone then becoming more cautious, "Have you been working hard with Trey? Is he looking out for you?"

"I guess you could say that. He can be pretty overprotective, but I'm getting used to it. There's the doorbell. It's probably him."

"Trey? But aren't you at your place?"

"I am. He comes here sometimes, when I'm not working at his house."

"Wait, what?"

"Okay, see you soon. Bye!" Claudia hung up and quickly opened the door, eager to show off her costume to Trey. Yet, when she saw him, he only greeted her with a look of confusion, as he dropped a full duffle bag with a thud onto her entryway floor.

"What the hell are you wearing? Where are your bags? I told you — we have to leave town."

"I didn't think you meant immediately. I have another appointment to meet with David tomorrow." Claudia turned to walk toward her living room and continued talking. "I dug some more into that Sydney matter I told you about...turns out the CEO who was killed was named Ahmet Mehta, and he was David's roommate at *MIT*. It can't be a coincidence. Plus, he's exactly the kind of person David would've confided in about his problems after the car accident, likely by email, what with the time difference and all. I just need to talk to David about it. His lawyer said David was very eager to discuss Dr. Mehta with me. I think this is the break we've been waiting for!"

"No way. I told you not to tell anyone about what we are working on."

"Not to the detriment of the case. It has to be our first priority."

"*My* priority it to get you to D.C. David will be here when we get back."

"One more day won't make a difference," Claudia muttered absently, making sure her purse had all the essentials for the evening.

"It will," he answered.

Claudia spun around and leveled a suspicious stare at him, trying to read his mind, or at least his facial expression, but as always, he was closed off to her.

"What aren't you telling me, Trey?"

"What? Me? Nothing."

"You do realize I've been trained to spot lying, right? You could try a little harder. Something has been up with you ever since last night — like you're nervous, or worried about something."

"I'm not nervous, and I'm not lying," he answered, deliberately meeting her gaze and setting his jaw in a stiff manner. "Besides, I thought you hated it here and couldn't wait to transfer back to D.C.?"

"*Hate* is a strong word. And, I don't know, lately it's kind of been growing on me. I mean, I have new friends with Jenna, Tea, and Aubrey, and I like the time I spend here with you..."

Trey approached her, a sexy smile creasing his cheeks. After leaning down to give her one of his maddening brief kisses, he said, "Good answer. I like the time I spend in this city with you, too." Trey moved from her as quickly as he'd come, and began to collect the files she was working on from her kitchen table.

"Hey! I'm not done with those."

"I know you're not. That's why I'm bringing them with us when we leave tonight."

"You know, this is confusing, because I'm almost positive the language I was speaking to you just now was English, yet you act like you don't understand a thing I said."

"I got every word of it. And you can unclench your fists, because I can interpret your body language pretty fluently, too."

Claudia growled in frustration, but he simply grinned back at her.

Trey replaced the files on the table, moving his hands to the tops of Claudia's arms, and in a soothing tone explained, "Look, I'm just eager for you to meet Stephen. I trust him. He runs a task force under the CIA umbrella. Working with him could be the *actual* break you're waiting for."

"But it's Halloween."

"What?"

"October 31st? All Hallow's Eve? You know, people dress up...ask for treats as an alternate to tricks? Communicate with other humanoids in a group setting, such as Wyatt and Jenna's party tonight? You do live in the same world as the rest of us, right?" she answered with a teasing smile.

"Is that why you're dressed like...wait, what *are* you dressed like?"

Claudia crinkled her nose and pulled her stuffed *Ewok*, with a granola bar pinned to him, even more closely to her body.

"I'm *Leia* from *Return of the Jedi*, jeez. You know, when they land on the forest moon of *Endor* and she has to take out a bunch of storm troopers on a speeder bike?"

"Wow, that's some high-level geekdom right there, Claudia."

"Don't act like you don't know what I'm talking about. Are you sure you're really a techie?"

"Little one, this is *not* the Princess Leia outfit I fantasize about you wearing. You can wear the slave girl getup for me on a future evening, but for now, we need to get to work."

Claudia had toyed with the idea of the slave girl costume. She'd never been so openly sexy in her life. Yet, as soon as she built up the nerve to wear it, she just as quickly realized her clunky insulin pump rendered the option impossible.

"But I put in all this effort. You could pass for being in costume, maybe go as a rock star?"

"No. I'm just *me* on a Friday night…trying to get you to do what I say."

"But Tea, Jenna, and Aubrey asked me to come!" Claudia heard the begging tone of her own voice and it filled her with embarrassment. In her ridiculous jodhpurs, tunic, and hat, it was hard not to feel like the lonely, nerdy little sister she worried she appeared to be — the one she'd always felt like on so many other Halloweens. Claudia couldn't meet Trey's eyes, but she also couldn't keep quiet.

"I worked hard on this costume. I never really got to have a Halloween… We would donate all my candy. The sugar was 'poison' for me, after all. As mamá would say, 'El dulce es venenoso para tu salud.'" Claudia hitched her hip to the left a little and wagged her finger, impersonating her mother as she spoke. "I always told myself, when I was a grown-up… Never mind. I sound like a stupid kid. I'll go pack my bag, for wherever it is we're going." She started to walk away, ashamed of how silly she must sound to him.

"No. Stop," Trey grabbed her arm, keeping her close to him. His face softened and he moved his hand to hold the back of her neck gently, allowing his thumb to run over her cheek. "Tell me."

Claudia leaned into his palm, her goofy helmet slipping a little. "I always told myself, when I got big and ran my own life, I would find a way to make Halloween fun for me. I would fit in and…and I wouldn't be alone anymore."

"Then you *need* to go to this party." His finger moved to run across her lower lip. She could see worry in his eyes, but she didn't know its cause. Trey swallowed hard, finally adding, "What asshole said you couldn't?" Trey teased with an apologetic smile on his face. He kissed her lightly on her nose and Claudia felt as if she were the prettiest, coolest geek to ever dress like *Princess Leia* — slave girl, or otherwise.

"Thank you. You're coming with me, right?"

"Of course. I can't let you loose with all those single guys in such a sexy outfit, without my supervision. Let's go."

"Not yet, tattoo boy. You need to at least pretend to have a costume. I think a little black eyeliner and spiky hair should round out your rocker look in just the right way," she stated, grabbing his hand to pull him to her bedroom.

"If you wanted me in your bedroom, all you had to was ask."

Claudia gaped at him for a moment, her face flushing hot with desperate thoughts of what he might do if he ever were in her bed — if he finally didn't stop himself...

"We're running out of time. You can either stare at me all night, or go to your party."

"Right, then let's, uh, get that makeup on you," she stammered out, cringing at the sound.

"Don't worry, little one, I'll make sure to let you touch me a lot while you do it," he whispered into her ear.

"Damn it, Adler, get in there already," she added before turning around and using all her strength to keep from swallowing her tongue.

Claudia felt pretty sure this guy would be the death of her, but she knew she was already too far gone to care.

"Claude, I love your costume!" Jenna exclaimed after opening the door to the home she and Wyatt shared. "*Princess Leia*, right?"

"Thank you! I hoped someone would get it," Claudia answered with a laugh.

"Come on in, girl."

Jenna began to close the door, not seeing Trey, until he stopped the door with a press of his hand, probably a little more forcefully than necessary.

"Oh, Trey. Hi. It's good to see you, too."

"You like his costume?" Claudia enthused, showing she was clearly proud of her handiwork.

He could still feel the sensation of her hands on his face, as she slid her ridiculous black eyeliner on the rims of his eyes. Every part of him had wanted to grab her hand, throw her to the floor, and lose himself deeply inside her. He'd resisted the urge, instead simply meeting her eyes with his own. Her slightly quivering hand told him all he needed to know about how much she wanted him in return.

"Though, it's not much of a stretch. I'm pretty sure Trey already thinks he's a rock god somewhere deep inside," Jenna said with a lightness Trey knew was forced. "I thought you said you couldn't make it?" Jenna asked him directly.

"This little one can be very persuasive," he answered vaguely, avoiding her perceptive gaze, as he guided Claudia into the foyer.

"Is that right?" Jenna asked slowly.

"It is. I'm a total nag," Claudia responded.

Trey was already regretting letting Claudia talk him into this. It was bad enough the way his head was spinning with anxiety over the dangerous new theory she'd come up with in the Taylor case. He didn't need Jenna trying to discern just how close he'd gotten to the protégé she'd thrust upon him.

Jenna had become one of his best friends over the past year, but he knew she didn't think he was right for Claudia. Damned if this suspicion hadn't turned her into some kind of enemy in his mind overnight. It didn't matter that Trey was pretty sure he wasn't right for Claudia, either.

"Claude! There you are," Aubrey brayed at her, grabbing Claudia's hand and yanking her away from them.

"Hi! It's so good to see you all. So, what are your costumes?"

"Tea is over there. She's *Elle Woods* from *Legally Blonde*. I'm a mad scientist," Jenna responded. "Your brother insisted I wear my lab coat, this was the compromise."

"Girl costumes are so ridiculous these days. I guess I could've come as a sexy letter of the alphabet, or something," Aubrey joked. "I decided to be *Pat Benatar* for a night, instead."

Claudia laughed. "Good choice," she stated. "I mean, love is a battlefield, right?"

"Exactly. Which is why I need you to look alive, girl. This is a target-rich environment if I ever saw one. Wyatt invited all his teammates, and I've already done some legwork to identify the available ones. You came at the perfect time. The guys who have kids are all out with them trick-or-treating, taking advantage of how private it is here on *Washington's Landing*, which means most of the guys left are unattached and *all* of them are hot. It'll be like hitting on fish in a barrel."

"You really put a lot into this plan," Claudia said with a laugh.

"You have to stick with me. We're the only single ones left in this bunch."

Aubrey's words grated at Trey like a root canal, but he kept his expression neutral.

"Whoa, Brey," Jenna said, "don't steal her away completely. You know Wyatt and I want to make sure she talks to one fish in particular."

"Jenna, what are you and Wyatt up to now?" Claudia asked, her eyes darting back and forth between Jenna and Brey nervously.

"It's a good thing, Claude, I promise. Jason is here and he asked about you, specifically, when we invited him," Jenna stated, with a glimmer in her eye, which was a punch in Trey's gut.

"Well, I think Trey and I were going to..." Claudia began, but Aubrey grabbed her hand and pulled her away from him.

"It's a party. He'll survive," Aubrey chided.

"We aren't staying long. We have a lot to get done," Trey growled out, feeling whatever patience he'd pretended to have with Claudia drain out of him more with each second.

"Oh, come on. You two can take one night off. Don't work her to death, man," Aubrey declared, making his teeth grit together with frustration.

"Maybe if you let her speak for herself then you'd know whether I'm working her too much, or not," he growled, causing both Jenna and Aubrey's eyebrows to raise.

"We aren't speaking for her. We're interrupting her. There's a big difference. Chill, dude," Aubrey answered crisply.

"Trey, calm down," Claudia whispered, her eyes wide, and he felt a little like shit at the trepidation he saw reflected in each of the pretty chocolate orbs. Claudia turned from him and said coolly to her girlfriends, "Let me go speak to the boss for a second, ladies."

After pulling Trey aside, Claudia asked, "Why are you so pissed? We only just got here. I figured it would take you at least twenty minutes to get cranky," she teased, but it didn't lighten his mood at all.

"Oh, I'm just fucking great. I agree to delay the trip I tell you is vital to our mission and you walk in the door here and immediately run off with them to meet guys."

"You know that's not what's happening. But why am I defending myself to you? Is there a reason I shouldn't be talking to anyone?"

"Because we don't have time for it."

"If that's the only thing you can come up with, then I might as well just have a good time elsewhere," she gritted out.

Trey grabbed her elbow, stilling her, before whispering, "I guess I just don't like to see you with anyone else. I like to keep you all to myself. Is that so wrong?" he asked, throwing her a half smile, which caused her eyes to settle on his lips in a way that made him want to do all sorts of things unsuitable for a crowded party.

"No. I think it's a good thing," she muttered, her voice suddenly thick.

"You like having me to yourself, too, don't you?" he added, his voice rough like gravel.

"Very much."

"Good. But I did promise you a fun Halloween, so go enjoy yourself. I was serious about not staying long though."

Claudia nodded, opening her mouth to speak, when Aubrey grabbed her arm and started to pull her away from him.

"All right, you monopolized her enough. It's time to get this girl a drink."

"Nothing sweet," he said abruptly before he could stop himself, and cringed inwardly to see Claudia blush with embarrassment and anger in response. Trey realized immediately Aubrey didn't know about Claudia's diabetes, and she probably wanted to keep it that way.

"Damn it, Trey," Claudia growled at him under her breath.

"I'm sure Claudia can pick her own drink," Aubrey retorted. Her voice sounding more confused than irritated, though he wouldn't have blamed her if she were pissed at him. "You know, Trey. I think I liked you better before, when you didn't care about anything."

"I'm feeling the same way," he muttered to himself, noticing Jenna had rejoined them.

"I'll be back soon. Are you cool?" Claudia asked, and he nodded, her thoughtfulness affecting him in a way he didn't quite understand.

"Come on! Enough of that. He'll live. Let's get the party started."

Trey watched them walk into the main area, which was already filled with people. It didn't take that Jason guy any time to swoop in on her, but Trey forced himself to look away.

"Are you really okay, Trey?" Jenna asked.

"What are you trying to say, blondie? Just cut to the chase."

"What's going on with you two?"

"Nothing that concerns you."

"It does. Claudia is a special person."

"Don't you think I know that?"

"I see how she looks at you. But I don't want to see her heart broken."

"Who says I'd do that?"

"I know how you are with women...loads of women, to be exact."

"Spoken by the girl living with Wyatt Fucking McCoy. Should we talk about the kind of asshat he was with women before he met you?"

"You're kidding, right?

"No, I'm not. Besides, so what if I do get involved with her, Jenna?"

"She's young and vulnerable right now — in a new city, trying to find her way. Someone like you would be totally overwhelming to her."

"Someone like me? Real nice, blondie."

"You know that's not what I meant. I think you're great, it's just she would be in over her head with you."

"She's a twenty-three-year-old genius who's been trained to take down men three times her size. Maybe you all are underestimating her."

"It's not her head I'm worried about. It's her heart."

"What's going on, Doc," Wyatt asked, coming up behind her. "Who are you talking about?"

"Nobody. It's nothing."

"You seem upset, belleza," Wyatt continued, pulling her to him by the waist, even as he threw a wary glare at Trey.

"It's fine. I promise. Trey is like a brother to me, which means we fight like pissed off siblings sometimes."

Trey's phone began buzzing. "I have to take this, sorry, Jenna."

"But I wasn't finished..." she groused as Trey walked away.

"Hey, Stephen, what's up?"

"Are you ready to get out of Pittsburgh, yet?"

"Almost."

"That's not good enough. David Murphy's dead."

"What?"

"Found hanging in his cell about forty-five minutes ago. I've been scrambling ever since. He'd been dead at least a few hours."

"Suicide? I'm not buying it. I interviewed him myself today."

"I'm betting it's staged, too. Does Agent McCoy know you were doing your own digging about her theories?"

"No. I don't want anything else to distract from getting her out of town."

"Then definitely hold off on this news."

"No shit. Damn it. How the hell did no one find him until now?"

"My source says the video feed into his cell was tapped into. Someone overrode it and had the same image of him asleep on a loop, so no one saw any reason to check up on him."

"Why didn't Jacobs tell me? Fucking FBI."

"We can't worry about that right now. It gets worse. My contact in Murphy's federal detention facility also told me Agent McCoy was set to meet with him tomorrow. It was in all the logs. Anyone with resources of their own would be able to find it. And I'm pretty sure they did. The cameras we set up outside of Agent McCoy's house just picked up someone casing the place."

"Fuck. Anyone we've seen before?"

"Not sure. He was smart enough to keep his face mostly hidden, and screwing our chances of running him through our facial recognition databases. Either way..."

"I know. Claudia and I have to get the hell out of here."

"Everything is set up for you. I just left her place. I was able to make my way in. I found your duffel and the suitcase she'd packed. I added a couple things I'd want her to have if I were in your position," he added, with a lascivious tone to his voice.

Trey clenched his free hand in response to Stephen's ribbing. Stephen was only slightly less of a man-whore with women than Trey was — or at least used to be, before Claudia had him so distracted — and the thought of him in her house made Trey consider doing violent things to his old friend.

"Don't even fucking joke about that, dude."

"You've got a lot more to worry about than me going through your precious little Agent McCoy's panty drawer. You know it, too, or you wouldn't have brought me into this. Because, if she's right about that bloody Sydney job being connected to Jack Taylor's murder..."

"I know. I get it."

"Do you? Did you tell her about Operation Lexis?"

"Hell no."

"It's only a matter of time before she figures out something. It looks like she sniffed around about Sydney more than you realize."

"Christ. She is so fucking stubborn."

"If you care about this girl at all, you need to keep her as far away from Lexis as possible."

"No shit. It feels like my full-time job since I met her is trying to keep her safe."

"But it's not enough just to protect her. You have to ask yourself if you believe in Claudia, and trust her, enough to let *her* help *you* for real."

"Spoken like a true CIA handler. Claudia's not a spy."

"But she's a part of your team. And she's taken this personal project of yours to a whole new level you either couldn't, or *wouldn't*, see before."

Stephen paused, allowing his statement to sink in before going on.

"I'm on the way to get your new car to you. It will be about a block from the entrance to *Washington's Landing*, so you can walk to it. I made sure Claudia's FBI sidearm is in her suitcase. You'll also find a briefcase of weapons hidden in the wheel well, under the trunk cover. Leave the keys to Claudia's car under her driver's seat for me. Your destination is already programmed into the nav. I can get Claudia's car back to her house. We don't need any questions about it."

"You're a good friend, man. I owe you."

"Just keep the two of you alive. At least long enough for us to figure out what the hell is going on here. I'm going to put tabs on her place, make sure no one has compromised the inside. I'll do the same at yours."

"It's probably not a good idea for me to use this phone anymore," Trey muttered into his cell. "I'll call you with the burner as soon as we get to the safe house."

Trey swallowed hard, staring across the room at Claudia laughing and smiling with Tea and Aubrey.

She looked so relaxed and happy, like someone enjoying the pleasure of leading a normal life.

I hope it was good while it lasted, he thought bitterly.

CHAPTER ELEVEN

"Jenna, get over here!" Tea exclaimed, gesturing rapidly for the pretty blonde to join their conversation. Claudia was still laughing from Aubrey's last joke when Jenna found her way to them.

"What's up, girls?" she asked.

"I was just telling Claude about how Johnny insisted on raking your and Wyatt's leaves outside before the party started," Tea gushed.

"Oh yeah, that was sweet," Jenna answered, though her attention was still focused on Trey, her mouth set in a tight, frustrated line.

"You know my boy doesn't work for free. What are you going to pay him?" Tea asked.

Jenna turned her gaze to her friend, letting a mischievous smile creep across her face. "I don't pay for cuteness, Tea. I care about performance. He did a terrible job. Three dollars, I guess," Jenna stated slyly.

"You're a rotten girl. You get me every time!" Tea exclaimed, slapping Jenna's upper arm with enough force to knock her body a bit off-balance.

"Then don't be so easy to tease, Tea," Jenna answered, her voice breaking with laughter.

"No chance of that ever happening," Claudia interjected.

"See! I told you this smart-ass would fit in just right," Aubrey cheered. "Claude, enough girl time. It's time to focus."

"What?" Claudia asked, laughing roughly under her breath.

"I meant it when I said I'd make sure you and me get the most out of tonight. Besides, I could really use a win right now," she added darkly.

"Brey, I don't know if I should really…"

"Save it, girl. I get you're kind of new to this whole game, but now that everyone around here insists on pairing off, I need to bring you under my wing. Look, Jason's coming back now. Set your phaser to stunning, girl."

"A *Star Trek* reference? I didn't know you were a closet geek, Brey," Claudia teased before turning to see Jason's handsome face approach her again.

Handing her a cocktail, Jason smiled and probably gave most of the women in the vicinity a mild heart attack.

"Here's your dry *Boyd & Blair* vodka martini, just a little dirty, and extra olives. How'd I do?" he asked with an easy confidence, which was at once calming, and captivating.

"You did perfectly. It's definitely my favorite. Thank you for remembering, especially about the extra olives. That's where all the nutrition is," she joked in response.

Yet, no matter how charming Jason might be, Claudia felt her eyes finding their way to Trey's side of the room. His back was to her, but she could see tension in his muscles as he gripped his cellphone tightly. Whomever he was talking to, the conversation didn't appear enjoyable.

"My pleasure. It's good to see you again. I just found out yesterday I've been picked up to play for the *Roughnecks*, so I'll be in Pittsburgh now. Maybe I'll be able to catch up with you more regularly?"

"That's wonderful! Congratulations."

"Thanks. My agent, Gabe, gets a lot of the credit. Well, him and the brutal hit J.J. Cole took to the head during the last game. A suspension isn't enough to punish that lineman for what he did."

"How's J.J. doing? Have you heard anything?"

"Wyatt knows better than me, but word around the locker room is he's not doing very well. This is his third concussion in two years. We always have to worry if it's finally the one you don't come back from. Football gives a lot, but it can also take away so much more."

"Jesus. I grew up around football, but I still get nervous every time Wyatt takes a big hit. I don't know how she does it," Claudia mused, nodding to Jenna, who was still nearby, and pretty clearly eavesdropping on their conversation.

"When you make football your life, it's important to be with someone who understands everything that goes with it. Jenna gets it. So do you," he added, his blue eyes meeting hers steadily, and she had no words in response. "On a less depressing note," he continued. "No matter how long the *Roughs* need me, I'd really like to see more of the city while I'm here. I was thinking maybe you could show me around?"

"I'm still pretty new here myself. I'd just be able to show you the FBI office parking lot and the inside of my house."

His eyebrows raised in response, immediately causing Claudia to choke a bit on her drink.

"Oh my god. That's not what I meant."

"I know. Relax. Though I'm not opposed to the idea."

"Oh, uh, well," Claudia stammered out, only to jump at the feel of a firm hand on her upper arm. Her nostrils filled with the scent of Trey, before she'd even turned to identify him.

"Trey, hi. This is Jason. A friend of Wyatt and Jenna's."

"Hi," he grunted out rudely, though he caught himself, remembering to put out his hand to shake Jason's. "Nice to meet you," he mumbled before abruptly stating, "Claudia, we have to go."

"Go? Now?" Claudia asked, truly perplexed.

"But you guys just got here," Tea lamented, adding to the tense tableau, which Jenna and Aubrey quickly joined, as well.

"You can't leave. The kids aren't even back from trick or treating, yet," Jenna explained.

"Something's come up with work. It can't wait. Come on, Claudia."

"What's going on?" Wyatt asked suspiciously, suddenly appearing at Jenna's side. Claudia was starting to feel pretty exposed and uncomfortable, what with almost every person she knew in Pittsburgh surrounding her with varying levels of distress in their eyes.

"We have to leave for D.C. right away," Trey answered before Claudia had a chance to speak.

"Why in the hell would you do that?" Wyatt demanded.

"Trey and Claudia have been working together at the FBI," Jenna answered.

"How did that happen? And why am I just learning about this now?"

"Because it's none of your business, Wy," Claudia snapped. "And Trey thinks it's important we leave town immediately, so we're heading out."

"Oh, I bet he does," Wyatt sneered. Turning to Jenna with recognition in his eyes, he added with irritation, "You were talking about Claudia before, weren't you?"

"It was a private conversation, Wyatt," Jenna answered.

"That's not an answer."

"Tell him, Jenna," Trey interrupted, his fists clenching. Claudia spied Jason, Aubrey, and Tea attempting to put a suitable distance between them and the dispute, and it just embarrassed Claudia more. But Trey wasn't finished. "If Jenna won't, then I might as well. See, she asked me to babysit your sister while I'm helping the FBI, but now she doesn't like my techniques. Looks like you aren't the only one with secrets, Wyatt."

"What the hell, Doc, he's fucking with me, right?"

"Calm down. I just asked him to look out for her, nothing more."

"I'm sure he's doing more than just that."

"So what if he is?" Claudia demanded, leveling a fierce stare at her older brother.

"He's way too old for you."

"He's as old as you are!"

"Exactly."

"And Jason's age is okay?"

"Jason is the right kind of guy for you. It's totally different."

"So it's not an age thing."

"Yeah, maybe it's just a Trey thing." Wyatt turned to Trey, "Tell me, Trey. So you couldn't have Jenna, now you want to settle for my sister?"

"That bullshit again? Watch it, Wyatt. I'm not opposed to beating the shit out of you in your own house, but we don't have time right now."

"You could never even dream of being good enough for Claudia. The two of you will never be a *we*."

"Wyatt! Enough," Claudia exclaimed, but he ignored her. Claudia turned to Trey, but was floored to find Wyatt's words had knocked him off-balance a bit — as though he might agree with him.

Wyatt leveled his gaze at Claudia, apparently trying for another tactic, "Abeja..."

"Don't call me that right now," Claudia seethed, irritated at her brother's use of her family's childhood pet name for her at a time like this.

"Fine. Claudia, what do you think Mama would say about you being with someone like him?"

"You're going to go tattle to our mother? You really do think I'm still twelve years old."

Trey moved closer to Wyatt, their eyes locked in anger, "Fuck you, McCoy. This has nothing to do with you."

Wyatt pushed him.

"It has everything to do with me. I'm her brother. It's my job to protect her."

"I'm looking after her now. And we need to go."

"Trey, calm down," Jenna intoned. "And Wyatt, you *really* need to relax."

"All of you can stop with this *protecting me* crap. I'm a grown-ass woman." Claudia heard her voice rising and a hot flush ran to her cheeks. "This conversation is over, Wyatt. I'll call you from D.C., but *we* are leaving. Good night."

"Come on, little one, let's go," Trey stated brusquely, grabbing her hand in his and pulling her out the door.

Since she'd met him, every one of Trey's touches always seemed to fill her with a flood of powerful sensations, but none of those moments had anything on the fierce impact, which came from his palm on hers for the whole world to see.

Trey shifted the black *Mercedes S600* sedan Stephen had hidden behind a cluster of trees for them into gear, and eased onto the road. His heart was still racing from the surreal combination of his argument with Jenna and Wyatt, mixed with the adrenaline racing through his bloodstream from Stephen's bombshell.

"Why aren't we taking my car?" Claudia asked suspiciously, as she examined the view from her window and side-view mirror.

"We needed something new."

"I checked the area before we left and didn't set eyes on any threats. Do you think we're being followed?"

"I can't be too careful. And we aren't going by your place either. There's no time."

"How come?"

"Just trust me."

"Damn it, Trey. I do everything you say…follow you around like an obedient freaking puppy. The least you can do is tell me why you had to drag me out of my brother's place and start a McCoy civil war."

"From my viewpoint, you were more than happy to take up arms."

"Maybe I was, but it doesn't change that I need you to be honest with me in return. So tell me what the hell is going on, or I swear I'll…"

"David's dead."

"What? He can't… I don't understand…"

"He was found hanging in his cell."

"That's bullshit. He was too much of an egomaniac to kill himself."

"My thoughts exactly. Which means someone took care of it for him."

"We need to get to the office. There's going to be a debriefing. They'll be looking for you to help."

"No."

"Just, *no...*"

He turned to her and apparently the worry on his face must have been enough to shut down all her anger.

Looking back at the road, Trey explained, "I have reason to believe someone may be targeting you because of your theories on this case. You were the next person scheduled to meet with David. If the killer knew that, you could be next, and I can't let that happen."

"That's no reason to abandon my obligations to the Bureau."

"It's the only one, which matters to me. Period. It's just too unsafe to have you in Pittsburgh right now. David's dead, nothing will change that. We'll never know what he might've told you. But I can't care about it right now. The important thing is you don't end up like him. Got it?" he added, his voice raised and taut.

"Okay," she answered softly, placing a hand on his knee, rubbing a tight circle on the side of his leg with her fingers, which was at once soothing, and insanely hot. He looked at her from the corner of his eye, and saw a slight smile gracing her pretty face. His breath skipped in his throat in response.

"Good," he answered, letting his shoulders loosen slightly, as he picked up speed on the parkway out of town. There were no other cars in sight, but he couldn't get too complacent.

"So we'll deal with it in D.C.? I guess headquarters does make the most sense now."

Trey remained silent, working the inside of his lip ring with his tongue, rather than respond. He'd already told her more than he'd intended.

The constantly fluctuating temperatures of Pittsburgh in autumn had brought a heavy blanket of fog to the world around them. It lay against the asphalt with tendrils arching into the inky black sky, reaching for the curved branches of the trees above, providing the deceptive appearance of security.

Claudia's voice broke through the silence. "So, where'd you get this ride? Did you knock off a drug lord?"

"No. My friend Stephen picked it up for me. I gave him access to my emergency cash, so he could help us get out of town. We'd planned on having a little more time, but luckily Stephen is great at spending my money."

Trey grabbed her hand from his knee and kissed her knuckles lightly, one at a time, before laying her hand back down on his leg.

"What do you think?" he asked, gesturing to the dashboard.

"I think it's a good thing you're very rich," she joked. "But it's really hard for me to just leave town. What about my insulin?"

"My duffle has a small cooler bag with plenty of fast-acting insulin, and several slow-release pens in case your pump malfunctions."

"Since when did you become the diabetes expert?"

"Since I met you," he answered, sending a smirk her way, and enjoying the shy smile he received in return.

"Okay, then what about my clothes?"

"The suitcase you'd started packing is here in the car. If you need anything else, we'll buy you the rest tomorrow."

"How's? My suitcase was in my townhouse."

"Stephen made sure it got in here."

"But I thought he was in D.C. Isn't that why you wanted to go there in the first place?"

"Stephen is very mobile."

"That doesn't make any sense," she replied, and her smile disappeared and her brow furrowed. "Wait a second, you didn't get on the turnpike. This isn't the way to D.C."

"We aren't actually going there."

"What in the holy hell, Trey? You *just* told me we were on our way to D.C. headquarters."

"No. *You* said that, and I said nothing."

"So you lied."

"I omitted information."

"It's the same thing!" she exclaimed, ripping her hand from his leg and crossing her arms over her chest.

"Whatever you think it is, it's what I had to do. The last place I want you right now is anywhere you can be found. I needed you to believe we were going there and make sure you honestly said it to other people...even that Jason guy," he added, gritting his teeth.

"Are you mad I was talking to Jason?" she inquired, her voice changing into an interrogating tone.

"No."

"*Really*?"

Trey paused, responding solemnly, "You can talk to other men all you want. You can try to go anywhere in the world, but even if we aren't together, you'll still belong to me. I will always be the one who will do anything to keep you safe."

"Trey..."

"Shh," he interjected, pulling her hand from her chest so he could kiss the palm. "You'd better get some sleep. It'll be a couple hours before we get to the cabin."

"Cabin?"

"Yep." Trey increased his speed slightly, eager to leave the danger further behind them. "You like having me all to yourself? Well, you're going to get a taste of what that's really like, little one."

CHAPTER TWELVE

The rough crunch of tires slowly rolling over rocks, then abruptly coming to a stop, jarred Claudia back to reality. She instinctively grabbed for her sidearm, only to feel the smooth fabric of her homemade Halloween costume against her palm instead.

Wiping a bit of drool off her face with the back of her other hand, she sat up just in time to see Trey's glimmering gaze eyeing her in the car's dim light. He was sitting sideways in the driver's seat, unabashedly staring at her.

"You missed a spot," he mused, pointing to an additional remnant of saliva streaked across the elegant black leather of Claudia's passenger seat.

"Thanks," she grumbled, rubbing the offending goo away with the sleeve of her shirt. "Are we there yet?" she probed, petulantly.

"Ooh, you're grumpy when you're tired," he teased.

"At least I'm not grumpy almost all the time," Claudia countered, a blush warming her cheeks, even as a sly smirk snuck across her cheek.

Trey chuckled, leaning forward to kiss her lightly. "We're almost there. I just wanted to stop and get some gas and supplies. Stephen paid to have the cabin stocked, but I'm not sure when we'll be able to sneak away to civilization again, so better safe than sorry."

"That phrase should be one of your tattoos. I bet it's like your own personal mantra."

"I've been sorry for a lot of things. I'm trying safe on for size with you."

"I noticed."

"You coming in with me?"

"I need to check my glucose. *I* may not think I'm being cranky, but I'll take your word for it." He looked confused for a second, which spurred her to explain, "You know the phrase: *pride goeth before a fall*? Well, bitchy goeth before the low blood sugar. You should probably get me some O.J. and a snack, since we're being safe and all. A banana would be good. I'll need to eat a meal when we get in, but those will be work until then."

"See, is it so hard to humor me? O.J. and a banana, coming right up. Here are the keys, in case you change your mind."

Trey bounded out of the car, and Claudia couldn't help but smile to herself at the sight of the lightness in his steps. She could really get used to having Trey all to herself.

After testing her blood sugar and confirming it was a bit too low, Claudia adjusted the insulin setting on her pump and made her way to meet Trey, locking the small fortune on wheels behind her.

She caught sight of him wandering the store's small aisles, seemingly oblivious to the two drooling salesgirls behind the counter, eagerly waiting for him to acknowledge their presence.

"Hey there, tattoo boy," Claudia said, scampering up to meet him by the canned soups.

"There you are, little one. Miss me already?"

"Testing out how cranky I can get, are you?"

"You got it. I was actually about ready to wrap it up in here."

"Good, because you have some adoring fans at the checkout waiting for you."

Trey turned and threw the girls his most killer smile, as they scrambled to get out their camera phones to take pictures of the mysterious stranger, dressed like a rock idol in their very midst.

"Now, don't go and smile at them like that," Claudia joked. "You don't want them to faint before we get a chance to buy our stuff, do you?"

"They may be our closest neighbors. I might as well be friendly, right?"

"You just like being adored. Come on, let's spend some more of your money."

"My register is open," Claudia heard from Trey's fan club.

"Oh, calm down, Becky," the other clerk chastised, eyeing Claudia with a suitably apologetic face.

"Sorry," Becky responded breathlessly. "I just think he's so cute."

"It's okay. I think he's cute, too," Claudia agreed, tossing Trey her own sexiest grin, before grabbing a banana from the bunch his cart and peeling it with a flourish.

"You think I'm cute, huh?" Trey whispered to her, as he passed her to greet Becky and her friend.

"Don't pretend to be surprised. You know I'm always mooning over you."

"I like this side of you."

"I thought you liked all sides of me?"

"That is most definitely true. Time to buy these goodies and get you off the streets."

"My thought exactly."

Trey tossed their luggage on the couch and looked around at their new rustic surroundings. His whole body hurt from the long drive, but he was too wound up to relax. Once the adrenaline of their hasty departure had subsided, it left behind a nagging sense of dread, as though he'd forgotten something vital.

"Come in, Trey, do you copy?" Claudia asked, though he could barely hear her over the thoughts rambling through his brain.

"What?"

"I said: this place is beautiful."

"Stephen told me it has a great view, too, though it's too dark to enjoy now."

"You've really only just bought it?"

"About forty-eight hours ago. Though I've seen pictures and specs, so Stephen and I could prepare it for optimal security. Stephen replicated my war room as much as possible in such a short time. I brought backup hard drives. You won't be able to use your work cell phone. I have a burner phone and another laptop for you, too, all with different credentials."

"Sounds like my kind of vacation. How long will we be here?"

"As long as it takes."

"Trey, I can handle it if people really are coming after us. It's what I've trained for."

"I told you I wouldn't let anything happen to you, little one. And maybe you practiced being threatened, but no amount of training will prepare *me* for seeing you at risk. So, you're just going to have to accept my approach."

Trey paused for a moment. Sliding a hand along her face, he leaned down to give her a gentle kiss, which he hoped would fry her brain enough to erase any of her remaining questions — at least for a little while.

"Humor me again, little one?"

"Okay," she whispered, nodding ever so slightly. "What is there to do around here, besides getting back to our work?"

"Not much in terms of entertainment. It pretty much only came with a bunch of old movies and cassettes."

"What?"

"Oh fuck, please tell me you know what a cassette is."

"I have heard tales of such ancient artifacts… Oh come on, I'm just teasing. Maybe I never made a mix tape with a boom box, but I do know what they are. By the way, old man, are we planning meals? Should I put you down for dinner at five?"

"Very funny. Maybe you'll expand your horizons...learn what this old guy has to offer."

"I can't wait," she answered, slipping her arms around his waist and pressing her body fully against his.

Trey brushed the hair back from her face, long since disheveled from falling asleep in the car. He'd enjoyed watching her resting. With her face so peaceful and calm, he had the ability to take in every edge and contour of her high cheekbones, upturned lips, and the inviting freshness of her soft, olive skin.

"What are you looking at, Adler?" she wondered timidly. "You're making me nervous."

"You," he stated simply. "You're very beautiful. I should probably have mentioned it before."

"You're saying it now. That helps."

Running his fingertips over her forehead, down the side of her cheek, he felt the breath catch in her throat. Her eyes turned dewy, bringing back the vulnerable young woman who made him all kinds of stupid. Swallowing hard, Trey changed the subject.

"Stephen's people rigged this place up with cameras inside and out. No one will come within a mile of us without me knowing about it."

"You sure are a sweet talker... Stephen must be a great friend."

"He is. But he also has an ulterior motive. He and I have been working on a project for a long time and resolving it is...vital."

"Operation Lexis?"

Trey backed away from her and began to busy himself with unloading documents and medical supplies from his duffle.

"Did you find your way into that file?"

"No, but you aren't as hard to read as you believe. I still think I can help you with it, whatever it is."

"You already are."

"I am?"

"You want me to be more open with you, right?"

"Of course."

"Well, those Sydney killings you connected to whomever compromised David and turned him into a thief and a killer? Stephen and I have been tracking the team behind it for a long time now. Someone named Lexis runs them, and they are incredibly dangerous. If they are involved, like we now suspect, it's a safe guess they killed David."

"And you think they know I made the link between the Sydney killings and David?"

"Stephen and I both do. If we're right, then I'm not sure any cabin, or bunker, or remotely located island in the South Pacific is going to make sure you're secure."

"That's the real reason you needed to pretend we were going to headquarters?"

"Yes. Are you still pissed at me about that?"

Claudia turned her back to him and fingered the handle of her suitcase slowly. He couldn't read her mind, instead staring at her silently trying to process so much new information.

"I'm not mad at you, Trey," she finally explained, pivoting to face him. "It hurts when I feel like you don't trust me. The way you keep trying to rein me in — as though you think I'm going to do something crazy — it's frustrating."

"You're willing to do anything to prove yourself to the world, risking your own life in the process. I know how seductive it is to you to test your limits. I want to help you do that, even if it's on my own terms."

"So you really are the boss, then?"

"*Boss* is so negative sounding," Trey responded, approaching her and placing a hand on her hip. He wasn't above using some dirty tactics to get her back on his side. "I prefer *older and wiser mentor*, whom you like to dream about teaching you all kinds of new things."

Claudia turned her face, trying to hide a smile from him, but he held her chin and forced her to look at him.

"I wish you'd told me this sooner, Trey. I could've helped you...been even more careful. Instead, it seems like your favorite word with me is 'no.'"

"I'm sorry."

"Don't apologize. That's not my point. I'm not trying to be a whiny-ass baby. I'm just tired…tired of working my ass off and not going anywhere. It's like my tires are spinning out and no matter how hard I press the gas, I can't fucking go anywhere. There's only so much a person can hear 'no' before they stop asking for anything anymore."

"I don't get off on saying no to you, Claudia. I wish I could give you everything you want in life, but it only works if I'm able to keep you safe. That's not negotiable. If it means I have to be a bastard most of the time, then so be it."

"I get that, even if it doesn't always seem like I do. But if you try to control everything that happens, you risk causing us to lose even more."

"I won't let that happen," he assured her, easing his mouth toward hers and feeling relieved when she didn't back away.

"So stubborn," she whispered against his lips, before he closed the space between them. Her mouth was soft, but her tongue quickly emerged to lick the seam of his lips. A growl rumbled in his throat, urging him to taste her more deeply. Holding her tightly around the waist, he allowed his lips to part from hers before lightly kissing her again.

Pressing his forehead against hers, Trey took a moment to catch his breath. This wasn't the way he wanted their first time together to be — full of fear and unresolved issues, and too exhausted to truly appreciate it.

"You have your own bedroom. Maybe you should use it."

"*Excuse* me?" she demanded, leaning back with a scowl.

"I still intend to do right by you, which means I can't have you all cute and sleepy next to me."

Trey placed his hands on her hair, letting the feel of the smooth strands ground him, even as he tried to soothe her obvious irritation.

"I guess if you paid so much money to get a place with two bedrooms, I might as well spread out a little. But it's my choice to sleep there...for now. Got it?"

"Crystal clear. Don't worry about the cost, though, please. Buying this cabin with cash was no trouble. If I can't use all this money for someone who matters to me, then what's the use in having it?"

"I matter to you? Come on, Trey," she added, with a nervous laugh, punching him lightly on the shoulder.

He moved to grip her more tightly, using his thumbs to force her to look into his eyes.

"If you don't know how precious you are to me by now, then you're not half the genius I took you for."

"You better be careful, or I'll think you're going soft, Trey Adler."

He smirked slightly, sliding his right hand along her bottom just enough to make her gasp.

"You affect me in many ways, little one, but making me *soft*...is not one of them."

Before she could say another word, Trey covered her lips with his, moving his tongue into her mouth to let her warmth bring him the comfort, which only seemed to come when he touched her.

Backing away, he grinned at the hazy look in her eyes.

"I guess I'll have plenty to dream about," Claudia mused, moving to pull down her shirt, which had gone askew, revealing not only her pump, but the location where the needle went deeply into the skin of her abdomen.

"Does it hurt?" Trey asked.

"What, when I open my angel wings?" Claudia joked. Her tone was coy, but her eyes clouded when she saw he was looking at the entry point.

"Clever, little one. Come on."

"What? You taught me to be such a smart-ass," she answered, her lips turning up and making her even sexier than she'd appeared the moment before.

"This ploy will never work with me, little one. It comes to me naturally. In fact, I happen to be a master of many things."

"So humble."

"Aw hell, if you want me to be humble then we really are totally at a loss. Now be serious. I want to know about your pump. Does it hurt, the way the needle goes in?"

"It hurts like hell. Sometimes it comes out without me wanting it to and it's torture. But what's worse is the pain of my sugar being too high or too low. The physical effects, of course, they are brutal and can kill me. I accepted all that pain a long time ago, but…"

"What?" Trey felt somehow urgent to know what she would say.

"My asshole body may do things to cause me pain, but I can handle it. It's the effect my condition has on the people who care about me that bothers me. It sucks. I could've died when I was little and…I don't know, I lay in my hospital bed and I was somehow okay with the possibility of diabetes killing me. But the fear my stupid blood sugar puts in so many people's day-to-day life — I fucking hate that. It's the part I've never been able to live with… Pardon my language."

"I *do* know those words."

Claudia ripped the elastic out of her hair, allowing her thick, shiny tresses to flow over her shoulders.

"It does weird things to you, to your brain, when you realize your own dependence on shots, or a pump, can break so many people. It makes you want to be something really special. Even if your own body may never let it happen." Claudia's voice was deceptively calm, but her eyes were blazing.

"I can handle it. Maybe it makes us feel better to worry about you? Makes us feel like we have some level of control over what might happen to you."

"You can't shield me from everything, all the time, Trey."

"Just watch me.

CHAPTER THIRTEEN

A delicate and hypnotic dance of morning sunlight sparkled against the rippling lake outside Claudia's bedroom window. The world appeared to be at peace, yet she felt anything but tranquil. In fact, she was pretty irritated.

Placing one palm on the cool glass in front of her, she twisted her body to stare at the evidence of another lonely night behind her. Only one side of her bed held rumpled sheets. The other remained smooth and untouched – a crisp reminder of the way she'd lived her life.

Claudia was pretty sure she may not have a career at the other end of this case, what with disappearing after a witness's death, and all, but the only thing on her mind was how sick she was of sharing a bed with nothing but her own feverish mind.

On top of that, Claudia was through with listening to the broken record that was Trey's misplaced and warped sense of chivalry.

Claudia gritted her teeth and moved her hand to secure the remaining hooks in the front of her cream and black teddy. She'd ordered it online after one of Trey's epic teases, desperate to try her hand at seduction, instead of mere deduction, if only for just once.

Despite that bold moment, she'd ultimately chickened out when packing for this impromptu getaway and left it on her bed. Yet, there it was buried deeply in the bottom of her suitcase, as if left there by her own perverted fairy godmother.

Perhaps it was a sign, or fate, or Trey, or even his mischievous friend Stephen, who'd put it there, but either way she was glad. She'd never been one to wait for life to happen to her, and she wasn't going to keep letting Trey call all the shots.

She could accept having her job sidetracked to the mountains of southwestern Pennsylvania, but she'd be damned if she was going to spend another night alone while her skittish sex god was only a scream away.

Not again.

It was time to channel the McCoy side of her lineage and take some action, whether foolish or otherwise.

With a deep breath, she maneuvered her scantily-clad body down the stairs of the cabin. Music was playing low, and the woman's wistful voice soothed Claudia's nerves.

Trey sat on the couch and her throat and legs clenched at the sight. Papers were strewn around his feet as a laptop hummed on the coffee table in front of him, even as two more rested on either side of him. His tee shirt was stretched tightly across his tense back and shoulder muscles. She could just barely see his jaw tighten and clench in frustration, strong fingers clicking away at the keyboards in front of him and to his right. Her overactive brain couldn't help but marvel at the code whirring downward across the screens, as he bounced back and forth between each machine.

"Good morning, Trey," she announced, planting her nervous hands firmly against the sides of her thighs.

Claudia shook her head to knock the heavy weight of her wavy hair off her back for a moment. It was rare not to have her dark locks in a ponytail, but if this mission were to succeed, she needed to bring all her weapons – even the ones she'd never really learned to use.

Still staring intently at the screen directly in front of him, he muttered absently, "Morning. I hope you slept okay, because we have a ton of catching up to do. Stephen sent me some things to go through, so I need you..."

"You need me? Well, that's a good start," Claudia purred, feeling a little embarrassed, but soldiering on, as it seemed like the kind of thing a powerful minx would say.

As he turned toward her, she couldn't figure out which was hotter — his wide, gray eyes or those damned lips of his, which had parted in shock, revealing a few of his even, white teeth.

Underneath all his danger and tattoos, Trey was a sweet, brilliant guy who somehow along the way got hurt enough to make him do all he could to keep anyone from really getting close to him. The poignant pain of this lost chance at an innocent life appealed to her even more than his impossibly handsome face and dark hair, still mussed from sleep.

Trey's vulnerability disappeared as quickly as it had come. He stood, letting a stack of paper fall to his feet without a glance. With each step his stomach muscles flexed in opposition beneath his shirt, hypnotizing her. Finally reaching her, he looked down to her and the strain of meeting his eyes actually hurt the back of her neck.

"Little one...what are you wearing?" Trey asked. She could tell he was deliberately maintaining some kind of control when all she wanted was for him to use those perfect teeth of his to tear the ridiculous thing off her body.

"That depends," she whispered.

"On what?"

"If it's working..."

Trey backed away from her with a chuckle, rubbing his right thumb between his eyebrows.

"It's working too well. I think you're trying to kill me."

"No. The plans I have for you require you to be very much alive." Claudia touched his waist, then sliding her hands around to the small of his back. "If you're going to keep me locked away out here in the suburbs of the middle of nowhere, then we might as well enjoy our time together."

"Claudia..."

"Look, I get how for some reason — which you won't share with me — you feel you need to handle me with kid gloves. But I'm not as innocent as you think I am, and I'm pretty sure you're not as hazardous as *you* believe you are."

"Don't be so sure of that."

"I'm sure I don't want to wait anymore. If I have to tackle you and pin you to the floor, I will... You know I can do it," she added, bringing her hands to his face so her eyes could lock with his. His mouth curved into a sly smile, creasing his stubbly cheeks against her palms.

"No need for that. I don't want to fight this anymore, either," he whispered, before softly kissing her lips. The touch was light, but the effect was potent. The gentle pressure of his mouth against hers filled her with a sense of calm confidence, which was as hypnotic as the warm desire coursing through her limbs.

Trey's hands ran lightly down the curve of her shoulders, skimming the edges of her bare arms, leaving nothing but goose bumps in their wake. His lips moved from her mouth, feathering light kisses across her right cheek, until his teeth found her earlobe, nipping it hard enough to make her gasp and then groan.

Yet, when his hands finally found their way to her waist, Trey jerked back from her abruptly.

"What's wrong? Why'd you stop?" Claudia asked thickly.

"Where's your pump?"

"Don't change the subject."

"Wrong answer."

"I disconnected it," she murmured after licking slowly across the edge of a tattoo on his neck.

"Claudia, I can't believe you're still being so fucking stubborn..."

Irritation quickly displaced her prior passion, causing Claudia to push hard against Trey's chest, jarring him enough to make him take a step back.

"Ay! Pinche hombre!" Claudia exclaimed.

"Hey, easy now."

Claudia growled in frustration, running both hands through her hair. It had taken her so much courage to approach him like this, and now she had to deal with him slamming a door closed between them, yet again.

"No, *you* take it easy. My whole life people have been babying me, hovering over me — convinced I can't take care of myself. Well, you know what? I'm more than capable of knowing who I am, what I want, and how to make it happen, damn it." Trey opened his mouth to speak, but she raised a hand to silence him. "I wasn't finished. So, guess what — I know I'm stubborn and that's just fine with me."

"You forgot about reckless, impulsive, aggravating, impatient..." he added, a slight smirk creeping across his face. Claudia couldn't stop from grinning right along with him.

"No one likes a know-it-all, Trey."

"But I think you do. I have a feeling you like me very much."

"I suspect you may be right, which is why I don't want you to be just one more in the long line of people who treat me like a child. I want to be a woman with you."

"But if something happens to you..."

"Then we'll deal with it. We will make it be okay. I can test my glucose later and will reattach my pump then. I don't want that damn thing on me right now — getting in the way. I want to be focused on us…on you. Because I won't let you stop this time. I checked my blood sugar, and it's perfect — definitely good enough to be without my pump for a little while. I want to be with you…in every way," Claudia stated, running her hands back and forth along his waist, slipping her fingers under the band of his jeans.

She could almost feel the breath catch in his throat. He licked his lips and it filled her with the rush of need, which only seemed to come from being near him.

"I need you to realize, if we do this, I won't be able to let you go," Trey whispered, his right hand curling around the smooth skin of her cheek.

"Good."

Claudia took a shaky breath before turning her face slightly to kiss the palm of his hand.

A deep rumbling growl escaped from Trey's mouth, as he briskly moved his hand to cradle Claudia's neck, pulling her roughly to him.

"Be careful what you wish for, little one," he added, before kissing her harder than he ever had before.

A commanding sense of pleasure completely overwhelmed her. She may have started this, but the power was all his, and she couldn't make herself want to take it back. It was as though she'd gone snow-blind and was being swept away by an avalanche, all at once.

As his tongue explored her mouth, Trey grabbed her bottom with his hands and heaved her body up to meet his, emphasizing just how small she was next to him. When he wrapped her legs around his hips, Claudia felt every muscle below her waist clench.

After spinning them both around, Trey broke the kiss and made a few hasty steps back to the sofa. He threw her down along the length of its cushions so quickly she bounced a little, eliciting a giggle from her throat.

"Eager much?" Claudia asked, spying Trey bending over to grab something from a small duffle bag next to the coffee table.

"Hell, yes," he answered, straightening up and facing her again. "Being near you has been driving me crazy these last few weeks... Take off whatever it is you've got on."

Claudia fumbled with the strings at her breasts, already feeling so exposed, lying half-naked before him, as he stood there, watching her, fully clothed.

"*Now*, Claudia. I want to see you, and I'd hate to rip something that shows off just how beautiful you are."

Her fingers quickly yanked at the flimsy teddy, pulling it off her body like it was as inconsequential as a pair of sweaty yoga pants. Left with nothing but her own awkward smile, Claudia scooted backward on the sofa so she could sit upright. Trey's eyes had never left her body for a moment. If it weren't for the flaring of his nostrils as he breathed more heavily, she wouldn't have any hint as to whether he was going through the same kind of turmoil as she.

"No fair. I showed you mine, now show me yours," she commanded. A hot blush spread across the top of her breasts, all the way up to her cheeks and tips of her ears; yet, she refused to let her eyes stray from his.

He smiled broadly, revealing his row of movie star white teeth, sending a quick shiver up her spine.

"My pleasure," he responded, placing a square foil packet down on the arm of the sofa next to him, before pulling his *Arcade Fire* tee shirt off in one quick motion.

Claudia's mouth dropped open slightly at the full sight of his lean, muscular chest and arms. They were decorated with so much elaborate artwork, and the accent of his two nipple rings, that she almost missed the chance to watch him undo the button of his jeans — *almost.*

As if he knew just how crazy he made her, Trey slowed to a glacial pace when it came time to unzip his fly. Inch by beautiful inch, she got to see more of the man who'd managed to fill so much of her waking, and sleeping, thoughts for weeks.

Trey gradually revealed the V-shaped muscle below his taut abs, slipping his thumbs under the band of his boxer briefs, to bring those down, too. Suddenly she caught sight of a thatch of dark hair, and she felt her cheeks burn even more as a result.

His eyes met hers for a moment, before pulling his jeans over a stiff erection, which sprang out with an impressive level of spryness. Even though Claudia had only seen a couple penises in her life, she felt pretty confident this one was top-notch, especially because she couldn't look away from it — even as Trey's firm thighs and hard legs became visible to her.

The sight of him tall and bare before her was too much to process. She squirmed shamelessly on the sofa, desperate for him to touch her — everywhere. Trey must have noticed her uncomfortable wriggling because he smiled gently before crawling on the sofa to meet her.

"Do you need me to touch you, little one?" he asked softly.

"Yes, very much," she whispered back.

"Good, because I need you, too."

Still on his knees in front of her, he stroked her face softly, pressing his lips against her nose with a careful tenderness, which was completely opposite from the feverish intensity of his kisses from only a few minutes earlier. His hand moved to her throat, across the curve of her bare breast, and below to her waist.

With each section of her skin he touched, his mouth then blessed it with a kiss, the most devastating of which was his lips against the flesh which held the needle of her disconnected pump. His eyes never left hers as he peppered the area with reverent kisses, as if to thank that needle for keeping her alive. She had to break the connection and look to the ceiling for a brief moment, if only to suppress the fierce weight of confusing emotions filling her body and threatening to spill over in the form of tears from her eyes.

Every day since she'd been sucked into Trey's world, she'd felt increasingly convinced she could really be something great — that someone mysterious and sexy like him could *see* her, beneath the wires and needles, and beyond her famous last name.

Intellectually, she was fully aware Trey was incredibly practiced when it came to sex, but something about the earnest way he'd been looking at her filled her with the heady sense that despite anything which may have happened to either of them before, in this moment, they were both brand-new to all this.

They weren't two adults hiding out in a million-dollar cabin as they maneuvered landmines of secrets and deadly threats; rather, she and Trey were just two sweet, innocent teenagers sneaking down to her mother's basement to explore the meaning of their new tingly feelings for each other.

"Look at me, Claudia," Trey requested. She complied quickly, finding peace in his eyes. They were the color of storm clouds, which was fitting, because her body felt like it had been suffering through a drought since she'd met him — so hopeful for this moment to have finally arrived.

His lips curled into a mischievous smile as his hand traversed to the front of her stomach.

"I like it when you do what I tell you."

"Is that all it took to get you to finally stop being such a tease?" Claudia asked.

"You got me. I'm a controlling prick," he answered, moving his fingers downward, until he touched her already hardened clitoris. She was so sensitive she couldn't help but scream out loud. "Hopefully I was worth the wait," he added roughly.

Claudia released a soft cry, lifting her pelvis to press it more firmly against his hand. Trey lightly swatted her mound. Even if the action was meant to correct her behavior, it had the opposite effect — making her gasp with pleasure.

Trey grinned widely, bending down to kiss her hip bone, and then sucking on it lightly. She writhed in response, lifting off the sofa a little. Trey slid his hand under her bottom, lifting her up more, before taking a firm bite of one cheek. Claudia yelped in shock. When he sat up to look at her, his devious expression caused her to laugh out loud.

"Tasty?" she inquired.

"A delicious mouthful. I've been wanting to bite your butt, since the day I met you."

"Probably good I didn't know that, I would never have been able to get any work done just thinking about it."

"Don't get too comfortable. Now I've had a sample, I may need to nibble you on a regular basis — you know, to keep up my strength."

"I'm not going anywhere," she murmured, meeting his eyes to make sure he sensed how serious her tone had become.

"Good," he growled, mirroring her prior response.

He slid a finger inside her, as his thumb continued to massage her clit. The outcome was enjoyable to the point of almost being painful, forcing her to wriggle awkwardly beneath his hand.

"Are you ready for me, little one?"

"Yes!" she exclaimed, more emphatically than she'd intended. Of course she was ready. How could she not be, when everything this man did to her body felt so freaking amazing?

Trey's smile broadened with wicked joy. He leaned away from her to grab the condom he'd left nearby, and Claudia tried not to pout at the temporary loss of his touch.

"Miss me already?" Trey teased.

"Maybe," she answered with a playful smirk of her own. Pointing to the foil square in his hand, she asked, "You came prepared, too? Does that mean I wasn't the only one hoping for this?"

Trey took a moment to open the wrapper and Claudia stared, mesmerized, as he rolled it over his length.

"I've been dreaming of taking you like this — feeling you underneath me, knowing you're all mine — ever since you tackled me at that old steel mill."

"Really?" Claudia gasped. "I could've sworn you thought I was just some irritating twerp."

"Oh, I did. But you were such a *sexy* bite-sized brat," he teased.

"Hey!"

"Shh." Trey prowled back to her on his hands and knees, finally covering her body with his and nibbling at her shoulder.

"Need another taste?"

"Absolutely," he hummed against her.

Claudia released a deep moan at the sensation of him on top of her, instinctively moving her legs to wrap around his hips.

He propped himself up on his right hand, showcasing the definition of his bicep. She could feel him pressing lightly at her entrance and her own muscles were clenching in anticipation.

Trey paused to scan her face intensely. With his left hand, he brushed a lock of hair from her forehead. And for a moment, they simply smiled at each other goofily, but everything quickly became very serious when she felt him enter her slowly.

Once he'd pressed fully inside her, her body shuddered uncontrollably. His lips met hers as he rhythmically moved in and out of her, alternately sucking on her lower lip and using his tongue to mirror the delicious motions he was making down below.

His movements were alternately rough and gentle, and every time she tried to think, or anticipate what would happen next, his body inside hers, or his hands along her skin, would shock her to her core again. The force he had over her with both his mind and body repeatedly overpowered her tenacious brain, until she had no choice but to surrender every atom and nucleus of her being to his will.

The flood of passion, emotions, excitement, and sheer closeness built into a cresting tidal wave rushing through her body, until it crashed, sweeping away with it all her fear and leaving only intoxicating hope.

She gasped, arching upward toward him with the sensation, but he didn't stop there. He sped his strokes within her, sending her back over the edge of blinding pleasure over and over. Claudia moaned so loudly, the sound could no longer withhold her release of sensation. She screamed aloud — unaware she'd even intended to do so.

Trey paused a moment, allowing her to process what she'd experienced.

Does he know I will never be the same, after this? she wondered.

After this moment of recovery, emboldened by the sheer euphoria coursing through her veins, Claudia decided to take advantage of the absence of her clunky pump. She hooked her left leg around Trey tighter, and used the leverage, along with the pressure of her hand on his waist to flip them over.

It took every ounce of her strength to keep the movement tight enough to prevent herself from flopping onto the floor and humiliating herself. Yet, it was worth it to experience the blissful sensation of straddling him again — albeit in such a different way than when they'd first met. He had slipped out of her body in the process, but she still felt the impact of his presence — as though he would always be a part of her.

Trey stared up at her with a delighted, but somewhat gobsmacked look on his face, before his lips broke into an open and honest grin.

"Easy little tiger, now you're just showing off."

They both started laughing. Claudia's hair fell around them, capturing the mirth in a warm, dark cocoon around their faces.

"I guess you just bring that out of me. See, *I've* been fantasizing about taking you like *this* since I knocked you on your ass that first day. I hope you don't mind," she forced out through her giddiness.

Trey gradually fell silent, his smile turning into a serious frown. Reaching up with both hands, he smoothed her hair back and rested his grip along the sides of her head.

"Please always be whoever you really are when you're with me."

"No matter how much it may seem like that scares the shit out of you?" she murmured gently.

"Especially because of that."

Claudia smiled tenderly, leaning down to kiss him and sliding her tongue along the bottom edge of his upper teeth, then venturing it into his mouth as she maneuvered him back inside of her with the movements of her hips.

His hands moved to her bottom, guiding her up and down over his still rock-hard length. He seemed to be touching some deep place within the hidden recesses of her body. It felt as though he was directly connected to her soul, yet she wasn't frightened.

With each upward thrust, they breathed and moved as one, until she began shaking, and her muscles clenched in strong spasms around him. She screamed, even as Trey's deep groans joined with her own primal sounds.

Claudia jerked a few times, before collapsing into the warm circle of Trey's arms.

He kissed the top of her hair and she caught sight of the glistening lake through the wall of windows alongside them.

With a kiss of her own to Trey's tattooed neck, she closed her eyes, feeling as though the stillness of their temporary world was holding them, as well.

CHAPTER FOURTEEN

Trey took a slow, deep inhalation of Claudia's soft hair as he ran his hand along the curve of her bronze upper right arm. He'd been drawing the outlines of imaginary tattoos with the gentle swipe of his fingertips for some time, as she sighed with contentment against him.

They hadn't let go of each other, except for the few minutes she'd taken to reattach her insulin pump and glucose monitor. He'd studied each of her practiced moments, even her decision to grab a granola bar from her purse on the coffee table, with the focused attention of a loyal apprentice. She'd teased him mercilessly for his open fixation on her blood sugar, but he'd been unfazed.

As soon as Claudia was back in his arms, he tried to ignore the fact that a mere yard away lurked the vital, yet unfinished, task before him. He was convinced Lexis and her team were behind David's death, which meant they were a very real and imminent threat — especially if their sights were on Claudia, as Stephen suspected.

Trey had learned enough from chasing after her team with Stephen over the years that once you were a target of Lexis it was only a matter of when — not *if* — she would get you.

His brain knew he needed to get back to work, but his heart wouldn't let him stop touching the petite beauty next to him. Instead, he stared out across the lake, studying each undulation in the still water caused by the occasional fallen leaf.

Lying there with her, he felt none of the cloying emptiness, or nagging desire to disappear, which usually consumed him after sex — it was quite the opposite, actually. For some reason he was filled with a surreal feeling of completeness, compounded by a need to be closer to her. It probably was a dangerous sign, but it did him no good to worry about it now.

He knew he didn't fit into Claudia's life for any kind of real future — not really. She may be a badass at heart, but the girl had spent her whole life convincing herself she wanted to be some kind of a comic book rules-bound G-Woman.

Trey might be in the throes of a full-on flirtation with legitimacy at the moment, but he was not stupid enough to think he could make it last. He knew himself well enough to be aware he was notorious for only being able to be "good" for a short period of time — and that didn't even count the shit he was still hiding from Claudia. Secrets and walls may have been perfectly fine with the other women, but Claudia was different — special. She deserved better than that, than him. It was bad enough he'd let them both get in this deep.

The unavoidable fact was he'd have to fall from her branches someday, leaving her to grow and be strong without the poisonous effect of a past like his — a man like him.

"I finally get it," Claudia murmured, breaking through the brooding silence, which had been settling like fog around his heart.

"What's that?" Trey asked, moving his arm to secure her closer along the length of his body on the thankfully deep sofa beneath them.

"All these years, I never understood how guys could make girls act so crazy. The way my friends would chase after Wyatt…"

"Um, can we please leave your brother out of this moment?" he asked, moving his eager fingers to tickle the edge of her armpit.

"Shut up!" she screeched, laughing and squirming from the contact. With a hard pinch, she stopped him in his tracks.

"Ow! You're brutal, woman."

"You knew that when you met me, tattoo boy," she challenged. After a beat, she eased her body up to meet his eyes. "Come on, you get what I mean," she added, curling back down into the crook of his arm like a well-fed kitten. Looking back up at him with soft brown eyes, framed with the longest lashes he'd ever seen, she purred, "I'd see these smart, capable young women suddenly turn into illogical goo over some random dude they met at a frat party, or worse…on *Tinder*. It all seemed so stupid to me — a pointless distraction from our goals…"

"Are you saying I drive you nuts?"

Claudia looked down, swirling the index finger of her right hand over the Sanskrit shield on his shoulder. Eventually she stated, "Something like that…" Her hand moved up, tentatively running over the side of his neck. "What does this tattoo mean…the one on your neck? Is it a starling?"

"Good guess. It's the first tattoo I ever got."

"Why a starling, first? I mean, they're kind of assholes…"

"I didn't know birds could be assholes. You should work for the *National Audubon Society* with that kind of insight."

Claudia laughed and responded, "I was pretty nerdy about nature when I was little. And don't doubt it, birds can definitely be assholes. Starlings are some of the biggest dicks of them all. They're very treacherous. They'll steal another bird's nest, or leave their own eggs in a nest for another bird to feed and raise."

The memory of A.J. gleefully naming their virus "Starling" sent a chill through his blood, enough to make him want to veer the topic away somehow.

"Have you ever seen starling flocks flying together?" he queried.

"I have. They wreak havoc on us in Texas. But they *are* beautiful. Like a dancing cloud, that lives and breathes with its very own mind."

"And you think something that seemingly perfect can be bad?"

"Oh, yes. Absolutely. The idea that a creature being pretty or powerful makes every other bad thing it does somehow 'okay' is just ridiculous. I mean — even jerks need a gang."

"You really are obsessed with doing the right thing, aren't you, little one?"

"Of course. I may have been little when my dad disappeared, but before then I saw all too well what happens when people just care about themselves…hurting those around them simply because they *can.* That's how starlings are, but people love them because on the outside they are so pretty and seem so exceptional."

Trey squeezed her closer to him, cradling her in the crook of his arm, smiling at her moral indignation over a bird.

"Beautiful things can cloud the mind, that's true. I know you make me downright stupid."

"Oh, please," she mumbled, but he could feel her mouth breaking into a grin against his chest. "But stop trying to change the subject. Answer my question. Why'd you get a starling, first?"

Trey breathed deeply, staring at the ceiling for a few

moments before answering.

"It's to remind me of someone I lost. And what I didn't do to protect them."

"Where is she now?"

"You just assume it's a she?" he asked, moving his head to scan her face, and the inquisitive, dark brown gaze she'd leveled at him.

"I may be younger than you, old man, but I'm not an idiot," she answered with a lightness, which didn't match her intense eyes.

Trey swallowed hard. His instinct was always to deflect or shut down, but a new urge was taking over him — the yearning to share part of him with this extraordinary person.

"You don't have to tell me if you don't want…"

"Her name was A.J."

"*Was*?"

"Yes…was. She's gone. A.J. is dead."

"I'm so sorry. How… I mean… What happened?"

"For a girl trying to be a hard-ass fed, you're awfully polite," Trey teased, eager to change the subject, yet fully aware Claudia would never let it go until she got the closest thing to the whole story he was willing to give her.

"I met her my sophomore year of college. She was a genius with computers. A natural…like you," he added, taking a moment to deal with the acidic shot of pain in his throat. "We made a powerful mimicking virus together when we were at *Stanford*. She named it 'Starling.' And that, as they say, was the beginning of the end."

"Oh," Claudia said on a heavy breath. He knew she wanted to ask more questions, but he breathed a small sigh of relief when she went back to stroking his shoulder tattoo.

"And this one? Is it Sanskrit?"

"Right again. This was my second, after the asshole starling, of course."

"What does it mean?"

The tickling of Claudia's fingertips over the flesh of his shoulder sent his body into intense arousal all over again, even if the content of their conversation was anything but pleasant. It hit Trey just how formidable a hold she had over him.

"It's from the *Bhagavad Gita.* It translates roughly to: 'I am become death, the destroyer of worlds.'"

"That's pretty dark, even for you, Trey. I mean, jeez, that's what *Oppenheimer* quoted when he saw the A-bomb being tested."

He chuckled lightly. "Nothing gets past you. You must feel pretty lucky, being the only one getting to see what a miserable shit I am."

"Like I won the lottery. Stop trying to distract me."

"Fine. I got it in India, the year after I dropped out of *Stanford.*"

"Because of whatever happened with A.J.?"

"Yes. I learned no matter how well-meaning a person may be, they can still cause mass destruction. And we Adlers, well, we've cornered the market on it, because even the most seemingly beautiful emotions can leave nothing but waste behind them. I'd had enough. I decided it was safest for the world if I never engaged with anyone again."

"But what about your friendship with Griffen, and the Taylor investigation?"

"I tried to draw lines there."

"Then…what about…"

"You?"

"Yes," she stated with a matter-of-fact sternness, sitting up with her legs draped across his lap. "What about me?"

"I've fucked up my philosophy royally with you, little one.

But I don't want to fix it, and that is terrifying as fuck."

"Why?"

"Because nothing is so simple. Maybe if I'd met you before...when I was eighteen."

"Nope. That wouldn't have worked. I was eleven," she answered, tickling his rib cage and grinning.

"You know what I mean, you tiny monster," Trey answered, smiling for a moment, before falling back under the weight of his own resignation. "But the fact is no matter how much I may care for you, eventually, you're going to want a normal life — with a sweet little Labradoodle panting in the backseat on your day off, as you go to meet friends at the dog park. I'll only disappoint."

Claudia straddled his lap, ruffling his hair with her right hand. "Hmm, that *does* sound nice. But I've always pictured myself adopting a rescue."

"I'm serious."

"What else is new?" she grumbled. "Come on! Stop worrying all the time. Why can't you just *be* with me? Why do we have to know what happens next?"

"I can't help it."

"You know, most girls who get abducted without warning by a sexy tattooed older man with a mysterious past figure they'll at least get some fun out of it. You're too busy being moody. I'm sure there's a moor around here somewhere. Want me to look on *Google Maps*?"

Trey grinned in spite of himself, resting his hands on her narrow waist before stating, "So I'm disappointing you? Is that what you're saying?"

"Oh, *yes*. Well, not totally..."

"Good. All right, smart-ass, how about this? We take the morning off. I'll find us an old movie in one of the many dark closets in this place."

"Works for me," Claudia answered with a smile, slipping her smooth legs off his lap slowly enough to make him rethink ever doing anything that required her body not be plastered against his.

As much as he'd wanted to hold her a little longer, Trey had taken advantage of his extended time alone wandering through the cabin to sort through his own thoughts.

Not since A.J. had anyone made him feel so full of foolish optimism. He just needed to find a cure for the Adler mania, which would inevitably come next — or was already beginning.

Proud of the movie selection he'd found on his reconnaissance mission, Trey made his way back to her with a spring in his step he couldn't suppress. He grinned to himself at the sight of her hunched over a computer. She'd snuck away to dress in a pair of worn jeans and a thin long-sleeved shirt. Even from behind she looked like his thirteen-year-old wet dream.

Apparently, just like him, she was unstoppable when there was a problem to be solved.

"Okay, that took forever," he boomed, and her shoulders stiffened when he broke her reverie. "If you can believe it, I've been ransacking this place the whole time." She didn't turn around, but he kept prattling on. "We've got some great choices. A couple of my favorites, *Rear Window*, *To Catch a Thief*, or we could go full throwback geek and watch *War Games*. I feel like I can guess your choice. Don't worry, I won't tell anyone you watched a 1980's *Matthew Broderick* pretend to be a hacker."

Trey flipped a *VHS* tape in his right hand, feeling beyond happy and comfortable, until he saw Claudia spin around in her chair, the computer monitor glowing behind her in haunting backlight. Her sweet, young face was burning with a rage he'd never seen before.

"Hey, what's wrong?"

"Why don't *you* tell me?" she demanded, standing and immediately planting her hands on her hips. She stepped aside and Trey's mouth went dry at the sight of himself in grainy black and white, meeting with David the night he died. "Take your time and have a look. I've watched it a few times already, but I'm sure you'll want some time to make up an excuse." He opened his mouth to speak, but for once, he had nothing to say. "Oh, no quick and witty comeback this time?" she challenged. "You're seriously going to play dumb right now?"

"How? I mean…"

"That's the best you can do? Fine. I hacked into the federal prison's surveillance. I figured I could make a little headway on figuring out who killed David. And what do you know? There you are."

"It's not what it looks like."

"Wow. A blessed savant such as yourself, I thought you would be smart enough not to insult my intelligence."

"Come on, calm down. You don't need to worry about that…"

"Oh, I don't? So you get to run every part of my life, is that it? I'm just supposed to trust you? You get to have all the information and I sit here in the dark, like an idiot? I get to fall in love with you while you control the world and call all the shots?" she demanded, tears welling in her eyes.

"You're falling in love with me?" he questioned, though his voice was a hoarse whisper.

She tugged at the edge of her sleeves and averted her eyes from his.

"Stop trying to deflect me from what you've done. Do you know what a federal agent will think when they see this?"

"A 'federal agent,' or *you*?"

"Does it matter?"

"It matters to *me*."

"You know what matters to *me* — that you stop playing with me, because *none* of this is a game to me. Don't you get *that*?"

"Of course I do."

"Really? Because if you did, you wouldn't do this…you wouldn't keep lying to me and hiding things from me…like…like I don't matter."

"Fuck! How come *you* don't get it? I did *all* of this because you matter *too* much to me. I fell in love with you even before I met you. I figured out you were following up on that ridiculous lead. I saw your picture and I was toast. You were so beautiful and brave and brilliant."

"And you thought that was what? Bad? Loving me? Respecting me?"

"Christ, no! It's not that *I* didn't want to love you. I knew that was a given. I didn't want *you* to love *me*!"

Claudia reached for him, and held his face in her hands. She looked so small, delicate, yet at once strong as steel. The effect was hypnotic. He could tell she felt like him — as though they'd survived a car crash and were blood drunk on residual adrenaline and fear.

Trey took her hands in his and kissed each palm, bringing a smile to her face, before letting her go.

Claudia rubbed her forehead with her thumb and index finger and stared at the lake for a few torturous moments. She shook for a moment, almost like a sob, and rested her forehead on the wall of windows.

Without looking at him, she pleaded, "Why did you sneak away to see him?"

"I met with David all the time. What's the big deal?"

She spun on him, and he barely recognized the icy face of resolve she brought.

"Damn it, Trey. It's a *very* big deal. You have to realize how bad this looks."

"I've got this, Claudia."

She stalked toward him.

"No…you…don't. And the best thing you can do for the both of us is to accept that. My boss is an idiot. And he hates you. Do the math. This means I need to know about David, and every goddamned thing that brought you there to see him."

"I was worried about you planning to meet with him."

"Why?"

"Because he was going to put you in danger."

"Stop giving me bullshit. I need facts. You're fixated on this Lexis-Australia link. Was that why you went there?"

"I didn't want you in a room with David again, not after you'd been asking around about Australia. I couldn't risk Lexis knowing you were in there with him again."

"So you go behind my back to do what? Did you kill him?"

"Did you see me in there killing him?"

"I couldn't access all the footage for that night, so you'll just have to tell me, won't you?" After a beat, she asked cautiously, "When you said you'd do anything to protect me did that mean you'd kill for me?"

"Claudia…"

"Damn it! Talk to me. I can't help you if you won't let me. You have to know this is just the beginning."

"Fine. Yes, I would kill for you. But I haven't…not yet." He stepped closer, placing his hands on her arms. "Believe me, I sure as hell didn't murder David. He was too valuable."

"Which is, of course, why someone else did," she muttered to herself, deep in thought. "The best thing is that you *did* leave…"

The burner phone in Trey's pocket began ringing and they both jumped a little.

"It's Stephen. I have to answer it so he knows we're okay."

She nodded, nibbling absently on her thumbnail as she paced back and forth.

"Hey. It's only been a few hours since we last talked. What's up?"

Claudia stared at Trey, her face streaked with worry. Without breaking eye contact, he moved the phone away from his ear and put it on speaker. The look of relief on her face at his openness with her made him smile a little.

"The FBI has the footage of you visiting David shortly before he died."

"I figured that wouldn't take long."

"Then after you're seen leaving his cell, someone using your computer at the FBI hacked in and disabled the camera in there for twenty-five minutes. Once it was back online, you see David hanging in his cell."

"Fuck," Trey blurted. Out of the corner of his eye, he caught sight of Claudia rushing back to her computer to sit down, apparently attempting to access additional FBI information. "Stephen, hold on a minute. Let us check something." After a moment, Claudia turned in her seat and nodded at him severely. Trey swallowed and continued, "So, I guess the FBI isn't dumb enough to buy it was a suicide anymore?"

"No. It was deliberately shoddy. The noose was tied by someone left-handed. David was right-handed."

"And I bet it didn't take the feds long to remember I'm a lefty?" Trey asked, running a hand through his hair roughly.

"You got it. This whole thing reeks of a setup," Stephen answered.

"The steel mill bomb was prepared by someone left-handed, too," Claudia interjected.

"The bomb you and I decided to keep to ourselves?" Trey asked gently, and he could almost hear her grinding her teeth in frustration.

"Is that Claudia?" Stephen asked.

"Yes."

"It's good she knows about this, because, frame job or no, you are definitely a prime suspect, Trey. I told your dad for you."

"Christ, man, I don't want him dragged into this."

"Too late. He's gotten you a great lawyer. I think he's more pissed you were helping the feds than you being suspected of murder."

"That sounds like my dad all right," Trey muttered dryly. "Aldous Adler hates the government, but he likes you Stephen."

"Of course he does. I'm incredibly likable... Think about this man, you and Claudia being unaccounted for isn't helping things — especially since you threatened David when Claudia interrogated him. You look like a jealous and violent lunatic."

"Which is probably why I'm the perfect person for the real killer to blame."

"What are you going to do? You know how it will look for Claudia, too, if she stays with you, right?"

"I know all too well. Thanks, Stephen."

"I still have a spot for you on my team, you know. That's one way to get you out of this shit."

"Stop trying to recruit me," Trey answered with a laugh. "And I seriously doubt how safe your team is. I've seen your methods, dude."

"They're no worse than yours, man."

"True. Talk to you soon." Trey ended the call and walked to Claudia slowly.

She stood and held him closely to her.

"Fuck. I'm going to need to get you somewhere else that's safe. With someone else," he finished.

She leaned away from him. "Why?" Her eyebrows squeezed together under her crinkled forehead, revealing her honest confusion. Trey looked down at her, his chest hurting at what he knew he needed to do.

"I'm a prime suspect in the murder of an FBI captive. You're going to have to distance yourself from me."

"No," she answered, almost nonchalantly.

"I'm not joking. Staying here with me now could destroy your career. I know being an agent is everything you want. They're going to say you should've brought me in."

"Stop trying to guess what I want in life. You dumping me off could be exactly what the killer hopes you do. If Lexis's team is behind it and she's as connected as you say, then they may be trying to flush us out this way. They probably figure you'll be willing to compromise yourself for me." Claudia kissed him briefly, before continuing in a matter of fact tone. "You told me you're innocent. I believe you. Once I can prove you're telling the truth, everything will all be okay. And if it's not, so be it. You're too important to me."

"Claudia…"

"Shut up. You need me. I'm not going anywhere."

Trey walked across the room and unlocked a file cabinet. He breathed deeply before opening it.

"All the paper files on Lexis are here." He explained, before moving to his main laptop and entering the password to open the electronic files for her. "And everything else is here."

"Why are you giving me all this?" she inquired.

He crossed the room to her, meeting her eyes to state, "Because I finally figured out I trust you almost as much as I believe in you."

Trey wrapped his arms around her, resting his chin on the top of her head.

"Thank you," Claudia whispered against his chest. Looking up at him, she added, "But you know I need more than this. You're going to have to tell me everything you know. No secrets, okay? Because I do love you, too, whether you like it or not."

CHAPTER FIFTEEN

"You know what I'd like to do?" Claudia asked delicately, pulling a sweater over her head.

"Dive into my brain and swim around until your fingers get all pruney?"

"No," she answered over an awkward laugh, grabbing a hoodie for Trey before taking his hand and pulling him past the stone patio and out toward the dock. "I'd like for us to enjoy this world you created for me."

"I thought you wanted me to tell you...everything."

"I do. But we have time, and you went to all this trouble to buy this fancy hideout," she added, waving her hand around them, after dragging him to the corner of the pier with her. "I mean, it's got an impressive dock, and a speedboat, and a seaplane... Christ, Trey, has anyone ever talked to you about overkill?"

He blushed, his fingers curling slightly into her palm, and Claudia thought she might cry.

"I just want to use everything I've worked for all these years to keep you safe."

He looked away, but she pulled at him until he was face-to-face with her again.

"I'm with *you*, Trey. That's how I know I'm going to be okay...because I believe in you, and I know you'll do everything in your power to keep me around."

"How?"

"Because I'd do it for you."

"Yeah?"

"That all you got, tattoo boy?" she queried with a cocky tone broadcasting far more confidence than she actually felt.

"The best I have for you at the moment."

"Works for me, but you know all the money and control in the world...they have limits, too," Claudia took a breath, feeling almost oppressed from the weight of the moment and the memory of those stolen moments her mother had with Claudia's football star dad before he ran off the final time, leaving only his debts behind.

"Claudia?"

She sniffed for a moment and smiled bravely.

"Sometimes you just have to have faith...and iced tea — hold on, I'll get it. Wait for me out here."

"And do what?"

"Relax. As we say in Texas, sit for a spell."

Claudia ran from him, releasing his hand at the last possible moment, such that their arms were fully stretched between them before she left. Her heart was trampling inside her little chest, until she walked into the kitchen and had to clutch the handle of the *Sub-Zero* fridge to still her trembling hand.

She'd learned numerous methods for interrogating witnesses while at Quantico, and was more than ready to utilize those tools.

Theoretically, she knew it was just a matter of calming Trey down, and then to sell to him that opening up to her about a past he clearly hated was as awesome as a free concert in June.

It didn't matter, because none of that knowledge or training could've prepared her for this. She was stupid in love with the guy waiting for her outside, and willing to do anything to make sure nothing happened to him. *Anything.*

After a few more breaths, she returned with a tray, featuring the pitcher, along with a baguette and some cheese she'd found. Claudia grinned broadly even before she saw him.

His back was to her, his right hand rubbing the back of his neck. The motion pulled up the sleeve of his tee shirt, revealing the edge of the Sanskrit tattoo on his shoulder. Claudia wished she could just hold him until all this passed.

Trey turned and caught her eye. Claudia took a deep breath and smiled forcefully, swaying her hips as she walked past him. When he followed her as he slipped on his hoodie, her nerves began to die down.

She led the way toward the edge of the wide pier, which overlooked most of the lake. A *real* smile started to play on her lips at the thought she might be Trey's Latina pied piper.

After setting down the tray on the wooden planks, she kissed him on the cheek. He tentatively took her face in his chilly hands, stilling her so he could kiss her fully on the lips. Her arms slid around his waist, allowing her to lean fully against him.

Trey broke the kiss, but kept his hands on her cheeks, resting his forehead against hers. They both became lost in the moment, with nothing but the lapping of water against the dock's wooden supports to compete with the sound of their gentle breaths.

Easing away from him, she turned to take in the multi-colored leaves overhanging the rippling dark blue water as he sat down. Claudia could tell the delay was helping put him more at ease, and she didn't want to interfere with this progress.

"You do know how to put together a great picnic, Claudia."

"It was easy — that skill is a requirement of my Texas citizenship. Besides, between what you bought last night at the store and Stephen having this place stocked for us… It makes me feel very special — cared for."

Trey smiled sheepishly in response, warming her heart even more.

On a whim, she took off her *Converse* low tops and dipped one foot in the water. She quickly yanked it back onto the dock, shivering and cursing in response.

"Why's it so cold?"

"It's a mountain lake, little one," he responded with a chuckle. "You basically just put your foot into melted snow. If you put it back in and wait a little, the water will start to feel warmer to you."

"I don't know about that...my people like heat."

"Aren't you half Irish?"

"Only in name," she grumbled. "Wyatt's the one who looks anything like our dad. He hates it. Let me sit on your lap so you can warm me up."

"I'm framed for *one* murder, and now you get to boss me around?"

"Sounds about right."

Trey moved to sit cross-legged, and guided her on top of him. Claudia wriggled into position, so she could see his face.

A deep rumbling erupted from Trey's throat.

"If that's your method for making me talk, it's a good one."

"Whatever it takes. The sooner we get this done, then we can get back to everything *else* we like to do."

"Does this mean you aren't mad about me hiding my visit with David from you anymore?"

"Keeping you out of prison and finding the people who set you up has given me a lot of perspective."

"You were right to be so pissed."

"I agree. Though, I may have overreacted a tiny bit. I've always had a hell of a temper. I hope that's not a problem."

Trey smiled slightly, resting his hands on her waist. "I'd love nothing more than to get through this and have many chances to get you all worked up again."

"Good. But I don't want any more lies or secrets. You hear me? It's more important than ever you be open with me."

"Right."

She leaned into him, smiling at the feeling of his arms around her waist. Shifting again to meet his eyes, Claudia slid her right hand over the edge of his face, running her thumb over his bottom lip. His eyes were as dark as the cold water around them, but his flesh was beginning to heat under her caress.

For weeks now, all she'd wanted was to be able to touch him freely like this, but she didn't really have the luxury to enjoy it.

"Trey, are you ready to talk, yet?"

He nodded slightly, worrying his lip ring back and forth with his tongue.

Claudia gave him a quick kiss and held his face to meet her eyes again, before saying, "I want you to know...no matter what you tell me, it won't change how I feel about you. That's your past. *We* are our future. This is just...a detour, something we need to go through before we can move on… together."

"You think you can have a future with me? Isn't that a little foolish?"

Her shoulders stiffened. "I've never given up on anything before, and I'm sure as hell not going to start with you."

"It looks like I have no choice then. Where do you want me to start?"

"At the beginning, or at least whatever you believe is the beginning."

"I guess I need to go back to *Stanford*, then."

Trey turned his face away from Claudia's. It worried him too much to look at her, even though her presence usually brought him peace.

The sun was warm against his skin, but the breeze was cool and smelled faintly like rain may come. He swallowed, and began to speak.

"Before it happened... I mean, when we were together, A.J. always wanted more."

"More what?

"Just *more*. More respect, more success, more than I could ever give her, but I wanted to try. I wanted to impress her, so I had the crazy idea we should make our own virus. She named it Starling. Then she secretly went and made it more powerful, before selling it on the black market."

"And you had no idea what she was up to?"

"I knew she was acting strangely, but I tried to ignore it. My dad screwed up everything with my mom by being too controlling. I didn't want to lose A.J., the same way, so I just convinced myself everything was fine, when the whole time she was actually auctioning it off to Russian gangsters."

"Why did she assume you wouldn't want to sell it?"

"How about you tell me what you really think of me," he bristled, his hands clenching against her waist.

Claudia shifted and stroked his hair. Trey flinched a little, and he could hear her pained intake of breath in response.

"It's not like that at all," Claudia said quickly. It relieved Trey to hear her turn off her interrogator mode for a second. "Look, I know this is hard, but if you really think it somehow started with this Starling virus, we need to figure out how."

Claudia reached for his face, turning it to kiss him, and he let her.

"Okay," he continued slowly. "She knew I'd gotten busted by the FBI in high school for a pretty big hack I did of the San Francisco school system. It was just a prank that got out of control. It pulled in way more data than I'd ever intended. My dad got me off, but the feds were keeping tabs on me. Dad was convinced their plan was to use my brain down the road — see if I'd slip up and give them enough leverage to get me to work for them."

"Your dad wasn't crazy. They do that, and you would be quite the prize. It's how they got you to help them now with Jack Taylor's case."

"It's why they want you, too — brains like ours are quite a commodity," he grumbled.

"But he was right to worry — you're very special, Trey."

"Because I'm Aldous Adler's son?"

"No, because you're *you.*"

It was embarrassing how warm he felt at those words. He cleared his throat and started rambling on again. "Well, no matter what the FBI was thinking, I didn't want to put my dad through all of that shit again. Problem was, I've never been able to keep out of trouble for very long. It was never about money or notoriety for me. It's always just been curiosity — I'd get an idea and then I couldn't wait to see if I could do it. A.J. was different. For her, she wanted to prove to the whole world how capable she was — kind of like someone else I know," he added, leveling a meaningful gaze at Claudia.

She looked shy for a moment, before inquiring, "Do you know who she sold it to?"

Trey snorted. "They came for us," he started to talk quickly, eager to spit the words out as fast as possible.

"Did they hurt either of you?"

"They shot her and knocked me out. They kept me locked up in a fancy hotel room somewhere in Europe, judging by the electrical outlets."

"What about A.J.? Did the gunshot kill her?"

"I begged to see A.J. They said she was gone, but I could work for my own freedom. The virus wasn't enough for them. They wanted me to make more like it."

"What did the Starling virus do?"

"It would mimic a server perfectly, replacing the nest of its host, if you will. Everything the server did — such as, accessing other mainframes or co-opting devices — the virus would be able to do, as well, all while barely leaving a trace. The Russians had this scheme of using it to impersonate and control the U.S. power grid — hold America hostage for a much bigger ransom than they'd get for me."

"Hurting or killing millions of people in the process..."

"Exactly. Not like I would help those fuckers forge a library card, much less with something like that. Instead I used the computer they gave me to infiltrate and corrupt their systems. I tried to use it to figure out where A.J. was, too, but there was no record of her anywhere in their systems. Whatever other data I was able to access, I sent to my dad."

"Did it work?"

"Yes. He came for me, with his own team of paid muscle and bought me back to the States. The Russians didn't know I'd stolen all that intel from them until it was too late."

"What about A.J.?"

"They demanded millions for her body, but would never show evidence of her being alive or dead."

"Why'd you believe she wasn't dead?"

"Because they didn't get what they wanted from me. I thought if I could just get safe, maybe I could find her. But I hated myself because..."

"You believed if you'd helped them, maybe you could've saved her?"

"Exactly. I became obsessed with figuring out what happened to her, so I used all the data I stole to try and find her. For me, my dad rescuing me was just the beginning."

"You only mentioned your dad. Your mother is alive, isn't she? Wouldn't she have been worried sick, too?"

"I have limited interactions with her."

"Why?"

"Now you're just being nosy," he answered, grinning.

"Guilty. Like you say — humor me."

"They split when I was young. My dad swore I wasn't safe with her. He paid her a fuck ton of money to let him raise me alone. She fought for a while, but he was too powerful. She eventually took it. Used her solitary treasure to travel around the world. After I got busted, she met me outside of school, and took me on a little trip that ended with a boat ride — in the Mediterranean Sea. My dad went nuts. She told him he was turning me into him and that a boy needed his mother, and all that kind of shit. He told her there was no way she could keep me safe from all the people that would want me, and what I can do. I figure it took another small fortune and a few threats for him to get her to let me go again."

"Trey, I'm so sorry."

"Yeah, me too. I guess you could say I've been kidnapped twice... That's something special, right?"

Claudia fell silent for several minutes, until he couldn't take it anymore.

"I can hear your brain working, little one. What do you want to know?"

"What happened after your dad saved you from the Russians? How did this turn into a ten-year hunt for you?"

"After I dropped out of *Stanford* I couldn't go back home, even though my dad wanted me to. It was all my fault — what happened to A.J."

"That's just silly. You can't blame yourself. She made her choice. She was the one who took it too far, lying to you in the process."

"It's not that simple. We have to take responsibility for the damage we cause, even if we never saw it coming. No matter how much benefit one person gets for doing the wrong thing, someone always ends up paying a price. And I know that had to be me. That's when I started searching for A.J. on my own. I had no idea what I was doing. I thought if I could just find out what they did to her and take them down, then maybe I could fix everything — and move on."

"Did it work?"

"About three years later, I met a nice Irish girl in Budapest, she fell for me hard and I thought I might be able to love her."

"What happened?"

"I lost Maura, too."

"Lost her? You mean... Jesus... How?"

"They ruled it a suicide, but I never believed it. I'd gotten a mysterious email from her account before it happened. The cops called it a suicide note, but I never bought it."

"What was the MO?"

"She was found hanged...the noose tied by someone left-handed. Just like David."

"Shit."

"Did they suspect you?"

"Not officially, but it wouldn't take much for the FBI to find out about it — and add it to my laundry list of suspicious activity."

"It sounds like these people are fixated on you."

"They should be. I'd been chasing them for years. After Maura died, I knew it was too dangerous for me to care about anyone — until I met you."

"Trey..."

"People always like to say things happen for a reason — that you can get over everything, if you just try. But there are some things in life you shouldn't leave behind. They are there to remind you of just how imperfect you really are — how damaging you can really be."

"Maura wasn't your fault either."

"I didn't keep her safe. I let her love me and she was killed. It's that simple."

Claudia gritted her teeth, ready to speak, but she let him continue.

"And no sign of A.J. being alive?"

Trey paused. How could he explain his greatest fear — that A.J. had done what he wouldn't — she'd become one of them.

"No. I couldn't imagine them letting her go, and there was never a sign she escaped."

Claudia narrowed her eyes, appraising him coolly, but he kept his face passive.

"So you just accepted she was gone?"

"I became obsessed with finding the team who took me and A.J. One day, I finally had a breakthrough — hunting down the source of Maura's suicide note. It came from a group called 'Lexis.' That's how I hooked up with Stephen. He runs a CIA task force focused on international mercenary groups — and Team Lexis is his prime target. We've been two steps behind them for years. The Jack Taylor investigation was supposed to be my own thing, but when you saw the connections to Lexis..."

"You got scared?"

"Hell yes, I did. Claudia, if that team has you in their sights, they will get you. And they've killed every woman I've ever cared for. I can't lose you, too."

"Trey, you wreck me," Claudia whispered.

"Does that mean we can take a break from this conversation?" he asked, gripping her ass with his hands.

"Hell yes," she answered, kissing him hard. She was getting bolder with him by the minute, and he loved it. If he was going to throw away everything he'd learned about how to live his life over the years by allowing himself to fall for her, at least he wasn't alone in the madness.

Holding her hands firmly with his, he stood, before hoisting her up, so she could wrap her legs around his waist. He carried her back to the patio through the slightly ajar French doors, then straight to his room.

"It's a good thing you're so light, little one."

"Why? Are you worried about hurting your back, old man?" she teased, her breath hot against his neck. She began nibbling the juncture of his neck and shoulder, and he groaned audibly.

"Damn it, woman," he growled, coming to a stop at the foot of his bed.

Claudia slithered her denim-clad legs down Trey's sides, setting her feet on the bed.

She yanked her sweater over her head impatiently, with her tee shirt not far behind. He couldn't blame her, as he felt possessed, too — frantic to wipe away all the toxic memories with each slide of his hands across her perfect skin.

She was now a bit taller than him, placing her pert breasts conveniently close to his eager mouth. He closed his lips around an upturned nipple, letting the tip of his tongue play with the taut flesh. Her responding shiver sent another jolt of arousal through his bloodstream.

If the past half hour hadn't left him so crazed, he would've joked about how she'd finally given his neck a rest from constantly straining to look down at her. Yet, he had no room inside of him for playfulness. His brain was overtaken with the need to bury himself deeply inside her. Perhaps if he hid from the world with her long enough, he could figure out how to drag them from the nightmare currently spiraling around his life.

Claudia whimpered slightly, grasping at his shirt with a feverish desperation, which matched his own madness. The stretch of the cotton over his head separated him briefly from her warm skin. Trey growled in frustration, licking his lips to savor the lingering taste of her.

Once freed, he reached up to grip her hair, his hands ready to form into fists, but before his mouth could find her throat Claudia forced her way to his chest, alternately licking and sucking his left nipple, then using her teeth to pull gently at the metal piercing running through it. His head swung backward, releasing himself to the freedom of each hot swipe of her deft tongue.

Shock and heat ran through his chest at the sudden sensation of the tip of her tongue sliding across his chest, between his pecs, and down the length of his stomach. She flicked her tongue over every ripple of his abs, which were clenching with each warm, lapping motion.

Her hands yanked off his belt, then quickly undid the button of his jeans and slid down the zipper. Trey's hands twisted and tugged at her hair, trying to stem his urge to guide her movements.

Glancing up at him briefly, Claudia rubbed across Trey's length through his boxer briefs with the heel of her palm. Hesitating for a moment, she sucked at her bottom lip, revealing her two front teeth. He took a sharp intake of breath, growing harder under her excited touch.

When she finally pulled down the elastic band, Trey's cock sprang free so jubilantly that Claudia smiled and swiped her tongue across her lips in response. The sight of her innocent and beautiful, young face next to his rock-hard erection was enough to force him to access every ounce of self-control not to come right there.

Stilling his body, Trey let her take her time. At first she tentatively licked around the head and down his shaft, as though she were charting a course of him. He ground his teeth together at the almost painful pleasure it caused. As if emboldened, in one surprising motion, Claudia took him into her mouth. The velvety smoothness of her engulfed all his senses, filling him with pleasure, desire...and hope, all at once.

"Fuck," Trey muttered with a jagged growl. The word seemed to make her even more impassioned, as she quickened her pace. Her little happy slurping and humming sounds elicited another series of expletives, until Trey couldn't take it anymore.

The pleasure was too intense, yet Trey didn't want to finish like this. He needed to be truly connected to her — to wipe away every word and painful memory with each stroke of him in her.

Trey eased himself out of her mouth. He clutched her jaw in his palms, his fingers spread wide along her cheeks and jawline. With the press of his thumbs, he tilted her chin up so he could see her brown eyes — impossibly wide, and accented by her wet red lips.

The sight of Claudia kneeling in front of him assured Trey she could truly be his. She was giving up everything for him, and *to* him, and that realization acted as a steadying force to his heart, which was still reeling from the roller coaster of a morning.

Needing to confirm she was real, he slid his thumb across her plump bottom lip.

"Eres mi todo," he whispered, the words cracking slightly.

Claudia gasped a little, clearly stunned by his use of Spanish, and his choice of words.

"You're my everything, too," she responded after a beat. A lone tear welled in one eye. For a moment, it glistened like a newly discovered pearl until it gave way and slid down her face.

"Does that scare you?" Trey asked.

Claudia shook her head vigorously.

"Don't you get it? As long as I'm with you, I'll never be afraid."

Trey took a rough breath and leaned down to lick the tear away. Claudia's hands held both sides of his face, her lips so close to his. Trey sealed his lips over hers, massaging and teasing her with his mouth and tongue, nibbling at her with his teeth.

Claudia broke from him. "I need you, Trey," she panted. "Do you need me?"

"I need you so much it fucking hurts," he blurted out hoarsely. Trey grabbed behind her knees, flipping her on her ass.

Claudia unclipped her pump from her waistband. They both fought with her jeans, yanking them off, along with her panties, unceremoniously.

She was barely naked for a second before Trey thrust fully inside her, his hip bones grinding against her. Claudia arched her back, releasing a loud cry. The debilitating feeling and completeness stilled Trey for a moment, and he gulped for air.

"Yes! Trey...*please*," she begged, clutching at his arms, urging him to continue.

Her desperation reignited his madness. With his hands still behind her knees, Trey thrust hard and fast inside her, his body a broken piston of frustration and pain, which could only be repaired with this rough touch. Claudia started screaming in complicated Spanish words he couldn't understand, until she clenched around him tightly. The sharp bite of her nails in his arms told him he didn't have to hold back anymore. With one last hard push, he released himself into her.

She breathed heavily beneath him for a minute, clumsily wrapping her legs around his waist. Once Trey regained his senses, he shook off his pants, which had pooled around his ankles, and joined her on the bed.

They held each other tightly, as if the connection of their bodies was the only recovered buoy from a sinking ship.

Then reality sunk in. "Shit. I forgot to wear a condom. I've never done that before..."

"Don't worry," Claudia stated calmly. "I'm on the pill. I have been since I was sixteen. With all my other issues, having irregular periods wasn't something we wanted to worry about, too."

"That's good. I probably shouldn't get you pregnant *and* fired in the same month," he added, a wry smile playing on his lips as he wrapped an arm around her. She swatted him lightly, before taking a deep inhale and resting her cheek on the un-inked portion of his chest. Trey craned his neck to look down at her, "I'm clean, I swear."

Claudia made small swirls in the shape of an infinity symbol repeatedly on his skin before speaking.

"I'm sure you are. I know you would never put me at risk." She paused the motion of her fingertip and met his eyes before intoning, "I trust you."

Her words lumbered through the air like two-day-old helium balloons — bouncing in slow motion around their heads.

"Thank you," Trey said finally, his eyes staring at the ceiling, sensing the words slicing clumsily into the air like a dull knife.

"Don't thank me, silly. Even though you piss me off royally sometimes, you're a lot easier to believe in than you realize," Claudia muttered, wiggling her body flush with his, her hair spreading across Trey's chest. She smelled like fresh air and sweat. He couldn't breathe her in deeply enough as he let his eyes close before falling into an uneasy sleep.

CHAPTER SIXTEEN

"Theodore, sweetie, can you hear me?"

"Mom?" he mumbled.

"Did you fall asleep in front of the computer again, you silly boy?"

"Yes. I'm sorry."

"It's your dad's fault, making you crazy like him. I need you to wake up. I was bored with your father gone all week, so I have some new friends over."

"Again?"

"Oh, don't be crabby. One of them has been dying to meet you. All he can talk about is how he hears you're so smart. He actually wants to know about all those computer games you keep making up."

"Dad says I'm not supposed to talk to people about those."

"Well, he's not here right now, is he? Don't you want to learn how to make friends? You don't want to be cooped up all by yourself forever, do you?"

"No?"

"No, is right. My friend is European. It's about time you were exposed to culture that didn't come from a hard drive. Now, be a gentleman and come

downstairs with me."

Rubbing a little hand across his face, he stumbled out of his desk chair. His mother held his face and kissed him on the forehead.

"At least you're still dressed. Here, put this jacket on," she commanded, holding out a navy sports coat to him. He complied. "Much better. Oh, you are such a handsome angel."

"Thank you, Mom," he muttered sheepishly. She looked at him with a vague smile until he added, "And you look very pretty."

"Why thank you, as well. See, such an elegant little man," she responded proudly. She really was beautiful. Tonight, her dark hair was spilling over her shoulders and framing her gray eyes, which looked like a mirror of his own.

She took his hand and steered him to the main staircase.

His head was still fuzzy, but he could make out the sound of steps running toward them.

"Dad?"

"It's okay, son, I came home early to check on you. Abigail! What the hell do you think you're doing?"

"Having a dinner party. So?"

"You bypassed security. If it weren't for Ian figuring out who you invited into my house…"

"Excuse me, Aldous. Your house?"

"Don't start that shit now, Abby."

"What about my guests?"

"Your guests? Ian's taking care of them. Do you have any idea what kind of dangerous people you brought into our home…who you allowed to have access to our son?"

"Dad, it's okay," he interrupted. "Don't yell at Mom, please."

His father took a breath and crouched in front of him, resting his hands on his shoulders.

"Little man, I'm sorry I yelled. But you need to know your safety is the only thing that will ever matter to me."

"I'm okay, Dad."

"You won't be, not forever…"

"Damn it, Aldous, he's just a child."

"No, he's not. He's very special, and he needs to be protected."

"You're going to turn him into a freak. Stop being such a lunatic."

His father stood, face red with anger.

"Don't tell me about putting him at risk, Abigail. What kind of a life are you trying to live here?"

"None that isn't approved by you, I suppose," she taunted in a sarcastic tone. "I mean it. I don't know how much longer I can put up with this. The way you control me and Theodore is unconscionable."

"There are consequences to the things we do. You are playing games with his safety."

"And what about you? Isn't it just as unsafe what you're doing? He's going to be alone his whole life at this rate. Don't you want him to have friends? For someone to love him? People need more."

"All you ever want is more! This isn't even about him, for you," his father roared.

"Dad, Mom, stop!"

Yet, they kept shouting, until his eyes welled with tears and he couldn't focus anymore. They steadily disappeared from view, into blackness.

Trey awoke slowly, disoriented by the lingering remnants of sleeping during the day.

He had no idea how long he'd been out, but when he reached over to hold Claudia and ground himself again, he found she was gone.

Ignoring the immediate sense of emptiness and worry, which came from this discovery, Trey dressed himself. His clothes from earlier were conveniently set out for him, neatly folded on a nearby chair. The thought of Claudia taking the time to do such a domesticated task for him brought a smile to his lips.

He found her quickly. She was bundled up on the patio bench feverishly clacking away on a laptop, while taking brief breaks to peer at something on the armrest next to her.

The wind had picked up, accompanied by threatening gray clouds, which were causing the water on the lake to quiver and shake.

"Aren't you cold?" he asked, startling her.

"Christ, Trey. Give me a heart attack, why don't you?" She gasped, then turned and grinned at him.

He approached her, leaning over the back of the bench to kiss her, and tried to catch a glimpse of her computer screen.

"Mmm," she hummed in response. Trey eased away, which gave her a chance to look him up and down. "You know, it should be illegal for someone to look as good as you when they just wake up."

"It would just be one more entry in my rapidly expanding criminal record," he deadpanned as he leaned over, resting his forearms on the back of the bench. "But, apparently I didn't look good enough, since you left me," he pouted.

She tickled his cheek with her left hand and kissed him back.

"Trust me, it wasn't easy. My pump was beeping, so I got up to refill it and eat something. I didn't want to wake you. I was too wound up about everything going on, anyway. I had to start working."

"And what is it you keep checking on?" Trey peered over her shoulder to spy a fat bumblebee resting on the edge of a liquid-filled metal spoon.

"Oh, this is Ernie. I found him out here and saw he was in distress."

"And you brought him a *spoon*?"

"Yep. It's full of sugar water," she clarified, returning her attention to the screen. "I'm multitasking. Bumblebees and honeybees can become hypoglycemic, just like me. They're especially at risk in the autumn, when there are fewer flowers available. My mother used that fact to help me understand what was different about me. All Ernie needs is a little sugar and he'll be okay."

"So you just stop whatever you're doing and nurse bees back to health?"

She blushed a little. "I've been doing it since I was a kid. Who knows, maybe it will be good karma for me some day."

"I like that idea," Trey whispered, toying with a lock of her hair, which had escaped from her ponytail and was blowing in the breeze.

"It's where my family got their stupid nickname for me — 'abeja,' it means 'bee.' Seriously, I am the *only* Latina in the world called that."

"Would you prefer 'bebé' or 'muñequita'?" he asked, slipping his hand along the slim back of her neck and smiling at her responding happy sigh.

"Probably not, but I do like the way those words sound when you say them. I think you've been secretly learning Spanish, mi chico guapo?"

"I've learned a lot of things since I met you."

"Not as many as you've taught me. I especially like what I've learned from you the last few days."

Trey leaned forward to kiss her, but they became distracted by the sight of a now spry bumblebee flying away.

"I did it!" Claudia exclaimed. A bolt of lightning, and a few large drops of rain cut her joy short. "Quick! The laptop, get it inside!" she ordered, shoving it into Trey's hands before she scrambled off the bench.

They scurried toward the house, but the light shower rapidly escalated into a downpour, before they could make it inside. Trey used his body to protect the closed laptop, rendering it the only dry thing between the two of them.

Shivering, Claudia closed the French doors behind her, and the air filled with the sounds of their giddy laughter and the pelting rain outside.

The sight of her hair and clothes dripping with rain warmed his chilled blood. Transfixed by the sight of her hardened nipples through her wet tee shirt, Trey stated firmly, "Claudia, take off your clothes."

"What?"

"You heard me. Take…off…your…clothes. You're very wet," he added with a smirk, still reveling in the way his words had the power to make her blush. "I'd hate for you to catch a cold."

"No chance of that happening with you around."

"Oh, is that my abeja's stinger?"

"You know I don't really like that nickname, right?"

"Oh, come on now," he cajoled, peeling her wet shirt off her. "You wouldn't want to hurt Ernie the Bumblebee's feelings would you? Besides, I like thinking of you like a bee — someone who can defend herself, but whom I can still help when you need it."

The lights began to flicker, and a quick shot of fear ran up Trey's spine, stilling his hands as they made their way to the button of her waistband.

"Shit, if the power goes out… What will we do with your insulin? How can we investigate…" Trey murmured.

"Stop that."

"What?"

"Being so obsessed with what will happen next. My insulin will be fine in the cooler bag for a short period of time. And I've managed to do low-tech things like work with paper before." Claudia stated matter-of-factly before removing his wet shirt and throwing it across the room. She spoke again, punctuating each word with a warm, seductive kiss to his neck. "We…us. You…and me," she cooed, slipping one arm around his waist and using her other hand to turn his face to hers, forcing his eyes to meet her own. "We are all that matters right now. Please enjoy this moment with me, because we don't know how many more moments we may have — especially with everything going on right now. All we know is that we have this *one*, and I am *never* going to let it go."

With that, she sealed her lips over his, and he didn't care if he never had electricity ever again.

The slow trails Trey's tongue was making along Claudia's spine sent chills through her body, despite the steaming spray of water coursing over them from above. His accompanying touch was gentle and soothing — caring for her in a way, which felt almost like worship.

After they'd peeled off each other's cold, wet clothes, she'd dragged Trey to the master bathroom for a shower.

Claudia had mumbled something about warming them up after the onslaught of rain, though all she really wanted was an excuse to stare at Trey naked and soaking wet. Trey had different plans, though — taking her from behind against the vanity. The cold granite had cooled her fingers as they watched themselves joining together in the glass of the bathroom mirror.

It had amazed her how each time felt a little different,

stimulating various parts of her body and mind. His hands on her body had been rough, but his eyes in the mirror were full of love. When he had made one last deep thrust into her, they both came, causing her to arch back, hard. The sudden movement had jarred Trey's hand against the cord of her pump, which she'd rested on the edge of the sink.

Suddenly, she'd found herself screaming out for a much different reason. Oblivious, Trey held her, his arms wrapped tightly around her, his face nestling into her neck. Desperate to hide her pain, she'd stilled against him, remaining silent, but the mirror had given her away.

"What's wrong?" he'd asked.

Before she could form a lie, she saw his reflection catch sight of the needle resting innocently beside her.

"Oh, fuck, I'm so sorry. Are you okay? No, of course you're not."

"It's not your fault. I got carried away. It could've been worse. I just need to breathe through it and put the needle back in."

Overcome with a childish sense of shame at ruining such a perfect moment, Claudia had made quick work of disconnecting the pump from the needle. Yet, as she tried to leave, his hand moved to her arm, stopping her.

"No, I want to watch. I need to understand."

His eyes had held so much worry and agony, Claudia wondered if it had hurt him, more than her.

"O-okay." Averting her eyes, she went through the grueling process of inserting the long needle into her stomach.

Even now in the shower, she could remember the feel of his intense gaze as her hands worked. When she'd finally finished, he tilted her chin so she had to face him.

"Thank you for that. I promise to be more careful with you."

"It's not like that…"

"Shh, let's go take that shower," he'd responded simply.

After Trey had managed to kiss most of her body under the water, she turned and wrapped her arms around his waist.

"Do you feel better?" he asked.

"Yes, I'm sorry you had to see that."

"Don't be sorry. You can't help it."

Claudia leaned in, resting her cheek against his chest.

"My whole life…this body has been my biggest enemy. It didn't help I grew up in a world of athletes and had a model mother. Everyone in my family...their bodies are their careers. I know my dad was disgusted with me…and my condition. I refuse to believe I'm sick, but I know he always saw me as broken. He left so soon after that, for good. Or bad, who knows."

"If that's true, then I look forward to kicking his ass someday."

"It would be tough for you to find him. He only surfaces to do random *NFL* commentary, or to gamble in Vegas." Trey moved his chin to the top of her head and grunted a little. She continued. "I did everything I could to be like everyone else, but at night, I'd go to sleep and wonder if I would always be nothing but a monster with a big, lumpy pump connected to my stomach."

"I personally am a big fan of that pump," Trey said, leaning back to show her the teasing grin on his face, as he started caressing her bottom. "I sure as hell don't like the idea of the alternative. And, for what it's worth, I think this body of yours is perfect."

"You're proving to be a secret softy, Trey Adler."

"Only for you, Claudia McCoy. And not just in that way. You've ruined me for the world in all kinds of other ways."

She swallowed, hard, "Then I'd better get back to work. This escape has been amazing, but you are in serious trouble, and I don't want to lose you to it."

Trey nodded, turning off the water, and helping her out of the shower. She grabbed two towels, studying his strained expression. The loud rumbling of thunder interrupted their nervous conversation, followed by the flickering of lights, and then darkness.

"Shit," Trey muttered.

"It's okay. We've got candles, there's one in here, and the lantern in the living room. Let's set up shop in there. I'll make a fire while you collect all the paper files."

"You seem pretty relaxed, considering the mess I've dragged you into."

"Believe me, I'm freaking out inside a little," she answered, rummaging through a drawer, then lighting a candle before hanging up her towel and carrying the small candle into the bedroom and finding one of Trey's button-down shirts to wear. She had her own clothes, of course, but she liked the idea of being close to him. "But we can't control everything," she added. "All we can do is try to find a solution. Now, go out there and get me some wood." She smirked and handed him another lit candle.

"You know how to make a fire?"

"Of course I do, city boy," Claudia taunted, pressing her hand on his chest and letting her homegrown twang come through her voice. "I'm a native born and bred Texican, so that means you're in *my* world, and you have to do what *I* say."

"With pleasure," he assured her with a smile.

CHAPTER SEVENTEEN

Claudia placed her pen down on the coffee table and stifled a yawn. Glancing outside, she found the sky was turning from streaky orange and rose to a glowing blue twilight. Distant lightning occasionally illuminated the lake for one brilliant moment, but the stunning sight was blurry to her exhausted eyes. She rubbed her index fingers back and forth across her eyelids, giving herself a moment of relief.

For hours she'd pored over files chock-full of documents, including pictures, government records from various nations, newspaper clippings, intercepted communications, and the scrawl of Trey's feverishly handwritten notes. Lexis and her team were innovative, prolific, talented, and — at times — ruthless.

Staring at hard copy evidence of Trey's almost decade-long manic pursuit of a vendetta was both daunting and depressing, but she couldn't let that slow her down.

Claudia had spent weeks trying to solve Jack Taylor's murder. If she could help bring justice to his family, and maybe find Trey some freedom and peace, then a little tiredness would be a small price to pay.

She sighed, leaning forward to swap out a folder on hacking of a Chilean businessman's accounts and personal investments. It was one of their clean smash-and-grab jobs. Its success was made all the easier for the mark's reluctance to cooperate with the investigation, most likely due to his suspected links to organized crime.

No — Claudia was more interested in the few operations where Lexis and her team had failed in some way. Which brought her hand back to the Sydney file — the job , which started her link to Lexis in the first place.

"I'm back," Trey announced, entering the room from behind her. He held a plate filled with sandwiches and chips and placed it on the small portion of the table not buried in papers.

"Honey, you baked!" Claudia teased.

Trey straightened up, a bashful smile on his face. "This city boy of yours is used to ordering out, so hopefully this is edible."

Claudia smiled softly. "It'll be great, I'm sure. Honestly, I'm so distracted, it could be sawdust and I would eat it."

"You flatter me," Trey remarked, and she threw him a little smirk. "How's my old-school detective doing?" he asked, throwing another log on the fire.

"Not being able to work with a computer is threatening to give me hives right now, but I guess it's good to remember how to think without a computer every once in a while. Keeps me sharp." She turned to him. "Where were you all this time?"

"Talking to Stephen. The burner phone still has enough juice to check in with him every eight hours. In the meantime, he's working on getting a generator for us."

"Thank God. Be sure to tell Stephen he's my hero," she said with a smile.

"Careful, you wouldn't want to make me jealous, would you?"

"You'll survive. Now focus. I want to talk through some things with you."

She saw him briefly tense up, before sitting next to her on the sofa. "Okay, shoot."

"I'm struggling to make sense of the history of this group."

"What do you mean?"

"They don't really fit the profile of the kind of violent thugs who abducted you and A.J."

"What do you mean? They slaughtered that couple in Sydney."

"True, and the pictures were definitely disturbing, but that was several years ago, when the team wasn't nearly as effective. This group has developed over the years into a much more sophisticated, savvy organization. Now they are sort of a dark version of the *A-Team.* It appears everyone has a specialty, but Lexis is the mastermind. Plus," she continued, "those Sydney killings were in *response* to the mark coming home to find the agent with his wife — the team had been compromised. My point is, these files show they certainly are willing to be vicious, but it's not their business model."

"I hear you. To gather information and power, which they can sell — is their overarching goal. They infiltrate a person's life or an organization through espionage. Then they get in, and get out. That is their ideal approach."

"Exactly!" Claudia started to feel excitement rushing through her veins. "Which is why I've been focusing on the isolated incidents where they had to go off script — those limited acts of mayhem."

She took one bite of a sandwich, before pushing the rest of the uneaten food to the side and reaching for a couple more files. After stacking them in order, she said, "It seems they take that step for only two reasons. One is to cover their tracks. With the

Sydney op, it all started pretty standard. Her agent seduces the mark's wife, and then accesses his files. He must have been a rookie, because he got caught. I'm guessing it was one of his first assignments, just from how clumsily he executed it."

"And the second reason?"

"To punish a betrayal of some kind. Look at the Brazil file here. Agent X meets with Stephen secretly, attempting to defect from the team. Then he's quickly eliminated."

"What do you think that means? How can it help us find them?"

"I'm thinking they like to believe they aren't evil. Maybe they tell themselves nobody gets hurt who doesn't deserve it. Their targets are either large, faceless entities — organizations, businesses, and government contractors — or individuals who are weak in some way — corrupt officials, adulterers, criminals themselves. Look at David, he was willing to sell out his whole university for money to gamble and do drugs."

"He was even willing to kill his protégé to protect himself."

She nodded, and added, "They could definitely convince themselves David deserved all that was coming to him. That means we need to focus on finding the members of the team most dependent on that rationalization, and try to turn them. I've been working on a list of which specialists may be the most susceptible to that approach." Claudia handed the list to Trey, before opening one of Trey's files on his repeated meetings with David. "But that doesn't solve the immediate problem," she continued.

"You mean keeping me out of prison?"

"Yeah, that one," she stated wryly. "Clearly, Lexis has been able to infiltrate government agencies before. It's how she knew Agent X met with Stephen, and I think it's how she was able to make it look like you killed David."

"And getting you that phony tip, which almost got you blown up."

"Shit, you're right," Claudia flipped through the pages of another folder until she found the forensic report on the explosive device. "That actually brings us to what's been bugging me so much."

"What's that?"

"Why not kill David sooner? Under her MO, Lexis would've cleaned that mess up shortly after David got busted. Every other time, they did it within weeks, or days, even. There were some indicators that was the plan after David got caught." Claudia handed Trey a file showing evidence of someone tampering with David's closed-circuit camera system two weeks after his arrest.

"But then they left him alone for over a year."

"Right. Why do that? The only change I could find was that the FBI brought you in at about that time."

"Then why give you that bogus lead so many months later? You weren't on the case at all."

Claudia paused, letting the question rattle around in her head for a while.

"Not until I spoke to Drew after getting the email," she mused. "You know, he was the only agent in the field office who knew I hadn't given up on the tip. Drew is in cybercrime, too, it would be easy for him to set me up with the phony tip and then try to frame you for David's murder. He would've been able to access your office computer whenever you were out, or mine, too, for that matter."

"I hope Drew is the mole. I never liked that fucking guy." Trey growled, making Claudia relax and laugh for a moment. "But why would he want to kill you?" Trey wondered.

"What if it wasn't about me? We think this team is obsessed with you, right? Maybe they see you get involved and want to teach you a lesson — make this the last time you fuck with them?"

"But I was doing everything by the book till I met you."

"Maybe that was the problem. You didn't give them an opening. But then I get assigned to the office... Let's suppose I was killed all those weeks ago..." Trey's jaw clenched, but she barreled on. "If Drew really is their inside guy, he would have seen an opportunity to pull you in deep — make you do something crazy. He knew all about how close you are to Jenna, and with me being Wyatt's sister and so close to Jenna... Oh no, what if they use the two of them to smoke you out now?"

"I'm way ahead of you," he growled. "Hurry. I'll call Stephen from the road."

"He needs to assign a detail to Wyatt and Jenna's house."

"Right. Come on, put on the nicest clothes you brought. We're going to D.C. headquarters...for real this time."

Claudia drummed the fingers of her right hand in rapid-fire succession, against the armrest of the car door. The nervous percussion blended with her quick breaths, such that she was creating an ugly, restless symphony, all by herself.

Her eyes flicked back and forth, counting each tree, which whizzed past her passenger side window. Throughout the half hour since they'd left the cabin, Claudia's brain had been performing complicated equations to determine just how many trees they would need to pass, before getting to their destination.

It appeared they'd left the storm behind them, as the sky was clear. Yet the creeping inky blackness of night was taking over the last shades of deep blue, making her self-imposed mathematical assignment increasingly challenging.

As soon as they'd started driving, Trey had plugged his burner phone into the car charger and called Stephen again to debrief him on their discovery. He'd also asked him to call ahead to some of his friends in the D.C. FBI, hopefully making them receptive to their theories.

Stephen was overseas somewhere, but swore he had everything well in hand. He promised to make sure Jenna and Wyatt were safe, and that his team would look for hard evidence against Drew. All that was left for Trey and Claudia was to get the FBI chasing after the right people, and check in with Stephen every hour. It sounded simple, but it left Claudia feeling powerless at that moment.

"It's going to be okay," Trey stated, stroking Claudia's knee with his right hand.

"Easy for us to say," she muttered. "Where exactly are we, anyway?" Claudia added.

"We're still in the Laurel Highlands, making our way to Maryland. It's a pretty large region in southwestern Pennsylvania. We were only about an hour and a half from Pittsburgh, but the navigation says it's going to take at least three and a half more hours to get to D.C. I'm sorry."

"Don't be. We needed remote, and you found it. But, are you sure you can't drive any faster?" she asked.

"Not without putting wings on this thing. There's only one road out, unfortunately."

She chuckled in spite of herself. "You're right. I'm sorry..."

"Don't be. I'm jumping out of my skin, too."

"I wish we could've taken that damn seaplane of yours."

"Um, you may be more familiar with the FBI than I am, but I'm pretty sure I wouldn't have gotten speedy clearance to land that baby on the Potomac River."

"No, probably not. So, we just need to try and relax, right?"

she questioned, turning to him, and allowing the shadows playing over the now-familiar line of his jaw to soothe her slightly. Placing her left hand over his, she let those fingers bounce up and down on his — this time performing a tiny stress-induced form of ballet, on his flesh.

"Is this you relaxing?" he probed jokingly.

She laughed a little, before commanding, "Talk to me. That will help."

He shifted his palm so he could hold her hand.

"Claudia, you heard Stephen say he had people waiting at the ready back at Pittsburgh. They were there in minutes. They're securing the house now. You should be more worried about the interrogation they must be facing from Jenna."

Claudia laughed again, this time a bit more freely. "I hope they're armed, because Wyatt probably tackled them and may still be screaming at them in Spanish, as we speak," she added, watching Trey's face relax into a smile of his own.

"I'm just so mad at myself," she continued. "How the hell did I not see this coming? I worked next to Drew every day. He was my friend. I talked to him about *The Walking Dead* on Monday mornings for Christ's sake…and this whole time…" She moved her right hand to the side of her face, resting her elbow on the armrest, "I'm such a freaking idiot."

"No, you're *not*. If anyone is at fault here, it's me."

"That's ridiculous," Claudia challenged.

"Is it? Come on, I was so caught up with helping Griffen find Jack's killer, that I totally missed how this whole thing had Lexis's fingerprints all over it. If you hadn't made the connection to the Sydney job, I would've never figured it out."

"I would never have even known about Lexis's team, if you hadn't managed to identify dozens of her other operations. That was amazing. No wonder Stephen wanted your help. You're a natural."

"Some natural," he snorted. "I chased their shadows for years, and never got this close."

"That's only because I had all your information and the luxury of looking at it from a different angle."

"How's that?"

"They warned us at Quantico how it's easy too get too emotional about a case. And it doesn't get any more emotional than this one is to you. You understandably focused on Lexis as a monster, but I could look at these files from the perspective of her as a businesswoman."

"Monster or businesswoman, I should've seen she was involved with this. Then I would've assumed she'd try to have an inside man helping her."

"No, you couldn't. It wasn't until they pushed the envelope with framing you that you could even put a face on it. That desperate move gave us the best clue you've ever had. I'm the one who got the tip. If I'd just opened my damn eyes, I would've seen that explosion was connected to Drew."

"Are we back to blaming you, now?" he asked, his mouth twisting into a smirk.

"Yes. You got a problem with that?" she teased.

They both laughed, and it was the best she'd felt since they'd left the cabin.

"No. How about some music?"

"That sounds good." Claudia muttered, forcing her head to lean back against the plush leather headrest.

Trey inserted a CD into the *Mercedes's* sound system.

"Luckily I thought to grab some old CDs before we left. It's too dangerous to turn on our *iPhones*, in case someone is tracking them."

"I like this song. What's it called?"

"*You Belong to Me*... It's the *Jo Stafford* version. My dad gave me the CD last Christmas. We used to listen to this kind of music all the time."

Trey began to sing the words to her, turning to her to croon how she belonged to him.

Claudia broke out in giggles at the sound of his off-key karaoke rendition.

"Hey! I thought that was pretty impressive."

"Oh yes, you should take that act on tour. You just need some *Auto-Tune*." She took his hand and kissed each of his fingertips. "I loved it."

"I love you."

"I know," she answered, with a devilish grin.

"Oh, more *Star Wars*, you nerd!"

"*The Empire Strikes Back*, to be exact. *Han* and *Leia's* romance is the greatest love story of our time, thank you very much."

Claudia leaned forward and laughed so hard, it bumped the pump she'd tucked into her bra out of place. Letting go of his hand, she started fussing with it, securing it again between her breasts.

"Damn dresses," she cursed as she straightened, referencing the sleeveless black dress she was wearing. "Now you see why I wear pants all the time — nowhere to tuck this damn thing."

"I like you in a dress."

"Thank you. It's not exactly appropriate for our impending arrival at FBI headquarters, but for some mysterious reason, it was the most formal thing in my suitcase. I suppose it was Stephen who removed all the pantsuits from my luggage?"

"What can I say? He's a good friend. I didn't even have to ask."

"Well, *you* look perfect. I could definitely get used to you in a suit," she added, pleasantly distracted by the sight of his strong shoulders encased in a black, Italian suit jacket.

"After all this is over we should go somewhere and really relax. Somewhere that we can make sure you won't miss your pantsuits."

"Maybe Ashtabula? Like in the song," she joked.

"I was thinking more like Nice, as in France. It's where my mother first took us when she abducted me. I still remember the Mediterranean Sea appearing below us. You'll never see that color of blue anywhere else. She said she wanted me to have a different kind of life, to let myself be free, and not be obsessed with creating one thing, after another." Trey took a deep breath. "Right before we landed, she told me: 'If you define yourself by the worlds you create, you will only destroy the one you actually have.'"

Before Claudia could formulate a thought, Trey began to turn the car to the left.

"What are you doing?"

"Going to that gas station we stopped at on the way to the cabin."

"There's no time. We have to get to D.C. as soon as possible."

"Not without buying you something to eat. I rushed out without grabbing the sandwich I made you, like a dumbass."

Before she could protest any further, Trey pulled into a parking space at the empty lot of the late-night service station. Claudia crossed her arms, and released a rough, frustrated breath.

"Don't huff at me, little one. You know I'm right. I also want to make sure we have enough gas to actually get there. This ride may look nice but it's not exactly fuel efficient, and there's no other options to get gas for a long while."

"Fine. You're right," she muttered. "I better come in with you though," she added, opening her door and giving him a sweet smile, to make up for her mini snit. "I wouldn't want that salesgirl, who loved you so much, to try and steal you for herself."

He laughed as he walked around the luxury vehicle, and promptly took her hand to help her out of the car, quickly moving his arm to her waist and kissing her deeply. Once he released her, Trey stated, "You aren't getting rid of me that easily. Come on. Let's make this quick."

Trey opened the door for her, and she made a little skip through the entry, as the bell above the door rang, announcing their arrival. Her anxiety quickly returned, though, as soon as she caught sight of the empty store and abandoned counter.

Stopping short, Trey bumped into her back lightly. She held up a hand to silence him, pointing to the counter. Glancing back, she saw him nod, then point to the security camera, along the corner of the ceiling. It had no blinking light, indicating someone had turned it off previously.

Trey twirled his finger in the air, and pointed to himself, clarifying he would take the perimeter of the store. She nodded, gesturing she'd investigate the counter.

Claudia remembered Trey's piece was still locked in the trunk. It might as well have been a mile away with the potential urgency of the situation. She cursed herself for not thinking to demand he carry a gun of his own at all times. He'd been so focused on her security, that she'd foolishly forgotten to insist he care about his own. Low on options, she offered Trey a can of *Mace* from her purse.

He smirked derisively at the innocuous-looking item, but took it from her wordlessly.

She reached back into her bag for her *Glock* and quickly moved it into position. Trey walked away from her, disappearing behind an aisle lined with a variety of breads and chips. The country store was deceptively large, featuring numerous rows of metal racks, which quickly obscured Trey from her view.

Moving as quietly as possible in her pumps, Claudia approached the checkout counter at the back of the store. A handwritten note was taped to its edge, simply stating: "*Will be back in one hour.*"

Why leave this note and not lock the front door? That's just asking for trouble, Claudia thought.

Setting her jaw, she moved behind the counter to investigate. She crouched down to confirm the cash register was untouched, and the shelves and drawers around it were tidy.

A woman's hooded sweatshirt was resting on the stool next to her. Claudia stroked the insignia of her brother's *NFL* team, the *Pittsburgh Roughnecks*, emblazoned on its front, sending a pang of worry for his and Jenna's safety back through her bloodstream. Even so, their situation didn't change how this female employee could be in danger, and needed her help, too.

It was possible the cashier simply took an unauthorized one-hour break, but why wouldn't she take her jacket? It was a chilly evening and even an employee negligent enough to leave the store's money and products unprotected would've wanted to take it with her.

Claudia began to straighten up, when a small object on the floor caught her eye. Claudia picked it up, only to find it was a shiny pink button. The hanging threads and small scrap of material still connected to it indicated it had likely been yanked off in a struggle.

Clutching the button in her left hand, Claudia looked up to see the area marked: "*Employees Only*," behind her. The temptation to explore more on her own was intense, but she knew the safer bet was to get Trey so they could determine their next move as a team.

She shifted her weight, preparing to stand up, when she

heard the front door bell chime, echoing through the abandoned store. Before she could even make a move to look for the new entrant, muffled shouts and the squeak of shoes on the waxed floor echoed around her.

A knot of fear wrapped itself around her throat. She slipped off her pumps and left her purse behind, still holding the button, as though it were a protective talisman. Remaining in a crouch, she approached the sounds slowly, edging her way along the wall, which was blessedly encased in shadows.

Claudia heard a woman's voice as she turned the corner. Trey suddenly came into her line of sight. He was struggling against the two huge guys holding him. One of them had a bloodied nose. Before anyone could see or hear her, Claudia ducked behind a stack of toilet paper boxes, mere yards away from her worst nightmare.

She heard the woman's voice again. Her authoritative tone was consistent with that of a leader, but its owner was too deeply hidden in darkness for Claudia to discern what she looked like.

"Damn it, you two. Get him under control so you can grab the girl. We aren't leaving without more leverage."

"You touch her and I'll fucking kill you," Trey shouted, managing to get a good elbow to the gut of the guy on his left.

"How adorable," she taunted. "Shut him up, Cam. But be careful not to kill him, okay? He needs to be alive for what I have planned," she added.

Claudia stayed glued against the wall, until she could come up with a plan. As the "girl" in question, she had no intention of being grabbed. She felt pretty confident these three were the only other people in the store. Most likely, they hadn't predicted Trey would give them so much trouble, thus tying up both of this woman's brute muscle.

If she could just get a jump on her, it should give Trey

enough time to overtake at least one of the guys, then she could shoot the other.

One guy elbowed Trey hard in the kidneys and the other punched him in the gut, causing him to cry out, sending a jolt of empathetic pain through Claudia's heart.

"That's better," the woman stated, stepping out of the shadows to reveal herself. She was about thirty years old, blonde, buxom, and quite striking. In fact, she bore a striking resemblance to Jenna, and the realization made Claudia want to vomit.

"Go find the girl, Hugo. I'm getting bored," the strange woman continued. Claudia exhaled heavily to see Hugo head toward the other end of the store, leaving her with just Cam and the woman to deal with.

The blonde stood over Trey, as Cam held him down by the shoulders. She reached down to snatch Trey's burner phone.

"You won't be needing this anymore," she stated, removing the battery deftly. "I can't have that prick Stephen finding you, can I?" She lifted her head and shouted, "Hugo, what's taking you so long?"

"I can't find her, Lex."

"Idiot," she muttered. So this was Lexis... Lexis didn't appear to have a weapon on her body, but there was a badass illegal *Strike One* handgun resting on a box closely within her reach.

Claudia swallowed hard at the confirmation Trey was currently at the mercy of his very dangerous fixation — Lexis. Claudia wanted desperately to shoot her down, but the tall bitch was standing too close to Trey. Any shot at this close of a range could likely harm him, too, while also not disposing of Cam.

Instead, Claudia turned the pistol in her hands so the butt end was up. She threw the button as far as she could. Cam and

Lexis both turned toward the sound for a moment — just long enough for Claudia to sprint forward and land a perfect spin kick against Lexis's back, knocking her over, as well as the box on which her *Strike One* rested, sending it sliding several feet from them.

"You fucking cunt!" Lexis shrieked.

Claudia managed to get in a good whack of her pistol, with the butt end, against the side of Lexis's head, but it wasn't positioned well enough to knock her out.

Lexis grabbed for Claudia's ponytail with one hand, backhanding her powerfully with the other. Claudia tasted the metallic sting of blood in her mouth, and realized what Lexis lacked in trained fighting skills, she made up for in sheer mania and dirty tricks.

The element of surprise had worked well enough to allow Trey to head-butt Cam and free himself. She could hear Hugo's heavy footfalls as he ran to them. Claudia rolled forward and kicked Lexis off her, just in time to spin her pistol around and shoot Hugo in the knee mere yards before he could reach them.

Cam was on his knees, preparing to lunge at Trey. Claudia noticed the can of *Mace* on the floor near her head.

"Trey, coming at you," she yelled, rolling it across the floor to him. Trey grabbed the can, then spraying its contents on Cam's unprepared face. The thug's agonized cry in response was a lovely symphony for her ears, as was the sound of Trey punching him again. She turned back to Lexis, positioning her pistol to take her out.

Lexis dove for Claudia, grabbing her wrist. The impact forced Claudia to discharge her weapon impotently across the room. Furious, Claudia kicked hard into Lexis's stomach, throwing the bitch off.

Lexis turned back, with the *Strike One* in her hand, which

she'd apparently managed to grab at some point after Claudia had thrown her on her ass.

They both quickly aimed straight at the other's head. The blonde held a healthy amount of respectful hatred in her eyes. Claudia spit a mouthful of blood on the floor, and threw Lexis a cocky grin.

Lexis's hesitance confirmed Claudia's suspicion she would rather not kill her just yet. If she had plans for Trey, Lexis probably had some for her as well, which meant Claudia could still take her down.

Lexis took off the safety and Claudia moved to squeeze her trigger in response, when suddenly Trey screamed, "A.J., no!"

Shock stilled Claudia's finger.

"A.J.?" she stammered out, turning toward Trey for a split second, when she felt a hard force come down on the base of her skull, and everything went black.

CHAPTER EIGHTEEN

"Claudia..." Trey whispered through the darkness surrounding him, hoping he wouldn't attract the wrong kind of attention.

Trey was woozy but he could remember A.J. using a syringe to drug him. She'd been smart to do so, because Trey was pretty eager to kill them *all* after seeing "Cam" clock Claudia from behind. It had been a pretty impressive feat, considering Trey had just blasted him in *Mace*.

He'd been so proud of how Claudia had handled the situation. Yet, it was the monsters from his past, and his own inability to stay quiet in the present, which ultimately put her in peril. This recognition left him with a blistering and acute sense of misery and failure.

Trey had come to for long enough to register Cam had dragged him out of his *Mercedes*, in front of another mountain cabin. He had no idea how far it may be from his own, or from the gas station where they'd been taken. With addled senses, he'd registered Cam restraining his hands and legs in a pitch-black room, before Trey gave into the darkness again. Now, he was fully awake, with a pounding headache and a frantic need to know Claudia was alive.

"Little one…are you there? Can you hear me?" He presumed Claudia had been in the A.J.'s team's car, but he held out hope she may have chosen to lock Claudia up with him.

"Oh good, you're up, sleepyhead," Trey heard a familiar, but unwelcome, female voice, declare to him through the blackness.

"Hello, A.J." he growled, biting every syllable as it left his dry mouth.

Bright lights came on, blinding him for a moment. He tried to move, but realized through the fog of his addled brain that he was restrained.

His eyes focused slowly through the thundering pain in his head. Eventually, he could discern A.J. standing over him imperiously.

In spite of her familiar face, so much about her was foreign and strange, including her clothing. She wore black leather pants and a tight leather vest. She displayed none of the sweet innocence, which used to soften her hard edges. Even so, her light blue eyes were a surreal reminder of the young woman he had once known, and believed he loved.

"Hello, to you, too, *lover*," she cooed. The words turned his stomach, but he resisted the urge to grant her the pleasure of showing how her actions had hurt him.

Instead Trey waited for his eyes to adjust to the light, then glanced around quickly, desperate for any sign of Claudia. She was nowhere to be found.

"Why do you look so worried?" she asked coyly. "Oh, because I'm not your sweet 'little one'?" A.J. cupped her cheek, working her jaw back and forth. "Though she's not that nice, and the bruise she gave me won't be that little. It's okay. I'll make it up to her soon enough."

"Leave Claudia out of this. You wanted me. Now you've got me. Kill me if you have to, just let her go."

A.J. laughed before moving closer to him.

"You still don't get it. I could've killed you fifty times over the years."

A.J. checked on the tightness of his ropes. Trey jerked back at the sight of old, deep scars across her chest and upper arms, leading to her neck. They were jagged, as if made with a dull serrated knife, and he felt bile in his mouth.

She caught him looking at the evidence of her wounds and yanked the ropes on his hands hard enough to send shooting pain through his back and shoulders.

"How dare you feel sorry for me, you son of a bitch? You lost that right when you left me with those bastards — the ones who gave these scars to me." She released his tethers, providing a brief moment of relief. "I hope you took a good look. You let your dad's fucking money save you," she continued, standing and walking around him in a tight, threatening circle. "While you left me there to rot. Being smart only gets you so far. At some point they use you like all their other pretty little girls. Do you know what that feels like, Trey?" she sneered.

"I tried to find you. I spent so much of my life trying to figure out who did this to you."

"Aren't you such a hero? Well, let's put that to the test, shall we? Cam, bring her out."

Trey's throat clenched, torn between wanting to see Claudia and afraid at what A.J. may do to her.

Cam quickly dragged Claudia into the room. Her hands were tied, but she was struggling against him, and it filled Trey with satisfaction to see just how much of a challenge she was for the large guy.

"Have a seat, Agent McCoy," A.J. stated, before Cam pushed Claudia into the chair and held her down by her shoulders.

"Where's the salesgirl? Did you hurt her?" Claudia demanded immediately.

"How adorable of you to care, because you have a lot more serious things to care about, trust me," A.J. replied, eventually releasing a sigh. "She'll be fine. She's blindfolded and locked up in a back room of the gas station. Her boss will find her soon enough. She never saw us and we aren't on the cameras, so I won't have to kill her. No matter what you may think, I'm not a monster. Not like your boyfriend here. Any other questions?" she added, stroking a finger across Claudia's cheek, until she jerked away.

"Yeah, how's your head? It would be a shame if I smeared your makeup when I kicked your ass," Claudia spat out.

"I see why you like her, Trey, she's quite sassy," A.J. stated, her words dripping with sarcasm. With a more even tone, she added, "It's good to see Trey still has good taste in women."

"Not always, it appears," Claudia bit out.

"How'd you ever make it to twenty-three years old, Agent McCoy? Because you really have no idea when to shut up."

A.J. quickly slapped Claudia hard across the face, eliciting a bright line of red down her bottom lip.

"Damn it, A.J., end this now."

"Why? I've only just gotten started," A.J. taunted, as she stood in front of Claudia, arms crossed over her chest. "You looked so surprised when Trey called me A.J. It's short for Alexis Jane. Though as you probably guessed, no one but your failure of a caretaker, Trey here, calls me that anymore. *He* didn't seem too shocked to see me. I was always pretty sure he suspected I'm Lexis." A.J. smirked as she stared at Trey. "I guess I was right, huh, Trey?"

Trey tried to keep his face even, but the pain Claudia tried to hide from her eyes proved to him he'd failed.

"Just as I thought," A.J. continued, smiling at Claudia. "And he must not have shared that little tidbit with you, *little one.* Looks like he's still pulling the same crap he did with me — keeping secrets from others for their own good." Claudia glared at her in response. "Trey, I can't help but be amused... I mean, if you'd been honest with her from the beginning, then you two might have found me first, and you wouldn't be in this predicament." A.J. smirked and added, "Agent McCoy, a word of advice from one woman to another, you're going to find you'd have been better off without him."

A.J. turned and stepped away from them, giving Trey a chance to whisper, "I'm so sorry, Claudia. I'll fix this."

Spinning around to face them again, A.J. said, "Don't you remember, Trey? It's not nice to lie to a lady." She moved to stand over Claudia, "The truth is, you aren't going to be okay at all, you tiny brat. Okay, I'm ready Cam."

He stepped back, relinquishing his hold on Claudia so A.J. could grab Claudia's arm and heave her off the chair.

"Stop it!" Trey commanded.

Claudia met his eyes, allowing him to see the raw determination in her gaze. She wasn't going to give A.J. an inch, and he loved her that much more.

"Trey, do you know there's another name for your girl's condition? It's called: 'insulin dependent diabetes.'" That A.J. knew this about Claudia sent an icy chill through him, but he tried to remain silent. "Do you understand what that means? Tell him, Claudia." Claudia set her jaw firmly and refused to respond. In return, A.J. squeezed the sides of Claudia's face until her lips looked like a duck's bill, turning her head to force her to look at Trey. "*Tell him!*"

"It means I need to take insulin to live," Claudia finally spit out, letting strength and rage fill her eyes.

"That's technically true. But I prefer to view it as meaning — if you don't receive insulin, then...you die," A.J. added, with a pout, releasing Claudia's cheeks to softly stroke the length of her face, then running her fingers through her thick, dark hair, until Claudia twisted her head away as best she could. A.J. jerked Claudia's head back to face her. Running her hands down the length of Claudia's side, A.J. cooed, "This dress is quite lovely, but I need to get to what's beneath it. Cam..."

Cam handed A.J. a knife, and Trey pulled so hard on his ropes, he almost knocked over his chair.

Claudia fought against A.J.'s hold, until Cam held a gun to Trey's head, causing her to still obediently.

"A.J., stop. You've got me, don't punish her," Trey growled.

"But where is the fun in that, Trey?" she queried, holding Claudia's dress in place so she could slice down its front, leaving it in black scraps around her.

The sight of Claudia in nothing but her underwear, insulin pump still tucked in her bra, filled him with nauseating fury. A.J. handed the knife back to Cam, before stating, "You never cared enough about yourself, it won't bother you one bit to die. Watching *this one* suffer a slow and painful end? Now that will break you like you let them break me. Because, guess what? Modern medicine really is amazing, but it doesn't stand a chance against me."

She yanked Claudia hard against the length of her body, forcing Trey to watch as she slid her hand down Claudia's bare, slim waist. Settling on the part of her skin where her pump was connected, A.J. stroked it gently.

A.J. stared into Trey's eyes for a beat then suddenly yanked the needle from Claudia's body, making her scream out in agony.

A.J. slid the pump from Claudia's bra and threw it hard on the floor, stepping on it firmly with the stiletto heel of her leather boot, until it broke under the force.

"Oh no, look what I've done," she crowed, tossing Claudia's still bent over body to Cam. "How long do you think your little one has? As long as you thought I had when you let them take me?"

Trey tugged at his restraints. "Damn it, A.J. You've got it all wrong… I did all I could to save you."

"Such a shame then, isn't it, Trey? Because it looks like you're always destined to let down the girls you love. Take her to her room, Cam."

Trey felt like he was suffocating. The rage coursing through his bloodstream was all consuming, yet also completely pointless.

After Cam hauled Claudia away, a tall, dark-skinned man whom Trey had never seen before arrived to help Cam drag him to a simple room. It was decorated only with a twin bed, a chair, and multiple monitors on a desk.

He'd been by himself for half an hour, desperately trying to find a way out of his glorified cell, and to Claudia. Yet, even though they'd untied his hands to allow him to retain feeling in his arms, they'd then proceeded to chain him by an ankle to a steel loop secured into the floor. Trey had pulled at it repeatedly, but it was no use.

Every area of the cabin he'd been through so far had been rustic, and he couldn't hear any street noise. Despite the apparent isolation of their location, he believed if he could just get them out before the lack of insulin incapacitated Claudia, they might be able to find help.

Just when he started to peer at each monitor for any kind of components he could use in their escape, the door opened. A.J. and this new *third* asshole entered. He was elegantly dressed in slacks and a long-sleeved cashmere sweater — a far cry from the jeans and sweatshirts of the other two ogres she'd brought.

"Hello again," she said cheerfully, then turning to lean back against the desk. "You really kept me guessing there for a bit. I knew you were sweet on that fed in there, but to run off with her to keep her safe? Now *that*, I didn't see coming. If you weren't so gorgeous, I might never have tracked you two down."

"What?"

"The gas station clerk your girlfriend is so worried about? She took a picture of you a couple days ago, posted it on *Facebook*, telling her friends all about the mysterious stud, who wandered into her store. Don't you just love facial recognition software? So, it took a little more work than I imagined, but here you two are."

"Lucky us," he muttered, as he narrowed his eyes.

"Humph," she grunted. "Well, I hope you like your room. I believe you met Louis earlier."

"We weren't formally introduced. He was too busy shackling me," Trey groused.

"Oh well, Louis is all business, what can I say?"

"Say what you expect me to do, so I can get Claudia out of here, and to medical attention."

"Just watch."

A.J. turned on two of the monitors, each showing Claudia in her cell from multiple angles. She had a tray of untouched food on a table next to her and was seated in a chair.

"Look at her trying to delay the rise of her blood sugar — staying calm and refusing food. She's a stubborn bitch."

Trey smiled, in spite of himself — ever amazed at just how

tough Claudia could be.

"But she *does* need insulin," she taunted in a singsong tone. "Without it, her blood glucose will skyrocket. At first she'll become thirsty and tired, until she can no longer fight the need to sleep. Soon after, diabetic ketoacidosis will begin, leading to pain, nausea, hallucinations, coma, and finally, *death*. And you are going to watch it all from here…unless..."

"Unless what?"

She took out an old-looking pistol and placed it on the table next to her. "Does this look familiar? It's the Russian *Tokarev TT-30* those fuckers shot me with back at *Stanford*. Do you remember now, Theodore?"

"Theodore…" he muttered, "no one calls me that…"

"But your mom? I only just found out Theodore used to be your name before your dad changed it. Some knowledge is even beyond me."

"How…"

A.J. flicked another monitor on, this one displaying his mother in a posh hotel room somewhere, clearly terrified. Two men were in her room, standing guard over her.

"Oh, your mom, Abigail, was nice enough to refer to you by your birth name at the hotel we deposited her into today. I supposed she never accepted your father exercising his will in such a petulant way once he got her out of the way. You Adler men are all the same — domineering little fucks, thinking you know what's best for everyone. Enough about that, though…because the thing is, Abigail really *does* like sexy, young men. A couple weeks ago, one of my operatives connected with her — seducing older women for me is kind of his specialty."

Trey's heart leapt at this news. He and Stephen had managed to turn an operative from A.J.'s team named Colin recently. They'd used his desire to protect his first love — a young woman named Feng Huang, whom Stephen had strategically recruited to become a secret agent for his team — from being a Lexis target, as incentive to help them.

Colin was A.J.'s go-to guy for using romance to steal information. If he was involved with abducting Trey's mother, then maybe Trey had this situation under control, after all.

Yet, Trey's hopes sunk just as quickly, when he remembered Colin and Feng were in Vietnam, far away from his mother's torment.

"But that's not all," she crowed, turning on the last two monitors. These revealed multiple angles of Althea and Griffen's house, with one frame showing Johnny sleeping peacefully in his bed.

"What the fuck, A.J.!"

"I know. It's a shame I have to threaten such a sweet boy, not to mention that pretty mother of his and her handsome fiancé. What are their names, Tea and Griffen, right? They make such a perfect picture of a family, and I know they mean the world to you. What with you playing at nice-guy uncle, and all."

"What in the ever-loving fuck are you even thinking, A.J.?"

"Hey, calm down. I don't *want* to do any of this," she assured him, her voice filled with passion. "But it's necessary."

"How in the hell could threatening all these people…a fucking child…ever be necessary?"

Her brow furrowed in honest confusion at his denseness, "It's simple. I need to force you to finally make a choice. Just like I had to."

"A choice?"

"Life is just a series of choices, Trey. Each one creates the path we must follow. When you left me for dead with those Russian bastards, I had to decide — do I mimic who they are? Become like them and steal their nest…or do I die? You'd be amazed what paths you're capable of following when the whole world — all your hopes and everything you've believed in — all desert you."

"I *didn't* leave you for dead."

Disgust made her face look like she'd smelled something foul. "You didn't? But *you* were rescued," she challenged. "*You* refused to give them the virus they wanted. Which left me for them to torture, and use — for whatever my body or mind could get them. And when you did finally track me down, you had the nerve to try and fuck with all I've worked so hard to build."

"A criminal empire? Good for you," he retorted, his voice heavy with disdain.

"I did what I had to do. But you've been able to live comfortable as hell, right on that gray line. Keeping our Starling virus small…helping the fucking FBI all these months... Well, I'm putting an end to your privileged way of life, now."

She lined up three insulin vials and a hypodermic syringe on the table, next to a cell phone.

"The insulin is from the cooler bag in your own duffel, actually. I think that's pretty adorable — how you try so hard to look after your little bird with her broken wing…just charming. I can use the syringe for Agent McCoy, or the cell phone…for everyone else."

A.J. met his eyes and calmly continued, "You just need to choose: Claudia, *or* your mother and that happy family over there. It's up to you. Your sweet little *one*, or four innocent lives. Once you have to make that call, then maybe you can understand what you *truly* did to me…the harm you caused."

Trey lunged for her, but the chain stopped him short right before his hands could reach her throat. Louis's solid fist connected with the side of Trey's face, dropping him hard on the floor. His head bounced comically against the wood, sending waves of pain through his skull and neck.

Pushing himself up, he looked at the five monitors, his heart hurting far more than the throbbing in his head.

"I was right when I told Claudia you were dead," he growled. "Because nothing good that was in you from before is still alive."

"And whose fault is that?" she screamed as she stood over him, snatching the pistol from the table and holding it to his head, before breathing deeply and composing herself.

"You want to kill me? Then fucking do it. I'll give you all my money, my life…just let everyone go."

"That wouldn't accomplish anything, because you don't give a shit about yourself. I needed you to care about someone else for this to work. Unfortunately, you've managed to live a pretty lonely and depressing life this past decade, and your dad still remains too elusive for me to capture," she mused.

"My apologies," he sneered.

"Do you know how long I had to wait? I killed that Irish girl, Maura, but it wasn't enough. You didn't really love her. Oh, but now... You're crazy over this girl in there…but are you willing to let four other people who matter to you die because of it? Are you ready to be responsible for that innocent boy's death?"

"You're fucking nuts. You're beyond evil."

"Quit your whining and deal with the situation you created."

"What if I won't choose?"

"Then I drop a fucking atom bomb on your life, and get rid of them all," she spit out. "You don't *get* to make the rules this time. You need to feel the pain you cause, because you've never saved anyone — all you've ever done is destroy them."

She tucked the *Tokarev* pistol back in the waist of her leather pants and led Louis to the door.

"I'll leave you to think about your decision, Trey. But don't take too much time. Claudia doesn't have any to spare."

CHAPTER NINETEEN

Hours after the pain of having her pump yanked from her body had subsided, Claudia was still reeling from the discovery Lexis was, in fact, Trey's first love — and his greatest shame — A.J.

The knowledge Trey had kept that suspicion from her, made it all the more disturbing. As she tenaciously searched for possible escape routes from her room, or potential weapons, her brain continually veered back to the grotesque sound of that woman's name on Trey's lips.

Yet, she didn't have the luxury of wallowing in the hurt, disappointment, or anger resulting from his most agonizing omission to date. There was too much to do, and in light of her rapidly increasing symptoms of insulin deprivation, Claudia knew she was in a race against the clock.

The fact she'd eaten so little during the day meant she'd started with low blood sugar, but this only bought her a few extra hours. Her limbs were already heavy, her mouth dry, and head swimming. She hadn't gone this long without any source of insulin since she was a child. That time it took a hospital to save her life. If she couldn't escape A.J.'s improvised prison, it would be the end of her.

Unable to escape through force, Claudia had transitioned to using her mind — trying to make sense of A.J.'s actions. Sure, she was bitter and vengeful, but she was also far too smart and ambitious to risk her entire business just for the cheap thrill of forcing Trey to watch Claudia die.

No...there had to be more to it.

If A.J. only wanted to torment her ex-boyfriend, she could've just stabbed Claudia in front of Trey, while she stood there half naked. The memory of that exposure still made Claudia blush with frustration and shame, but she knew it was simply part of A.J.'s process.

A.J. had clearly planned and orchestrated every aspect of this experience — from her flamboyant show of cutting off Claudia's dress in front of Trey, only to leave her a luxurious spa robe in her room, to the well-placed cameras and sugary foods lining that same space.

She could've stuck Claudia's arm with a glucose drip, bringing on the deadly effects of hyperglycemia in a much faster manner, but she didn't.

It was clear Claudia was just a pawn in A.J.'s contrivance to torment Trey as much as possible, and apparently Claudia dying right away just would not do.

A.J. had already framed Trey, potentially ruining his life. Killing Claudia would've hurt him, surely, but something Trey had said came back to her. He'd informed her of a tidbit of great value — A.J. always wanted "more."

There had to be more to *this*, too.

Her business operations showed she and her people liked to feel good about what they did. Perhaps this was a form of divine justice?

Which meant there was a lesson she wanted Trey to learn. If Claudia could discern what it was, then maybe she could thwart it.

A knock on the door brought Claudia to attention. She clumsily pulled the robe tighter around her body.

"Come in," she answered.

A handsome African American man she didn't recognize walked in with a large plastic cup of orange juice.

Claudia smirked. A.J. was right not to trust her with glass.

"I guess I should thank you for being polite enough to knock. What's your name?" she inquired sweetly, curious to see if she could make some diplomatic headway with him. The other two guys, Cam and Hugo, were worthless to her — clearly too comfortable with the darkest parts of A.J.'s business to worry about her current maniacal pursuit.

Yet, Claudia knew she wouldn't have too much longer with her wits fully about her, and this guy could be her last shot.

"Louis," he responded, his voice lilting with a posh English accent.

"Should I presume your gentlemanly behavior is related to a proper British upbringing?" Claudia queried, crossing her ankles and putting on her most innocent expression.

"No, I'm just trying to be professional."

"That's a pleasant change, because you must've noticed this operation doesn't appear to be too professionally motivated."

His eyes flashed for a split second with what looked like agreement, but he quickly schooled his face back into a cool mask.

"If I get someone's name for a job, it means they deserve what they get."

"Maybe most of the time. I've seen the files of your team's

previous marks. You've definitely given some very bad guys some well-earned comeuppance. I wish I could do what you've done to some of the bastards I've come across."

"I thought federal agents were all by the book?"

"Just because I took an oath doesn't mean I don't hate it when people get away with terrible things. I bet sometimes you've done the world a real favor." Claudia stood and took the juice from him, before adding, "Are you hungry? I have plenty to eat. I'm just not feeling too well, you know. I've been nauseated and my body is aching from the hyperglycemia…but I would hate to be a bad hostess."

"No thank you, Agent McCoy," he responded, slipping into respectful formality.

"Oh, call me Claudia. If I'm going to die here, we might as well be on a first name basis, *Louis*."

He swallowed and looked away from her.

"Louis, just so you know, I don't deserve this. If you've heard anything about why your boss brought us here, then you know I don't, and neither does Trey. This is her vendetta, and it's going to threaten all you've worked so hard to build with this team."

"That's not my call."

"It should be, if you ask me," she retorted, sitting back down, the juice still in her hand.

"I know what you're trying to do, *Claudia*."

"What's that? Call it like I see it? You know there is no value to you in watching me slowly slip into a coma… And think what you will of the American FBI, but your team is going to gain some very unwelcome attention when my murder is discovered. The kind of attention that can be quite career-limiting for a talented man like yourself."

Claudia knew she was laying it on thick, and she prayed her educated guess that the cameras were a video feed, without any audio, was correct.

"You won't have to die if that guy over there chooses you over those other people."

"What other people?"

"I better go. Enjoy your juice," he muttered, leaving the room quickly.

Claudia sighed. All she could do was hope the seed she planted could sprout quickly enough to make a difference.

She also was curious who the other people were. It couldn't be Jenna and Wyatt. They were safe. Someone else Trey cared about? The list of people was short, and she tried to run it through her mind, but everything was just so fuzzy.

The stress of the conversation had taken a toll, simultaneously draining her last bit of energy while also encouraging her body to shoot another toxic jolt of glucose into her bloodstream.

With leaden legs, she moved to the bathroom sink and dumped out the sugary orange juice and filled the cup with tap water, her eyes never wavering from the camera on the wall above her. She peed for about the umpteenth time, aware it was a sign her body was trying to rid itself of excess blood glucose any way it could. She finally washed her hands, and took a deep swig of water.

Resting her hand along the wall to support her, Claudia returned to the main room.

She placed the cup on the table, yet it landed on nothing, crashing on the floor and spilling water across her bare feet. Disoriented, she moved to sit on the bed, yet her bottom found nothing but the brutal impact of hard wood.

Claudia laughed, the sound was manic, frenzied even, as floating shapes flashed menacingly across her eyes.

The sound of the door opening made her slowly spin

around, but there was no one there.

She realized her mind was not seeing the room as it really was.

Oh no, Claudia thought, pushing down the panic swelling from deep inside her.

It's beginning.

Trey had been surreptitiously tilting his bed forward, so as to wedge the hard end of one of its metal legs into the floorboard to which he was chained, when he watched Claudia fall. He'd been making some progress, finally getting the leverage to lift the board up slightly.

Although the sight of her on the floor had stopped him short, it was the confusion and fear in her eyes that shocked him to his core.

He'd seen her go through a lot of emotions during their time together — anger, love, passion, humor — but terror had never been one of them. Somehow, he'd managed to let his faith in her innate strength and determination lull him into denying how dire her situation truly was.

The lingering light coming through the cracks in the windows was finally waning. Concern washed through him, clouding his ability to process what was the best thing to do next.

Then the wrath from within him came free, and any reason still remaining in him sprouted wings and flew into the wooden rafters above his head. With a feral howl, he stood and pounded his fist on the door repeatedly.

"A.J., I know you're out there, you twisted, sadistic bitch. Get your ass in here. Now! I know you can hear me."

He beat on the door with so much hatred and loathing, it was a shame he couldn't harness its power and free himself with it.

The door swung open, revealing A.J. and Louis on the other side. She looked smug, while his expression was unreadable.

"You rang?" she mocked.

Trey resisted the urge to strangle her, knowing it wouldn't get him anywhere. His breaths were hot and rapid, like a bull ready to run in Pamplona.

"Calm down, Trey. You'll give yourself a heart attack."

He tried to speak through his rage, his hands alternately clenching and relaxing. When he could finally form words, they came out in a sharp staccato.

"If you want me to make a choice, I need to know if you're lying to me, or playing tricks with these cameras."

"You can see the happy family dressed up and having dinner. You know they're still safe. Once they try to leave for the night, we will have to make them aware of the change of plans. I warn you, if you choose to save them, you should do so quickly. I'd hate to traumatize that sweet little boy unnecessarily."

Trey stared at the monitors for a few breaths. No matter how much he wanted to yell at her, he needed more information. He looked back at her.

"Then I want to speak to my mother."

"My pleasure. I would love nothing more than for you to have some more incentive. Louis, hand me my phone."

Louis reached into his pocket, pulling out an *iPhone* for her, which she took from him with a pleasant smile, as though she were about to use it to take a picture of kittens playing in a cardboard box.

"You carry her purse for her, too?" Trey taunted, disgusted with anyone who'd choose to help such an evil creature such as A.J.

"I advise you to watch what you say to me, Mr. Adler," Louis responded, his British accent coming as a surprise to Trey.

"Right, because it's *my words* that are the offensive part of what is happening here today."

"I'd listen to him if I were you, Trey. Louis here is my second in command. You wouldn't want to make him so angry he changes the rules, would you?"

"Congratulations," Trey retorted, turning to Louis. "This must fill you with such pride — watching an innocent, beautiful young woman be tortured for no reason other than being stupid enough to love me. I hope you don't have a soul, like A.J. here, because if you do, it'd be damned."

"Enough with the theatrics, Trey. Do you want to talk to your mother or not?"

"Yes," he growled.

A.J. appeared to pull up a contact, and waited as the phone rang.

"Bryce, I need to speak to the woman. Thanks." She waited a moment and Trey watched as a man appeared on the video feed with his mother and handed her a phone.

A.J. moved to put the phone on speaker, but Louis took the phone from her and handed it to Trey.

"It's his mother, I think you can let him have a little privacy." A.J. looked aghast for a moment. "If you want him to understand the impact of this decision, he needs to be able to really feel it, and us listening in won't do that."

"Fine. Good point. Proceed," she stated, with a slight nod.

Trey glared at A.J. and said, "Mom, are you there?"

"Theodore! Are you okay, my angel? Please tell me you're okay."

"Mom, I'm fine," he lied. "How are you?"

"Oh dear, I don't know what's happening. These people just came to my apartment in Paris and took me to God knows where. Between all the flying and driving, I don't even know what day it is."

"Have they hurt you?"

"No, not yet. I'm just so scared."

"I know, Mom. I am so sorry you have to go through this."

"It's not your fault. I'll be fine. Over the years, I have managed to create some very sticky situations for myself. I am sure it is just a misunderstanding."

His mother's blithe ability to ignore ugly things still amazed him, but in this instance, it filled him with a strong desire to protect her.

"Sure, Mom," he muttered.

"You do need to be careful, though, Theodore. I think this may have something to do with my friend Brian."

"Who's that?"

"I met him a couple weeks ago. He has green eyes and was so charming, but he wanted to know so much about my life. I never told him about you, I swear. But I know he's involved."

"Why?" Trey asked carefully, not wanting A.J. to pick up on the content of his conversation.

"Because he just arrived here. I see him through the French doors in my suite. They have some kind of an office through there."

It had to be Colin, arriving from Vietnam. He would never let them hurt his mother. Trey's heart soared for a moment, but quickly sank at the realization that Althea, Griffen, and Johnny were still in danger. A.J. had provided herself with another layer of insurance. Trey continued to face a horrible choice.

"Mom, I need to go. I don't want to make this any worse for you. Please just stay calm, and do what they say."

"Of course, Theodore. I love you, my sweet angel."

"I love you, too," he answered, feeling his voice break on the last word.

Louis took the phone from him and disconnected the call, before placing it back in his pocket.

"That was touching," A.J. cracked.

"I still need time to think," Trey stated, after collecting himself. "But Claudia may be hurt. She fell hard. I need to see her."

"No way."

He gritted his teeth.

"Then send someone to check on her, at least. I can watch from the monitors to make sure she's not hurt any more than what you've already done to her."

"Fine," A.J. grumbled. "She might as well be comfortable for her last couple hours. Louis, send Hugo to check on her. He hasn't done anything for hours but bitch about his knee and play poker with Cam."

"No, I'll do it. Hugo can try to help Cam get firewood."

"I'll be watching you, Louis. Don't you dare hurt her."

A.J. laughed, clearly amused by his impotent threat, but Louis wasn't so unfazed.

Louis grabbed Trey and pushed him to sit on his bed. Louis crouched on his knees, checking fastidiously to make sure the chain was secure. Trey held his breath, hoping he wouldn't see the progress he'd made easing up the floorboard.

When Louis stood, Trey released his breath. He then allowed the horror of his predicament to sink in again, as the door closed behind A.J. and Louis.

Trey threw his head into his hands, elbows pressing hard into his thighs. His eyes opened slowly, as if he were coming out of a nightmare.

A tiny streak of light glinted off something metallic hidden along the edge of his right foot, and Trey froze.

The gentle touch of a man's hand on her shoulder awakened Claudia.

"Trey, is that you?" she croaked, her breath coming in short, challenging little bursts.

"Yes, it's me, little one," he answered, touching her face. They were in the living room of his Pittsburgh row house, and the warm glow of a sunset was coming through the bay window.

She smiled, overcome with happiness by his presence. Although she wanted to touch him, her arms wouldn't move right, so she continued to lie still on his sofa.

"Why'd you let me sleep so long?" she queried.

"You needed your rest. The storm is over. Do you want to go outside with us?"

"Us? Who's here?"

"Don't you remember? Tea and Griffen brought Johnny over. He wants to play with everyone."

"Oh, good. I know how much you love him. I'm crazy about him, too."

"Of course you are. I don't know what I would do if anything happened to either one of you. It's *so* very important to me both of you are safe."

"What an odd thing to say. You're always so dramatic, Trey," she teased.

"You've got me pegged. Now come with me."

"Okay," she replied, her mouth almost too dry to speak. "Are we going to be together forever now?"

"We will. We can have all of these things. I just need you to hear me. Can you hear me, Claudia?" Trey shouted. As he began shaking her, he faded away from her view. In his place, she saw

Louis leaning over her.

"Louis, what are you doing here? How do you know where Trey lives?"

"Claudia, you're still being held hostage. You're hallucinating. Do you know what is going on?"

"Wait, oh no, that means Trey is still…"

Claudia tried to get up, but her head fell immediately back onto the pillow.

"He's okay. He wanted me to check on you. I wasn't able to come right away." He touched her head with his hand. "You're burning up."

"It's the high blood sugar and dehydration," she muttered, before laughing maniacally. "At least I remembered *that* fun fact," she added.

"I'm sorry I couldn't come sooner… I hunted down some more blankets and pillows for you. I have some cold water, as well. Louis put a glass of water to her lips and helped her sip it.

"I wish you hadn't brought me out of it, Louis. I was in such a lovely place," she whispered, thinking back to Trey's illusory words with whimsical glee.

Then a burst of clarity broke through the fog, and she yanked feebly on Louis's sleeve.

"Louis, you have to tell me. The other people your boss is threatening — are they a family? Do they have a little boy?"

"You shouldn't strain yourself. That's supposed to make it worse."

"There's no stopping it from getting worse, not without insulin and a hospital. Please answer me."

"Yes. They have a little boy," he responded, making her sip more water.

"Louis…I need you to promise me you won't let Trey choose me over them."

"I…"

"*Promise* me… Because I could never live knowing I caused those people to die."

He moved her pillow and looked away from her, before standing to leave.

Claudia snatched at his hand desperately.

"Promise me, Louis."

He paused and met her eyes.

"I promise I won't let him make that choice," he finally answered, before releasing her hand and leaving.

CHAPTER TWENTY

Trey gripped the curved end of the pry bar Louis had hidden for him so tightly, he worried his hand might cramp up, but even that wouldn't have stopped him from trying to get out of his room.

The tool was a little less than eight inches long, which made it small enough for Louis to have presumably hidden it in his sweater sleeve before slipping it under the bed, unnoticed. However, its size also made it difficult to achieve maximum leverage against the floorboard, especially without immediately alerting someone watching him over the video feed to his efforts.

The process was maddeningly slow, but still so much faster than the other methods he'd employed.

He wasn't sure what Louis's objective was in leaving it for him, nor what Trey would do when he got out of the room. For once in his life, he had no clever tricks or plans in place to control the world around him. Instead, he only had faith, and that was going to have to be enough for everyone.

Louis finally appeared in Claudia's room, checking on her as

Trey had asked. It seemed as though it took the guy an eternity to get there, but the look of deep concern on his face as he spoke to her spurred Trey to push with greater force. As if it sensed his urgency, the plank of wood popped up, and he was able to remove it, freeing his leg, as well.

Trey moved the floorboard to his bed. With his back to the cameras, he forced the chain off the board. Stretching the long chain along the length of his leg, he wrapped it once around his waist, and tucked the remainder of it in the pocket of his suit pants.

Althea and Griffen were puttering around the house, gathering items to visit someone, most likely Johnny's grandmother. They were seemingly still unaware of the danger they faced.

Trey moved to the door and made quick work of prying it open. Now that he had full use of his limbs and body, everything was coming more easily to him. Flipping the bar in his hands, he held it like a weapon, carefully moving through the halls of the unfamiliar cabin.

It wouldn't take long for A.J. to notice he'd left the room, but there was no time to wait. He just needed to get to a phone before she did.

He heard a door open around the corner. Plastering his back against the wall, Trey watched Cam exit what appeared to be a bathroom. As he bent over to zip up his fly, Trey hit him hard at the base of the skull. Cam immediately went limp, forcing Trey to grab under his armpits quickly, before he made a crashing noise. Hunching over, he juggled Cam and the pry bar as he walked backward.

After dragging him into the bathroom, Trey slid the pry bar behind the toilet and removed a phone, a semiautomatic handgun, and keys from Cam's pockets, which included one to his *Mercedes*. Apparently Cam thought the sweet ride was a spoil of war. Trey was more than happy to repossess it from him.

The bathroom was equipped with various tools for hostage management, including rope and cable ties, but no insulin. Not willing to take any chances, Trey tied Cam at his wrists and ankles as quickly as he could, and shoved the cable ties in one of his pockets.

His heart pounded so loudly, he thought for sure it would wake the injured beast. Trey dialed Stephen's number, feeling eternally grateful he had it memorized.

"You're calling from an encrypted line. Identify yourself immediately," Stephen demanded crisply, and Trey couldn't help but smile.

"It's Trey."

"Fuck me. Your mother's been taken. Colin's with her, but we haven't made a move yet."

"Good. You should be able to now. Do you have all your usual capabilities?"

"I'm with Feng and the rest of my team at your war room in Pittsburgh. We might as well be at *NORAD*. I'm putting you on speaker."

"Perfect. But we have to make this quick. Get a detail to Griffen Tate's house. It's surrounded by several of Lexis's men. Griffen and his family have no idea anyone is outside — but they're about to leave and that means all hell will break loose."

Trey knew he'd have to share with Stephen exactly who Lexis was, and what she represented to him at one time in his life, but that would have to wait.

"The team that protected Jenna Sutherland's home is nearby. Consider it done," Stephen assured him.

"Also, have someone go ahead and acquire FBI agent Drew Jaworski, from the Pittsburgh field office. If he's really a Lexis mole, we can't keep delaying while we look for evidence against him. It's too risky."

"Damn," Stephen cursed. "That'll ruffle some feathers."

"I don't care if you have to pluck the whole goddamn bird, pick him up."

"You got it."

"And I need a medically-equipped helicopter sent my way. Now."

"Medical? Are you hurt?"

"Claudia's very sick. She needs insulin and treatment for the effects of extreme insulin deprivation. We're somewhere in the mountains outside Pittsburgh. Are you able to locate me through this phone? It belongs to one of Lexis's men, and I don't know what they did to it."

"Donovan, can you do it?" Stephen asked, addressing the question to one of the best hackers on his team.

"I'll make it happen, man. Just be sure to leave this call connected," Donovan added, and Trey let himself breathe for a moment.

"What about you, Trey? Are you secure?"

"No, but I'm working on it," he answered. "Make sure to check in on my dad, too. See you soon."

Trey moved the phone to his back pocket, making sure to leave it connected.

He exited the bathroom and moved toward the sound of voices. One belonged to Louis.

"He's not on the monitor, we need to find him, damn it! Hugo, go get him." A.J. shouted.

"Hugo's on so many painkillers for his knee, he can barely keep from drooling…let me look," Louis responded.

Trey eased around the corner and peered into the kitchen. Syringes were on a counter, giving him the thought the insulin could be in the refrigerator, as recommended on the vials.

"Fine," A.J. grumbled. "He's got to be in the cabin. He hasn't been gone long. When you grab him, meet me at the girl's room. I'm going to call in the order to take down that family, then I'll shoot the girl. I want Adler to *watch* the consequences of his actions. Louis, give me my phone."

"It's in my room."

"What? You never leave it anywhere. Damn it, Louis. What is going on with you right now? Hugo, go get my phone. You should be able to do *that.* Morons," she muttered.

Hugo lumbered out of his chair, his injured leg clearly slowing him down.

Trey ducked into a linen closet behind him until he could hear they all had exited the kitchen.

Slinking back into the hall, Trey followed the sound of Hugo's labored breathing and heavy steps. He caught up to the big guy in no time. Using the butt of Cam's handgun, Trey was able to knock him out before he even got a chance to turn around. After securing him with cable ties and removing his gun, Trey dragged him into a room and closed the door.

A.J. was the only thing left for him to face.

After dumping the second gun behind Louis's bed he ran down the hallway, no longer worried about noise. He moved to the opened door and saw A.J. standing in its frame. Trey held his remaining handgun at the ready.

She turned and raised her gun, perhaps to threaten, maybe to kill, but he didn't care. Fury had made him quick, and he kicked her hard in the stomach, knocking her down. Stepping on her gun, he shoved it out of her reach, and pointed his own handgun straight at her head.

She clutched her stomach in pain on the floor beside Claudia's bed.

Claudia looked tiny, even on the twin bed, her breathing labored, and her skin jaundiced and sickly. The sight filled Trey with such a boiling, fierce rage, it made him wonder if his blood had transmogrified into liquid, sadistic desire — the craving for A.J. to feel pain, to experience *his* vengeance.

"You hate me?" she taunted. "Then you hate yourself, because you did this to me. You ruined me, and you'll ruin her. It's all you know how to do. Killing me won't fix you. Nothing will. You're poison, Trey, and you always will be."

Shame raced through him for a moment, but he shoved it away. This wasn't a woman to be helped or pitied. She wasn't the girl he had loved. A.J. had become Lexis, and she needed to be stopped.

"You wanted me to learn something? Well I did. You were right. We do have to make a choice in life. And this is mine."

Trey pulled back the hammer and squeezed the trigger. The gun was pointed squarely at A.J.'s cruel face, but just as it fired, a strong hand grabbed him, moving his arm so the shot went through A.J.'s shoulder. She passed out quickly, but her life was spared.

He turned, pointing the gun at Louis.

"Why'd you do that? She needed to die! I have to stop her!"

Louis placed his hand on the gun, moving it, so its nose pointed at the floor.

"You're not a killer," Louis answered smoothly. "And if you do this, you will never be the same. Trust me…" He then held out his right hand to Trey. It contained a vial of fast-acting insulin, an individually-wrapped alcohol swab, and a syringe. "Besides, you have something much more important to worry about. You need to save your girl."

"Why are you helping us? What do you want from me?"

"I want to be able to look at myself in the mirror and know

this is where I drew the line."

Trey turned to Claudia and his humanity slowly started to return. He replaced the safety on the handgun and slipped it into his waistband, before grabbing the items from Louis.

He then pulled the keys out of his pocket. Removing the *Mercedes* key, he handed it to Louis. "The *Mercedes* is yours. A chopper will be here any minute. Are you able to get out of here fast?"

"Yes, I collected what I need before I visited Agent McCoy one last time."

"Good, then you'd better go, but if you ever need anything, you find me."

"Take care of her," Louis responded, before shaking Trey's hand. He ran out of the room, disappearing from sight.

As soon as Trey restrained A.J., he sat beside Claudia on the bed. Filling the syringe with insulin, he moved the sheet covering her. He'd watched *YouTube* videos on how to do this when he learned of her condition, but he'd never actually done it. Swallowing hard, he opened her robe to reveal her legs.

She didn't respond to his touch and he feared the worst. He didn't know what a coma looked like, but he really hoped this wasn't it.

"Please just be asleep. Then you can wake up. I love you. I love you," he repeated over and over again, as he swiped the alcohol swab over her skin, inserted the needle into the subcutaneous layer of her thigh.

Once the injection was complete, he replaced the cover on the syringe and laid it beside her bed. Placing one arm behind her neck, and the other under her knees, he rose. Carrying her out of the room, he made it to the front door, unlocked it, and walked outside.

It was such a mundane and routine task — leaving a home,

but nothing was simple anymore, at least not for them.

The sound of an approaching helicopter filled the air, but Claudia did not awaken. Its force caused the trees around him to shake, and filled his nostrils with the cleansing sensation of fresh mountain air.

The sound of the chopper's blades slicing through the air grew to a crescendo. It was a sound more beautiful than a choir of angels, but Trey couldn't feel peace.

His heart was breaking with every moment Claudia remained asleep. Several drops of water fell on her face, and it took a moment for him to realize it was his own tears.

Squeezing her frail form to his front, Trey buried his face in her hair as the helicopter touched down.

"Come back, little one. Please, come back," he pleaded. "I'll never let you be hurt again. Never. I'm so sorry."

A soft humming sound whirred into Claudia's ears, gently spurring her awake. She willed her eyes to open, though her eyelids felt as heavy as cement. The stark white of an unfamiliar room greeted her. She tried to move her hand and rub her face, but the sting of a needle in her hand and the attached tube stopped her.

"Careful, you don't want to pull out your IV," a man's voice said, sending a jolt of panic through her.

Claudia sat up quickly, but immediately became woozy and leaned back against a pillow.

"Easy there. It's okay. I'm Trey's friend, Stephen. You're in a hospital in Pittsburgh. You arrived by chopper about twenty-four hours ago."

"Oh no, that means… Oh God, what did they do to Johnny?

Tea and Griffen?"

"Don't worry, they're okay. Trey took care of all of that. He saved them. I suspect he had a little help, but you know how he loves his secrets."

Claudia laughed dryly, taking a moment to register the many machines surrounding her, as well as to examine the shockingly good-looking Asian man in front of her.

He appeared to be about thirty-five, and of Chinese heritage, although he had an American accent. Despite being shorter than Trey, he was clearly lean and muscular under his black cashmere sweater, and expensive slacks. His eyes were nearly black, and appeared to be almost unnervingly perceptive.

"It's nice to finally meet you, Agent McCoy," he continued, a small smile on his lips.

"You can call me Claudia."

"You're one lucky lady, Claudia. The doctors assure us you won't have any permanent damage."

"I guess my Irish half is worth something, after all," Claudia joked.

Stephen laughed, and she noticed he had a killer smile.

"Trey got you out just in time, but you will need to rest and take a short leave from work," Stephen said.

"What about Trey, is he okay?"

"Physically and legally. When we captured Lexis and her two thugs, we were able to clear him of David's murder."

Claudia raised her eyebrows at his reference to only "two" henchmen, but she kept her mouth shut. If Trey needed to protect Louis, then she would, too.

"The FBI wasn't too threatened by a CIA man poking into their case?"

"I'm not really into labels, and besides, I don't let those jokers at the Bureau bother me. No offense."

"None taken. I'm pretty disillusioned with them myself. Seeing as I may not have a job with them anymore… What did you mean when you said Trey is 'physically' okay?"

Stephen opened his mouth to answer, when a voice interrupted him from the door.

"You're up!" Trey exclaimed, and her heart almost exploded in her chest.

"I'll let you see for yourself," Stephen answered. He placed a business card under the edge of her sheet. "I believe we're going to need to talk again…soon."

Claudia knitted her brow in confusion, but the sight of Trey walking to her transformed her face into a broad smile.

Trey put down a bottle of iced tea beside her bed and simply stared at her for several moments. His hands were in his pockets and the pain in his eyes was palpable. A few times, he started to speak, but seemed to think better of it. Finally, Claudia broke the silence.

"Thank you for saving me, Trey."

"Anytime," he answered, his voice sounding strange and tight. "How are you feeling?" he continued.

"Pretty sore, like I ran a marathon."

"Your body kind of did," he muttered, still standing stiffly beside her bed.

She moved to touch him, but he grabbed the iced tea bottle again, busying his hands with opening it. "I remembered you like this stuff. I wanted you to have some when you woke up. It's sugar free. Now that you have your glucose all fixed, I want you to make sure to be careful and…"

"Trey…you're rambling," she blurted out, laughing a little, but his frown never budged. He placed the iced tea down again and crossed his arms. "Trey, what's wrong?"

"I was waiting for you to wake up. I wanted to tell you myself that I'm leaving today with Stephen."

"Why? To go where?"

"We're going to hunt down the rest of A.J.'s team. You won't be safe until they're all captured."

"That was *A.J.'s* mission, they won't want me now. And what about *your* safety?"

"That doesn't matter."

"Bullshit. If you won't stay for you, then stay for me. I want you here with me. I *need* you with me."

"I can't be with you. Not now. Not ever."

"What?" she questioned, knowing the word sounded silly, but it was all she could force out of her mouth.

"You need to stay as far away from me as possible."

"You're being ridiculous."

"I destroyed your life, and I almost got you killed."

"You *saved* my life. You *are* my life."

"I can't be. I'll never put you at risk like that again. Some people are just meant to be alone. My dad was, and I am, too. I get that now."

"That's just A.J. talking. It's not true."

"Isn't it? Look at how much I messed up your life. I almost ruined your career."

"Everyone knows you didn't kill David."

"*Now* they do. Stephen and I were able to convince your boss you never knew I was a murder suspect, but that'll be a hard lie to keep up if I stay here with you."

"I don't even know if I want that career anymore, especially not if I have to lose you."

"You don't really mean that. You dreamed of this your whole life. I won't take that from you."

"So you'll take everything else?"

"I need to be responsible for what I caused, and that was putting you in danger."

"I love you too much, Trey. I'm not letting go."

"That's why *I* have to be the one to let go. I'll only hurt you again. Trust that what I am doing is right."

"No! I don't trust you know what is right at all, because there is nothing right about us being apart, you stupid son of a bitch," Claudia pleaded. "I lived twenty-three years in the dark, waiting for you. I didn't even know it was you I was waiting for. Maybe it was the idea of you, but I can't go back to who I was before. She doesn't exist anymore. I lived to find you and love you. And now you want to kill what we can become."

"It's because I love you too much that I have to let you go. I'm poison for you, your career, your dreams."

"*You're* my dream now, you idiot!"

Trey stroked his hand across her face and the slight touch twisted at her insides like a knife.

"You believed in me. Nothing will ever match that for me in my life. But you deserve better…someone who can take care of you. Someone who won't let you get hurt."

Claudia softened her tone, trying to take another tack with him.

"We've both been through a lot over the last few days, Trey. Let's just take a couple days and revisit this then…"

"No. If I do that I'll fall right back into the delusion a life here with you is something I can have. I've been thinking about how strong you are, but your weakness may be me."

"My only weakness is a pancreas, which can't effectively produce insulin," she countered, and Trey's small chuckle in spite of himself gave her a brief moment of hope. "What about Griffen? Johnny? Tea? Jenna?" she added. "They've treated you like family. You can't just leave them."

"Yes. I put them all in danger, too. If I'd been able to open my eyes and see A.J. for who she was years ago, this would never have happened."

Whatever optimism Claudia had experienced in the last minute quickly dissipated. Trey seemed to be both defeated and obstinate, all at once, and the sight of it was infuriating.

"Screw you, Trey. Maybe you're intent on destroying the world you've built here. But we're real people. Not just ones and zeroes. And the only thing you're really going to lose is yourself."

"Maybe, but that's a risk I have to take."

"I guess you're just going to let A.J. win. That woman controlled your life all these years and you're letting her do it all over again. You know what you are? You're a damn coward."

"Even if I am, it's still going to be the best thing that ever happened to you. I need to let you go."

He turned and walked away. At the sight of him leaving, Claudia released a torrent of Spanish curse words and threw the plastic bottle of iced tea as powerfully as she could, in spite of the tube restraining her. It hit the wall nowhere near him, spraying liquid everywhere.

Trey looked at her one last time, his eyes glistening slightly.

"You hate me now, but soon you'll realize I'm doing this because I love you. It has to be this way."

He left, and in his place Claudia heard the approaching sounds of her mother speaking to someone in quick and worried Spanish.

Once again, Claudia was alone in a hospital bed with her mother outside the door in a tizzy. But this time she wasn't a child — she was a grown woman with an aching body and pulverized heart.

CHAPTER TWENTY-ONE

"Abeja, where do you want me to put the oatmeal?"

"With the cereal, Mama," Claudia responded, wincing a little at her mother's use of her nickname.

Her mind wandered back to Trey's cabin, and the sweet moment when he'd watched her save a bumblebee. At the time, she'd been sure the brute force of her own determination would be enough to keep him with her. Yet, she'd been wrong.

That had been over three weeks ago. The empty reminders of her time with Trey continued to plague her, and each of them triggered different forms of melancholy.

Claudia sighed and placed a tote full of groceries on her kitchen table. She attempted to take a bag from her abuela, but received a slap on her hand for her troubles.

"No," the elderly woman added, setting the bag on the kitchen counter. She removed a whole raw chicken, holding it up like a plastic-wrapped trophy. "I will make this for you tomorrow. This will make you feel better," she declared, ending the discussion.

"Thank you," Claudia answered, knowing a battle over food with these two women was one she would never win.

"We'll have this all put away in no time, but then we do have to leave. Go and rest in the living room. You did a lot today," her mother stated, concentrating intently on Claudia's half-empty pantry.

Claudia resisted the urge to roll her eyes. "Mama, I've been resting for weeks now. At some point, I'm going to need to put my own food away."

"Maybe, but that day is not today," her abuela intervened, shuffling Claudia out of the kitchen.

Knowing it was easier to just give in, Claudia complied, overhearing her abuela clucking her tongue from behind her and lamenting, "Ay, Sofia, why does your daughter have so much cereal? It is not food… Pass me the rice…"

Claudia smiled, in spite of her desolate mood. This trip to the store had been one of the few times she'd left the house, other than to meet with the FBI post-trauma counselor, since returning from the hospital.

That didn't mean she was alone, though. Between her mother and abuela's constant visits, and Stephen assigning his beautiful agent, Feng Huang, to check on her daily, Claudia's town house had more foot traffic than a bus depot.

Feng was a Shanghai pop star, which, according to Feng, worked as the perfect cover for her activities as a secret agent on Stephen's task force.

She was certainly skilled at subterfuge, somehow managing to convince Claudia's mama and abuela, they'd become friends through a long distance language partner program the FBI put together. The story was farfetched enough to make it believable — especially when delivered with the force of Feng's seemingly straightforward, guileless charm.

What *was* true was how close a relationship she was developing with the young talented beauty. Feng understood how complicated it was to want success and excitement, but also love, and a future with someone. The way she described her work with Stephen's team, also made Claudia yearn for these same types of challenges, which she'd only found while working with Trey.

Taking advantage of the fleeting moment of privacy, Claudia snuck over to her laptop. Two weeks ago she'd snatched Feng's encrypted phone while she was in the bathroom, and implanted a worm virus she'd created to monitor the private network Stephen had developed for his team.

It had been effectively collecting information relating to Stephen and Trey's efforts to capture the rest of A.J.'s team. Perhaps Trey had kicked her out of his life, but that didn't mean she wouldn't use all at her disposal to monitor his safety.

Claudia gritted her teeth at the data she'd recovered over the last twenty-four hours. For two weeks she'd tracked Trey and Stephen as they zigzagged around the world. Yet, over the last few days, she'd been unable to find any indicators of Trey's whereabouts. She couldn't help but fear for the worst.

Claudia proceeded to manipulate the code on her end to expand the bandwidth of data she would collect directly from Stephen's devices, hoping the resulting information would give her some peace of mind.

Her front doorbell rang, and Claudia completed the modifications swiftly, desperate to avoid any snooping eyes.

"Claudia…" she heard her mother call after a few minutes, spurring her to quickly put her computer to sleep.

"Yes, Mama," she answered, moving to stand beside the sofa.

Her mother looked at her with a large smile and flushed cheeks, which highlighted her already lovely face.

"Are you all right, Mama?"

"Your friend, Feng Huang, is here," she answered, skittering around the room to fluff pillows and straighten the magazines on the coffee table.

"What else is new? She's here every day," Claudia pointed out, though her mother's attitude had Claudia's curiosity piqued.

"She brought someone with her, and let me just say… Ay dios mio, el hombre es muy guapo."

"Mama!" Claudia exclaimed, laughing and wondering what man could elicit such a response from her mother. The woman was still stunning, as her successful reinvented modeling career attested, but as far as Claudia knew, her mother had lived like a nun since her father left.

"He's far too old for you," her mother stated, "but he sure is something. I think I may be sweating. Do I look shiny to you? How embarrassing."

"You look beautiful, as always. Does this mean you're staying for a while longer?" Claudia teased.

"No, no. That would be silly. I'll let you talk to them. You *will* go to Wy and Jenna's house for the last *ESPN* taping, right? Wyatt is insisting on everyone being there."

Terror at rejoining the world seeped in for a moment, but Claudia knew she couldn't hide out forever, especially not from something so important to her brother's career.

"Of course. I can't wait," she answered, with a tone that was a bit unconvincing.

Claudia's mother kissed her on the cheek and prepared to leave when Feng walked in followed by a very handsome man in his late fifties. She couldn't see his whole face, but something about him looked remarkably familiar.

He kissed her mother's hand, causing her blush to darken.

"Sofia, it was lovely to meet you. I hope it isn't the last time our paths cross," he crooned. Claudia couldn't hear her mother's reaction, but the smirk on Feng's face assured her it was appropriately giddy.

After the door closed behind her mother and abuela, Claudia moved to welcome her guests.

"Please, come in," Claudia said.

"Thank you. I have someone here who wanted to meet you," Feng responded.

The man reached out a hand to shake Claudia's, and no sooner did she get a good look at his face when she squealed, "You're… My god."

"Hardly."

Claudia giggled like an idiot.

"No, I mean…you're Aldous Adler. I'm pretty sure I'm in heaven. I grew up studying your work. Feng, please stop me before I say something really stupid."

"I think you're doing great," Feng interposed. "I will make some tea while you two have a chance to speak. May I use your electric tea kettle, Claudia?"

"Of course. Thank you."

"Yes, thank you, Feng," he added, before turning back to Claudia. "I agree with her. You are quite an impressive young woman."

"Thank you, Mr. Adler," she answered, feeling her cheeks heat in response.

"Please, call me Aldous, or Aldy, if you prefer. Have a seat," he ordered, and she obediently sat on the sofa. "How are you feeling?" he inquired, inspecting her face with an intensity, which made her slightly nervous.

He was very attractive, with the same dark hair and strong build as his son, but he lacked Trey's distracting beauty — particularly his haunting gray eyes and perfect smile — traits she could only guess came from his mother, Abigail Adler.

Feng had informed Claudia how her secret boyfriend, Colin, had used his position in Lexis's group to rescue Trey's mother. The woman was safe now, if still a little shaken.

Claudia hoped Trey would let Abigail be fully in his life now. It wasn't technically any of Claudia's business, but it had never stopped her before.

"Better," Claudia finally managed to squeak out in response to Aldous's query. "It's been a long few weeks."

"I can only imagine. Made all the worse for facing them without my son, I presume," he added, and Claudia had to bite her lip to keep from crying.

"My dear, I didn't mean to upset you. I came here in the hopes of making you feel better. Ever since Stephen informed me you two had been taken, I have been very worried about how Trey would handle the situation."

"Trey was wonderful," she assured him. "He's a hero."

Aldous smiled with pride, before continuing. "I didn't mean it that way, but thank you. I agree. Trey has always been wonderful in a moment of crisis. It's what he does afterward to hurt himself, which keeps me up at night. Is that what he's done here?"

"I don't know if it was hard for him or not, but he doesn't want to see me again. It hurt me," she whispered.

Aldous held her hand. "I am sure it was the hardest thing he's ever done." He remained silent for a moment, and asked, "Do you know Trey's birth name was actually Theodore?"

"What? Um, no. Now I feel stupid."

"Not at all. Almost no one knows that. His mother insisted on the name. I never liked it, but I'd already been such a dictator on everything else I thought I'd let her have that. After she left us, I couldn't bear the name anymore."

"So you changed it to Trey?"

"Yes. It means the number three."

"Wait, after the 'Rule of Three?'" Claudia asked, excited by the prospect.

"Very clever. Yes. What does it mean to you?"

"It's a rule of thumb that states when the same computer code is used three times it should be extracted into a new procedure…replaced with something else," she answered with the eager desire for approval of a star student.

"Correct. No wonder my son is so taken with you."

Claudia's cheeks warmed, but the bitter disappointment still ate at her throat.

"I'm not so sure of that," she muttered.

"I am," he countered. "The point is, I named him Trey because I wanted him always to remember, you don't have to keep making the same mistake over and over."

"Why are you telling me this?" Claudia asked quietly.

"Because I don't want you to give up on him," he answered, as Feng appeared and set out the teapot and three mugs.

"Thank you, Feng," Claudia whispered, trying not to cry.

"He's right you know," Feng said. "I've watched you all these days, and I know you are blaming yourself."

"How could I not? Trey and I were together and then he decided he doesn't want me."

"He thinks it's for your own good," Feng challenged.

Aldous interjected, "Correct. He blames himself for you being kidnapped and tortured, and doesn't want to risk causing you harm again."

"He isn't the one who harmed me," she lamented.

"I know that, and you know that, but he doesn't see it that way. His actions, and inactions, ultimately led to you being taken, and that's enough for him. It's the same reason he's dumb enough to feel bad I help him when he's in trouble. But I will always do it. And I can't help but guess so will you, whether he knows it or not..."

Claudia thought of how she was attempting to monitor Trey from afar, and blushed at Aldous's strength of perception.

"Of course. I'd do anything for Trey. But I can't make him take me back."

"Can't you?" Feng asked, leaning against an armchair. "Did you tell him to reconsider?"

"I did — at the hospital. I even threw a bottle at him," she added sheepishly, which elicited a smile from Aldous.

"Good girl," he said.

"It was all pretty humiliating. And now, well...even if I knew where he was, I don't know if I could take him rejecting me again," Claudia answered.

Feng released a throaty sound, subtly harrumphing her disapproval, before proceeding to open Claudia's blinds, one after another, before turning to look at her with a sharp expression.

"You Americans. You're so scared of seeming weak, you're willing to risk losing the very thing, which makes you strong."

Feng moved to pour three cups of tea with delicate precision, before distributing them and meeting Claudia's eyes intently.

"You have to fight for what you want in this life. Don't be afraid — or ashamed — to fight for your man. Colin was my first, and only, love. He broke every promise he made me, but I never gave up on him. Once he disappeared, I chased after him for years. I did many things I'm not really proud of, but it was all to protect Colin, and my love for him. It was *all* for the hope of a chance at a life with him. If that's what it took to bring him back to me, I'd do every single part of it all over again...and then some. Sometimes you need to be the one who is brave enough to beg."

"You should listen to her. Forget about the rules, Claudia. And please…enjoy your tea," Aldous instructed, a conspiratorial half smile playing on his lips.

"Claudia, how are you feeling, sweetie? Come in," Tea said, ushering her into Jenna and Wyatt's home.

The sight of so many guests, along with the camera crew and lighting staff, made her feel suddenly shy, but Tea's arm around her shoulders gave her comfort.

She searched her brain for a good answer. Perhaps she should say: *Hanging in there. I finally got Netflix, other than that, I have been dying inside. You?*

Instead, she chose to go with a lie, "I've been doing okay," she stated, also hugging Aubrey when she appeared by her side.

"We wanted so much to come by and see you," Tea continued, "but Wyatt told us how you needed some time alone."

"It's true. I didn't want you all to feel unwelcome, but…"

"Don't explain, we completely understand," Aubrey assured her.

"Have you heard from Trey at all? He won't answer Griffen or Jenna's calls. They are so worried. Johnny misses him, too."

"No, I haven't. I'm sorry," Claudia muttered.

"Don't bum her out, Tea, jeez!" Aubrey exclaimed.

"It's okay, I promise," Claudia answered, smiling slightly.

"No matter what happened, you should know he barely left your side when you were asleep in the hospital. He was so worried about you," Tea assured her.

"Thank you," she answered, suffocating under the weight of how much she missed him.

"May I have your attention, please?" Claudia heard a booming voice announce from Wyatt and Jenna's living room.

"That's the producer," Tea whispered. "We'd better get in there."

"Thank you all for coming, but please remember, this is for all intents and purposes, a 'live set,' so we will need you to be as quiet as possible during this last interview we are taking for our feature on Wyatt McCoy. It will be of Wyatt and Dr. Jenna Sutherland together. I am happy to announce that we will be airing this piece during the Thanksgiving holiday, next week." The room gasped in response. "You can be loud right now if you'd like," the producer joked, and the room erupted in cheers.

When the room fell silent, Claudia watched with rapt attention as Wyatt and Jenna were placed in position and the *ESPN* interviewer, Peter Wilde, sat in a chair angled next to them.

Her heart froze for a moment when Jenna's blonde hair, light blue eyes, and curvaceous figure brought back flashes of A.J. It was shocking how much they looked alike, and for a moment, Claudia thought she might faint.

Forcing the fear away, Claudia reminded herself that experience was long gone. Yet, it also drove home just how painful life must have been for Trey for so many years. If the palest reminder of A.J. could do that to Claudia, what must it have meant for him?

The interview ambled through Wyatt's upbringing, and the ups and downs of his career, culminating in his current undefeated season. Jenna held his hand, and fielded the interviewer's questions posed to her with the ease of a pro.

Claudia's heart swelled with pride at the discussion of Wyatt's involvement in the *NFL's* September celebration of Hispanic heritage. She smiled when Peter addressed Wyatt's insistence on wearing every pink uniform option during October for breast cancer awareness, in honor of its role in Jenna's life. Yet, it was the end of the interview that brought tears to her eyes.

"You turned us down when we first reached out to you, Wyatt. Why was that?" Peter asked.

Wyatt looked at the correspondent with a strong, steady gaze and responded, "Sometimes you have to press the reset button on your life. That's how it was when I met Jenna. I decided to become a better man for her, one who would never let anyone hurt her, including myself. I also refused to let anything interfere with the life I wanted to build with her."

Tears welled in Claudia's eyes. Although Wyatt's words filled her with joy at their happiness, they also drove home just how alone she was now.

"Why did you feel this *ESPN* feature could be a problem?"

"Growing up in the public eye like I did made me very protective of the people I love. After what I put Jenna through, I was intent on doing all I could to shelter what we'd created. I was worried inviting the press into our lives would threaten that."

Claudia felt a pang in her heart, remembering how hard it was for Wyatt after their grandfather died and dad left. He'd wanted to take care of the whole family, though he was still just a teenager himself.

"And what happened to make you change your mind?"

"Well, Jenna has a knack for making me see things her way. She felt this was an important decision we would make as a team — as co-captains of our life together."

"We've been learning that in a relationship it's not who's right or wrong, it's how you sort through things together," Jenna added. "Plus, I bet him I could beat him at a backyard game of flag football."

Peter laughed, and most of the audience needed to stifle a chuckle of their own. "And who won?"

"I did," Jenna answered proudly.

"Yeah, but she plays dirty," Wyatt countered.

"I do not. You held me the whole time when I was on offense!"

"Spoken like a true dirty player. Though I do like to hold her, Peter, I won't lie."

Peter chuckled, and asked, "Wyatt, do you think Jenna has played a role in your winning streak?"

"Absolutely. Since I met Jenna, I've been nothing but a winner. And it's not just on the field. It's in every aspect of my life, and I'm never going to let that go."

Wyatt rose from his seat and pulled a velvet box out of his pocket, before lowering to one knee in front of Jenna. Claudia gasped along with the rest of the room. She'd always wanted Jenna and Wyatt to get married, but for him to do it so publicly, showed just how far he'd come in terms of opening himself to the world. For a moment, all her pain left, as she became overcome with pride for her brother.

Jenna's jaw dropped. She darted her eyes back and forth between Peter and Wyatt.

"Wyatt, what are you doing?" she whispered, with a combination of shyness and glee invading her voice.

Wyatt smirked at Jenna, opening the box to reveal a large princess cut diamond, nestled in the middle of smaller matching diamonds on a platinum band. It was beautiful, but also strong and elegant, just like her.

"Mi belleza, te amo. I wish I spoke a thousand languages, because I would use every one of them to tell you how much I love you. But this is all I know. I'm in front of you today, offering you everything I have — my words, my heart, my life, and my future. Will you marry me?"

Jenna nodded intently.

"Of course, Wyatt, my beautiful, crazy, stubborn man," she answered, taking his face into her hands, and kissing him softly.

When they finally separated, Wyatt grinned and placed the ring on her finger.

For so many years, Claudia's brother had been surly and intense, weighted down by the pressure and resentment lingering after their father left them. Yet, now all of this pain was gone from his face. It was everything Claudia had always wanted for him. No amount of wins on the field, or Claudia pleading with him to relax, ever had any effect. Jenna had done that for him — love was the difference.

"Wyatt, this diamond is huge. How can I wear this on rounds?" Jenna teased.

"Sorry, Doc, everything is bigger in Texas, and I *am* a Texas boy."

They laughed, and Peter finally interposed with a question.

"Jenna, what are you thinking right now?"

"That I am so happy. I mean, what can I say? I guess when a McCoy wants something, they don't give up until they get it."

Claudia felt like a bullet had shot right into her heart. As the production assistants ushered Claudia's mother and Jenna's father onto the set to hug and kiss the happy couple, Claudia knew she needed to fight for her own happiness.

Grabbing Tea, she said, "Please tell Jenna and Wyatt I am so happy for them, but I have to leave, but I'll see them soon."

"Okay," she answered. Tea was clearly confused, but Claudia couldn't wait another moment.

She grabbed a business card from her purse as she rushed to her car and dialed the number. "Stephen? Hello. It's Claudia McCoy. You were right, we *do* need to talk."

CHAPTER TWENTY-TWO

Trey stared across the undulating expanse of the mountain lake outside his cabin, as the sun merged into the edge of the horizon. The image was eerily similar to the manner in which the minutes of his life had blended into the hours, and the hours into days, since he'd left Claudia.

He'd barely even owned the place a month, but when Stephen had instructed him to go home, it was the first destination to come to mind.

After collecting various belongings and projects from his Pittsburgh place, he felt pretty confident he could disappear here long enough for the damage he'd caused to those he loved to subside.

At least when he and Stephen were chasing after the shadows of A.J.'s remaining team members, there was something to keep him occupied. Now all he had was his own regret to fill the empty spaces of his life. Its power had wrapped around Trey's chest, crystallizing into a frozen vise — one so powerful, it amazed him his heart could even beat at all.

Perhaps Claudia had already forgotten about him. What if she'd moved on with that Jason guy? Would he give her the nice, safe life she deserved? The mere thought of her with someone else moved the frigid grip of his misery up to his throat, throttling him until it hurt to breathe.

Every time Trey closed his eyes, his mind immediately went to the memory of Claudia asleep in his arms, unable to awaken, in spite of the loud helicopter above them.

His strategy for avoiding the image had been to stay awake as much as possible. This night, he was adding the idea of getting very drunk to his plan. The process had only just started, but he was already feeling delightfully numb, which was probably the best he could hope for these days.

Leaning over, he hit play on the CD player he'd brought with him. The strains of *You Belong to Me* filled the room. After flopping into a leather armchair, he refilled his tumbler with bourbon and waited for night to fall.

"I wish you were here with me," he murmured. "I miss you so much."

"I've missed you, too," a gentle voice said from behind him.

Trey shot upright in his chair, reaching for his weapon, which was no longer on the table behind him.

"I moved that gun of yours. Can't have you accidentally shooting me," the voice teased.

Trey turned and his chest expanded against the cold chill encasing it.

"Claudia?"

Her dark hair was down, cascading over her shoulders and glimmering in the low light of the room. She looked thinner and more delicate than usual — as sad and desolate as him — but still hauntingly beautiful.

"Yeah, it's me," she answered, dropping her keys and purse on a small chair beside her. She peeled off her thin, black leather jacket and tossed it on top of them.

"How'd you get in here?" he demanded.

"You're not the only one who can commit a little friendly breaking and entering. Though, I wish you were a bit more cautious about your own personal security."

"That hasn't been high on my list for a while," he muttered. Finishing his drink in one gulp before placing it down, Trey attempted to regain his resolve.

"So, what *is* on your list? To sit here in the dark surrounded by a bunch of boxes? Are you waiting for something?"

"Maybe."

"And what would that be — death, or a moving van?" she challenged, her chin raised in defiance.

"Right now? Trying to get drunk, if you couldn't tell."

"You seem to have accomplished that feat."

Trey looked down at the bottle, his throat tightening with his sadness. He hated being rude to her, but she needed to leave. Having her near him fucked with all his good intentions. "Not quite, no, but working on it. It's helping me settle into my new life. Maybe I'll grow a beard…go full *Unabomber.* I just need a manifesto."

"Be serious, Trey," she pleaded, sliding her hands into her pockets. Her nervousness was showing through for the first time since she'd arrived.

"Fine. You want serious, how about this, what are you doing here, Claudia?" he questioned gruffly.

Trey used refilling his glass as another excuse to avoid her eyes. Whenever he looked into them, he forgot all the logical reasons why he pushed her away, instead wanting to cradle her in his arms until the sun came up over the lake.

"I should never have let you leave me," she declared with her signature confidence.

"It wasn't your decision," he clarified.

"Why the hell not?"

"Because I almost killed you, damn it!"

"No, you didn't. Stop punishing yourself."

"Call it what you like, but you still shouldn't be here," he asserted through gritted teeth.

"That's the thing. I *know* I *have* to be here. You were wrong."

"Do you think I made this decision on a whim? It fucking broke me to do it, but I know it's what I had to do — for you."

She appraised him for a moment, before crossing the room. She wore a soft gray sweater and black jeans. As always, she was simply perfect.

He wanted to push her away, but she was close enough for him to smell her. The scent blended with his tipsy brain, and the combination dulled his wits just enough to prevent him from exercising common sense.

"You will always be the best thing for me. I'm not going to give up, so you might as well accept it now." Claudia stated gently, as her hand ran over his stubbly cheek, before smiling. He knew he should pull away, but her skin felt too good against his. "You look like shit, Trey," she added, removing her hand.

He laughed coarsely, shuffling away from her. "Well, I've had a rough few weeks."

"Me too," she responded.

"How'd you find me?" he inquired, struggling against his pull to her. He was still trying to process that she'd come for him, even after all he'd done.

"Stephen. He told me I was right to come looking for you…and how to get here."

"That sounds like him. He always was a secret romantic."

"What happened? Why aren't you with him hunting down the bad guys?"

"Were you worried about me, little one?" he queried, with a smirk, in spite of himself.

"Of course, always," she intoned.

He ran one hand through his hair and looked out over the water again. After several moments, he turned back to her.

"We got one of A.J.'s guys in Prague. When we tracked down a second one in Thailand, he wouldn't stop saying…" Trey paused, remembering how the bastard invoked Claudia's name, knowing just enough about her brush with death to fuck with him. After a moment, Trey found words again. "I lost my temper. Things got a little…physical. Apparently, Stephen feels I'm too much of a loose cannon these days," he finished, with a mirthless laugh. "He felt it was important for compliance with the Geneva Convention that I take a break."

"So you came here?" she whispered, approaching him slowly. Her hesitance toward him broke his heart, especially because he knew it was his own actions, which caused it.

Clearly unsure of herself, Claudia paused to look around the room. Her eyes fell on the dining room table, littered with insulin pumps and glucose monitors, which were next to his laptop, and pages of his handwritten notes.

"What's all this?" she probed, approaching the table.

"It's nothing."

She turned to him, one of the sheets in her hands. "No, it's not. Tell me."

Trey rubbed the back of his neck, finally meeting her eyes to say, "I've had some time on my hands since I got here a couple days ago…"

"Trey…"

"It's just a few ideas for software I had."

"What would it do?"

"It would track your glucose remotely. If it dropped too low, or went up too high, it would send an alert to a set of recipients, including 911. That part was pretty easy. I just reverse engineered some of the insulin monitoring devices already out there. But this one would have a GPS tracker, and if the monitor or pump were disconnected without the entry of a password…it would send a different alert — one that you'd been compromised."

"And when did you start this?"

"Right after I met you."

Claudia stared at him with her mouth agape, yet she said nothing.

"I got distracted from it. I was too caught up in our investigation…in us… I didn't finish it in time. It's just one more way I failed you," he whispered.

"You could never fail me," she insisted, crossing to him and holding his face in her hands, as the CD proceeded to play the next song.

He shook her off him. "Don't you get it? I thought in the same way as A.J. My mind is just as twisted, maybe I'm even worse than that venomous bitch."

"That's not true."

"Isn't it? It's bad enough I anticipated the way someone would try to harm you, but I also didn't protect you from it. I *am* poison."

"That's ridiculous!" she exclaimed. "What happened is no more your fault than it is mine for having a condition they exploited. A.J. made her own decisions. She ruined *herself.* No matter how much you want to torture yourself, you have to understand that. I'll stand here holding my breath until you see reason, if that's what I have to do!"

Trey suppressed a smile at her unrelenting pigheadedness.

"Do you really believe in me that much? I left *you*, remember?"

"And it was a terrible lapse in judgment on your part, that's for sure," she pronounced.

Trey laughed, wondering if maybe he could set aside all this guilt and truly find joy in life.

He frowned again. "But…"

Claudia took his hand and moved it to her face.

"No 'buts.' We *deserve* to be happy," she whispered.

Trey moved his hand to caress Claudia's hair and allowed the soft tresses to calm him.

"What about your career, Claudia?" he inquired, dropping his hand. "I wasn't lying when I said being with me isn't a good idea for you."

"It doesn't matter. I told you, if I have to choose between the FBI and you, I choose you, every time."

"It's not that simple."

"Maybe it can be. The Bureau isn't the only option for me. Stephen offered me a job."

"He did what?"

"Well, he actually offered *us* a job. You game?"

"Do I have a choice?"

"Not really."

The idea rattled around in Trey's brain. It would be fun to be Claudia's partner, both professionally and intimately. It also guaranteed he could keep an eye on her.

"Stephen has been trying to recruit me for years now. I swear, that dude always ends up getting his way, somehow."

"As long as I get my way in the process, too, then it works for me," Claudia joked.

"You know this would technically make me a fed, right? I thought you liked my dark side?"

"Oh, I'm not worried about that, there's plenty of darkness left in you. I have a feeling your outlaw spirit will come in handy on our missions."

Trey placed his hands on her cheeks, gliding his thumbs back and forth on her soft skin.

"So you've thought of everything?"

"I have."

"You sure like to cause trouble, don't you?"

"Yep."

"You know this would mean you can't get rid of me, either, right?" he asked.

"That's the plan. You see, I've been thinking," she said. "Maybe it's called *falling* in love because sometimes someone catches you, but if they don't, you simply crash down on the pavement. I'm here to catch you."

"And what should I do?"

"You need to catch me, too," she answered.

"I can handle that," he assured her, moving his hands under her armpits to lift her up to eye level.

Claudia wrapped her arms around his neck, allowing him to move his arms to her waist and secure her small body tightly against his own.

Trey kissed her — tentatively at first, drinking in the taste of her sweet lips. Quickly, the need for more of her took over. He pressed his tongue against her lips, and she purred in response.

As he explored her mouth, he found her to be even more intoxicating than his bottle of bourbon, and so much more satisfying.

He set her on her feet, so he could peel off her sweater. She stood before him in a simple white bra, which was gaping a little at the top. Trey slid his right hand back and forth over the top of her supple breasts, lingering for a moment to explore her pronounced collarbones with his fingers. Her skin erupted into goose bumps under his touch.

"You've gotten too skinny, little one," he chastised, as he moved his left hand to run along the length of her arm.

"You sound like my abuela."

"Did I do this to you?" he whispered, guilt seeping back into his conscience, as his left hand stroked her rib cage.

"I told you I missed you. Now you're just going to have to make it up to me," she challenged.

"Every day of my life," he promised, before sealing his lips over hers again.

Claudia slid Trey's tee shirt over his head, breaking them apart. She ran the tip of her nose slowly across his chest, then between his pecs. The sensation was light, yet he thought he'd explode from the contact.

Her tongue began to follow the same path, tasting him, when suddenly she took a hard bite at his left pec, and he didn't know if he should laugh, shout, or moan. Leaning back, she threw him a mischievous smile.

"So you plan to eat me up, little one, is that it?" he remarked.

"You're all mine, finally. And I plan to enjoy every inch of you," Claudia purred, running her nails over his shoulders and chest, trailing them across each of his tattoos. Finally, she placed one hand over the bare skin covering his heart, and he could feel the pressure of it beating against her palm.

"You deserve a tattoo right here, now. You have the strongest heart of anyone I've ever known."

"And it belongs to you. I believe I was saving this spot for you all along."

"What will this tattoo be?" she asked, her eyes crinkling with curiosity.

"Isn't it obvious, abeja?" he countered, mischief twinkling in his eyes.

Her mouth dropped open a bit.

"A tough guy like you is going to get a tattoo of a *honeybee*?"

"Absolutely. You're my little bee, but you have to promise me if I get lost like that bumblebee you found, you'll save me, too."

"Always. I promise," she insisted.

Trey grinned and scooped her into his arms so he could hurry them to the bedroom. She circled her arms around his neck and giggled with a lightness he'd rarely heard from her.

Standing beside the bed, he paused to look into her eyes. She was awake, and safe, and she belonged to him.

Claudia ran a hand through his hair and swallowed hard, her face suddenly very serious.

"I love you, Trey," she whispered.

"I know," he retorted, with a smirk on his happy face, and an intense sense of warmth in his heart.

EPILOGUE

TWO AND A HALF MONTHS LATER

"Uh…this is your captain speaking," the pilot announced, in that slow baritone it seemed they all were required to have before flying a plane. "On behalf of the flight crew, we'd like to be the first to wish you a good morning…and happy Valentine's Day. We hope you've had a pleasant night's rest on our journey from New York City. We would like to update you on our progress. We will be landing in Nice, France in about thirty-eight minutes…"

Claudia stretched awkwardly in her first class seat next to Trey.

"May I, uh, be the second to wish you a good morning?" Trey said into her ear, in a perfect impersonation of the pilot's voice, making her giggle. "Happy Birthday, little one."

"You remembered!"

"It's kind of hard to forget when your birthday is on February 14th."

"Seeing as I'm not very sentimental, it was never a big a deal to me. I must admit, though, whisking me away to the South of France for my birthday is quite impressive."

"I've been waiting for just the right time."

"I'm amazed we found any time to get away, what with Stephen's constant assignments for us. I would be happy with just a night on the couch in Pittsburgh."

"You don't like my brownstone in New York?"

"I love it, but it's not home to me. I think that will always be where I met you."

"I thought you said you weren't sentimental?"

"I guess you've made me weak," she teased.

"If you're homesick, maybe we better head back right away."

"Oh no you don't. You promised me France, and I am going to enjoy it — even if we have to screen all of Stephen's calls."

"That guy needs something to distract him."

"You keep saying he's such a romantic, then maybe he needs to meet a nice girl."

"Like I did?" Trey teased.

"I'm not *that* nice, but yes," she remarked with a sly smile.

"True, you're becoming quite a little devil. I love it." Trey paused, and turned serious for a moment, "I don't know. Stephen has demons of his own to deal with. My guess is being Captain Asian-America is the only way he quiets them."

"Speaking from experience?"

"Yes. And one I hope never to think about again."

They both fell silent. Claudia's mind couldn't help but wander to thoughts of A.J. The bitch still refused to talk to any of her interrogators, but at least she was rotting in a federal cell — one surrounded by enough trustworthy guards to ensure she had no chance of escaping. There was more than enough evidence to put her away for life — or something more final — but the powers that be were eager to learn what secrets she held in that twisted brain of hers.

Luckily, Claudia had many other things to worry about instead of A.J., such as tracking down international bad guys alongside Stephen and his incredible team. Though Claudia spent most of her time working with Trey, and she wouldn't have it any other way.

A.J. may not have been cooperating with authorities, but Drew certainly was. Desperate to avoid extensive jail time, he was eager to share what he'd learned about A.J., and her crew, during his stint acting as their mole within the Pittsburgh field office. Claudia accepted the assistance begrudgingly. Nothing would ever heal the damage of her former colleague's betrayal, but she knew she had to see the bigger picture.

Returning her thoughts to Trey's concerns over Stephen, Claudia remarked, "Well, Stephen may be a tortured soul underneath it all, but anyone who can get your dad on board with you working with the federal government, would at least appear to have it pretty together."

"Dad's always liked Stephen, and he's freaking crazy about you. As long as I'm working with you two, he's happy."

Claudia took Trey's hand and kissed each of his knuckles. "Works for me," she murmured.

Trey removed his hand from hers to put his arm around her. "Now, about this vacation…" he began, his brow furrowing with sudden worry.

"What's wrong, Trey?"

"I was wondering… It's okay if you don't want to…"

"Come on, what is it?" Claudia insisted. "You're freaking me out a little here," she added, making Trey smile.

"Would you like to meet my mom, you know…Abigail…while we're here? She spends this part of the year living near Nice. We've been talking on the phone since…it happened, but she wants to see me, and she really wants to meet you."

"I would be happy to, of course," Claudia intoned, giving him a light peck on the cheek. "I hope she likes me."

"Of course she will. Abigail loves pretty things, and they don't get more beautiful than you," he teased, though she could tell he was visibly relieved by her willingness to meet his mother. He paused for a moment, lost in his thoughts apparently, "After we see her," he finally continued, "I promise to let you relax. I can't wait to have champagne with you on our terrace, overlooking the Mediterranean Sea. Then I'll walk you through the *Cours Saleya* market to buy you flowers and cheese."

"It sounds perfect."

"And if that's not enough for you, we can take the train to Cannes and get you some lingerie."

"I already have lingerie."

"One piece — that's not enough. And wearing a tank top with my boxers doesn't count either. Though, you do look pretty hot in those, too." Trey eased her sideways, before he continued, "Be sure to look out the window. I don't want you to miss the view as we approach."

She peered outside, and gasped. "It's so completely blue," she murmured, awestruck by the mountains giving way to brightly colored buildings and the crystal waters.

"That's why they call it the *Côte d'Azur*," Trey explained. "It's the perfect place to escape…with you."

"And I intend to make the most of it," Claudia assured him. "I don't know how much free time I'm going to have after we get back. On top of all this work we have, Jenna and Wyatt are in full wedding-planning craziness. Mama is already naming their unborn children. I don't know how much Jenna will conscript me to do. Tea is helping a lot, but Aubrey has been acting really weird. Tea says she's been basically MIA for two months."

"I'm not really the right person to give you advice on how to be a good bridesmaid, Claudia, but I know you'll do great, and will look very nice in whatever sensible dress Jenna chooses for you."

"Thank you," she chuckled. "Jenna made sure to tell me it's a perfect color and length for wearing at multiple future events. It was like having an actuary discuss a wedding with you."

"It's all show. She's a huge softy."

"I know! Did she tell you Wy's going to sing and play guitar for a song at their reception?"

"She mentioned it. Apparently he's pretty good?" Trey inquired.

"He's wonderful. Though as arrogant as he is already, I try not to say it to his face much."

"Arrogant and *stubborn*..." Trey mused quietly.

"I know," Claudia growled. "I love him, but, dammit, I wish he'd come around about us being together."

"Well, regardless of how much he and I fought before...I get how he still blames me for the way A.J. hurt you. I can't fault him for feeling that way."

"Well, *I* can. He's wrong and he needs to accept it, because as far as I'm concerned, you're not going anywhere."

"I hope he gets over it. I won't give up, don't worry. I mean, how else will I convince him to sing at our wedding, too, one day."

"Wait, what?"

"Buckle your seat belt. You know the rules," he answered calmly, turning his face forward toward the seat in front of him, a smug grin threatening to crack his perfect poker face.

"You can't say something like that and then just change the subject, you jerk."

"Oh, come on, you can't be surprised I feel this way."

"That *you* do? Hell yeah, I'm surprised."

"All right, now that the shock is gone…"

"What if I don't want to get married?" she teased, not even bothering to hide her gleeful amusement.

"I didn't ask how you *generally* feel about getting married to some random person."

"You haven't *asked* me anything."

"Technicality… Fine." He turned back to her, as the plane descended rapidly. Her ears were popping, but all she could hear was the whirring in her brain as she waited for him to continue. "Right now, I don't want to know if you've ever cared about getting married — in the abstract. I'm not asking if you put a pillowcase on your head and held a bunch of plastic flowers in your bedroom when you were eight. When I met you, I sure as hell never thought I'd want a freaking wedding and to build my life around one person. But you've changed all that."

"I am a real pain in the ass, aren't I?"

"You sure are. So, what I want to know is… Do you want to marry *me*?"

"Trey…" she whispered, but by now Claudia could tell when Trey was on a roll, so she bit her tongue.

"I know you'd rather be writing code than spending hours shopping, so I went ahead and did it for us." He pulled a light blue box out of the side pocket of his cargo pants, and all words left Claudia's brain.

Apparently, her slack jaw made it clear he now also had to do the talking for both of them. Trey untied the white ribbon adorning the box and lifted the lid slowly, revealing a velvet container.

Every one of his movements was slow and deliberate. Over a hundred people were waiting for the flight to land, but as far as Claudia was concerned, they didn't exist.

The world could've stopped right then and she wouldn't have cared — all that mattered was Trey was hers and he was proposing they belong to each other forever.

Claudia reached forward, embarrassed to find her fingers were shaking, she fumbled to lift the lid. Even after taking a deep breath and blinking several times, she had trouble focusing on the shiny ring resting inside, through the tears in her eyes.

"Claudia McCoy, you and I both know I'm never going to be stupid enough to let you out of my sight ever again, so we might as well make sure the rest of the world knows it, too, right? What I mean is…you're my home, and I want you to be my home forever. So, what do you say? Will you marry me?"

"Hell yes!" she answered, loudly enough that the rest of the first class cabin turned to stare, and then smile, at them.

Neither of them cared what any of those other people thought. Trey took her face in both his hands and kissed her so deeply, she thought her toes would curl and burst right out of her flats.

When he let her up for air, she gasped out, "I love you, Trey."

"That's good, because I fucking love the hell out of you, and it would suck to feel this way by myself," he declared, before sliding the ring on her finger. The band was covered in little diamonds, with two rows of small diamonds surrounding one large yellow one.

"A yellow diamond?" she asked.

"For my little abeja," he responded with a smile.

A tear slid down Claudia's cheek as she rested her left hand over Trey's heart, where his tribal bee tattoo rested.

"I can't believe you did all this. You may be a little crazy, you know that, tattoo boy?"

He leaned away from her a fraction and whispered against her lips, "That's a confession for another day. I mean it, though — it's time to buckle your seat belt."

"You're such a nag."

"I need you to be safe. You're my everything, remember?"

"Well, in that case..." Claudia slid the metal buckle in place and decided keeping herself in one piece for this guy was probably a just fine way to live.

THE END

Keep Reading for a Sneak Peek of Book Four in the Gateway to Love Series

CITY OF BRIDGES
(Anticipated Release: Fall 2016)

It feels like life keeps passing Aubrey Vasil by more and more each day. Left devastated, emotionally and physically, by a horrible relationship years ago, Aubrey decided to start anew and recreate her life and identity in Pittsburgh with her best friends — and a promise to herself never to let her heart lead her astray again. Yet now, everyone is pairing off, and the perfect little world she built is suddenly crumbling before her eyes.

Bax Taylor is angry — at Griffen Tate for having a relationship with Bax's dead brother's widow, at his mother for thwarting his plans to bring the family restaurant into the twenty-first century, and most of all, at *himself* for not doing more for his beloved older brother Jack when he was still alive. Each day that Bax is back in his hometown of Pittsburgh it seems that his volatile emotions are more likely to overtake him and derail any hopes or dreams he may have for the future.

In a moment of weakness, the two find drunken solace in each other when Aubrey opens her heart — and her bed — to Bax the night of Althea and Griffen's engagement party. Their connection is powerful, but they both get a lot more than the just one night of escape they anticipated.

Aubrey is intent on continuing to go it alone, and is terrified of a future with someone as heartbroken as Bax — but neither can deny the connections between them.

Will they have the courage to let themselves love each other, and hopefully heal their damaged souls — together?

CONNECTING WITH CHLOE

Hopefully you enjoyed *A Steel Town.* If you did, please consider leaving a review so that other readers can find it.

Also, be sure to sign up for the Chloe T. Barlow newsletter. It is the best way to catch any deals, giveaways, new releases, or other exciting news about Chloe's creations. You are also welcome to join Chloe's street team, Chloe's Crew, on Facebook.

Newsletter and Blog:
http://chloetbarlow.com/newsletter/
Chloe enjoys nothing more than interacting with her readers, so please keep in touch!
Facebook:
https://www.facebook.com/ChloeTBarlow
Twitter:
https://twitter.com/chloetbarlow
Goodreads:
https://www.goodreads.com/author/show/7376511.Chloe_T_Barlow
Email:
chloe@chloetbarlow.com
Google+:
https://plus.google.com/u/0/116405903319564147007/posts
Chloe's Crew (Chloe Barlow Street Team)
https://www.facebook.com/groups/chloebarlowcrew/
Pinterest:
http://www.pinterest.com/chloetbarlow/
Amazon Author Page:
http://www.amazon.com/Chloe-T.-Barlow/e/B00IXAHC64/ref=ntt_athr_dp_pel_1
Learn more about Chloe, *A Steel Town*, and the continuation of the Gateway to Love Series at:
Chloe's Website:
http://www.ChloeTBarlow.com

ACKNOWLEDGEMENTS

It's impossible to thank every individual who has helped me in this crazy journey since I released *Three Rivers* in March 2013. Each time I think of a new person beginning to read the *Gateway to Love* series, it fills me with indescribable joy and gratitude. So, to all the readers, bloggers, and reviewers who have taken a chance on these characters who mean so much to me, I say: thank you from the bottom of my heart.

I would also like to send my love to some specific folks, without whom I could never have accomplished bringing these stories to you all.

To my dear husband: It has been so much fun to go on this crazy ride with you. Seeing all the time and hard work you take to support me during this process is just one more reminder of how very lucky I am to have you in my life. I love you.

My Agent: *Michelle Grajkowski* of *Three Seas Literary Agency* is not only a fabulous advocate for me and my books, but she is also a remarkable person and dear friend. I am thrilled to have met her and can't wait to share more stories with her.

My Team: *Eisley Jacobs* of *Complete Pixels* truly is a magician. She somehow manages to turn all my crazy ideas into a beautiful visual reality.

Marilyn Medina of *Eagle Eye Reads Editing*, thank you for being such an incredible editor, full of tough love and a remarkable eye for story and detail. Working with you is a pleasure I look forward to with bated breath every time.

Kara Hildebrand for being that last set of sharp eyes and warm hand of support that makes the last month before publishing so much less stressful.

Between the Sheets Promotions gets a big round of applause from me for their unending skills and tireless professionalism. They are also incredibly kind and supportive friends that make this journey ever more special.

Kristina Ohrberg, and Ashley Lake for helping me so regularly with all the craziness being an author entails. You two are such a blast to work with, and I can't wait to get started on my next book with you both.

Linda Eng Reed, what would I do without your support, and delicious treats to keep me going? You are a culinary artist, and a delightfully kind person, whom I am honored to know.

Katie Kurtzman, the greatest literary publicist on earth, I am so grateful for all of your help and guidance.

Consultants: Thank you to *Micaiah Kuchinick* for your open honesty about living with type 1 diabetes. You are a beauty, and an inspiration. *Ryan Firkel* for being my tattoo consultant, and for generally helping me to complete my vision of Trey. You are a Pittsburgh treasure.

My Beta Readers, Blogger Buddies, and Author Mentors: Thank you so much to *Kristina Ohrberg, Ashley Lake, Jennifer Stewart, Nicole Beckett, Katie Bloch Pettigrew* of *Southern Belle Book Blog, Marissa Vann* of *Smut Book Club, Patricia Booth, Karrie Mellott Puskas* of *Panty Dropping Book Blog*, and authors *Helena Newbury*, and *Julia Kent.* Your help through early reading, wonderful input, and general good old pep talks has meant the world to me.

Chloe's Crew: I can't fathom how much my street team has grown since *Three Rivers* released, but what I can believe is the depth of love I have for each of you great Crewbies. Thank you for all you do every day. I am honored you would take time out of your busy lives to be a part of this experience with me.

The City of Pittsburgh: The inspiration I receive from this beautiful city is very special to me. I am also thankful to all the Pittsburghers who have been so supportive of this series. I especially want to thank *Lorinda Hayes* for granting my long-held dream of being featured in the *Pittsburgh Post Gazette* newspaper. I am also very grateful to *Rege Behe* and the thoughtful, interesting pieces in which he has featured me.

Thank you, as well, to the remarkable group, *Littsburgh*, for organizing the literary community of my beloved city into the juggernaut it is today.

And to *Susan*, of *The Penguin Bookshop*, for being so supportive of me and other authors. You and your store are something so very special.

My Readers: Finally, it is with great pleasure that I again thank each of my readers for enjoying the world of Claudia, Althea, Jenna, Aubrey, and the whole gang with me. You are the reason I do this.

A STEEL TOWN SOUNDTRACK

- *Everlong* – Foo Fighters
- *Hurt* – Nine Inch Nails
- *Just One Of The Guys* – Jenny Lewis
- *All The Pretty Girls* – Kaleo
- *Protection* – Massive Attack
- *Riverside* – Agnes Obel
- *Concrete Sky* – Beth Orton
- *I Will Possess Your Heart* – Death Cab for Cutie
- *Snake Eyes* – Mumford & Sons
- *Things Happen* – Dawes
- *Blood Bank* – Bon Iver
- *Blue Beard* – Band of Horses
- *Cover Me Up* – Jason Isbell
- *You Belong to Me* – Jo Stafford
- *Slow Show* – The National
- *A Comet Appears* – The Shins
- *Mess Is Mine* – Vance Joy
- *Dearly Departed* – Shakey Graves
- *The World Ender* – Lord Huron
- *Ship To Wreck* – Florence + The Machine
- *Keep the Car Running* – Arcade Fire
- *It Makes No Difference* – My Morning Jacket
- *Perfect Day* – The Constellations
- *Let It Go* – James Bay
- *Coming Home* – Leon Bridges
- *Airplanes* – Local Natives
- *Ice Cream* – Sarah McLachlan

Follow Chloe on *Spotify* to hear this and other soundtracks from future novels:

http://open.spotify.com/user/chloetbarlow

ABOUT CHLOE T. BARLOW

Chloe is a contemporary romance novelist living in Pittsburgh, Pennsylvania with her husband and their sweet dog. She is a native Washingtonian who graduated *Duke University* with a degree in English and Chinese language. She met her husband at *Duke* and he brought her to Pittsburgh over a decade ago, which she has loved ever since and made her adopted hometown. She also attended the *University of Pittsburgh Law School* where she continued to be a book-loving nerd.

Chloe has always loved writing and cherishes the opportunity to craft her fictional novels and share them with the world. When Chloe isn't writing, she spends her time exploring Pittsburgh with her husband and friends. She enjoys yoga, jogging, and all Pittsburgh sports, as well as her *Duke Blue Devils*.

Since the release of her debut novel, *Three Rivers*, Chloe has been featured in *Pittsburgh Post Gazette*, *Pittsburgh Tribune Review*, *RT Book Reviews Magazine*, *Heroes and Heartbreakers* blog and the *Lupus Now* newsletter. Chloe thoroughly enjoys every opportunity to communicate with her readers. She has also appreciated the honor of meeting and talking with numerous fans, and looks forward to getting to know many more.

28915798R00219

Made in the USA
Middletown, DE
06 February 2016